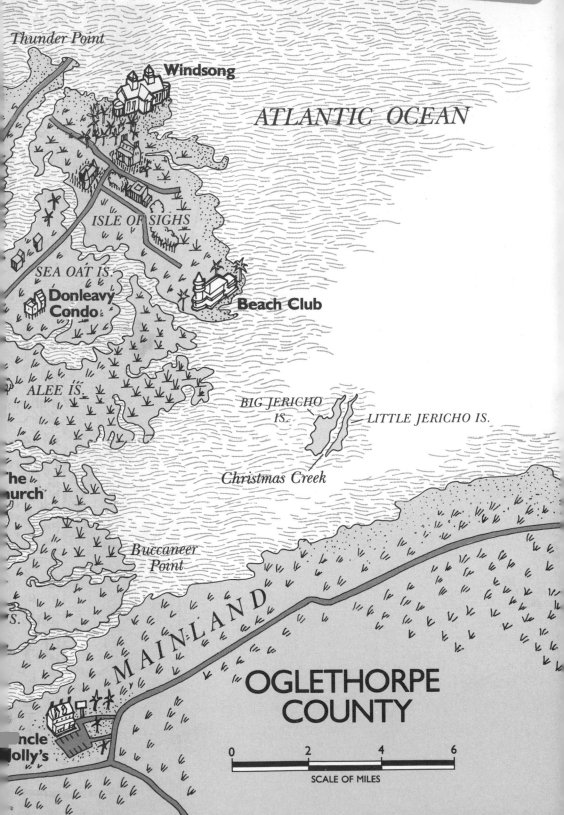

Thunder Point

Windsong

ATLANTIC OCEAN

ISLE OF SIGHS

SEA OAT IS.

Donleavy Condo

Beach Club

ALEE IS.

BIG JERICHO IS.

LITTLE JERICHO IS.

Christmas Creek

he urch

Buccaneer Point

S.

M A I N L A N D

OGLETHORPE COUNTY

ncle olly's

0   2   4   6

SCALE OF MILES

HOOLIGANS

William Diehl

HOOLIGANS

VILLARD BOOKS, NEW YORK 1984

Library of Congress Cataloging in Publication Data

Diehl, William.
Hooligans.
I. Title.
PS3554.I345H6 1984   813'.54   83-50862
ISBN 0-394-53049-7

Endpaper map by David Lindroth

Manufactured in the United States of America

9 8 7 6 5 4 3 2

First Edition

*This book is dedicated to Virginia,
who is the love of my life;
To Michael Parver, for his support and
friendship through the tough times,
and for Stick;
And to my father, the most gentle
and loving man I have ever known,
who died before it was completed.*

ACKNOWLEDGMENTS

My thanks and gratitude to my family and friends for their constant encouragement and support: to my mother, Temple, Cathy, John and Kate, Bill, Melissa and David, Stan and Yvonne, Bobby Byrd, Carole Jackowitz, Marilyn Parver, Michael Rothschild, Billy Wallace, Frank Mazolla, the Harrisons of Lookout Mountain, Mark Vaughn, Barbara Thomas, Jack and Jim.

To a true and trusting friend, Don Smith, whose wit and wisdom always help.

To my good friend, C.H. "Buddy" Harris, of the Treasury Department, for his selfless assistance and attention to detail, and to his wife, Joan and daughter, Robin.

To Director Charles F. Rinkevich, Deputy Director David McKinley, Kent Williams, Charles E. Nester, Morris Grodsky, and the other officers of the Treasury Department's Federal Law Enforcement Training Center, Brunswick, Ga., for their invaluable technical assistance.

To George Gentry and the many other men who served in Vietnam and shared their experiences and feelings with me.

To George, Bill, Bear, B.L., Nancy and Slavko, Sandy, Jim, Frankie and Jingle, Larry, Averett, Ted, Mike, Kurt, Richard, Ruth, Dayton, and all my friends and associates at the late, great Higdon's on St. Simons Island, Ga., for sharing their names, friendship, time, and experiences with me.

To my editor, Peter Gethers, a man of awesome insights, and to Susan and Audrey, and the rest of his sterling staff.

To Marc Jaffe, for his continued faith.

To Irene Webb, my favorite wonder woman.

And to a treasured and lasting friend, Owen Laster, at once and always, a gentleman of the realm.

SPECIAL OPERATIONS BRANCH

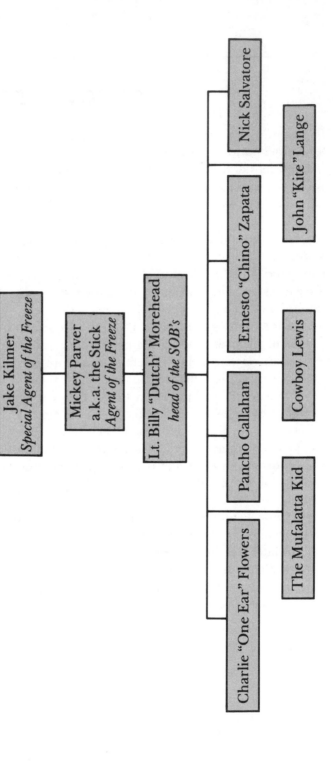

Jake Kilmer
Special Agent of the Freeze

Mickey Parver
a.k.a. the Stick
Agent of the Freeze

Lt. Billy "Dutch" Morehead
head of the SOB's

Charlie "One Ear" Flowers

Pancho Callahan

Ernesto "Chino" Zapata

Nick Salvatore

The Mufalatta Kid

Cowboy Lewis

John "Kite" Lange

CINCINNATI TRIAD

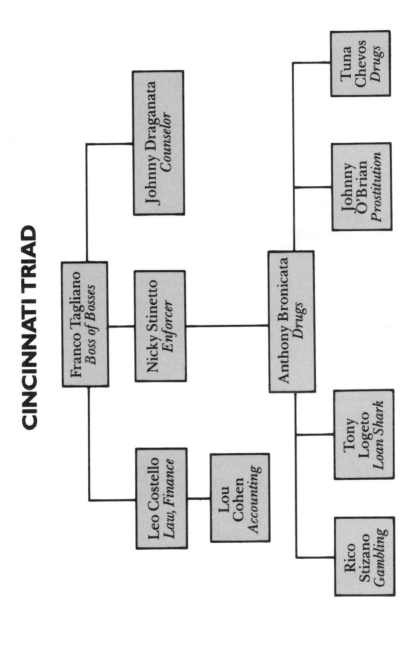

Franco Tagliano
Boss of Bosses

Johnny Draganata
Counselor

Nicky Stinetto
Enforcer

Leo Costello
Law, Finance

Lou Cohen
Accounting

Anthony Bronicata
Drugs

Rico Stizano
Gambling

Tony Logeto
Loan Shark

Johnny O'Brian
Prostitution

Tuna Chevos
Drugs

The fish trusts the water,
And it is in the water that
it is cooked.
—HAITIAN PROVERB

HOOLIGANS

PREFACE

DUNETOWN

Dunetown is a city forged by Revolutionaries, hammered and shaped by rascals and southern rebels, and mannered by genteel ladies.

Dunetown is grace and unhurried charm, azalea-lined boulevards and open river promenades, parks and narrow lanes; a city of squares; of ironwork and balustrades, shutters and dormers, porticoes and steeples and dollops of gingerbread icing; of bricks, ballast, and oyster shells underfoot; a waterfront place of massive walls and crude paving, of giant shutters on muscular hinges and winding stairwells and wrought-iron spans; a claustrophobic vista where freighters glide by on the river, a mere reach away, and sea gulls yell at robins.

It is a city whose heartbeat changes from block to block as subtly as its architecture; a city of seventeenth-century schoolhouses, churches, and taverns; of ceiling fans and Tiffany windows, two-story atriums, blue barrel dormers, Georgian staircases and Palladian windows and grand, elegant antebellum mansions that hide from view among moss-draped oaks and serpentine vines.

Dunetown is a stroll through the eighteenth century, its history limned on cemetery tablets:

HERE LIES JENIFER GOLDSMITH
LOVING WYF OF JEREMY
WHO DIED OF THE PLAGUE THAT KILED SO MENY
IN THESE PARTS IN THE YEAR OF OUR LORD, 1744

or

JAMES OLIVER
A FAST TONGUE AND HOT TEMPER
DEAD AT 22 YRS. OF HIS AGE
IN A DUEL WITH LT. CHARLES MORAY
WHO SHOT QUICKER AND WITH KEENER EYE

These are its ancestors. The survivors become the city's power brokers, the rulers of the kingdom, dictating an archaic social structure that is unchanging, and defined by its metaphor, the Dune Club, restricted to the elite, whose money is oldest, whose roots are deepest, and who, for more than a century, have sequestered it from time.

Thus the years have passed Dunetown, leaving behind a treasure: an eighteenth-century serfdom whose history trembles with ghost stories, with wars and brawls and buried loot on shaggy Atlantic beaches; whose people have the heritage and independence of islanders, their bloodlines traced to Irish colliers, Spanish privateers, to Haiti and Jamaica, and Cherokee reservations.

Its bays, marshes, and rivers still weave a city composed of islands: Alee, Skidaway, Thunderhead, Buccaneer, Oceanby, Sea Oat, and the wistful, *Gatsby*-like Isle of Sighs, a haunt of the rich, its antique houses serene against the backwaters of the sea, where one might easily envision a solitary and forlorn Jay Gatz, staring across the water at the solemn light on Daisy's pier.

> *The past is everywhere,*
> *If you listen,*
> *For that is not the wind you hear,*
> *It is the whispering ghost of yesteryear.*

Reality, to Dunetown, is history to the rest of the world.

INTRODUCTION
A Walk Through Dunetown
J. THOMPSON, 1972

Sunday: Dawn   *The small trawler was heading north an hour before dawn on the eighth day out of Cumaná, Venezuela, when the captain of the four-man crew first spotted the red trouble light blinking on the mast of the sailboat. He made it a mile or so away when he saw it the first time. The trawler was ten miles at sea and thirty-five miles northeast of Fernandina, Florida, at the time. The captain watched the light for half an hour as his rusty scow drew closer.*

In the gray light just before the sun broke, they were close enough to see the sailboat, a rich man's toy, dead in the water. It was a forty-footer, with a man on deck. The man had removed his shirt and was waving it overhead.

The captain, a deeply tanned man in his early forties wearing four days' growth of beard, stroked his jaw with a greasy hand. Two of the crew members watched the sailboat draw closer with mild interest. The mate, a black man with a scar from the corner of his mouth to his ear, squinted through the dim light and then urged the captain to pass up the stricken boat.

"Fuck 'em, man. We ain't got time to mess with no honky sailors," he said quietly.

But the captain had been a seaman too long to pass up any vessel in distress. Besides, the shirtless man was obviously rich; a soft, Sunday sailor, becalmed far beyond his limit and probably scared to death.

"No guns," the captain said softly in Spanish. "Just stand easy and see what they want. If gas is their problem, we can help the gringos out."

He turned on a powerful light and swept its beam along the sailboat from bow to stern. He steered the trawler close beside the sailboat and tossed the man a line.

"Habla español?" the captain asked.

"No," the sailor answered.

"What ees your problem?" the captain asked in broken English.

"Not enough wind." The sailor, who was wearing white jeans and designer sneakers, pointed at the limp sail. "And no gas. Can you sell me some gas?"

"I geev you enough gas to make Saint Simons Island," the captain said, pointing toward the horizon. "Fifteen, maybe twenty miles northwest."

"Thank you, thank you very much. Muchas gracias, señor." The man bowed and waved a thank-you.

The captain ordered one of his men to take a gas can aboard the sailboat. The man went below and emerged a few minutes later with a ten-gallon can in hand. He and one of the other crewmen scrambled aboard the sailboat.

The captain and the mate watched from aboard the trawler.

"Messin' with trouble," the black mate mumbled.

"No problem," said the captain.

The two crewmen had not quite reached the stern tanks of the sailboat when the hatch to the cabin suddenly slid back and another man jumped on deck from below. He was holding a submachine gun. The mate uttered an oath and reached for the pistol in his belt but he was too late. The man with the machine gun raked the deck and bridge of the trawler.

Bdddddddddddddt . . .

Bdddddddddddddd . . .

The windshield of the captain's cabin exploded, showering glass across the deck. The first burst blew away the captain's chest. He flew backward through the door and landed on his back on the bridge. His foot twitched violently for a few seconds before he died.

The second burst ripped into the mate as he clawed under his coat for the .38. It lifted him high in the air, twisted him around, and tossed him halfway across the deck. He fell like an empty sack, face down, most of his head blown away.

The remaining two crew members, the ones who had boarded the sailboat, turned wild-eyed toward the gunner. The shirtless man stabbed one of them in the chest with a bowie knife. He fell across the stern, babbling incoherently. The man with the submachine gun fired a burst into the chest of the last crewman, who dropped the gas can and flipped backward over the railing into the sea.

The shirtless man pulled his knife free, cleaned the blade on the dead man's pants, and tossed his victim overboard.

The shooter sent another burst into the light and it exploded into darkness.

It was all over in thirty seconds.

They worked very quickly, searching the boat. It took less than half an hour to find their prize. They transferred the three small, heavy bags to the sailboat, threw the captain and his mate into the sea, doused the trawler with gasoline, and set it afire.

The shirtless man cranked up the engine of the sailboat and guided it away from the trawler; then, setting the wheel, he joined the shooter and they checked out the prize.

"What d'ya think?" the shirtless man said, leaning over and staring into one of the bags.

"Beautiful," the shooter said. He moved behind his partner, took a .357 Magnum from his belt, and stepped closer.

"Sorry," he said. He held the gun an inch or so from the back of the shirtless man's head and squeezed the trigger. The gun roared and the bullet smacked into the back of the man's head, knocking him forward against the railing.

The shooter reached out for the body but it fell sideways, was caught for an instant in the line of the foresail, and then rolled over it and plunged face forward into the sea.

"Shit!" cried the shooter and made a frantic last grab, but it was gone. The body bobbed to the surface like a cork on a fishing line, then went under.

The shooter ran back to the tiller, shoved the throttle on full, and turned the boat sharply around. He searched for ten minutes, hoping to get a glimpse of his victim, but he finally gave up.

He was a mile or so away when the gasoline on the trawler exploded, spewing up a broiling ball of fire that for a moment or two rivaled the rising sun.

He watched the trailing smoke grow smaller and smaller until he could see it no longer.

ACE, DEUCE, TREY

Going back to Dunetown was worse than going to Vietnam. I didn't know what was in store for me in Nam; I knew what was waiting in Dunetown.

As the plane veered into its final approach, memories began to ambush me, memories that pulled me back to a place I had tried to forget for a lot of years, and to a time that was, in my mind, the last green summer of my life. After that, everything seemed to be tinted by the colors of autumn, colors of passage. Dying colors.

The colors of Nam.

Brown, muddy rivers. Dark green body bags. Black cinders where trees and villages had once stood. Gray faces with white eyes, waiting to be zipped up and shipped back to the World and laid away in the auburn earth.

Those were the hues that had painted my life since that summer. 1963, that was the year.

A long time ago.

For over twenty years I had tried to erase the scars of that year. Now, suddenly, it was thrust back at me like a dagger, and the names and faces of another time besieged me. Chief. Titan. Wally Butts and Vince Dooley. Teddy.

Doe.

Time had dulled the blade, sanded down the brittle edges, but it had only sharpened that one persistent pain. Doe Findley was the last fantasy I had left. I had flushed most of my other dreams, but that one I hung on to, protecting it, nurturing it, seeking shelter in it, and I wasn't ready yet to surrender it to reality.

It was raining, a steady downpour, as the small jet swept in low over the marshes. I squinted through the oval window, tear-streaked with raindrops, looking for something to orient me in time and place. I suppose I was expecting that same one-room shed that passed for a depot, with its coffee machine and half a dozen chairs they jokingly called a waiting room. Time plays crazy head tricks on you. In your head, time is a freeze frame. People don't grow older; the paint on houses doesn't chip or fade; trees don't get taller. The grass doesn't even grow.

What I really expected to see through that window was the past. What I saw was a low, glass and chrome terminal, exploding strobe lights limning the runways, other jets jockeying for position. There was more action on the runway than in Las Vegas on a Saturday night. Twenty years is a lot of reality to swallow in one dose, but that's what I got.

As I scampered down the stairs from the plane and across the ramp through the rain, I remembered something my father used to say:

"Anything that comes easily isn't worth having."

Well, actually it was my mother who said it. My father died in action in the Pacific three months before I was born. I was never very much for geography, but by the time I went to school, I knew just about everything there was to know about the island Guadalcanal. I knew its geographic coordinates, its shape; I knew it was barely one hundred miles long and thirty miles wide and that it was our first offensive target in the Pacific. And I knew that on August 20, 1942, at 22:15 hours which is quarter past ten at night, Captain J. L. Kilmer, First Marine Division, ceased being my father and became my mother's legend. I grew up with his Purple Heart and Navy Cross framed beside his picture over my desk so I would never forget him. Guadalcanal will always be an ugly, worthless, sliver of real estate in the middle of nowhere that nobody should've died for. Later, I was to learn firsthand about that kind of dying.

Anyway, his LST was blown out from under him on the first wave going in. He never even got his feet wet.

But I know about my old man, about what he believed, and about the place where he died. My mother made sure about that. The lessons she taught me while I was growing up always started the same way: "Your father used to say . . ."

Then she'd hit me with the payoff line.

I was probably sixteen or seventeen before I figured out that in order for my father to have passed on to my mother all the bromides fed to me during my formative years and attributed to him, he would have had to talk constantly, twenty-four hours a day, for the entire two years they were married. My father image was created by my mother. But it worked. By the time I got on to her, I figured my dad at twenty-two was wiser than Homer, Socrates, Newton, and Ben Franklin all rolled up in one. Funny thing is, I guess I still do.

"Your father used to say, 'Anything that comes too easily isn't worth having.' "

I should have listened to that reprise as I ran through the rain, but I had other things on my mind. It went in one ear, out the other, and never slowed down along the way.

When I entered the Dunetown terminal, I was slapped back to reality in a hurry. It was a city block long, with a moving sidewalk, a twenty-four-hour snack shop, a fancy European-type restaurant, and two bars.

In the time it took me to walk the length of the terminal and pick up my bags, I saw a first-class dip from Albuquerque named Digit Dan Delaney, two hookers from San Diego whose names eluded me, and a scam artist from Detroit named Spanish Eddie Fuereco, spinning the coin with a mark in a seersucker suit and a Hawaiian shirt.

They were all working. That told me a lot.

The lady at the airline counter had an envelope for me with car keys, registration, confirmed reservations at the Ponce Hotel, and a map of the town showing me how to get there. There was also a message that had been phoned in twenty minutes earlier:

"Urgent. Meet me at emergency entrance, city hospital, soon as possible."

It had been phoned in by a Lieutenant Morehead of the local police. And that reminded me of why I was there, which certainly wasn't to weep over my lost youth. A man named Franco Tagliani was the reason I was there, a mobster who headed an outfit called the Cincinnati Triad. For five years I had dogged Tagliani; for five years I had listened to his voice on wiretaps, watched him through binoculars, snapped pictures of him through a telephoto lens. For five years I had tried to bring Tagliani and his bunch down. I had tried everything due process would allow.

Zip.

In those five years I never got close enough to him to tip my hat good morning. It was embarrassing, five years and nothing to show for it but a goose egg.

Then he had disappeared. And with him, his whole bunch. Poof, just like that. The magic trick of the year. And now, nine months later, he had popped back up. And in Dunetown, the last place on earth I cared to be. Thanks a bunch, Franco.

This time we were going to play hard cheese. This time the score was going to be a little different.

I finessed the hotel and drove straight to the city hospital. The lieutenant was waiting at the entrance, an enormous man who towered over me.

"I'm Morehead," he said as my hand disappeared into his. "Call me Dutch."

"Jake Kilmer," I said.

Five minutes later I came face-to-face with Franco Tagliani for the first time. He was in a drawer in the basement freezer with a hole in his back, a nick in the shoulder, one more in his forehead, and an insurance shot in the right eye.

The tag on his toe said his name was Frank Turner but I knew better.

In the drawer beside him and just as dead was his number one boy, Nicky Stinetto. He had been shot three times, two of them good-bye hits. His tag said he was Nat Sherman, another lie.

Both bodies were badly burned, both had multiple body hits.

Two different guns. You don't need to be a coroner to tell the difference between the hole a .22 makes, and one made by a .357.

"Couple of pros?" I suggested.

"That or Wyatt Earp," Morehead said. He went on, sounding like an official police report. "The homicides occurred at approximately seven fifteen p.m. at the residence of the deceased, Turner . . . or Tagliani, whichever way you want it. The shooting was followed by an explosion. We're working on the bomb angle now. Tagliani's old lady got caught in the blowup. She's up in ICU, hangin' on by her pinky."

I looked at my watch. It was a little after nine.

"You've put together a pretty good sheet on this thing, considering it happened less than two hours ago," I said.

"We got a play-by-play on tape," he said and winked. Billy Morehead, head of the Special Operations Branch, local police, had Kraut written all over his battered face. He stared down at me through pale blue, hooded eyes that lurked behind gold-rimmed glasses. Morehead was the size of a prize bull with hands like cantaloupes, sandy hair going gray, a soft but growling voice, and a penchant for swearing in German, all of which had earned him the nickname Dutch. He was cordial, but cautious, and although I had known him for only thirty minutes, I was beginning to like his style.

I said, "Well, so much for them. Let's hope his widow makes it. Maybe she saw something."

"She'll never stool if she did. They're all alike."

There was nothing more to do there until the autopsy, so we went up to the intensive care unit on the second floor. Mrs. Tagliani looked like she was on her way to the moon; lines sticking out of both arms, a mask over her face, and behind the bed, three different monitors recording her life signs, what was left of them. The coronary reader seemed awfully lazy, *bip, bip, bipping* slowly as its green lines moved across the center of the monitor screen, streaking up with each *bip*.

Nobody from the family was in sight. I asked Dutch about that. He shrugged and smoothed the corners of his Bavarian mustache with the thumb and forefinger of each hand.

"Probably hiding under the bed" was his only comment.

The intern, a callow young man with a teenager's complexion, told us the widow had suffered first-degree burns over seventy percent of her body, had glass imbedded in her chest and stomach, and had been buried under debris which had caused severe head injuries.

"What're her chances?" I asked.

"A Kansas City shoe clerk might take the odds," he said, and went away.

"I got a man on the front door, another one in a green robe on this floor," Dutch said. "Nobody can get near her. Whyn't ya come with me? I gotta debrief my people."

Mrs. Tagliani made the decision for me. While we were standing there the heart monitor went sour. It stopped bipping and the green lines settled into a continuous streak.

The machine went *deeeeeeeeee*.

"*Schmerz!*" Dutch muttered. I had heard the expression before. Roughly translated, it meant a sorry state of affairs. I couldn't have put it better.

A moment later the intern and two nurses rushed in, followed by the trauma unit with their rolling table filled with instruments.

We stayed around for ten minutes or so until they gave it up.

"*Eins, zwei, drei,*" Dutch growled. "One more and we'd have us a home run. Looks like you made a long trip for naught, Mr. Kilmer."

"Yeah," I said.

"I gotta call homicide, tell 'em Tagliani's missus went across. I'll be a minute. You're stayin' at the Ponce, right?"

"Right."

"Nice digs," Dutch said.

He went into the ICU office, made two phone calls in the time it took me to straighten my tie, and came back.

"I hear you know the town," he said as we headed for the parking lot.

"I do if it hasn't changed in twenty years," I answered.

He laughed, but it was a sardonic, humorless laugh. "You're in for a surprise," he said. "Follow me over to the hotel. You can plant your car and run out to the Warehouse with me."

"The Warehouse?"

"That's what we call our layout."

I told him that was damn white of him and we headed out into the hot, rainy night.

2

SIGHTSEEING

It was only a few blocks back to the hotel but I saw enough through the windshield wipers and rain to tell me what twenty years had done to Dunetown. These were not the wrinkles of time; this was a beautiful woman turned whore. Tagliani's death had started the worms nibbling at my stomach. One look at downtown Dunetown turned the worms to writhing, hissing snakes, striking at my insides.

Twenty years ago Ocean Avenue was a dark, romantic, two-lane blacktop, an archway of magnolias dripping with Spanish moss, that meandered from Dunetown to the sea, six miles away. Now it was Ocean Boulevard, a six-lane highway that slashed between an infinity of garish streetlights like a scar. Neither tree nor bush broke up the eerie green glow, but a string of hotel billboards did, their flashing neon fingers beckoning tourists to the beach.

Front Street was worse. I was so shocked by what had happened here that I stopped the car, got out, and stood in the rain, staring at a street gone mad. It was so far from the Front Street in my freeze frame, I couldn't relate to it.

The Front Street I remembered was like the backdrop of a Norman Rockwell painting. There were two old movie houses that showed double features. There was Bucky's drugstore, which had a marble-top soda fountain where you could still get a milk-shake made out of real ice cream and sit in an old-fashioned wire-back chair to enjoy it. And there was the town landmark, Blaine's Department Store, which filled an entire block. The people of

Dunetown once got everything from their diapers to their funeral clothes at Blaine's.

Gone. No more Bucky's, no more Blaine's, and the two theaters were twenty-four-hour porno houses. A neon blight had settled over the heart of the town like a garish cloud. Hookers peddled their bodies from under marquees to keep out of the rain, hawkers lured out-of-towners and footloose horseplayers into all-nudie revues, and "bottomless" and "topless" signs glittered everywhere. The blaring and oppressive beat of disco music was the street's theme song.

I had been there before, along Hollywood's strip and in the Boston combat zone. The scenario was always the same. You couldn't buy a drink in any bar on the street without staring at a naked bosom or getting propositioned by a waitress—or waiter, depending on your inclination.

My God, I thought, what's happened here? How could Chief and Titan have let this happen to a town they had once treated like a new bride?

The neon blight held the next six blocks in its fist.

And then, as if some medieval architect had built an invisible wall right through the middle of the city, the neon vanished and Dunetown turned suddenly elegant. It was as if time had tiptoed past this part of town with its finger to its lips. Old trees embraced mansions and two-hundred-year-old townhouses. The section had been restored to Revolutionary grandeur with spartan and painstaking accuracy. Gas lamps flickered on the corners, the streets were mostly window-lit, and there were flower-laced squares every three or four blocks, fountained oases that added a sense of symmetry and beauty to the place.

My reaction was simple.

The town was schizo to the core.

3

DOOMSTOWN

Dutch was waiting for me under the awning in front of the Ponce, the political watering hole of Dunetown, a grand, old, creaky hotel, dripping with potted plants, and one of the few things in

Dunetown that hadn't changed. His hands were stuffed in the pockets of a bagged-out, nondescript suit, and a Camel was tucked in the corner of his mouth. If he had a care in the world, it didn't show. I parked behind a large black limo, gave the keys to the garageman, checked in, gave a bellhop five bucks to drop my bag in my room, and tossed my briefcase into Dutch's backseat.

As I crawled into the front seat, I was still shell-shocked from the sights and sounds of Dunetown.

"Okay, let's roll," he said, pulling into the dark, palm-lined street.

He didn't have anything to volunteer; his attitude was still co-operative but cautious. And while I was interested in getting the lowdown on Tagliani-Turner, for the moment I was more interested in what had happened to the local landscape.

After a block or two of silence I asked, "What in hell happened to Dunetown?"

He stared over at me with a funny look on his face, then, as if answering his own question, said, "Oh, yeah, I keep forgetting you lived here once."

"Not here," I said. "Not in *this* town. Anyway, I didn't live here. I was, uh . . . I guess you could say I was a summer guest."

"When was that again?"

I was trying to be casual, trying to keep away from personal history. I didn't know him well enough to show him any scars.

"Twenty years ago, just for a couple of months. It's hardly worth mentioning," I answered in an offhand way.

"You were just a kid then."

"Yeah, a senior in college." While I didn't want to get too personal, I didn't want to play games, either.

"Teddy Findley was my best friend," I added after a second or two.

"Oh," he said. "Then you know what's been going on."

"No, I got out of touch with the family," I said.

"You know the Findley kid is dead?"

"You mean Teddy?"

"Yeah."

"Yes," I said. "It's after that I kind of lost track of things."

"Well, what happened was the racetrack, that's what. The town got bent. Twenty years ago there was probably, what, seventy-five, a hundred thousand people?"

"Sounds about right."

"Probably three hundred thousand now, about half of 'em from the shady side of the tracks. What you got here, you got a major racetrack, and a beauty. Looks like Saratoga. A classy track, okay? That's a gimmee."

"Where is it?"

"Back behind us, on the other side of the river. It's dark now, anyway."

"Okay, so you got a classy track. Then what?"

"I think maybe what the money in town expected was kind of another Ascot. Everybody standing around sipping tea, wavin' their pinkies in the air. What they got is horseplayers, which come in every shape, size, and variety known to mankind, and about half of them smoke tea; they don't drink it."

"So that's what Front Street's all about?"

"It appeals to some of that element. It isn't Front Street's gonna make your gonads shrink. It's what happened to the rest of the town. They turned it into a little Miami."

"They? Who's they?"

"The wimps that took over. Look, Chief Findley's an old man. Most of the rest of the old power structure's dead. They turned it over to their heirs. Keepers of the kingdom, right? Wrong. Wimps, the lot of 'em, with maybe an exception or two."

"I probably know some of them," I said.

"Probably. But it wasn't just them, it was anybody had a square foot of ground they could sell. Condos all over the place. High-rise apartments. Three big hotels on the beach, another one going up. Real estate outta sight. Two marinas as big as Del Mar. You feel bad now, wait'll you see Doomstown in the daylight."

That was the first time I heard it called Doomstown, but it was far from the last.

"I'm still surprised Chief Findley and the old power structure let it happen," I said.

"Couldn't do anything about it," Dutch growled. "They died or were too old to cope."

An edge had crept into his tone, a touch of anger mixed with contempt. He seemed to sense it himself and drove quietly while he calmed down.

I tried to fill in the dead space. "My father used to say you can inherit blood but you can't inherit backbone."

For the first few blocks we drove through the Dunetown I wanted to remember, the large section of the midtown area that had been restored to its Revolutionary elegance.

I remembered driving through the section with Chief and Teddy

17

one Sunday afternoon a long time ago. It had fallen on hard times; block after block of broken-down row houses that were either boarded over or had been converted into cheap rooming houses. We were in Chief's black Rolls convertible and he was sitting on the edge of his seat, shoulders square, his white hair thrashing in the wind.

"We're going to restore this whole damn part of town," he had said grandly, in his soft, Irish-southern accent, while waving his arm at the drab ruins. "Not a damn museum like Williamsburg. I mean a livin', breathin' place where people will be proud to live. Feel like they're part of her history. Share bed and board with her ghosts. This is the heart of the city, by God! And if the heart stops, the city dies. You boys just remember that." He paused to appraise the street, then added, half under his breath, "Someday it'll be your responsibility." And Teddy looked over at me and winked. In those days I was one of the boys.

It seemed he had kept that bargain, although God knows what miserable trade he had made, allowing the business section to go to hell. That part of it didn't make sense. This part did. The parks and squares opened the town up, letting it breathe and flourish naturally, giving it a personality of its own. Here and there, expensive-looking shops and galleries nudged up against the town-houses. You could tell that zoning here was communal, that the rules were probably shaped by common consent.

"This is better," I said. "But Front Street, Jesus!"

"They had to give the two-dollar bettors someplace to play," Dutch said matter-of-factly.

We took a left and a right and were back to reality again. We were on the edge of Back O'Town, a kind of buffer between Dunetown and the black section. You could feel poverty in the air. The fancy shops gave way to army-navy stores and cut-rate furniture outlets. It was the worn-out part of town. A lot of used-car lots and flophouse hotels.

We drove in silence for a minute or two, then I asked, "How long you been here, Dutch?"

"Came down from Pittsburgh almost four years ago, right after they passed the referendum for the track."

"They built it when?"

"It opened for business year before last and the town went straight to hell. From white Palm Beach suits to horse blanket jackets and plaid pants overnight. You gotta bust an eardrum to hear a southern accent anymore." His own was a kind of guttural Pennsylvania Dutch.

"You mean like yours?" I joked.

He chuckled. "Yeah, like mine."

"Town on the make," I said, half-aloud.

"You got that right."

"How long you been a cop?"

"Forever," he said, without even thinking.

He turned down a dark residential street, driving fast but without circus lights or siren.

"Hell of a note," I said. "Chief and his bunch pampered Dunetown. It was like a love affair."

"Well, pal, that's a long time ago. It's a one-night stand now." He paused and added, "You know the Findleys that well, huh?"

I thought about that for a minute before answering.

"Well, twenty years dims the edges," I said.

"Ain't that the truth." Dutch lit a cigarette and added, "Sounds like you thought a lot of the old man."

I nodded. "You could say that."

"The way it comes to me, his kid was a war hero, got himself wasted over in Nam. After that the old guy just folded up. Least that's the way I hear it."

"Too bad," I said. I was surprised at how indifferent my words sounded.

"I guess."

"I gather you've got reservations about Findley," I said.

He shrugged. "It's the machine. I don't trust anybody's been in politics longer than it takes me to eat lunch. And I'm a fast eater."

Old feelings welled up inside me, noodling at my gut again, a passing thing I couldn't quite get in touch with. Or didn't want to.

"It was like a fiefdom, y'know," he went on. "A couple of heavyweights calling all the shots. Now it's a scramble to see who can get richest."

It was an accurate appraisal and I said so.

"It's what power's all about," I told him.

"So I got a dollar, you got two. That makes you twice as good as me?"

"No," I said, "twice as dangerous."

He thought about that for a few seconds.

"I guess it all depends on who you are," Dutch said. Then he dropped the bomb. "Findley's daughter tried to take up the slack. After his son was zeroed, I mean."

Bang, there it was.

"How's that?" I asked, making it sound as casual as a yawn.

"Married herself a hotshot All-American. He grabbed the ball from Findley and took off with it. Harry Raines is his name. Talk about ironic."

"How so?"

"Findley's own son-in-law's head of the racetrack commission."

That one caught me a little off guard.

"How did that happen?" I asked.

"Wasn't for Raines, there wouldn't be a racetrack. We'd all be dustin' our kiesters someplace else."

"Raines . . ." I echoed.

"Harry Raines, the son-in-law," he said.

"Yeah, I know. I was just thinking about the name. Harry Raines," I said.

"Know him?"

"Vaguely."

Harry Raines. I remembered the name but I couldn't put a face with it. Faces come hard after twenty years.

"Raines put it all together. This whole racetrack thing."

"Why?"

"You'll have to ask him that," said Dutch.

"This Raines a stand-up guy?"

"I couldn't say different. What I hear, old Harry's gonna be governor one of these days."

"You mean because of the racetrack?"

"I guess that's part of it."

"What's the rest of it?" I asked.

"It's a long story," he said. "Worth a dinner."

"Fair enough," I said. "What do you think?"

"About what?"

"About whether Harry Raines is going to be governor or not?"

"I think the sun rises in the east and sets in the west," he said.

And that was the end of that.

4
LEADBETTER'S LEGACY

The rain had turned into a driving storm by the time we got to
Dutch Morehead's war room, which was in a small, rundown shop-
ping center in the suburbs, a mile or two from the center of town.
Lightning etched in purple monochromes a shabby, flat, one-story
building that had once been a supermarket. Its plate-glass windows were boarded over and the entire building was painted flat
black.

"Looks like Gestapo headquarters," I said.

"Psychological," Dutch grunted.

A less than imposing sign beside the entrance announced that
it was the SPECIAL OPERATIONS BRANCH. Below it, even less imposing letters whispered DUNETOWN POLICE DEPARTMENT. I had to
squint to read that line.

"Nice of you to mention the police department," I said.

"I thought so," Dutch said.

"What exactly does Special Operations Branch mean?" I asked.

"I'm not real sure myself," he said. "I think they just wanted
to call us the SOB's."

A moment later Dutch roared like a lion demanding lunch.

"That sorry, flat-assed, pea-brained sappenpaw!" he said, curl-
ing his lip.

"Who?" I said, thinking maybe I had offended him.

"That six-toed, web-footed, sappenpaw, *klommenshois* Callahan,"
he raved on. "The mackerel-snapping, redheaded putz stole my
damn parking place *again*! If I told him once, I told him—arrgh . . ."
His voice trailed off as he whispered further insults under his
breath.

A half dozen cars in various stages of disrepair were angle-
parked along the front of the building. Dented fenders, cracked
windshields, globs of orange primer where paint jobs had been
started and never finished, hood ornaments and hubcaps gone;
it looked like the starting line of a demolition derby.

"Your boys got something against automobiles?" I asked.

He growled something under his breath and wheeled into a spot marked only THE KID.

"I'll take Mufalatta's place," he said defensively. "He's never around anyway."

We were fifty yards from the front door, a long way in the raging storm. He cut the engine and leaned back, offering me a Camel.

"No thanks, I quit," I said.

"I don't wanna hear about it," he said, lighting up. He cracked the window and let the smoke stream out into the downpour.

"I can understand about your feelings toward old man Findley," he said. "The old boy had a lotta class, I'll give him that. He dealt one last hand before he retired."

"How's that?"

"His last hurrah. He brought in Ike Leadbetter to head up the force here. Findley was smart enough to know the burg needed some keen people to keep an eye on things when the track was built—the local cops were about as sophisticated as a warthog in a top hat. Leadbetter had been through the mill already. He'd done a turn up in Atlantic City before he came here, so he was savvy. Was Leadbetter brought me in."

"And Leadbetter is good?"

"Was."

"Where'd he go?"

"No place. He's dead. Leadbetter knew what was gonna happen, I mean law-wise. He had learned a lot in Atlantic City. And he was honest."

"What happened to him?" I asked.

"Three years ago, ran his car into the river, if you can believe that."

"You don't?"

"I stopped believin' in accidents an hour after I got here."

I was beginning to wonder how Tagliani fit into the picture. Killing a police chief was not exactly his way of doing things.

Anger crept back into Dutch's tone. "The way it was, the case went to the homicide boys. You lump that whole bunch together, what you end up with is a bigger lump. Not a one of 'em can count to eleven without takin' off his shoes." Pause. "It went down as an accident, period, end, of course."

"Who took Leadbetter's place?"

"Herb Walters."

"What's the score with him?"

"Old-timer. Up through the ranks. Scared for his job. He don't swim upstream, if that's what you mean. Herb likes calm waters."

"Is he honest?"

"That's an excellent question. I just don't know. I guess old Herb's okay; he just hasn't had an original thought since the first time he went to the john by himself." He stopped, then after a moment added: "Actually he's just a kiss-ass to the people on the green side of town."

I laughed. "I gather you don't like him."

"That's very smart gathering."

"Why would anybody want to blitz Leadbetter?"

"Why would a lotta people *not* want to? A smart, tough, no-nonsense cop, honest as the Old Testament, in a town going to hell. When Leadbetter was running the show, you couldn't find a pimpmobile anywhere on Front Street. Now every other vehicle you see's either a pink Caddy or a purple Rolls-Royce."

"How does your outfit fit into all this?"

"It's borderline. We try to monitor the out-of-towners, but local stuff is handled by vice. Don't even ask me about them."

I slid down in my seat and shook my head.

"Wonderful," I said. "Maybe I'll just take some sick leave and sleep this one out."

"Stick around and watch the fireworks," he said.

"You think that's going to happen, eh?"

"Well, what I don't think is that Turner and his pistol and his wife had a suicide pact."

I laughed. "His name's Tagliani," I said.

"Whatever."

"I agree," I said. "It's my experience that when a *mafioso capo di tutti capi* gets wasted, it doesn't just quietly blow over."

"*Verdammt!*"

"If you're right and Leadbetter was assassinated, that could have been the kickoff, right there."

Dutch threw away his butt and checked the weather. It was still like a monsoon outside. He sighed.

"Look," he said, "here's the long and short of it, okay? The way it went was that big daddy Findley plugged in Leadbetter, tells him keep the town clean. But Leadbetter inherits a department so old and leaky, if it was a bucket you couldn't carry rocks in it. He can't just vacuum out the whole outfit. That's where I come into the picture. Ike brings me in, gives me a decent budget, says, 'Go out, get yourself a dozen or so of the toughest no-shit lads you can find. Boys who know something about the LCN and can't be bent.' So I went lookin'. What I got is one mean bunch of hooligans. They're savvy and tough enough to take heat. And they're about as friendly as a nest of copperheads."

I said "Uh-huh" pensively. There was a message in all that for me.

"I just want you to understand the way the land rolls, see," he went on. "What it was, Leadbetter didn't trust anybody on the old force. Our job was to keep our eyes open, build up our snitches, hassle the out-of-town conmen, grifters, dips, hustlers. Put a little heat under the undesirables so they'd move on. Try to keep a line on who's who and what's what. The tough thing is to do it without walkin' on toes. We hassle a hooker, vice gets pissed. We break down an out-of-town dice game, bunco goes crazy. So we pretty much been spinning our wheels up till now. I mean, we do okay, but . . ." He paused, looking for the next sentence, and finally said, "Maybe I'm just tired of doin' rounds with the front office."

I let it all sink in. What I thought I was hearing was that the local police were either stupid or on the take. It was Morehead's job to cover all the bases.

"Leadbetter and Findley played it real smart," Dutch continued. "They gave us very loose power, so to speak, and fixed it so we report to a select committee of the city commission."

"You're not part of the department, then?"

"Yeah. We deal with them when we have to. But Walters can't fire any of us, so we pretty much play it our way. He don't like it, but it's a tough-*sheiss* situation for him. Otherwise, we'd probably all be sorting files in Short Arm, Kansas, by now."

"He fights you?"

"Not in the open. But he wants control. He's a back-fighter. Hell, I'm talkin' too much," he growled suddenly, and fell silent. I could tell from his flat monotone that he was having trouble trusting me. He was being just friendly enough not to be unfriendly.

The storm rolled over and the rain turned to a fine mist.

He locked the car and we headed for the front door, squeezing up against the building to keep out of the rain that swirled under its eaves.

"Once ya get t'know the gang, you can come, go as ya please," Dutch said as we hurried toward the door. "For now, they ain't gonna give you a dime for the toilet unless I'm with you."

I stopped and he almost ran into me. He loomed over me, his hands jammed in his pockets and an unlit butt in his mouth.

"You got a hard-on for Feds?" I asked.

"Let's just say we've had a few bad rounds with 'em," he said, studying me through eyes the color of sapphires. Rainwater dribbled from the brim of his battered brown felt hat.

"Well, who hasn't?" I said.

"You *are* the Fed," he said.

"Look, I'm on *your* side. I'm not the Feebies or the Leper Colony. You've dealt with the Freeze before. You and Mazzola are practically old pals by now."

"Like I said, it's one-on-one in there. These guys don't even trust each other sometimes."

"How about you?" I asked. "Am I on probation with you, too? Where do you stand?"

"Out here in the rain getting soaked," he said. "Can we maybe continue this inside? There's a lot more of me getting wet than there is of you."

And he turned and stomped off toward the door.

5

THE WAREHOUSE

Dutch Morehead herded me toward the door with his sheer bulk. I'd been this route before, getting the red eye from the local police. Local cops don't like to deal with Feds because they get treated like kids and because they get the runaround from the Feebies and the shaft from the Lepers. My outfit, the Federal Racket Squad, was different. Part of the job was working on the local level, pointing them in the right direction on interstate cases. Sometimes it took a while for that to sink in.

I decided to save a little time, so I put on my tough-guy act.

"I just like to know where I stand without reading a road map," I snapped as we hurried along through the rain. "If I'm on some kind of probation with this bunch of yours, then screw it. I'll go it alone."

He stopped me and smiled condescendingly.

"Cut the bullshit," he said.

"No bullshit," I said. "The hell with this one-on-one, sink-or-swim crap. I didn't come here to audition for you and yours."

"What the hell got under your saddle all of a sudden?"

"You know what the Freeze is all about?" I demanded, and went on before he could answer. "We're the only federal agency around who works with the street cops. The FBI, the IRS, Justice Department, they're all in it for themselves."

"And you're not?" he demanded. "You came here to bust this Tagliani's balls, right or wrong?"

"I came here to find out what he's doing here—"

"Was," he interrupted.

"Was," I agreed. "But if he was here, then the rest of his bunch is close by. I know this outfit, Dutch. I know this gang better than anyone alive. Sure, I want to bring the whole bunch down. What do you want to do, send flowers?"

He lit his Camel and took a long pull, staring hard at me all the while.

"Look here," he said. "Before, when I was talking about what our assignment is, I left one thing out. We were supposed to keep organized crime out of Doomstown. All of a sudden, your boss tells me we got Mafia up to our eyeballs. How do you think that makes me feel? All of us, the whole bunch. Like monkeys, that's how."

"Cisco didn't invite them down here, y'know. He just recognized a face and turned them up for you, that's all. If it was the Feebies, you can bet your sweet by-and-by they'd be all over town and you couldn't find out what day it is from any of them."

"You're right there."

"So we throw in together and bring them down?"

"If somebody doesn't beat us to it."

"Okay. So tell your boys to forget this college Charlie shit," I said, still acting irritated. "This isn't pledge week at the old frat house and I'm not here to impress anybody. If these guys are as tough as you make them sound, it'll help if you give me a vote of confidence off the top."

Not bad, Kilmer, not bad at all. Hard case but not hard nose. They can live with that.

Dutch started laughing.

"Sensitive, ain't you," he said, and led me into the building. We walked through the front door into what looked like the entrance to a prison block: a small boxlike room, a door with a bell on one side, and a mirror in the wall beside it. One-way glass. Dutch shoved a thumb against the bell. A second later the door buzzed open. Inside, a black, uniformed cop sat in a dark-ened cubicle, watching the entrance. An Uzi submachine gun was leaning on the wall beside him. I nodded and got a blank stare back.

"Looks like you're expecting an invasion," I said.

"Security. Nobody gets in here without one of us saying so. That includes everybody from the chief of police and the mayor to the President of the United States."

"Nice weapon," I said, with a nod toward the Uzi.

"We liberated it. My bunch is pretty good at dog-robbing," Dutch said, then added, almost as an afterthought, "among other things."

Inside, the front of the place had been divided into half a dozen office cubicles. Behind them, in the center of the building, was a fairly sophisticated computer system and a telephone switchboard. Behind that was what appeared to be a large meeting room, walled with chalk- and corkboards. A six-foot television screen was mounted in the wall at the front of the room and twenty or so old-fashioned movable chairs were scattered about, the kind with writing plat-forms attached, like they had in school when I was a kid—and still do, for all I know.

The big room in back was affectionately known as the Kinder-garten.

Two rooms filled the back end of the old supermarket. One was a holding cell that looked big enough to accommodate the entire D-Day invasion force, and the other was behind a door marked simply VIDEO OPERATIONS. I counted three uniformed cops on duty, including the man on the door and a black woman who was operating the switchboard.

A pretty classy setup: Morehead's war room.

"Are the uniform people part of your gang or on loan-out?"

"Probation. If they can hack the everyday stuff, they maybe can work their way into the gang. Also we find out pretty quick whether they can keep their mouths shut."

I decided to take one last shot at my immediate problem. "Be-fore the rest of your guys show up," I said, "can we settle this Fed problem?"

"It's settled. We don't have a problem," he said, trying to brush it off.

"Right," I said with more than a little acid. I decided to let him blow off a little steam.

"Okay," he snapped, "let's put it this way. At first we tried workin' with the IRS, but cooperating with the Leper Colony is no different than loanin' your watch to Jesse James. They're either young turks just out of college, in it so they can learn how to beat the system and get rich, or they're misfits none of the other agencies'll touch. Either way, it's every man for himself. Like workin' in a patch of skunk cabbage."

"No argument," I said.

"A bunch of *pfutzlükers!*" he bellowed.

"Absolutely," I agreed. "Whatever that means."

"If I broke half the laws they do, I'd be doing time."

"Life plus twenty, at least." Now it was his turn and I let him rage on.

He leaned over me, jabbing his chest with his thumb. "I wouldn't let one of 'em in here, not if he showed up with a court order and the entire Marine Corps to back 'em up!" he roared. "And the Feebies aren't much better! All they wanna do is make nickels in Washington. If it looks good on the daily report and they can get a press conference out of it, that's all they care about. Ask them for a little help, you get senile waitin' for the phone to ring."

"I've had the same experience," I said with sympathy.

"Dipshits and robots!" he said. Now his arms were in the act. He was waving them around like a symphony conductor. "Bastards steal our information, make deals that sour our cases, violate civil rights, and we get the enema. They always ride off with the chick in the end."

I nodded agreement. He was running out of steam.

"All my boys get is to kiss the horse at the fadeout, know what I mean?"

"Sure." Pause. "How about you?"

"How about me what?"

"You feel all you get out of them is to kiss the horse?"

He stopped and stared me up and down and then he figured it all out and started to laugh.

"Aw, hell, pal," he said, "I been around so long I'm glad for all the kissin' I can get, even if it's a horse's ass."

"Okay, Dutch," I said quietly. "I'm not looking for any fadeout kisses. If these people are looting your town, I'll help you put them away. All the Freeze wants out of it is information. Connections. How they operate. How did they infiltrate the town?

Who did they have to buy? How are they connected with the other mobs? No conflict, okay?"

"We'll just play it by ear," he said, still coy. It was like kicking a brick wall.

"Shit, if that's the play, that's the play," I said with a shrug.

"You'll do fine. You got a hair up your ass just like the rest of us."

"I just do the best I can," I said, throwing in a little humility.

"According to your boss, that's pretty damn good," he said.

"Far as I'm concerned, if we get enough to make a case against somebody, it can go state or federal," I said. "My style is give it to whoever has the strongest case—and the best prosecutor. I get a little crazy when somebody walks on me."

"That's fair enough," he said. "Who doesn't?"

"What kind of DA do you have?"

"A woman. Her name's Galavanti and she's meaner than a three-day hangover."

"On us or them?"

He smiled. "On *every*body. You put a case on her with holes in it, you'll hear language would turn a lifer purple."

"Good. Maybe we can help each other."

"Thing of it is, I never heard of your bunch until a couple months ago. This guy Mazzola shows up one day outta the blue, buys me lunch, gives me the same buck and wing you're givin' me."

Mazzola was Cisco Mazzola, my boss in the Freeze. He had told me Dutch Morehead was a man who said his piece and I was beginning to believe him.

"Which you sneezed off," I said.

"Not exactly. For starters, he put something in the pot."

"Like what?"

"Like the Stick."

"The Stick? What's the Stick?"

He looked at me kind of funny, one of those "what year were you born" looks.

"Not what, who. You know . . . the Stick. Parver. So far he fits right in."

I didn't have the foggiest idea what he was talking about and before I could pursue it any further, he picked up a bright red bullhorn, turned up the volume, and summoned his men to the back room.

I took the opportunity to step into an empty office and call the hotel. They patched me through to Cisco, who was in the restaurant, eating. He had flown in from Washington to brief me on the local situation. Since it had changed radically in the last couple of hours, I didn't know what to expect.

Cisco and I were friends in a remote kind of way. He was one of several shadows that wove in and out of my life, altering its course without ever touching me directly, our main connection provided by the telephone company. In the seven or so years I had known him, I had never seen the inside of his house, never met his family, and knew little about his personal tastes other than that he had a penchant for vitamins and health food. He also had an obsession about saving his hair, most of which was gone.

It took him a minute to get to the phone.

"Sorry to take you away from dinner," I said. "I would have called sooner but I've been busy. There's been a takeout. Tagliani, Stinetto, and Tagliani's wife."

"Yes, I've heard," he said in his flat, no-nonsense voice. "Any details yet?"

"At his place, about three hours ago. Pistols and a fire bomb. The woman was killed by the bomb. Whoever scratched the other two knew what he, or they, were doing. It looks like a couple of Petes to me."

"I want you to stay with this," he said.

"Good. How many have you made so far?"

"The whole mob's here except for Tuna Chevos and his gunslinger—"

"Nance," I hissed, cutting him off. Anger roiled inside me at the mention of Turk Nance. We went back a ways, Nance and I, and it wasn't a friendly trip. "They're here too," I said. "I'll give you odds."

"Maybe so, but this isn't a vendetta. Nance is just a tinhorn shooter. Forget him."

"Right."

"Forget him, Jake."

"I heard you!"

"What are you so edgy about?"

"Oh, nothing at all. I've been hounddogging this mob for what, four, five years?"

"Closer to five," he sighed.

"I'm just a little burned that the iceman beat me to it."

"Understandable. Just remember why you're here. I want information. Where are you now?"

"Morehead's war room."

"A good man," Cisco said. "A little short on procedure, maybe."

That was the understatement of the year.

I said, "So far he's treating me like I just broke his leg."

"Cautious," said Cisco. "Give him a little time."

"What happens if things pick up speed and I need some backup?" I asked.

"Mickey Parver will help you," he said.

"He the one they call Stick?"

"Right."

"I felt a little like an idiot. How come I never heard of this guy before now?"

"Because you never read the weekly report, that's why," he snapped. "He files a report every—"

I cut him off, trying to change the subject.

"Oh, yeah, I do seem to remember—"

"Don't bullshit me," said Cisco. "You haven't read the weekly poop sheet since the pope was a plumber."

"How long's he been in the squad?" I asked, trying to avoid that issue.

"He's been in the squad for a year or so," Cisco said, with annoyance. "You'll like him. He's young and not too jaded yet. Please don't spoil him by getting lost out in left field someplace. He's a lot like you, a lone wolf. You two can be good for each other."

"I don't have time to baby-sit some—"

"Who said anything about baby-sitting? Did I say that?"

"It sounded like—"

"It sounded like just what I said. Don't stray off the dime, Jake. I want information, period. You're a lawyer and you always stick to due process. I'd like a little of that to rub off on Stick."

"I got a feeling he's not going to get a lot of help in that respect from Morehead's bunch."

"That's what I mean," Cisco said. "Give the lad a little balance, okay?"

"What if I need some *professional* backup?" I asked.

"He wouldn't be in the Freeze if he wasn't first class, and you know it," Cisco growled. "You get in trouble, he's as good a man to have at the back door as you could ask. All I'm saying is, if we do happen to turn up a RICO case, I want it to be airtight. No illegal wiretaps, no hacking their computers. Nothing that won't hold up in court."

"Yeah, okay," I said.

Cisco couldn't resist throwing in a little jab.

"Maybe he can get you to file a report now and again, once a week or so, y'know."

"Mm-hmm."

"Dutch has a computer setup. You can tie directly into our terminal in Washington."

"Right," I said, and before I could move on to something else, he added sarcastically, "Maybe he can help you a little in that area."

"Sure thing."

"Stick sent the Tagliani photos up to me in his weekly report; that's how we made them."

I was beginning to hate this kid they called Stick, already. He sounded like a miserable little eager beaver.

"How long you in town for?" I asked.

"I'm in town to say hello," Cisco answered. "I head back to Washington tomorrow."

"Aw, and just when the fun's starting."

"Somebody has to put food on the table. We're in the middle of the annual battle of the budget—which reminds me, you're two months behind in your expense reports and you haven't filed a field report for—"

"Tell me more about this Stick fellow," I said, trying to avoid another issue.

Mazzola paused. "I want those expense reports," he said. "Clear?"

"Right. You got 'em."

"Now, about Parver. Before he came with us, he was a D.C. plainclothes, then a narc, then he worked on the D.C. mob squad. Before all that he did time in Nam. Army intelligence or something. He's tough enough."

"Not too jaded, huh?"

Cisco chuckled like he'd just heard a dirty joke. "I loaned him to Dutch. I don't think anybody else in the outfit knows he's one of us. Dutch'll fix it so the two of you can pair up. You'll like him."

"Says who?"

"All the ladies do."

"Great."

"Sorry about Tagliani," Mazzola said. "I know how long you been working on his case."

"Well, saves the Fed a lot of money, I suppose," I said. "But it would have been nice to put the bastard in Leavenworth with his brother."

"One more thing," Cisco said before hanging up. "You're not here to solve any murder cases. You're here to find out if there were any outside mob strings on Tagliani and who holds them. That's number one. We could have a classic case working here, Jake."

"Morehead said something funny," I told him. "He said, 'I've got the whole thing on tape.'"

"What whole thing? You mean the Tagliani hit?"

"I guess so. He was evasive when I asked him."

"Well, ask him again. You can fill me in at breakfast."

"Sure."

"I'll meet you in the hotel restaurant. Eight o'clock suit you?"

"Nine might be better."

"See you at eight," he said, ending the conversation.

INSTANT REPLAY

When I got back to the Kindergarten, Dutch Morehead's SOB's were beginning to gather in the room. One or two had drifted in. Dutch had a handful of photographs which he was about to pin on a corkboard. A quick glance confirmed that the Tagliani gang was in Dunetown and was there in force. Only two pictures were missing: Tuna Chevos and his gunman, Turk Nance. And as I told Cisco, I knew they had to be in Dunetown somewhere.

"That's Tagliani's outfit all right," I told Dutch. "All but two of them. Otherwise known as the Cincinnati Triad. Mind if I ask you what put you on to him in the first place?"

"Ever hear of Charlie Flowers?" Dutch asked.

"Charlie 'One Ear' Flowers?" I asked, surprised.

"Could there be more than one?" he said with a smile.

"Everybody in the business has heard of Charlie One Ear," I said.

"What've you heard?" he asked.

Charlie One Ear was a legend in the business. It was said that he had the best string of snitches in the country, had a computer for a brain, was part Indian, and was one of the best trackers alive. If rumor was correct, Flowers could find a footprint in a jar of honey, and I told Dutch that.

"Ever meet him?"

"No," I said, "I've never met a living legend."

"What have you heard lately?"

He asked it the way people who already know the answers ask questions.

I hesitated for a moment, then said, "Word is, he got on the sauce and had to retire."

"You been listening to a bunch of *sheiss kopfes*," he said. "That gent in the tweeds, second row there, that's Charlie One Ear. He's never had a drink in his life."

I looked at him. He was short and squat, a barrel of a man, impeccably dressed in a tweed suit, tan suede vest, and a perfectly matched tie. His mustache was trimmed to perfection, his nails immaculately manicured. He had no right ear, just a little bunch of balled-up flesh where it should have been. I had heard that story too. When Flowers was a young patrolman in St. Louis, a mugger bit his ear off.

He was chatting with a middling, wiry tiger of a man who was dressed on the opposite end of the sartorial scale: Hell's Angels' leather and denim. His face looked like it had been sculpted with a waffle iron.

"Flowers remembers every face, rap sheet, stiff he's ever seen or met," said Dutch. "Photographic memory, total recall—whatever you call it—he's got it. Anyway, he didn't make Tagliani, but he made a couple of Tagliani's out-of-town pals. A lot of heavyweights from out of state spent time with Tagliani at the track, none of them exactly movie-star material. Tagliani was also a very private kind, but he flashed lots of money. Big money. So Charlie One Ear got nosy, shot some pictures one day out at the track. Stick sends the photos up to D.C. to Mazzola and tells him Turner, which is how we knew him then, is keeping fast company and spending money like he owns the Bank of England. Cisco takes one look and bingo, we got a Tagliani instead of a Turner on our hands. That was last week."

"Great timing," I said.

"Ain't it though," Dutch said woefully.

"Who's that he's talking to?" I asked.

"You mean the dude in black tie and tails?" Dutch said with a snicker. "That's Chino Zapata. He mangles the king's English and thinks *Miranda* is a Central American banana republic, but he can follow a speck of dust into a Texas tornado and never lose sight of it. And in a pinch, he's got a punch like Dempsey."

"Where'd you find him?"

"LAPD. The story is they recruited him to get him off the street, although nobody in the LAPD will admit it. When I found him, he was undercover with the Hell's Angels."

"How'd you get him down here?"

"I told him he could bring his bike and wear whatever he pleased."

"Oh."

By this time the room had gathered three more men—about half of Dutch Morehead's squad—a strange-looking gang whose dress varied from Flowers' tweeds and brogans to Zapata's black leather jacket and hobnail boots. They stood, or sat, smoking, drinking coffee, making nickel talk and eyeballing me. It was my first view of the hard-case bunch I would get to know a lot better, and fast.

Morehead sidled around so his back was to the room and started quietly giving me a rundown on the rest of his gang.

"Sitting right behind Zapata is Nick Salvatore, a real roughneck. His old man was *soldato* for a small-time *mafioso* in south Philly, blew himself up trying to wire a bomb to some politician's car. You'll probably get the whole story from him if you stick around long enough, but the long and short of it is he hates the Outfit with a passion. Calls our job the dago roundup. He's more street-wise than Zapata. I guess you might call Salvatore our resident LCN expert. He doesn't know that many of the people, but he knows the way they think."

Salvatore was dressed haphazardly at best: a T-shirt with GRATE-FUL DEAD printed over a skull and crossbones, a purple Wind-breaker, and jeans. A single gold earring peeked out from under his long black hair. It was hard to tell whether he was growing a beard or had lost his razor.

"The earring is his mother's wedding band," Dutch whispered. "He's touchy about that. He also carries a sawed-off pool cue with a leaded handle in his shoulder holster."

On my card it was a split decision whether Zapata or Salvatore was the worst dresser, although Dutch gave the nod to Salvatore.

"Zapata doesn't know any better," he said. "Salvatore doesn't give a damn. If you blindfold him and ask him what he's wearing, he couldn't even guess."

Dutch continued the thumbnail sketch of his gang:

"Across from him is Cowboy Lewis." The man he referred to was as tall as Dutch, thirty pounds trimmer, and wore a black patch over his left eye. He was dressed in white jeans and a tan Windbreaker zipped halfway down, had very little hair on his chest. A black baseball cap with a gold dolphin on the crown covered a tangled mop of dishwater-blond hair. There wasn't a spare ounce of fat on the guy.

"Pound for pound, the hardest man in the bunch. He doesn't have much to say, but when he does, it's worth listening to," Dutch said. "He thinks in a very logical way. A to b to c to d, like that. If there's a bust on the make, Lewis is the man you want in front. He's kind of like our fullback, y'know. You say to Cowboy, we need to lose that door, Cowboy, and the door's gone, just like that, no questions asked. I suppose if I told him to lose an elephant, he'd waste the elephant. He's not afraid of anything that I can think of."

"Are any of them?" I asked.

Dutch chuckled. "Not really," he said. "Lewis is kind of . . ." He paused a moment, looking for the proper words, and then said, "He's just very single-minded. Actually, he started out to be a hockey player but he never made the big time. His fuse was too short, even for hockey. Y'see, if Cowboy was going for a goal, and the cage was way down at the other end of the rink, he'd go straight for it. Anybody got in his way, he'd just flatten them."

"Doesn't sound like the perfect team man," I said.

"Nobody's perfect," said Dutch.

The last man in the room was also lean and hard-eyed, in his mid- to late thirties, and over six feet tall. He looked like he had little time for nonsense or small talk.

"The tall guy in the three-piece suit and the flower in his lapel, that's Pancho Callahan," Dutch continued. "He's a former veterinarian, graduated from UCLA, and can tell you more about horse racing than the staff of Calumet Farms. He spends most of his time at the track. He doesn't say too much unless you get him on horses; then he'll talk your ear off." Callahan seemed restless. It was obvious he would rather have been elsewhere, which was probably true of all of them.

Altogether, about as strange a bunch of lawmen as I've ever seen gathered in one room. And there were a few more to go: the Mufalatta Kid and Kite Lange, more of whom later, and, of course, Stick, who was still an enigma to me. Eight in all, nine if you counted Dutch.

"Tell me a little about the Stick," I said. "What kind of guy is he?"

Dutch stared off at a corner of the room for a moment, tugging at his mustache.

"Very likable," he said finally. "You could call him amiable. Bizarre sense of humor. But not to be messed with. I'll tell you a little story about Stick. He has this old felt hat, I mean this hat looks like an ape's been playing with it. One day he leaves the hat in the car while he goes to get a haircut. He comes back, somebody lifted the hat. Don't ask me why anybody would *want* the hat, but there you are. About a week later Stick is cruising up Bay Street one afternoon and there this guy is, strolling up the boulevard wearing his hat.

"Stick pulls up, starts following the guy on foot. The guy goes into a record store. At that point Stick remembers he left his piece in his glove compartment. So what does he do? He hops in a hardware store, buys a number five Stillson wrench, and when the little putz comes out of the record store, Stick falls in behind him, shoves him in the first alley they come to, and whaps the bejesus out of the guy. The guy never saw him and never knew what hit him, but he sure knew Stick got his hat back."

He paused for another moment and then added: "Resourceful, that's what Stick is, resourceful."

I filed that information away, then said to Dutch, "Look, I don't want to seem pushy this early in the game, but I know this Tagliani mob. There's something I'd like to run by your people. Maybe it'll help a little."

He gave the request a second's worth of thought and nodded. "Okay," he said. "But let me ease you into the picture first."

"Anything you say."

I went over and grabbed a desk near the side of the room.

Dutch, as rumpled as an unmade bed, stood in front of the room.

"All right, listen up," he told his gashouse gang. "You all know by now what happened tonight. We lost the ace in the deck and we had a man sitting two hundred yards away."

He did an eyeball roll call and then bellowed loud enough to wake the dead in Milwaukee:

"*Sheiss*, we're missin' half the squad here. Didn't they hear this is a command performance?"

"They're still out on the range," a voice mumbled from the back of the room.

"Hmmm," Dutch muttered. "Okay, you all know about Tagliani and Stinetto getting chilled. Those are the two we knew as Turner and Sherman. Well, first, I got a little good news, if you want to call it that. Then we'll talk about who was where and how we screwed up tonight. Anyway, we had the house bugged and as happens, one of the rooms on the wire was the den, which is where the hit was made. So I've got the whole thing on tape, thanks to Lange, who did his telephone repairman act."

Dutch punched a button on a small cassette player and a moment later the room's hollow tone hissed through the speaker.

For maybe two minutes that's all there was, room tone.

Then a doorbell, far off, in another part of the house.

Seconds later someone entered the room.

Sounds of someone sitting down, a paper rustling, a lighter being struck, more paper noises. Then a voice, getting closer to the room:

"Hey, Nicky, *bom dia*, how ya do at the track?"

It was Tagliani's voice; I'd heard it on tape enough times to know.

"I dropped a bundle." Stinetto's voice.

"How the fuck you lose? It was a fix. I gave it to yuh just this morning. Din't I tell yuh, it's on for the four horse, third heat. Huh?"

"Ya tol' me. Too bad the other seven heats wasn't fixed."

Laughter. "I don' believe yuh. I give you a sure thing, you turn right aro—"

At that point there was a sound of glass crashing, a lot of jumbled noise, swearing and yelling . . .

Tagliani: "God—no, no . . ."

Stinetto: "Motherfu—"

Several shots, from two different guns.

A man's scream.

"Nicky . . ."

Brrrddt. A muffled rapid-fire gun, probably a submachine gun. It fired so fast it sounded like a dentist's drill.

Two screams; terrible, terrified, haunting screams.

Two more shots.

Bang . . . bang. Something heavy, a .357 maybe.

Somebody gagged.

Something heavy hit the floor, crunching glass as it fell.

Two more shots, spaced.

Bang . . . bang!

Footsteps running and the sound of something else hitting the floor.

The something else was sizzling.

A woman's voice,

screaming,

getting closer,

entering the room.

Baroomf!

The explosion blew out the mike. Dutch punched the off button.

"That's it," he said.

Charlie One Ear said, "Utterly charming. Too bad about the woman."

"Too bad about all of them," Dutch snapped caustically. "They were worth more to us alive than dead."

Dutch ran the tape back and played it again. We all leaned forward, hoping to hear something significant, but there wasn't much. I listened to the shots, counting them.

"That one, sounds like a dentist's drill, I make that some kind of submachine gun," Zapata said.

Dutch played it again.

It was a chilling tape. Just when you think you've seen it all and heard it all, you run across something like this, listening to three people die. Mobsters or not, it raised the hair on my arms.

"Definitely two guns," Charlie One Ear said.

"That's pretty good, Charlie. Stinetto's gun was still in his belt when we found him," Dutch said. "Loaded and clean. The old man was light."

"Pretty good shooting," Chino ventured.

"Had to be two of 'em," said Salvatore.

"Or an ambidextrous marksman," Charlie One Ear said.

"Fuckin' nervy one," Zapata added.

"Any other ideas?" Dutch asked.

I kept mine to myself.

"Okay, now pay attention. We got a man here can maybe shed a little glimmer on the night's proceedings, so everybody just relax a minute. This here's Jake Kilmer. Kilmer's with the Freeze and he's an expert on this outfit."

A moan of discontent rippled through the room.

"You wanna listen to him, or stay dumb?" Dutch snapped without a hint of humor in his tone.

The room got quiet.

And colder than an ice cube sandwich.

7

EXIT SCREAMING

The house was a two-story brick and stone structure nestled against high dunes overlooking the bay. The backyard was terraced, rising from the swimming pool to a flat that looked like a child's dream. There was a gazebo and an eight-horse carousel and a monkey bar set and a railroad with each car just large enough to accommodate one child.

Two men smoked quietly in the gazebo.

From high above, on top of the dunes that separated the house from the bay, the sound of the child laughing could be heard, followed by his grandfather's rough laughter. Their joyous chorus was joined by the sound of a calliope playing "East Side, West Side, All Around the Town." The child was on the carousel, his grandfather standing beside him with an arm around the boy. The horses, eyes gleaming, nostrils flaring, mouths open, jogged up and down in an endless, circular race. Below them, in the pool, an inner tube floated, forgotten.

The figure, dressed entirely in black, crouched as it moved silently and swiftly through the sea grass on top of the dune to a point above the house. Only the swimming pool was visible. The figure was carrying a weapon that had the general conformity of a rifle but was larger.

The figure slid to the ground and eased quietly to the edge of the dune, looking down at the old man and the child. He waited.

A woman appeared at the sliding glass door at the back of the house.

"Ricardo, bedtime," she yelled.

The child protested but the woman persisted.

"Once more around," the old man yelled back, and the woman agreed and waited.

The figure on the dune also waited.

His last ride finished, the little boy ran gleefully down the terrace and then turned back to the older man.

"Come kiss me good night, Grandpa," he called back.

The grandfather smiled and waved his hand.

"Uno momento," he called back, and then motioned to the men in the gazebo to shut down the carousel.

The child skipped to his grandmother and they entered the house together.

The figure on the dune fitted what looked like a pineapple onto the end of the weapon and adjusted a knob on the rear of the barrel. There was the faint sound of metal clinking against metal.

The old man looked around, not sure where the sound had come from.

One of the men in the gazebo stood up, stepped out onto the terrace, and looked up.

"Something?" the other one said.

The first one shrugged and walked back into the gazebo.

There was a muffled explosion—

Pumf!

A sigh in the night air over their heads.

Then the terraced backyard of the house was suddenly bathed in a sickening orange-red glow.

The two men in the gazebo were blown to the ground. The grandfather arced like a diver doing a backflip as he was blown off the terrace. He landed in the pool. The merry horses were blown to bits.

The night calm was shattered by the explosion, by a crescendo of broken glass, by the screams.

8

THE CINCINNATI TRIAD

Morehead had pinned seven photographs on a corkboard in the front of the big room, each one identified with a felt-tip pen. Since we had already made Tagliani and Frank Turner as one and the same, ditto Stinetto and Nat Sherman, Dutch crossed them out.

Until a couple of hours ago Tagliani had been *capo di tutti capi,* "boss of all bosses" of the Cincinnati Tagliani family, known as the Cincinnati Triad.

For fifty years the Taglianis had ruled the mob world in southwest Ohio, operating out of Cincinnati. The founder of the clan, Giani, its first *capo di tutti capi,* died when he was eighty-three and never saw the inside of a courtroom, much less did time for his crimes. The empire was passed to his son, Joe "Skeet" Tagliani. While the old man had a certain Old World charm, Skeet Tagliani was nothing less than a butcher. Under his regime the Taglianis had formed an alliance with two other gang leaders. One was Tuna Chevos, who married Skeet Tagliani's sister and was also one of the Midwest's most powerful dope czars. Across the Ohio River, in Covington, an old-time *mafioso* named Johnny Draganata controlled things. When a black Irish hood named Bannion tried to take over, Skeet threw in with Draganata. The war lasted less than three months. It was a bloodbath and to my knowledge there isn't a Bannion hoodlum left to talk about it.

Thus the Cincinnati Triad was formed: Skeet Tagliani, Tuna Chevos, and Johnny Draganata.

I had put Skeet away for a ten spot, but it had taken three years of my life to do it and I had spent the better part of the next two trying to prove that his brother, Franco, had taken over as *capo* in Skeet's place. It was a nasty job and costly. Several of our agents and witnesses had died trying to gather evidence against the Taglianis.

Then Franco had vanished, poof, just like that, no trace—and another year had gone down the drain while I chased every hokum lead, every sour tip, up and down every dead-end alley in the country. The Cincinnati Triad had simply disappeared.

A clever move, Tagliani selling out and hauling stakes like that. Clever and frustrating. Now, almost a year later, he had turned up in Dunetown—stretched out in the morgue with a name tag on his toe that said he was Frank Turner. The name change was easy to understand.

What he was doing on ice was not.

The other five faces in Dutch's photos were familiar although their names, too, were new. They were the princes of Tagliani's hoodlum empire, the *capi* who helped rule the kingdom: Rico Stizano, who was now calling himself Robert Simons; Tony Logeto, who had become Thomas Lanier; Anthony Bronicata, now known as Alfred Burns; and Johnny Draganata, the old fox, whose nom de plume was James Dempsey. The subject in the last picture was less familiar to me, although I knew who he was: Johnny "Jigs" O'Brian, a nickel-dime hoodlum who had been doing odd jobs for the mob in Phoenix until he married Tagliani's youngest daughter, Dana. At the time the Triad had done its disappearing act, O'Brian was doing on-the-job training running prostitution.

Cute, but not all that original. The new names helped explain initials on suitcases, gold cuff links, silk shirts, sterling silverware, that kind of thing. The Tagliani bunch was big on monograms.

Then there were the two missing faces, Tuna Chevos and his chief executioner and sycophant, Turk Nance. In the whole mob, Chevos and his henchman, Nance, were the most deadly. The setup here seemed too perfect for them to be very far away. Besides, Chevos was a dope runner and the coastline of Georgia from South Carolina to Florida was the Marseilles of America. Dope flowed through there as easily as ice water flowed through Chevos' veins.

"Recognize these people?" Dutch asked, pointing to the rogues' gallery.

I nodded. "All of 'em. Cutthroats to the man."

"Okay," he said, "let's get on with it."

I decided to play it humble and sat down on the corner of the desk.

"I don't want to sound like I know it all," I said, "but I've been hounddogging these bastards for years. I know a lot about this mob because I've been trying to break up their party ever since I got out of short pants."

Not a grin. A tough audience. Salvatore was cleaning his fingernails with a knife that made a machete look like a safety pin. Charlie One Ear was doing a crossword puzzle.

"Just what is the Freeze?" Charlie One Ear asked without looking up from his puzzle.

They were going to make it tough.

"Well, I'll tell you what it's not. It's not the Feebies or the Leper Colony," I said. "We have two jobs. We work with locals on anything where there's a hint of an interstate violation. And we go after the LCN. We're not in a league with the Leper Colony. We don't kiss ass in Washington by victimizing some little taxpayer who can't protect himself, and we don't hold press conferences every five minutes like the Feebies."

"What's the LCN?" Zapata asked.

"La Cosa Nostra, you fuckin' moron," Salvatore taunted.

Zapata looked back over his shoulder at Salvatore. "Big deal. So I never heard it called LCN before. My old man didn't suck ass for some broken-down old *mafioso*."

"That's right," Salvatore said. "Your old man swept floors in a Tijuana whorehouse."

"You shoulda been brung up in a whorehouse," Zapata shot

back. "Maybe you wouldn't wear an earring, like a fuckin' fag."

"Hey, you're talking about my mother's wedding ring!" roared Salvatore.

"All right, all right," Charlie One Ear said, holding up his hand.

"You keep outta this," said Salvatore. "At least I got an ear to put it in; some dip didn't eat it for dinner."

I wondered why Dutch didn't step in and stop things before they got out of hand. Then Zapata started snickering and Salvatore broke out in a laugh and Charlie One Ear smiled, and I got a sudden sense of what was happening. You see it in combat, this kind of barbed-wire humor. It's a great equalizer. It says: I trust you; we're buddies; you can say anything about me you want; nobody else has the privilege. It bonds that unspoken sense of love and trust among men under pressure, a macho camaraderie in which the insult becomes the ultimate flattery.

I was beginning to understand what Dutch meant. This was a tight little society and they were letting me know it in their own way.

They all got into it except Pancho Callahan, who never cracked a smile. He stared at me over a pyramid of fingers through cold gray eyes, the way you stare at a waiter in a restaurant when he forgets your order. I got the message. "Screw the buddy-buddy humor, hotshot," he was saying. "Show us what you got."

"You guys can rehearse your act later," Dutch said, throwing a wet towel in the works. "If we listen, maybe we can learn something. Did all of you forget that part of our deal was to keep organized crime out of this town? Look what we ended up with."

They all eyeballed me.

"Not him," Dutch growled, "the *pfutzlüker* Taglianis."

Dutch never swore in English, only German. I doubt that any of his gang knew what the hell he meant most of the time. Nobody ever asked, either.

"Go on," he said to me. "Keep trying."

"Look, this gang up here on the wall is no penny-ante outfit and they didn't come here for the waters. They came here to buy this town. I been after these bastards since the day I joined the Freeze."

"So what d'you want outta all this?" Cowboy Lewis asked.

"I'll tell you what I want," I said. "The RICO anti-crime laws refer to any monies earned from illegal sources as IGG," I said, "which stands for *ill-gotten gains*."

That drew a laugh from Charlie One Ear. "Ah," he said, "the wonders of the government never cease."

"What's RICO stand for?" Lewis asked, seriously.

"Racketeer Influenced and Corrupt Organizations—gangland fronts," I said.

"IGG simply means the kiwash they make from dope, gambling, prostitution, extortion, pornography . . . all the LCN's favorite tricks. The LCN has to wash that money, and it isn't easy. So they invest in legitimate businesses—even banks—to clean it up. RICO gives us the power to bust them if we can prove that any business depends for its support on IGG. If we can prove that, we can confiscate their money, their businesses, their equipment, their yachts and Rolls-Royces and all the rest of their toys. And we can also make cases against the racketeers and *everybody* connected with them. That goes for legitimate businessmen, politicians, or anybody else that gets in bed with them."

Zapata piped up: "Do we get credit for this course?"

"Yeah," Salvatore chimed in. "When's the final?"

More laughter.

"Give him a chance," Dutch snapped.

"Okay," I said, "let's forget the bureaucratic bullshit. Here's what you're dealing with. In the Freeze we spend most of our time working with the locals, tying known LCN racketeers to IGG, and the IGG to legitimate sources that have been corrupted. That's what I'm after—I want to know how they got their hooks into Dunetown and who they had to buy to do it. I'm not interested in making individual cases for prostitution or gambling or even homicide. Anything I get that can help you in those areas is yours."

"We've heard that song before, old man," Charlie One Ear said caustically.

"Enough of this true-and-false crap," Dutch said. "Let's get to the meat and potatoes."

I gave them a brief history of the Triad, very brief so they wouldn't fall asleep.

"Franco Tagliani was very cautious," I said. "Before we nailed Skeet, Franco had made quite a name for himself. He was a big shot in Cincy. He contributed to the arts, ballet, symphony, local sports teams, everything including the humane society. He loved animals. Everybody's lovable old Uncle Franco, right? When we dumped Skeet, we figured Franco would have to come out of the closet, so we started a matrix on him. What we call a link analysis. We charted every scrap of information that came our way that related to the Triad, even the most insignificant stuff. Bits of bullshit from snitches, restaurants they frequented, social gatherings, weddings, pals, acquaintances, habits, police records, vacation trips. Hell, we even had Interpol checking on them when they left the country. It all went on the matrix, and we kept refining it, and finally we ended up with this."

I took a chart out of my briefcase and pinned it on the wall.

CINCINNATI TRIAD

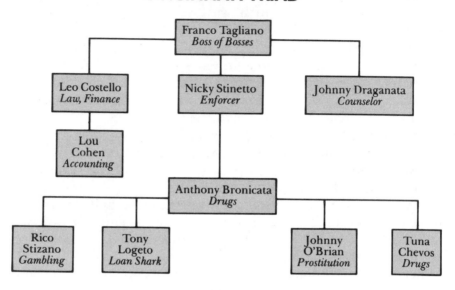

"There it is," I said. "The Cincinnati Triad. Anybody thinks they came here for their health should go back to school."

No grumbling this time. I had their attention.

I started down the list while I was still ahead, beginning with Franco, once the *consigliere*, the legal brains, for Skeet, and until a few hours ago, godfather to the Triad.

"Tagliani was a classic *mafioso*," I said. "His religion was family, friends, and fuck everybody else; Tagliani's three daughters are all married to family *capi*. The Triad's respected in La Cosa Nostra. Nobody messes with them. At least nobody has until now.

"Stinetto was Franco's executioner, the official enforcer for the outfit, and Tagliani's bodyguard. One of the few people Tagliani trusted. All the other *capi* were under Stinetto's direct command. Stinetto was an old-timer. He made his bones in the fifties, about the time Buggsy Siegel bought his. So what I'm saying, they were both tough old pros. Taking them out together like that was ingenious and gutsy."

Dutch jumped in at this point. "Whoever pulled this off

poisoned two guard dogs and got past three armed guards. Nobody laid an eye on him or them."

There was another face that was not on Dutch's board: Leo Costello, Mr. Clean, the *consigliere* of the outfit, summa cum laude graduate of Chicago Law School, mid- to late thirties, married to Tagliani's daughter Maria.

"Costello was a major in Nam," I said. "Adjutant general's office. He never saw combat, spent most of his time preparing court-martial cases. The man won't touch a gun, doesn't even hunt. He prefers the country club set to his own family."

"Mazzola put us on to him," said Charlie One Ear. "Him and his friend."

"Lou Cohen?" I asked.

"The same," said Flowers. "Neither one of them changed their names."

"That sounds like him," I said. "Costello avoids as much contact as possible with the rest of the mob. He doesn't have any shooters around him. And Cohen is a quiet, reclusive accountant. The money brains and the bagman for the outfit. The Lepers've been trying to burn Cohen for at least ten years. Zip. But Costello may have to show his colors now."

"How come?" asked Zapata.

"Because he's the most likely one of the bunch to take over as *capo di tutti capi* now that Franco's bought the farm. That's unless there's something we don't know," I added.

"Such as?" asked Dutch.

"Such as somebody else in the family pushing the old man across and taking over."

"Oh," said Dutch, "*that* such as."

I went on, running down the list of felons who were now in residence in Doomstown:

Johnny Draganata, the tough, no-quarter Mustache Pete from the old school, and professor and priest to all the Tagliani soldiers, the final authority on tradition and protocol; Rico Stizano, also known as the Barber, because that's what he had once been in Chicago, until he married Tagliani's sister. Now his specialty was gambling. A big family man. They all were.

Tony Logeto, Tagliani's son-in-law, was a cannon and a muscle man, married to Tagliani's oldest daughter, Sheila, and a specialist in loan sharking, extortion, and anything that required more mus-cle than brains. Logeto saw himself as a big ladies' man. A lot of ladies apparently did too.

"Anthony Bronicata is another old-timer," I told them. "He's a onetime *soldato* with a lot of notches on his gun. In dope circles he's known as the Peg, short for Il Peggiore, which means the Worst, and that—in the trade—means don't mess with him. He's king pusher, pipeline to the street, and we've never been able to put a finger on him for anything—possession, conspiracy, distribution, nothing. Bronicata's front is always a restaurant. The only good thing I can say about him is he makes pretty fair fettuccine. You want him? If we can nail his ass, he's yours."

I had very little recollection of O'Brian. In my mind I remembered him as a short little Irishman with a blustery red face and bad teeth. Dutch's photo showed that he had a pug nose and a go-to-hell smile, and his picture was the only pleasant one in the bunch, but I didn't let that fool me for a minute. As the newest member of the clan, he still had to prove himself, and that made him more unpredictable than any of the rest.

Dutch observed, "All these guns around, and it didn't help Tagliani for a minute."

"Never does if they want you bad enough," I said.

I pulled two new photographs out of my briefcase and held them up.

"These two look familiar to anybody?" I asked.

There were no takers.

I held up the clearer of the two photos, that of a round-faced man in his sixties with a pleasant smile, his snake eyes hidden behind sunglasses.

"This is Tuna Chevos," I said. "We'll turn him up."

"How would you know that?" Charlie One Ear asked.

My stomach started to churn just thinking about Chevos and Nance, his personal assassin.

"I have this little buzzer inside me goes off whenever I'm within fifty miles of the son of a bitch."

"Something personal?" Charlie One Ear asked, raising his eyebrows.

I stared at him dead-eyed for a full minute before he looked away. Then I held up the other picture, a somewhat fuzzy photograph of a lean, hard, ferret-faced man in his midthirties, his eyes also obscured by sunglasses.

"You see Chevos, this one is close behind. He's the Greek's numero uno, your friendly little neighborhood assassin. His name is Turk Nance and he's the deadliest one of the lot, a psychopath with a temper as thin as a shadow. They're both cobras. Chevos married into the family but they're outsiders. They play by their own rules."

"Maybe they did the old bastard in," Zapata suggested.

"Maybe, but I don't think so."

"Why not?" Dutch asked.

"I don't say I'm ruling them out," I replied. "I said I don't think they did it. It's still family. Salvatore, you know what I mean?"

"He's right," Salvatore said. "I mean, what you say, this Chevos was the old man's brother-in-law. Unless there was real bad blood . . ." He let the sentence dangle.

"So where do these two bombos fit in?" Cowboy Lewis asked.

"Chevos brings the stuff in, Bronicata gets it to the wholesalers," I said. "Nance is Chevos' personal *soldato*. If Chevos says go flush your head in the toilet, Nance's head is as good as in the bowl. There's one other thing—don't let Chevos fool you because he's got Nance for backup. The story goes that Chevos killed his own brother to make his bones for Skeet. I don't know if his brother needed killing, but if he was in the same league as Chevos, it was no big loss.

"Nance started in the streets, got a postgrad course in Vietnam, probably killed at least half of the Bannion gang himself. He favors a nine-millimeter Luger with a twelve-inch barrel and hollow points soaked in arsenic. A real sweetheart. He's also a muscle freak. Sooner or later, when he can plant Chevos someplace safe for an hour or two, he'll show up at the best fitness center in town. Everybody in the family is scared shitless of both of them.

"Turk Nance. Remember that name. If you have trouble with him, shoot first."

"You keep tellin' us what you don't want," Callahan said in a dead monotone. "What the hell do you want?"

I thought about that, about why I was here and what had happened to Dunetown and was going to happen to it. I thought about a lot of things in the next few seconds.

"I want the whole damn bunch off the street. I don't care if you do it or I do it or we do it together. They're the cockroaches of our society."

I looked at Charlie One Ear. "You ask me is it personal? I got five years invested in this bunch. In the whole rat pack only Costello and Cohen are clean. The rest of them have rap sheets that'll stretch from here to Malibu and back."

I started pacing. I had lost my temper for a moment, not because of Charlie One Ear or because Dutch Morehead's hooligans didn't trust me. I was used to that. It was because of Cincinnati. I stopped and looked at each of them in turn.

"Yeah, fuckin'-A it's personal," I said. "One of my partners on the Tagliani job was Harry Nome, Wholesome Harry we called him. Best inside man I ever met. He was undercover in Chevos' dope operation. Nance tumbled him. They took him for a ride and Nance stuck his gun up Harry's nose, ripped it off with the gunsight—I mean he *ripped it off*. Then he tossed Harry out of a car doing about fifty. Harry came out of it a paraplegic.

"We had another man, on loan from the Drug Enforcement Agency. He tried to burrow into the operation at the New Orleans end. We never saw him or heard from him again. Nothing. He just disappeared. That's been three years now.

"I had an informant, a hooker named Tammi. She was eighteen years old, recruited by Stizano, who hooked her on horse when she was fifteen. They had her working interstate and she wanted out, so she agreed to talk to the attorney general about how hookers are moved around on the national circuit, who runs it, that sort of thing. Very strong stuff. Nance got her away from us. He cut off her nose and both ears, stuffed them down her throat, and strangled her with them. Costello—Mr. Clean? He was Nance's mouthpiece. The bastard wasn't even indicted."

I paused for a minute, letting it all sink in.

"Naw," I said, "it isn't personal. It's never personal, right? I mean, why should I be pissed? I was lucky. When they took a shot at me, the bullet went in my side, here, just below the ribs, popped out my back, and went on its merry way. The bullet hurt, but not like the arsenic it was soaked in."

I sat down.

Not bad, I thought. Not bad at all. Save up the rough stuff until the end.

Nobody said anything else for a minute or two.

I didn't know it at the time, but there was another name I should have added to the list that night:

Longnose Graves.

I would get to know him well in the next few days. I would get to know a lot of people well in the next few days, very damn few of them for long.

9

SCREWING UP ROYALLY

Dutch stood in front of the room, a Teutonic frown etched into his heavy features.

"Thanks," he said.

"Any time."

"I don't want to upset anybody," he said, turning to his troops, "but these . . . *ash lochers* have been under our surveillance two weeks. A whole family of them, and we didn't even know it!"

The group looked stricken, none more than Charlie One Ear.

"I can't believe it," he said, shaking his head in disbelief. "Not so much as a hint from any of my canaries about this. I should think somebody, *somebody*, would have heard some goddamn thing!"

The rest of them stared at the floor and moved imaginary objects around with their feet. All except Lewis, who stared at a corner of the room through squinted eyes, and Callahan, who spoke up again.

"Why you getting steamed up, Dutch?" he said. "We didn't know who they were until last week. Up till then we were just following them because Charlie One Ear had a hunch."

"I'm including myself," Dutch said. "We been making a lot of racket for these past nine months. Busting pimps and pros, dropping dealers with a nickel bag in their shorts. We got a little too big for our hats."

"We didn't *know* until—" Salvatore started.

"He's right," Charlie One Ear said. "We were much too casual about this mob. I was one of the worst."

"You, Chino, you were on Tagliani tonight, right?" Dutch asked.

"Who?"

"Franco Tagliani," Dutch said, leaning an inch from the Mexican's face. "He's the one got killed tonight while you were parked in his front yard. Remember?"

"I keep forgetting the new names," Zapata said.

"Well, stop forgetting them. I don't want to hear any more about Frank Turner or Nat Sherman or any of the other monikers their people are using. From now on, we use their *real-life* names, okay?"

The group nodded in unison.

"So what happened?"

"On Sundays, uh . . . Tagliani and . . . uh . . . Nicky Stinetto go to . . . Bronicata's joint for dinner, so I went there and waited. Shit, you stand out like a blind man at a tit show, out there on Thunderhead Island. There's only one other house on Tur . . . Tagliani's street. Twice I been hassled by the fuckin' downtown blue and whites, fer Christ sakes."

"So it's your call to jump ahead of your mark that way?" Dutch asked.

"It was just a routine surveillance, Dutch. Shit, I was hungry, nothing to eat for seven hours. I went ahead, grabbed some groceries so I'd be ready when he split. Who had any thought he was gonna get hit?"

"I'm sorry you didn't get a printed invitation!" Dutch said. "How about Stinetto, who had him?"

Charlie One Ear sank a little lower in his chair.

"I'm afraid I have to plead guilty," he said. "It was a double-up, Dutch. We knew they were going to dinner together, so I told—"

"So you told Chino to go to the restaurant and you'd cover the house," he said, finishing the sentence.

"Right."

Callahan said, "It's routine with him, Chief. Tagliani goes to Bronicata's every Sunday for dinner. He usually meets one or two of his *capi* there. Draganata, Stizano, Logeto. Like that. Bronicata usually sits with them."

"Big deal, so who does the dishes? What I want to know is who was at dinner?"

"Logeto and, uh, the red-haired guy . . ." Chino said.

"O'Brian," I coached.

"Yeah. And, of course, Bronicata."

"I suppose you was eyeballing Bronicata, too, right, since you was there anyway," Dutch growled at Chino.

"I had Bronicata," Callahan said quietly. "They all split together. I put Bronicata home before I came back here."

"Who had O'Brian?"

Lewis raised his hand. "Same thing," he said. "He went straight home too."

"What happened there in the restaurant?" Dutch said.

Chino said, "I was inside, watching the whole team. So Bronicata gets this phone call, comes back looking like he just swallowed a jar of jalapeña peppers. There's some chi chi—"

"Chi chi? What the hell's chi chi?" Dutch asked.

"They was whispering."

"Oh."

"Then the Irishman and Logeto both split like the place was on fire. Coupla minutes later the waiter brings the check, tells me the joint's closing for the night. 'What the hell's goin' on?' I say. He tells me the chef had a heart attack. I guess the call was to tell them the old man got aced."

Dutch, who was twirling one side of his mustache and staring at the ceiling, said, "It don't make a lot of sense, y'know. Tagliani follows the same procedure every Sunday. There he is, in the car with only Stinetto and the chauffeur, who couldn't shoot the shit with the pope. An easy mark, yet the shooter chooses to waste two guard dogs and blow up Turner and Sherman in the house."

"It's Tagliani and Stinetto," Charlie One Ear said sedately.

All that bought him was a dirty look.

"Salvatore," Dutch went on, "who was your mark?"

"Stizano," he said. "He's home also. I left his place when you called us in."

"Cowboy?"

"The playboy—what's his name?"

"Logeto?" I suggested.

"Yeah, him. He's home too."

"Everybody's home tonight," Zapata said with a chuckle.

"Is any of this stuff from the past few weeks, from when you started watching these guys, is any of this on paper?" I asked.

Dutch said, "We don't make reports. You put it on paper and somebody can read it."

"Like who?" I asked.

"Somebody, anybody," he said vaguely.

"You know what burns me?" said Chino. "What fuckin' burns me is that these assholes have got themselves watertight alibis and they don't even know it."

"Wouldn't it be fun not to tell them," Charlie One Ear said wistfully.

Dutch said, "Okay, Charlie, put your good ear to the ground, see if you can turn up something. The rest of you, back out on the range; see if we can stop this daisy chain before it goes any further. If you run across the Mufalatta Kid, Kite Lange, or the Stick, tell them to get in touch. Any questions?"

There weren't any.

As the gang started to disperse, Cowboy Lewis got up and walked straight toward me. He moved two desks out of his way to get to me.

"It's Jake, right?" he said.

"Yeah."

He stuck out his hand.

"My name's Chester Lewis. They call me Cowboy."

"Right."

"You want this asshole Nance, right?"

"Yeah, I want him, Cowboy."

"Then he's yours."

"Thanks," I said, pumping his hand.

"You got a right," he said, whirled on his heel, and headed straight out the door. As he left, a new face appeared in the doorway.

I knew who it was without asking.

STICK

The new guy was ignored by the rest of the bunch, who were too busy talking about the tapes to notice him. He came straight toward me.

He was what some women would call a primal beauty. Indian features, high cheekbones, long, narrow face, hard jaw, brown eyes, thick, shining black hair that tumbled over his forehead and ears. Six feet tall and lean, he was my height and ten pounds trimmer. His seersucker suit looked like he balled it up and put it under his pillow at night; his tie had a permanent knot in it and was hanging two inches below an open collar. The points of his shirt collar curled up toward the ceiling, and I doubt that his loafers had ever seen a shoeshine rag. Obviously, dressing wasn't a real big thing with him.

He looked bagged out, and not just from a bad night. The

circles under his eyes were permanent and his dimples were turning into crevices. He had the deep, growling voice that comes
from too many drinks or too many cigarettes or too many late
nights or all three. He was wearing a battered old brown felt hat,
and a cigarette dangled from the corner of his mouth.

Twenty-nine going on forty. One look, you knew he drove the
women crazy.

Not jaded yet?

"I'm Parver," he said. "Everybody calls me Stick."

We moved away from the rest of the bunch, back toward the
coffeepot.

"You a poolshooter?" I asked, to get the conversation off the
ground.

"Not really, why?"

"The moniker."

"It's short for Redstick. Everybody thinks I look like a damn
Indian," he said with disgust. "Truth is, I'm Jewish and I'm from
Boston."

"I'm Jake Kilmer," I said. "That's all I ever was."

We shook hands.

"This about the Tagliani chill?" he asked. He said it casually,
as though murder in Dunetown were as common as sand fleas on
the beach.

I nodded.

"It looks like two gunners," I said. "They killed a couple of
guard dogs, got by a couple of armed guards, and killed all three
of them."

"Three?" Stick said. "When Cowboy raised me, he said Tagliani
and Stinetto got it."

"After wasting Tagliani and Stinetto, they dropped off a bomb
to finish the job. Tagliani's wife walked in. She died in the hospital."

"Too bad," he said. "Though I can't say as I'm too upset over
the two goons." So much for sympathy. "How do you figure there
were two shooters?"

"The house was wired. Dutch has the whole scene on tape, what
there was of it. It was all over in about thirty seconds."

"Not so great for you. In town for an hour and your mark gets
snuffed out from under you."

"That's the breaks."

"Guns and bombs," he mused. "Sounds like the Lincoln County
war."

I said I hoped not.

"The boys giving you a hard time?" he asked.

"How'd you guess it?"

"I got some jazz when I first came on. Kind of like an initiation. But they think Dutch hired me, so they weren't as suspicious as they will be toward you. You're a Fed, man. That makes you a badass. Don't let it get you down; they'll come around."

"So as far as they're concerned, you're just another one of the boys, that it?"

"You got it."

"What's your angle in all this?" I asked.

"Dutch's had me playing the field, kind of getting my feet wet. One day this guy, the next somebody else. But the last week, since Mazzola made the Tagliani gang, I've been hawking Costello and that little fink, Cohen."

"And . . . ?"

"Hell, you know the outfit better than any of us," he said. Then, smiling, Stick added, "Don't you ever do reports? I didn't know shit about Tagliani until Cisco filled me in. I mean, there's some chicken-shit stuff in the box about them, but nothing with any meat on it."

"Yeah, I know. I'm bad about reports. I'm like Dutch. Anybody can read them."

"In answer to your question, Costello keeps away from the rest of the players."

"How about Cohen?"

"The same. A mousy bookkeeper."

"Don't undersell him. He's got more tricks than a gypsy magician."

"I'll keep that in mind. Have you seen Cisco yet?"

"Talked to him on the phone. I'm meeting him for breakfast. Maybe you ought to join us."

"I think I'll pass. If any of these guys spot me with you this soon they could get antsy. Right now they trust me. I'd like to keep it that way."

"Whatever," I said as Dutch joined us.

"That was a nice job," he said to me. "I liked the little heart tug at the end." And then to Stick: "What have you been up to?"

"Hounddogging Costello. He and Cohen spent the day on his yacht, talking business."

"Great. That's two more we can alibi." Then back at me: "You talk to Cisco yet?"

"Just before the meeting. He suggested maybe Stick and I should team up. Is that a problem?"

"I guess not. It's a pretty loose operation. I'll move you around a little bit, just so's the rest of the boys don't wonder why I've put the two newcomers together. So what can I tell you, you don't know already?"

"Anybody on the local scene I ought to know about?" I asked, not really expecting an answer.

"Just Longnose Graves," Dutch said.

"Longnose Graves?" I said, chuckling at the moniker.

Dutch stared at me through his hooded eyes. "He ain't a laughing matter," the big man said.

"Oh? Who is he?"

Dutch scratched the edge of his jaw with a thumb. "The local bandit," he said. "Not *a* local bandit, *the* local bandit." He tossed a sideways glance at the Stick. "This business tonight, I hope it doesn't blow up like the Cherry McGee thing."

"Cherry McGee?" I said. "Would that be the McGee from up in Pittsburgh?"

"The McGee I'm talking about is planted in the local cemetery," said Dutch. "Compliments of Nose."

The Stick drew himself a cup of coffee and poured me one. It was strong enough to swim the English Channel.

"So what's the story on Graves? What's he called? Longnose?"

"Not to his face," Dutch said. Then he ran down the pedigree:

"Graves once had a beak, made Durante look like he had a nose job. He had an inch or so shaved off it in a fight, but the name sticks. He's black, a dandy, but not pimp-dandy, know what I mean? Sports jackets, shirt and tie, likes sports cars—that's more his style. Long before I got here, Graves controlled whatever underworld Dunetown had in the old days. Ladies, sharking, the book. He doesn't deal in hard drugs; in fact, he probably kept them out of Doomstown."

"That's a switch," I said.

"Moral fiber," said the Stick.

"Sure," Dutch snickered, and went on. "About two years ago this outsider, Cherry McGee, moved into town with a bunch of roughnecks and decided to take some of the action. First he tried easing Nose out. When that didn't work, he tried buying Nose out. Still no dice. So then McGee decides to burn down one of Graves' clubs, to show Nose he was serious. A mistake."

Stick chimed in with a character observation.

"Graves has great comeback talent," he volunteered. "Going against him was no different than McGee jumping off the Bay Bridge and thinking he could fly."

Dutch continued, "McGee did something uncharacteristic. He dropped a frame on Graves. Extortion. And it washed. Graves did a deuce off a nickel in Little Q."

"Little Q?"

"Felony Disneyworld," said the Stick. "A very hard-time joint in this state—or any other for that matter."

"When Nose comes out, he comes out like a Brahman bull comin' out of the chute," said Dutch.

"Did he keep the business while he was gone?" I asked.

"It was nip and tuck. The trip cost everybody. In the end it was a trade-off—three of Graves' boys went down in the street; a couple of McGee's shooters ended up in the swamp."

"Is it still going on?"

"Not since McGee and his top gun got their brains handed to them, wham, bam, just like that," said Dutch.

"Hey, Chief, it's the phone for you," Chino yelled from across the room. "It's Kite Lange, babblin' like Niagara Falls."

"Excuse me," Dutch said, and dashed for the phone.

"Who's this Mufalatta Kid?" I asked the Stick.

"Black cop, out from New Orleans. He's very good. Moves easy on the range. A real cool operator, but make him mad, you got a ton of bad nigger on a hundred-and-fifty-pound frame."

Dutch's *"Schmerz!"* could be heard for miles. The room got as quiet as a prayer meeting. Then he said it again, this time louder and, to everyone's shock, in English. "Holy shit!"

He slammed down the phone.

"Somebody just blew up Johnny Draganata in the family swimming pool while Lange was sittin' shiva half a block from his house," the Dutchman bellowed.

The war room sounded suddenly like a hen house.

"Now listen t'me," Dutch boomed. "I want Tagliani's bunch covered like a strawberry sundae, and now. I'm goin' up to Draganata's. Chino, you come with me. The rest of you know your marks. Let's roll before the whole town gets snuffed."

He rushed back to us.

"You two wanna join us?"

"We wouldn't miss it for the world," I said.

"Let's roll," the Dutchman roared, and moved faster than any big man I ever saw.

II

DEATH HOUSE ON FLORAL STREET

It was like Saturday afternoon at the county fair and the Stick was Joey Chitwood. He slapped the blue light on the top of his black Firebird and took off, driving with one hand while he lit cigarettes, tuned the police radio, and hit the siren with the other, cigarette bobbing in the corner of his mouth as he talked. Pedestrians and traffic ran for cover before the screaming Pontiac. I hunkered down in my seat and stiff-armed the console.

"You nervous?" he asked.

"Not a bit," I lied.

He hit Azalea Boulevard sideways and straightened out doing seventy. I could feel the seat moving out from under me.

I liked the Stick's cavalier attitude, but his driving was downright hazardous. I knew he had to be a good cop or he wouldn't be in the Freeze. The Federal Racket Squad, which everybody called the Freeze, was three years old, understaffed, underpublicized, underlobbied, and under the gun. The FBI wanted to make it part of their dodge, but so far we had maintained our integrity because our job was mainly gathering information, not strict law enforcement. At least, that's what it was supposed to be. Sometimes it didn't work out just that way. Cisco Mazzola, who had formed the outfit, was an ex–street cop and he hired only street cops. As far as I could tell, the Stick fit in perfectly.

He seemed to know the town. His course took us down a few alleys and past an impressive row of old homes, restored to Revolutionary grandeur, their lights blurring into a single streak as we vaulted down the street.

"How long you been here?"

"Coupla months," he said around the cigarette dangling from his lips.

"So you were here for the Graves-McGee showdown?"

"Just after it happened."

"I knew a Philly shooter who operated out of Pittsburgh named

McGee," I said, still making small talk. "But he called himself Ipswitch."

"I wouldn't know about that," Stick said. "Actually, it was all over when I got here. All I know is what I heard on the gaspipe."

More turns. More screaming tires. More fleeing pedestrians.

"What's this Graves like?" I asked.

"Like Dutch said, for years he had the town sewed up. I get the idea the local law left him alone as long as he didn't get too far out of line."

"Wasting McGee wasn't getting out of line?" I asked.

"Y'know, I don't think anybody blamed him for the McGee thing. In fact, I get the feeling the locals were glad he did McGee in."

"Could he be behind this Tagliani chill?"

"I suppose he could. Mufalatta's keeping an eye on him. If anybody will know, the Kid will."

We drove away from the downtown section and across the bridge to Skidaway Island, which lay between the city and the beach. The rain had stopped and the moon seemed to be racing in and out of the clouds. As we crossed the bridge, the old-town charm of Dunetown vanished, swallowed up by redwood apartment complexes and condos that looked like gray boxes in the fleeting moonlight. There was something sterile and antiseptic about Skidaway. Twenty years ago it was a wild, undeveloped island, a refuge for wildlife and birds. Now it appeared almost overpopulated.

Stick took Ocean Boulevard like it was Indianapolis. The souped-up engine growled angrily beneath us and the needle of the speedometer inched past one-twenty. The landscape became a blur. Five minutes of that and he downshifted and swerved off the four-lane and headed off through a subdivision, its houses set back from the road behind carefully planted trees and shrubs. In the dark it could have been any planned community.

"Cisco says you lived here once," Stick said past the cigarette clenched between his teeth.

"I just spent a summer here," I answered, trying to adjust my eyes to the fleeing landscape.

"When was that?"

"I hate to tell you. Kennedy was still the President."

"That long ago, huh?" he said, somewhat surprised.

"I was still a college boy in those days," I said. I was beginning to feel like an antique.

He made a hairpin turn with one hand.

"Surprised you, huh, how much it changed?"

I laughed, only it didn't come out like a laugh; it sounded like I was gagging.

"Oh, yeah, you could say that. You could say I was surprised, and I haven't even seen the place in the daylight."

"I couldn't tell you about all that. No frame of reference, y'know."

"This used to be a wildlife refuge," I said. "That give you an idea?"

He flipped the cigarette out the window and whistled through his teeth.

"I doubt if you'll see a sparrow out here now. Rents are too high."

He swerved into Highland Drive without even making a pass at the brakes and lit another cigarette at the same time. I started thinking about taking a cab when I saw half a dozen blue and whites blocking the street ahead, their red and blue lights flashing. We pulled up behind one of them, leaving a mile or so of hot rubber in the process. Ground never felt better underfoot.

I could smell salt air when we got out of the car.

"Lock up," the Stick said. "Some fuckhead stole my hat once."

"So I heard," I said as we headed toward the house, which sat a hundred yards or so back from the road against high dunes. An electric fence was the closest thing to a welcome mat.

I began to get the feeling that this whole bunch of hooligans, Stick included, were like Cowboy Lewis. They definitely believed the shortest distance between two points was a straight line. I also began to wonder where due process fit into all this, if it fit in at all.

We reached the fence, showed some bronze to the man on the gate, and started up the long drive on foot. Dutch was right behind us. I could see his enormous hulk silhouetted against the headlights of the patrol cars. The body lay, uncovered, at the pool's edge. A breeze blew in off the bay, rattling the sea oats along the dunes above.

The old man was unrecognizable. Whatever had blown up, had blown up right in his face. One of his arms had been blown off and either he had been knocked into the pool or was in it when the bomb went off. The water was the color of cherry soda.

There were blood and bits of flesh splattered on the wall of the brick house.

All the windows in the back were blown out.

A woman was hysterical somewhere inside.

"What kind of maniac we got here?" Dutch said, as quietly as I'd heard him say anything since I arrived in Dunetown.

"Right under my fuckin' nose," Kite Lange said. And quite a nose it was. It looked like it had been reworked with a flat iron, and he talked through it like a man with a bad cold or a big coke habit. To make it worse, he was neither. His nose simply had been broken so many times that his mother probably cried every time she saw him. He had knuckles the size of Bermuda onions.

Ex-fighter, had to be.

He was wearing ragged jeans, a faded and nicked denim battle jacket, no shirt under it, and a pair of cowboy boots that must have set him back five hundred bucks. The headband he wore had to be for show—he didn't have enough dishwater-blond hair left to bother with. He also had a gold tooth, right in the front of his bridgework. I was to find out later that he was a former Golden Gloves middleweight champion, a West Coast surfer, and, for ten years, a bounty hunter for a San Francisco bail bondsman before he went legit and joined the police.

Salvatore appeared through the bright lights, nosing around.

"I thought you were gonna check out Stizano," Dutch said. "What the hell are you doin' here?"

"A look-see, okay? Where's Stizano gonna go anyway? He's an old fart and it's past ten o'clock."

"You don't think the whole bunch ain't hangin' on by their back teeth at this point? Somebody just wasted their king."

"They're on the phones," Salvatore said confidently. "They're jawin' back and forth, tryin' to figure out what the hell to do next. What they ain't gonna do at this point is bunch up. Jesus, will you look at this!"

I was beginning to get a handle on Dutch's hooligans, on the common strain that bonded them into a unit. What they lacked in finesse, they made up for with what could mercifully be called individuality. There's an old theory that the cops closest to the money are the ones most likely to get bent. Dutch went looking for mavericks, men too proud to sell out and too tough to scare off. Whatever their other merits, they seemed to have one thing in common—they were honest because it probably didn't occur to them to be anything else.

"First Tagliani's wife gets whacked," Lange said. "And the old man's grandson almost got it here."

"This here don't read like a Mafia hit t'me," Salvatore said. "Killing family members ain't their style."

"Maybe it was a mistake," the Stick volunteered.

"Yeah," Dutch said, "like Pearl Harbor."

"More like a warning," I said.

"Warning?" Lange and Dutch asked at the same time. A lot of eyebrows made question marks.

"Yeah," I said, "a warning that he or she or it—whoever he, she, or it is—means to waste the whole clan."

"Tell me some more good news," said Dutch.

"So why warn them?" Lange said.

"It's the way it's done," said Salvatore. "All that Sicilian bullshit."

"Now we got four stiffs, and we're still as confused as we ever were," Dutch said. "Hey, Doc, you got any idea what caused this?"

The ME, who was as thin as a phalanx and looked two hundred years old, was leaning over what was left of the old man. His sleeves were rolled up and he wore rubber gloves stained red with blood. He shook his head.

"Not yet. A hand grenade, maybe."

"Hand grenade?" the Stick said.

"Yeah," the ME said. "From up there. He was blown down here from the terrace. See the bloodstains?"

"There were two," Lange said.

"Two what?" the ME asked.

"Explosions. I was sittin' right down there. The first one was a little muffled, like maybe the thing went off underwater. The second one sounded like Hiroshima."

"Woke ya up, huh," Dutch said.

The ME still would not agree. He shook his head. "Let's wait until I get up there and take a look. The pattern of stains on the wall there and the condition of the body indicate a single explosion."

"I heard two bangs," Lange insisted.

"How far apart?" I asked.

"Hell, not much. It was like . . . bang, bang! Like that."

I had a terrifying thought but I decided to keep it to myself for the moment. The whole scene was terrifying enough.

The woman screaming uncontrollably inside the house didn't help.

"Homicide'll clean this up," Dutch said. "I'm just interested in the autopsy. Maybe there's something with the weapons'll give us a lead."

The homicide man was a beefy lieutenant in his early forties, dressed in tan slacks, a tattersall vest, a dark brown jacket, and an atrocious flowered tie. His name was Lundy. He came over shaking his head.

"Hey, Dutch, what d'ya think? We got a fuckin' mess on our hands here, wouldn't ya say?"

"Forget that Lindbergh shit, Lundy. This isn't a 'we,' it's a 'you.' Homicide ain't my business."

Lundy said with a scowl, "I need all the help I can get."

Dutch smiled vaguely and nodded. "I would say that, Lundy."

"Can ya believe it, Dutch," Lundy said, "that little kid almost bought it!"

It occurred to me that nobody had expressed any concern for Grandpa Draganata, whose face was all over the side of the house. I mentioned my feelings quietly to the Stick.

"What'd you expect, a twenty-one-gun salute?"

"Four stiffs in less than three hours," Dutch mused again. "This keeps up, I'll be out of work before morning."

"Yeah, and I'll have a nervous breakdown," Lundy said.

I looked over the entire scene. The pool was directly adjacent to the rear of the house; then there was a terrace with a carousel, a miniature railroad, a gazebo, and three picnic tables. Beyond that, the land rose sharply to the dunes above, maybe a hundred yards behind and above the house.

"I'm gonna take the Stick and have a look-see up on the terrace," I told Dutch. To the Stick I said, "Get a light."

A young patrolman came down the hill and said, "There's a couple of Draganata's goons up there, acting like they own the place."

"We'll talk to them," the Stick said. "Let me bum your torch a minute."

"Three gets you five they ain't sayin' a word about what happened. It's that damn wop salad code of theirs," Dutch growled. Lundy went back to the scene.

"Want to come along?" I asked Dutch.

He looked up the hill and laughed.

"In a pig's ass. Call collect when you get there."

The Stick and I went up to the terrace and looked around. One of Draganata's bodyguards approached me. He was no more than six four or five and didn't weigh a pound over two hundred and fifty, with a face that would scare the picture of Dorian Gray.

A finger the size of a telephone pole tried to punch a hole in my chest.

"Private property," he said.

I stared him as straight in the eye as I could, considering the eye was four inches above me.

"You jab me once more with that finger, I'll break it off and make you eat it," I said in my tough-guy voice.

The goon looked at me and smiled.

"Sure thing."

"I'm a federal officer and you're obstructing the scene of a crime. That's a misdemeanor. You jab me again, asshole, that's assaulting a federal officer, which is a felony. Can you stand still for a felony toss, sonny?"

He shuffled from one foot to the other for a moment or two, trying to work that out in whatever he used for a brain. While he was sorting through my threat, the other gorilla came over.

"Don't take no shit, Larry," he said. He was just as big and just as ugly.

"You two already fucked up royally once tonight," I said. "How's it feel, knowing you screwed up and your boss got his head handed to him."

Larry's face turned purple. He made a funny sound in his throat and took a step toward me. But before he could raise his hand a fist came from my left and caught him on the corner of the jaw. The top part of his face didn't budge; the bottom part went west. His jaw cracked like a gunshot. He was so ugly, it was hard to tell whether the look on his face was one of pain or surprise. A second later his eyes did a slow roll and he dropped to his knees.

He made a noise that sounded like "Arfroble."

The Stick was standing beside me, shaking out his knuckles.

The other tough went for the Stick and I pulled my .38 from under my arm and stuck the barrel as far up his left nostril as the gunsight would permit.

"Don't you hear good?" I said.

He stared at the gun and then at me and then back at the gun. The Stick kicked him in the nuts as hard as I've ever seen anybody kicked anywhere. He hit the ground beside his partner; his teeth cracked shut, trapping the cry of pain. It screeched in the back of his throat. Tears flooded his eyes. He fell forward on his hands and threw up. The other one was shaking his head, his jaw wobbling uselessly back and forth.

"Gladolabor," he said.

I thought about what Cisco had told me, about how Stick was

young and not too jaded, and about how I might give him a few pointers on due process. Now was hardly the time. He was doing just fine. I put my artillery away and smiled.

"Y'know," he said, "we got a pretty good act here."

"Yeah. Maybe we should tighten it up a little, take it on the road," I agreed.

Stick and I checked over the terrace, ignoring the two stricken mastodons.

"Obstructing the scene of a crime," he mused. "Where did you come up with that?"

"It sounded good," I said. "Did it sound good to you?"

"I was convinced," he said. "Cisco says you're a lawyer; I figured you should know."

He stepped into the gazebo and threw on the lights. The calliope music started, but the merry-go-round was destroyed, tilted on one side like a bloody beret. It was eerie, the mutilated horses frozen in up-and-down positions, heads blown away, feet missing, while the calliope played its happy melody.

"Cisco likes to tell people I'm a lawyer, to impress them," I said. "I never practiced law."

"How come?" he asked.

A bloody horse's head, with flared nostrils and fiery, bloody eyes, lay at my feet. I lifted it slightly with the toe of one shoe and peered under it, as though I expected to find some important bit of evidence under there.

"I had the stupid notion it was still an honorable profession," I said.

He laughed this crazy laugh, his eyes dancing between the lids, his mouth turned down at the corners instead of up. It could have been mistaken for a snarl.

"I knew better than that the first time I was briefed by a prosecutor. He as much as told me to perjure myself."

"And what'd you tell him?"

"I told him to get fucked. It didn't happen the way he wanted it to happen and that was that. He ended up plea-bargaining the case away rather than taking a shot with the true facts."

"Just after I took the bar I was interviewed by this big law firm in San Francisco," I said. "This was one of the most prestigious law firms in the city. The old partner who did the interviewing spent an hour explaining to me how fee splitting works. Nothing is ever said between two opposing lawyers; they just exchange D and B's on the clients and decide how much they can milk them for. When the well's dry, they reach a settlement. When I left, I was so disgusted I almost threw up. I wandered around the hill for a while, then went down and joined the police force."

"But you felt good about it," he said, flashing that crazy smile again.

"No, I felt like shit if you want to know the truth," I admitted to him. "Three years in law school and I end up driving a blue and white."

The Stick listened to the music for several seconds and finally flicked the switch off. I looked above us, up to the top of the dunes.

"Up there," I said.

We huffed and puffed through the sand to the top of the sharp embankment and found ourselves staring at the ocean far below. It twinkled in the moonlight.

"What're we looking for?" the Stick asked.

"You were in the army," I said. "What makes a discharge when it's fired and another one when it hits?"

"Mortar?"

"Too close."

He snapped his fingers. "Grenade launcher."

"It fits," I said.

We checked the trajectory from the hill to the pool. The terrace could be seen only from the very edge of the dune. It didn't take us long to find a scorched place in the grass on the back of the dune with a smear of gun grease behind it.

"Right here," I said. "Whoever killed the old man lobbed his shot from here, right onto the terrace. He couldn't even see him; he lined up his shot with some point on the pool and it blew up right in the old man's lap."

I flashed the light around the dune, looking for footprints.

"There," the Stick said, pointing to several depressions in the side of the dune leading toward the ocean.

We looked closer.

"Looks like Bigfoot," the Stick said. The depressions were fairly shallow and about the size of a small watermelon. There was no definition to them.

I pointed the light to the hard sand at the bottom of the dune. The tide was almost full. Ridges of foam lay near the foot of the dune.

"Great," I said. "The tide's in. There goes any tracks on the beach."

"Knew what he was doin'," the Stick said. "A blind shot like that and the timing was perfect."

"This took a little planning. He had to know the setup. He knew when high tide was. And with those two goons down there, he only had one shot. Confident son of a bitch. We better not make too many tracks; forensics may turn something up."

"One Ear," the Stick said.

"Right. Let's get him over here."

We went back down and told Lundy what we had found and he sent two men and a photographer up the hill.

"Those two gorillas up there may need some medical assistance, too," the Stick said. "They give you any shit, book 'em for assaulting an officer."

Lundy's eyebrows arched in surprise. "Yeah, thanks," he said with a touch of awe.

"I'm goin' inside," said the Stick. "See if I can raise Charlie One Ear."

I joined Dutch, who was leaning on the corner of the house gnawing on a toothpick. He was obviously impressed.

"You guys weren't gone long to be so busy," he said with a grin.

I looked at my watch. It was past ten and my stomach was telling me it hadn't been fed since noon.

"I've gotta fill Mazzola in and get something to eat," I said. "Then I'm calling it a night."

"I could use some food too," the Stick said, rejoining us. "Charlie's on his way and not too happy about it. I told Lundy to keep people off the hill."

The Stick produced a small tan calling card.

"You ever need me," he said, handing me a card, "my home number's on the back. There's a machine on it. If it rings four times before it answers, I'm there, just takin' a shit or a shower or something. Leave a number, I'll usually get back to you in a coupla minutes. If it answers after one ring, I'm out."

"Meet us at the Feed Mill," Dutch said to the Stick. "Jake can drive down with me."

I was grateful for that.

As we walked back to the cars I said, "We can throw in with you on this. I think we can assume the weapon was a grenade launcher and that's an illegal weapon and that makes it federal."

"Gee whiz," Dutch growled. "Ain't due process grand."

12

FLASHBACK: NAM DIARY, ARRIVAL

The first ten days: *First off, I was a replacement. I sat around the Cam Ranh Bay repo-depot for about ten days before they sent me down to Third Corps HQ and from there over to Phouc Binh which is where I pick up my squad. I'm only five weeks out of Advanced Infantry school, I don't know shit and I am plenty scared.*

I can tell you this, flying in to Cam Ranh I look down and it's really gorgeous, I mean this is some beautiful place except you have all this beautiful green jungle and then you have mortar holes everywhere. It was like, you know, paradise going to hell and gone.

Anyway, while I'm in Cam Ranh waiting to get a squad, I hang out with this potato farmer from Nebraska they call Spud, because of the potatoes and all. He doesn't like it much but he doesn't complain either. That wasn't too bad because we were both, you know, newcomers, so mostly we talked about what it's like back in the World—the States. Except this Spud, he was really scared. His hands shook and everything. Then he gets shipped into Indian country, and after that I meet up with this kid from Wisconsin—a short termer with only two months left to go who is off the line a couple days to come see his brother who got wounded and is in the hospital. We hook up in this sorry ass lean-to they call a bar. First off I tried striking up some talk with a sergeant but he just looks at me with these dead eyes, I mean eyes like hunks of coal, no feeling, no nothin'. He was scarey. I says "hi" and he looks at me and gets up and leaves, and that's when this kid from Wisconsin, who is sitting down the way from me, pipes up and says, "He's a CRIP, they don't socialize much." And I says, "What's a CRIP?" And he says, "Jeeze, how long you been over here?" And I says, "Less than a week," and he says, "Shit, you got it all ahead of you," and just shakes his head but he doesn't say anymore about CRIP; I learned about that later.

Anyway he got off the line to see his brother, only it turns out he's been there three days and hasn't been to the hospital yet and when I ask him why he says, "No guts." Finally after a couple beers I walk him down to the hospital and I wait outside in the hall and there's some guy screaming the whole time I'm waiting. It gives me the crawlers. I wanted to just up and leave but that wasn't right so I sat there and after awhile I put my hands over my ears so I couldn't hear it anymore. Then the kid from Wisconsin comes out and he's crying and he's like, you know, hysterical or something, and we get outside and sit down near the hospital and this kid, he's really torn up. But I don't ask him anything, I just wait, because already I'm learning about not asking questions.

About five minutes after we sit down for a smoke this Huey comes over and settles down almost on the ground and they dump out half a dozen body bags, just like that, plop on the ground and whip off again. I never saw anybody dead before. I started getting sick and the kid from Wisconsin is sitting there staring at the bags and finally I says, "Let's get out of here," and we go down to this other hooch and have a couple more beers.

The kid gets pretty drunk and finally he starts talkin'. Real fast, it just comes bustin' out. He says, "Bobby says to me, 'Christ, how am I gonna tell Arlene, that's his girlfriend, Arlene, how'm I gonna tell her I ain't got any balls left,' and I'm sittin' there thinking, Jeeze Bobby, you don't have any fuckin' legs *left!' Ah, shit, it don't make no never mind anyways. Arlene married some asshole from over at the paper mill at Christmas and she never even wrote him or anything. You think I'm gonna tell him that? There's a lot of Arlenes in the world but Bobby, he only has two legs and two balls. Now he ain't got neither."*

And I just sit there listening because, what are you to say, right? Besides, my insides are really beginning to churn and I'm wondering when I'm going up. And then he says, "What's it like back in the world? Do they really spit on soldiers?" And I says I never saw anybody spit on a soldier, although once I did see a demonstration and I was in uniform and a bunch of them, y'know, they shot me a bird like it's my fault I got to go to Vietnam.

Finally I navigate the kid from Wisconsin back to his quarters and he's really soused and the last thing he says to me is, "I'm afraid to go home, scared shitless here and scared shitless to go home, shit, they're gonna hate me because of Bobby."

I never saw him again but I know what he means now, about them hating him because of what happened to his brother. You get so paranoid after awhile. After awhile you get so you think everybody back in the world blames you for the whole thing.

Like this Jesus freak from Mississippi I meet at the Red Cross. He's even worse. He kind of babbles, you know, runs things together, like he can't get it off his chest quick enough, keeps talking about the kids, about killing kids. "Kids?" I says to him. "Listen," he says and he's whispering, "don't ever shoot a water buffalo, hear? You can kill women and children but you kill a water buffalo, man, they'll bury you under the brig." Then he starts laughing. Laughing. *Then he says, "Nothin' over here makes any sense. Sometimes I wonder, hey, we the good guys or not? But you ask an officer that, he'll send you up to the psycho ward. I don't pray anymore. I'm too embarrassed to talk to God. I got too much to tell him."*

He goes on like that for maybe an hour, shaking his head the whole time. Always whispering.

By the time I get my walking papers I'm almost glad to be going into it. This place is nuts. It all seems to come to a head here at Cam Ranh because you get them comin' and goin'. Everybody's a little crazy. There's a lot of questions you want to ask but after awhile you figure out nobody has any answers, anyhow, why bother.

So anyway, here I am in this creepy little town near the river, if you can even call it a town, I'm not here five minutes, the lieutenant, who looks about sixteen, red hair and freckles, his name is Carmody, sits down and pops two beers, and he says, "Now listen good to me. I been out here, it's going on eight months. I got my own way of doing things after all that time, so you do what I say, don't even argue, don't tell me you didn't learn it that way back in the World, you just do it and I'll get you home alive. You don't, I give you two weeks, you'll be dead or missing something you don't want to lose."

I don't say anything, I just listen. I try not to shake but I am real nervous.

"I got a few rules," he says. "In the beginning, no matter what happens, follow me. If Charlie starts busting caps, you just follow me. Don't talk, don't start yelling at anybody else. If I go down, you go down. Find a pebble or a mound of dirt or a paddy and get below it. Get under his horizon. If you get hit, don't say anything and don't move. You do, and you're dead. Just lay there, somebody'll get you. That's my last rule—we don't leave anybody behind. Dead or alive, everybody goes out together."

I was so scared my stomach hurt.

"These VC are good, goddamn good," he says. "Don't let anybody tell you different because that's bullshit. All that shit they gave you back in AI, forget it. They got tunnels out there, they go on for miles. They got whole operating rooms under the ground, not just some little pooch hole you throw a grenade in and forget it, they pop up fifty feet away and your ass is in a bucket. These fuckers can run into a village and vanish. We don't get heroic, okay, we call in some air, let the Black Ponies burn it out. We move on. That's our mission, search and destroy. What it is not is search and be destroyed."

I remember thinking, this is for real. Jesus, in five minutes we could be doing it for real.

"Any questions?" he says.

I shake my head no.

"Welcome to the war," he says.

13

STONEWALL TITAN

We drove across town to a bluff overlooking the Dunetown River. The rain had stopped and the river steamed in the warm southern wind that had brought it. Ancient brick buildings, shrouded in fog and dating back to God knows when, lined the bluff, like sentinels guarding the waterfront from Front Street and the Strip, and history swirled around us in the fog as we edged down a narrow cobblestone alley from Bay Street to the river's edge.

I felt the cold breath of ghosts on my neck. Unseen signs, hidden in the mist, creaked before the wind. The dim shape of a freighter drifted eerily down the river, not twenty yards from us, its foghorn bleating a path to the sea.

This was the Dunetown I remembered.

Doomstown seemed a Saturn ride away.

The Feed Mill was a long, narrow place on River Street facing the waterfront. The menu was written out on a green chalkboard at one end and between it and the front door there were maybe twenty tables and booths. We sat near the front. Dutch squinted through his glasses at the bill of fare.

"The chicken fried steak is great; so's the mulligan stew. All the vegetables are good," he said as he studied the menu.

He ordered the steak, three vegetables, a side dish of mashed potatoes and gravy, another side of stew, and two orders of tapioca pudding. I got heartburn listening to him.

The Stick and I ordered a normal meal and coffee.

"I think I'm ruling out Nose," Dutch said, diving into his banquet.

"How's that?" I asked.

"It's just not his style. When Nose came out of Little Q after doing that stretch, he went straight after Cherry McGee, blew him away in broad daylight as McGee was comin' out of a bank on Bay Street. People were all over the place but he didn't take out anybody but McGee and one of his strongarms. We got a woman kayoed here."

"Could have been a mistake," the Stick argued.

"Why's Graves still on the street?" I asked.

"No proof. I had twenty people who were standin' right there when it went down, couldn't identify him in the stand-up."

"Twenty-two," the Stick corrected.

"He was wearing a stocking cap, and the car he did the trick from was boosted from a downtown parkin' lot half an hour earlier. We couldn't prove doodly-shit. He walked. And he was laughing as he went out the door."

"Nevertheless, I kind of like Nose," the Stick said.

"Why?" I asked.

"Because he's not afraid of anybody. One spook against the lot."

"I give him credit for still being alive," Dutch said between mouthfuls.

"So where does that leave us?" I said.

"No-fuckin'-where," said Stick.

"Tell you the truth," Dutch added, "I think about it, we got about a hundred good suspects we could hassle on this score so far."

"I thought homicide was out of your league," I said.

"Wel-l-l, you can't stop a man from thinking. Besides, we'll be in wheelchairs before Lundy and his bunch come up with anything. He needs a road map to find his ass when it itches."

"I got explicit orders," I said. "Cisco says he'll hang me higher than the Washington Monument if I stick my nose in a homicide investigation."

"Well, nobody can stop us from thinking."

"You can blow a circuit trying to separate all the suspects," I said. "You've got the whole Tagliani outfit, what's left of them. Stizano, Logeto, Bronicata, Chevos—"

"If he's here," Dutch interrupted.

"Yeah, if he's here. Then there's Leo Costello. He's not only Tagliani's son-in-law, he's *consigliere* for the whole outfit."

"You may as well throw in Cohen," Stick said.

"He's afraid of his own shadow," I said, and then after thinking it over, I tossed in: "On the other hand, if he burned the books, they'd all end up doing the clock. They've all got a motive. That's assuming it's in the family."

"Even if it isn't, there's got to be lots of nervous Taglianis out there tonight."

"With Tagliani, Stinetto, and Draganata out of the way, that just about takes out all the old line. Except for the Barber," I said.

"They gotta figure it's Nose," said the Stick. "Some hothead Tagliani torpedo will take a pop at one of Graves' boys and we'll have a three-way war on our hands."

"That's if they don't start shootin' each other," said Dutch.

"Hell," the Stick said. "It's probably a coupla Philly shooters on their way home already."

"Or a coupla China soldiers with nothing to do right now," Dutch said.

"Shit, it could be anybody," the Stick sighed.

"Which is why I'm finishing my meal and going home," I said. "We can sit here all night speculating on who shot who. Let's hit it fresh in the morning."

We paid the check; the Stick said good night and left. Dutch and I drove the ten minutes back to the hotel in silence.

The black limo was still parked under the marquee of the Ponce when we got back. As I got out of the car I noticed the tag: ST-1. I told Dutch I would check my messages and meet him in the bar for a nightcap.

There was a phone call from Cisco and a hotel envelope, sealed, with my name printed meticulously across the front.

I called Cisco, gave him the latest body count, and told him I'd give him the details over breakfast.

As I started toward the bar I finally saw him, the first of several specters from the past. I was tired and getting irritable and I wasn't ready to face up yet, but there he was in his three-piece dark blue suit and a gray homburg, leaning on a gold-handled ebony cane, his snowy hair clipped neatly above the ears, his sapphire eyes twinkling fiercely under thick white brows.

Stonewall Titan, sheriff and kingmaker of Oglethorpe County, Mr. Stoney to everything that walked on two feet in the town, was standing under the marquee wiggling a short, thick finger under the nose of a tall and uncomfortable-looking guy in a tweed jacket and gray flannels. Titan had made or destroyed more than one political dream with a wave of that finger. The man in tweeds went back into the bar.

Finished, Titan turned and, leaning on the cane, limped toward his car, where a tall and ugly bird in a tan and black county policeman's uniform held the door for him. As he was about to enter the car, he saw me and hesitated for an instant. His bright blue eyes glittered in brief recognition, then his hard jaw tightened and he climbed into the limousine and was gone.

Then I saw her.

I moved behind a fern, watching her through its slender leaves, like a high school swain eyeing his first crush. I don't know what made me think I could have avoided seeing her. It had to happen sooner or later. Later would have been better.

Doe Findley still looked eighteen, still had the long blond silky hair, the caramel tan, eyes as gray as ever. A flash of memories tumbled through my mind: Doe on water skis, her silken hair twisting in the wind; roaring across the beach in a dune buggy; playfully wrestling on the boat dock with Teddy and pushing him into the bay in his best sports coat and pants, then chasing me across the wide lawn down to the edge of the bay.

Doe watching the sun set off the point at Windsong, an image as soft and fragile as a Degas painting.

Time had erased a lot of images from my mind, but those were as clear as a painting on the wall, even after twenty years.

It came and went quickly.

She was talking to a chic blond woman; then she laughed and turned and joined a tall guy in Ultrasuede who was holding open the door of a dark blue Mercedes sedan.

So that was Harry Raines. My dislike for him was intense and immediate, a feeling I didn't like but could not control. I looked for flaws, blemishes on the face of this golden boy who had it all. His blond hair was thinning out the way a surfer's hair thins out, and he had traded his tan for an office pallor, but he was a handsome man nonetheless, with the bearing and presence that most powerful men exude. Harry Raines wore success the way a beautiful woman wears diamonds. If he had flaws, they were not apparent. I watched as he helped her into the car, trying to ignore the feelings that hit me in waves, like the aftershock of an earthquake. A handsome, good-looking pair. I tried to shove my feelings down in the dark places where they had hidden for all those years but it didn't work. As the Mercedes drove off into the dark I was aware that my hand was shaking.

Easy, Kilmer, I told myself; that was then, this is now. The lady probably doesn't even remember your name. I tried shrugging it off and joined Dutch.

Some things never change. The Ponce Bar was one of them. It was a dark, oaken room with a brick floor, a zinc-topped bar, and Tiffany lamps over the stalls and tables. The mirror behind the bar itself ran half the length of the room and was etched glass. They had built the hotel around it, rather than change a brick of the place. Politicians had been made and trashed in this room, business deals closed with a handshake, schemes planned and hatched. It was the heartland of the makers and breakers of Dunetown. For two hundred years the room had crackled with the electricity generated by the power brokers, arm-wrestling for position.

Only Findley and Titan seemed immune to the games. Together they called the business and political shots of the entire county, unchallenged by the other robber barons of Dunetown. It was in this room that Chief had given Teddy and me one of our first lessons in business.

"Right over in that corner," he had told us, "that's where Vic Larkin and I locked horns for the last time. We owned half the beach property on Oceanby together; our fathers had been partners. But we never got along. Larkin wanted to develop the beach front, turn it into a damn tinhorn tourist trap. He just didn't have any class. I favored leaving it alone.

"One night it came to a head. We had one helluvan argument sitting right over there. 'Damn it, Victor,' I says to him, 'we're never gonna get along and you know it. I'll cut you high card. Winner buys the loser out for a dollar.'

"Vic turned pale but he had guts, I'll give him that. I told the bartender to bring us a deck of cards and we cut. He pulled a six, I pulled a nine. That nine bought me a million dollars' worth of real estate for one buck."

"You call that good business?" Teddy had asked.

"I call it gambling," Chief had said. "And that's what business is all about, boys. It's a gambler's game."

From the look of the crowd, there weren't too many gamblers left among the Dunetown elite. What was missing was the electricity. There was no longer a hum in the air, just a lot of chatter.

The blond woman who had been outside with Doe had returned to the room and was talking to a small group of people. She was wearing a wraparound mauve silk dress and an off-yellow wide-brimmed hat and her eyes moved around the room as she spoke, taking in everything.

"The blonde you're eyeballin' is Babs Thomas," Dutch said. "Don't say hello unless you want everybody in town to know it five minutes later."

"Local gossip?" I asked.

"You could call her that. She does a snitch column in the *Ledger* called 'Whispers.' Very apropos. You wanna know the inside on Doomstown's aristocracy, ask her. She knows what bed every pair of shoes in town is under."

I jotted that down in my memory for future reference and then said, "I just saw Stonewall Titan out front."

"Yeah?" Dutch said.

"I figured Titan was probably dead by now," I said.

"Mr. Stoney will tell God when he's ready to go, and offhand I'd say God's gonna have to wait awhile. How well do you know him?"

"Too long ago to matter," I said, which was far from the truth. I don't think Dutch believed it either, although he was kind enough to let it pass.

"I saw him, too, coming out of the bar," said Dutch. "We had words. He gave me some *sheiss*."

"What does Titan expect you to do?" I asked.

"End it."

"Just like that?"

"Yeah, just like that. 'Get it done before Harry gets wind of it,' " he says.

"Gets wind of it!" I replied. "How the hell does he hope to keep Raines in the dark? And why?"

"He's hoping we'll nail this thing down fast so the Committee can shove it under the carpet."

"What Committee?" I asked.

Dutch hesitated, staring into his drink. He rattled ice in his glass for a few moments, then shrugged. "Local power structure," he said, brushing it off.

"You just took a left turn," I said.

"Y'see, Raines doesn't think beyond the racetrack," Dutch said, still ignoring my question. "The paper and the TV stations tend to play down any violence that happens. Now we got Mafia here, it could be Raines' worst nightmare come true. I could get my walking papers over this."

"So you said."

The waitress brought our drinks. I decided not to press him on who or what the Committee was for the moment.

"Fill me in on Titan," I said.

He jiggled the ice in his highball.

"Only trouble with Stoney Titan, he's been sheriff for too damn long. Forty years plus; that's one hell of a long time."

"You think he's on the take?"

"Not the way you mean," Dutch said. "Nothin' goes down in this town he don't know about. Not a card game, not a floating crap game, not numbers. Not a horse parlor. He knows every hooker by her first *and* last name, every bootlegger, dope runner, car booster. A man can't be around that long, know that much, he isn't bent just a little, know what I mean? On the other hand, he's a tough little bantam, not a man to take sides against."

I remembered Titan differently. I remembered him on soft summer afternoons with his coat across his knees, drinking bourbon with Chief and talking on the porch at Windsong. I remembered he always put his gun in the trunk before coming up to the house and took off his coat because he wore his badge pinned on the inside pocket and I guess that was his way of saying it was a friendly call. And I remembered him as thinner and not as gray, a wiry little man with a fast step and twinkling eyes. Hell, I thought, he's pushing hard on eighty. Funny how people never age in your memory.

"I wonder if he was on Tagliani's payroll," I thought aloud.

"He isn't bent in that direction. No way," Dutch said. "Stoney doesn't need money or power. And he's too old to get sucked into that kind of game. Titan coulda been a state senator, probably governor. God knows he's got the power. But he's like a man who can't swim—he never goes in over his head."

"Then maybe he had Tagliani killed," I suggested.

"Not his style. Squeeze Tagliani out, maybe. But this high-style execution isn't gonna be good for Dunetown. And I don't see a hope in hell of cleaning this up right away, do you?"

I admitted that there was very little to go on at that point. I also told him I didn't think the town could keep the gang slayings a secret for too long.

"A day or two," I said, "maybe."

"When Cherry McGee and Nose Graves were going at it, the press kept it buried," he said. "As far as most folks know, the hoods that went down during that melee were robbers and thieves, part of the body count that can be chalked up to your normal, everyday crime statistics."

"Can't you sneak some of this information to them?" I said. "Having the press on your side can help sometimes."

He leaned over the table toward me and said, "You don't understand, Jake m'boy. They know it already. It's their option to underplay it. It's the way things have always been done here."

"As I recall, a sheriff is a very big man in this state," I said.

"Nothing like Stoney. Big doesn't even cover it. The way I hear it, he's delivered the swing vote for two governors, half a dozen senators, and this county helped give the state to Kennedy in 1960."

"A lot of people owe him then," I said.

"Yeah."

"He could probably put Raines in the statehouse."

"He could give him one helluva shove."

"And the town blowing up around them could sink Raines, right?"

"Yeah, I suppose you could say that. But Raines is a heavy hitter. He might could slug his way out of a scandal if it didn't touch him directly."

I leaned across the table and said very quietly, "You know as well as I do they can't ignore this. It's going to blow up bigger than Mount Saint Helens."

"Stoney's point is well made," said Dutch. "The sooner we stop it, the better."

"For Raines?"

"For everybody."

"Do you like Titan?" I asked bluntly.

"He's a relic," Dutch said. "And I love relics."

THE COMMITTEE

Dutch looked as if he were getting ready to pack it in for the night, but there was still a question left hanging in the air. He had avoided it. I didn't want him to. I decided to back into it with a shocker.

"You think there's any chance Harry Raines is behind this?" I asked. It worked. He looked up as if I had thrown cold water in his face.

"I'm just trying to get a fix on all the players," I said.

"Why would Harry want to create this kind of problem for himself? I told you, it's his worst nightmare come true."

"Maybe he thinks he can keep it quiet like the Cherry McGee

affair. Get rid of these hoodlums and pass it off as some kind of kook slaying."

"You're reaching, son," he said. "Harry Raines has more to lose in this than anybody."

"Maybe that's what he wants everybody to think."

"You're serious, aren't you."

"You can look at it two ways. He's got the most to lose when this gets out, but he also has the most to gain by getting rid of the Triad."

"You know, if I didn't know better, I might think that's the way you want it to play out."

"Just asking. Like I said, I'm trying to cover all the bases."

"You're out of the ballpark on that one," he said, scowling at me over his drink. He looked around the room and jiggled his ice some more.

It was time to force the issue. Dutch Morehead knew more than he wanted me to know, I was sure of it.

"Look, Dutch," I said, "I don't mind standing muster for your SOB's. I understand all that. I'll make my peace with them in my own way. But I think it's time we started trusting each other. Right now I have the feeling I'm not playing with all the cards and you hold the missing ones."

He continued to play with his drink. Finally he said, "All right, what's stuck in your craw?"

"What about this Committee you mentioned? What's that all about? I mean, look around, Dutch. This is the crème de la crème of Dunetown in here. Society, politics, money. This is their watering hole. They act like nothing's happened. Three mainline mobsters and a woman have been butchered and there isn't a frown in the place."

"They don't know about it yet," he said. "And the local press is gonna keep it under wraps as long as they're told to."

"By whom?"

He sighed as only a big man can sigh. It shook the table.

"I got a few questions first," he said.

"My old man used to say, 'You can't listen when you're talking.' "

"Is that a fact," he said. "Well, my old man used to say, 'You can't get water out of a low well without priming it.' "

I started chuckling. "You're older than I am, Dutch, I suppose you can keep this up a lot longer. What do you want to know?"

"You been playin' coy ever since you got here, actin' like this is your first trip to town," he said. "See, I ain't buyin' that because I don't think you're on the level and it ain't a one-way street, y'know, it's give and take."

I had been underestimating the big man. He was either a lot more perceptive than I had given him credit for or he knew more about me than I thought he did.

"Give me a for instance."

"For instance, I got this gut feeling you know all about Chief and Titan and the Findleys."

I wasn't sure I could trust Dutch Morehead, I wasn't sure I could trust anybody. But I had to start someplace. I decided to prime the pump a little.

"No bullshit," he said.

"No bullshit," I answered. "I lived with Chief Findley and his family for one summer. That was 1963. Teddy Findley was my best friend. We played football together. We were in Nam together. I was with him when he died."

"Uh-huh."

That's all he said. He was waiting for more.

"I never knew my own father," I went on. "He died at Guadalcanal before I was born. I guess Chief was like a father figure to me. What he said was gospel. You could . . . you could feel the power of the man when he walked in the room. It made the room hum. I've got mixed feelings about all that now."

"I've heard that about him. There isn't much left anymore."

"No, now Raines is doing the humming."

"So what's that to you?"

"Bottom line, if Raines is the man now, then he has to take the rap for what's happened here. Sooner or later it's going to fall on him."

"So?"

"So how come he's got his head stuck so far in the sand?"

"Harry Raines is a local boy," he said. "Surprised everybody because he was kind of a hell-raising kid who grew up to be a shrewd businessman and a tough politician. His old man was a barely respectable judge, had a passion for all the things judges ain't supposed to lust after—women, racehorses, gambling. Hell, the old man died in his box at Hialeah with a fistful of winning tickets in his hand."

"So that's where the interest in horse racing started," I said.

"From what I hear, by the time Harry was old enough to pee by himself, he'd been to every racetrack in the country. He handicapped his way through Georgia, played football, was one of Vince Dooley's first All-Americans, got a law degree at Harvard, came back, went to work as a lawyer for Chief, married Doe Findley, and inherited the political power of the city, then ran for the state senate and was elected, thanks in no little way to Stoney Titan. There it is in about two paragraphs, the story of Harry Raines."

"Nice merger," I said, with more acid than I had planned.

Dutch's eyebrows rose. Then he pursed his lips and said, "I suppose you could say that."

"So Chief picked him out, right?"

"I don't know, that's before my time. We ain't exactly drinkin' buddies, Raines and me. I don't know the particulars."

"How'd he get to be racing commissioner?"

"Gave up his seat in the state senate and stumped one end of this state to the other, selling the idea. His big edge was that it would raise tax money for the school system. He also turned over the operation of Findley Enterprises to his best friend, Sam Donleavy. That way nobody could accuse him of any conflict of interest. Hell, he won't even let his wife race her Thoroughbreds. The man's clean, Jake."

"Yeah, I know, he's going to be governor one of these days soon."

"Probably, if this mess doesn't blow him out of the water."

"Anybody jealous of his success? The fact that he married a rich girl and got richer?"

"I suppose so."

"Anybody who might be out to destroy him?"

He stared hard at me.

"Lissen here, a lot of people in this town got rich in the boom and they thank Harry for that. If you think he's unpopular around here, think again. He's the favorite son of Dunetown."

"And the most powerful," I added.

"I would say that."

"Because of Chief's clout," I went on.

"In the beginning maybe. Not anymore. He's got his own power base; he doesn't need a worn-out old man."

"He uses Titan."

I realized that was a mistake the minute I said it. I was letting my own feelings intrude on the conversation. Dutch shook his head and stared down into his drink.

"You're gonna waste a lot of time if you try to stretch that one out," he said. "Raines doesn't *use* Titan any more than Titan uses him. As far as the town goes, the people that run Doomstown don't have to drive down Front Street anymore. They can afford to shop in Atlanta."

"So they drew the battle line at Front Street," I said. "Gave that to the hoodlums."

"More or less."

I stared him hard in the eye.

"What's the Committee?" I asked bluntly.

He paused again. I had the feeling he wanted more out of me before going on but I waited him out. Finally he talked:

"Before he stepped out of local affairs, Harry formed an ex-officio committee. The five most powerful men in town. They have no legislative power per se. They don't have a name, an office, don't even meet any one place in particular. They're just old friends who feel it's their responsibility to look out for the town, just like your friend Chief used to do, and Titan still does. It's the way things're done down here."

"What do they do?"

"As I get it, the idea was that they screen everybody who comes near this town with a dollar to invest."

I said, "To make sure people like Tagliani don't get a foothold, is that it?"

"Part of it. And to contain the roughhouse element, so nobody gets out of line."

"That what you've been doing, containing the roughhouse element?"

"Part of it."

"That gives them ten points for awareness and none for performance."

"Thanks. I appreciate that."

"I don't mean you. It wasn't your job to spot Tagliani."

"They're local boys, Jake. They don't know from the Mafia. Babes in the woods. That was what Leadbetter was supposed to do, keep an eye on the new shakers that moved in."

"That makes a strong case against the Tagliani clan for Leadbetter's murder," I said. "Maybe he tumbled them and they hit him before he could say anything."

"I've been thinkin' the same thing. When Leadbetter took the wash, it kinda fell in my lap. What can I tell you, Tagliani got by all of us."

"Hell, I can't knock that," I said. "I lost them for a year. But how could five men operating ex-officio have any effect on the town?"

" 'Cause they're the most powerful men in the city, son," he said. "This is still a small town to them. Since the day they laid the first cobblestone, a handful of men have run Dunetown. Them, their wives and families—hell, they own or control most of the property on the islands. They *are* the political power. They set the social standards. They screen people who want to do business here. And they directly or indirectly control most of the big banks. They are Roman emperors, Jake. Thumbs up, you're in; thumbs down, you're out. Now, that may not be to your likin' or mine, but that's the way it is. Nobody bucks that kind of power."

"So they'd know who owns the hotels, the marinas, condos, apartments, what have you?"

"I suppose so, unless they're all owned by blind corporations. The hotels are owned by a local combine."

"You're sure about that?"

"Straight from the horse's mouth."

"And which horse would that be?"

"Sam Donleavy. He's Harry's right-hand man, the second most powerful man in Dunetown. If there's a head of the Committee, he'd be it."

"How about Raines?"

"He doesn't sit. Donleavy's his voice. Raines is funny about conflict of interest. Right now he devotes all his time to the track. If he can prove it's worthwhile, he'll waltz into the governor's mansion."

"Who else is on this Committee?"

He wiggled his head like an old bear. "Shit, pal, you don't stop, do you? You prime the pump with a cup of water and get a gallon outta me. You could turn out to be a real son of a bitch."

"I have been accused of that."

His flaccid face flowed back into a smile.

"I'll just bet so," he said.

"It's what I do," I said, smiling back.

"Don't we all. Okay, first, there's Donleavy. That's him sitting right over there in the tweed jacket."

He nodded toward the man whom I had seen talking to Stoney Titan as I came in. He was a big guy with a bull neck and shoulders that threatened to split his jacket down the middle. He appeared to be in his thirties, wore his hair in a crew cut, and had a nose that had been flattened more than once. An ex-ballplayer, I guessed looking at him. He was entertaining the ladies at the table, there was a lot of giggling, but the lines around his mouth were tight and the laughter didn't spread to his eyes. He looked like a man with a lot of trouble trying to have a good time and I mentioned it to Dutch.

"I imagine Stoney's driven a spike up his tail," said Dutch. "Sam'll fall before Harry, and if he falls out of grace, he doesn't have the Findley millions to lean on."

"Which means they'll put the heat on you."

"Us, partner."

"Yeah, us."

"Our feet are already in the fire, make no mistake."

"Who else is on this Committee?"

"Charles Seaborn. He's president of the Seacoast National Bank chain, largest in these parts. He's old money. His father was chairman of the board when he died last year. Then there's Arthur Logan, who'll be president of the town's most prestigious and successful law firm in another year or two, soon's his old man dies or quits. Next, Roger Sutter, he's Sutter Communications. That's the newspaper and the television station. Between them, they own most of the ground with grass on it in the county. That's power."

"That covers all the bases but one," I said. "You said there were five members on the Committee."

"Before I answer that," he said, "I got one more question to ask you."

"Shoot."

"It's personal, Jake. You can tell me to suck eggs if you want to."

I guess I knew what the question was going to be before he asked it.

"Were you in love with Doe Findley twenty years ago?" he asked.

I was ready for him. I smiled a big fifty-dollar smile. "Hell, I'm just like you, Dutch. I always end up kissing the horse at the finish. Who's number five?"

"Who else?" he said. "Stonewall Titan."

DOE

I finished my drink and said good night. My room on the third floor had a dormer window with a chintz loveseat and coffee table in front of it, a vintage TV set, a double bed, and ceilings so high you could fly a kite in it. Everything—the drapes, walls, carpeting, sills, and baseboards—was a combination of green and white. The room looked like it had been designed by a rampant garden club. I got out a bottle of amaretto and poured myself a couple of fingers.

Burned out, my bones aching with jet lag, I couldn't erase the images of the night from my mind. Tagliani and Stinetto in the icebox. Mrs. Tagliani's monitor going *deeeeeeee* right in front of my eyes. The haunting tape of two killers delivering their coup de grace and the bloody back wall of Draganata's house. I had seen worse, but never in any civilized place I could remember.

Then I looked at the note I had picked up at the desk. The handwriting was so precise it could have been calligraphy. I recognized it immediately and the old electricity streaked from my stomach to my throat.

"I know you are here," it said. "I'll be in the boathouse at Windsong, tomorrow night, 9 p.m. Please. D."

She must have written it before she went into the restaurant, before I had seen her downstairs.

I suppose you always remember the good things in life as being better than they really were. To me, Dunetown was a slow-motion movie shot through a hazy lens. Everything was soft, the reflections glittered like stars, and there were no hard edges on anything. It was the end of adolescence and being exposed to the sweet life for what was an instant in my time. It was living high, dancing at the country club, open cars and laughter and cool nights on the beach.

Fat City is what it was.

And it was Doe Findley.

Doe Findley had risen out of my past like a specter. For twenty years she had been the hope in my nightmares, a gauzy sylph brightening the dark corners of bad dreams like the nightlight at the end of a long, dark hall.

I thought about that boathouse and about Doe, dancing tightly against me to the music from the radio as we fumbled with buttons and snaps and zippers. I couldn't remember the song now, but it had stayed with me for a long time before Nam erased it.

The thought of her spread through me like a shot of good brandy. She was the memory of that lost summer, the last green summer I could remember. It had all vanished that fall on a Saturday afternoon in Sanford Stadium.

It's funny, Teddy and I used to joke about those days later in Nam. Anything for a laugh over there. I remember Teddy once saying to me, "Y'know something, Jake, we should have been born a little earlier or a little later. Our timing was terrible. Think about it—we played during three of the worst seasons the Bulldogs ever had. You remember what our record was for those three years?" Did I remember? Hell, yes, I remembered. "Ten, sixteen, and four," I answered with disgust. "Yeah," he said, "and the season after we graduated, Dooley came in and they had a seven, three, and one. Now we're here. See what I mean? A dollar short and a day late, that's us."

Looking back on it, he was right. Maybe we were just jinxed from the start. That Saturday that changed my life, I was going wide to the right with Teddy in front of me and I made one of those hard stopping turns I had become known for. The foot hit wrong. I could hear the ankle go before the pain knocked my back teeth loose. It sounded like a branch cracking. All I remember after that is the backfield coach staring down at my face, saying, "Shit! So much for this halfback."

I got the letter from Chief Findley while I was still in the hospital. "Too bad, son," it said. "Keep the car. Doe sends her regards." The pink slip for the MG was attached. That was it. That's how I found out what an ex–running halfback with a bum ankle is worth in Dunetown. Findley had been my sponsor. They couldn't pay us for playing football at the university, but there was always some rich alumnus willing to provide a sports coat now and then, a car, a summer on the house. Sometimes even a daughter.

She didn't even send a card.

Twenty years. I hadn't seen or heard from her since, not even when Teddy was killed. I can understand that; I can understand not being able to deal with that kind of pain. Hell, I can understand it all. When you love someone you forgive everything.

I had kicked most of the other monkeys off my back, all but Doe. I couldn't purge her from my fantasies, what was left of them. Vietnam was bad for the soul. It was bad enough, what you saw and did, but the worst thing was what you thought. You get over the rest of it but you never forget what it does to the soul. Teddy Findley was the best friend I ever had, from the day I arrived at Georgia until the day in Saigon that he bled to death in my arms. Teddy was a golden boy. Teddy hadn't hit a false note. He was Chief's hope for immortality. The plan was perfect: football for four years at Georgia, show what the kid could do, then law school somewhere in the north to erase the jock image. Then back to take over the reins and keep the Findley hand in the Dunetown pot.

Vietnam screwed it all up. Instead of Harvard Law School, Teddy ended up in Nam with me, a couple of shavetail lieutenants doing the best we could to keep sane and alive.

Then all of a sudden Teddy was dead and the moment it sank in that he was dead, what I thought was:

Christ, Teddy, how can you do this to me, how can you leave me to tell Doe and Chief about this?

I still remember thinking that. I have pretty much erased everything else from my mind, but I still remember that when Teddy died, I didn't think about Teddy, I worried about me. That's what I mean about Nam and your soul.

Eventually, of course, I wrote the letter. I told them what I knew Chief wanted to hear.

I created the lie and I wrote the letter and I never got an answer, not even an acknowledgment that he had received it.

So I started forgetting in earnest. Football heroes exist only on bright fall afternoons, and pretty girls stay young only in picture frames.

Except there was Doe, who hadn't changed a bit. She still had that young, amazed look she'd had in the early sixties. Still had the long, golden hair. Silk. Slim, firm body. Breasts that some women would pay a fortune to try to imitate. Skin like cream. And suddenly she was no longer out of reach. She wasn't a sylph or a fantasy; she was as painfully real as a shin splint and just a phone call away.

And now, twenty years after the fact, she expected me to come trotting to the boathouse like it never happened.

Meet her in the boathouse? Who am I kidding, of course I'd meet her in the boathouse. I'd walk from Pittsburgh to meet her in the boathouse.

Shit.

I got in bed with a copy of Donleavy's *Meet My Maker, the Mad Molecule* and read myself to sleep. At two a.m. the phone woke me up. I put the book on the table and turned off the light.

The phone rang twelve times before it finally quit.

Fuck it, it had to be bad news.

BAD DREAMS

I had the dream again that night. The first time in four or five years. It had been so long I had forgotten it. It had started a year after I got back from Nam. I understand that's normal. It's called delayed nocturnal shock or something like that. At first it was just this one persistent dream. I could never remember all of it, just bits and pieces. After a while it was such a familiar nightmare that I knew I was dreaming and it didn't bother me as much.

Then it changed.

The way it starts, I am in a hang glider soaring over a city. It could be Saigon, but I don't recognize it. Suddenly people on the ground are shooting at me. I can't see them, but the bullets are tearing through the wings of the glider. Next the bullets are hitting me. They bounce off as if my skin were bulletproof. I don't feel the bullets. I don't feel anything. I don't hear anything either. This is a silent dream. The next thing I remember, I see Teddy. He is on top of a ridge and he's running. I don't know what he's running from. Maybe he's running toward something. He starts waving at me. I try to soar down to pick him up, but the glider won't move up or down. Teddy starts screaming at me, this soundless scream. I feel desperate to get to him. Finally I get out of the seat of the glider and I hang over the side and let go and I fall. There's no ground, just me, falling through an empty space.

Then I wake up.

After a while it began to get more complicated, after I got used to it and it didn't bother me anymore.

There were other hang gliders trying to collide with me. The other gliders were black and the pilots were all masked. It was like an obstacle course in the sky. Before I got comfortable with that version, the people in the other gliders started taking off their masks. One was my mother. Another was a fifth-grade schoolteacher whom I had not seen or thought about for fifteen years. Another was my father, only a face in a photograph to me. Then the parish priest in the New Jersey town where I was born. I couldn't remember his name; all I could remember about him was that he had "silent collections"—that meant folding money, no silver. It used to make me angry. And there was also a captain named Grant, a martinet Teddy and I had served under in Nam when we were still second lieutenants.

They were all yelling at me, but of course I couldn't hear anything. It was a silent horror movie that never ended.

A couple of years later, when I was working the street in San Francisco, I became friendly with another patrolman who had served in Nam. His name was Winfield. He was a black guy and he was taking college courses in psychology because he thought it would help him make detective.

One night over too many beers we started talking about dreams, so I told him mine and he gave me a nickel's worth of Psychology 101:

"Your values are all fucked up, Jake. One thing is, you think you're different. Shit, join the club. I figure it like this: it was one way here, the other way over there, okay? You get a lot of guilt over such shit. Gets so you're afraid to trust anybody because you don't want them to find out. It happened to us all, man. What you do, see, you decide what makes sense to you. Settle for that and fuck everything else."

After that we talked a lot. The dreams got fewer and farther between. Finally they stopped.

That night in Doomstown I had the dream again, only this time it wasn't Teddy running on the ridge.

It was Franco Tagliani.

17

PLAYING BY THE BOOK

The Palm Room of the Ponce Hotel was a big, cheery room, as bright as a hothouse and decked out in as many hanging plants, ferns, and potted flowers. It was decorated in soft hues of green, yellow, and pink, with windows down one side that faced the hotel courtyard. Once, in summertimes past, the cream of Dunetown society had sunned itself and gossiped around the pool. It had since been converted into a giant fish pond spiked with lily pads, and while there were still a few old deck chairs scattered about the area, the place had a forlorn, faded, unused look about it. The restaurant, however, was breezy, cheerful, and buzzing with early morning conversation.

I showed up the next morning at a few minutes after eight with my head pounding and the taste of old overshoes and amaretto in my mouth. I put on my sunglasses and groped my way through the restaurant.

Francisco Mazzola, the peerless leader of the Freeze, was seated near a window overlooking the courtyard. He had half a dozen vitamin pills of varying sizes and colors lined up in front of his plate and was gulping them down with orange juice. He pumped my hand, threw an arm around my back, and slid the morning paper in front of me as I sat down.

"I ordered your breakfast," he said. "Fresh orange juice, a dozen dollar pancakes, one egg over easy, no meat. Your system needs a break, I'm sure. She's bringing your coffee now and I got some great vitamins here for you."

"If I eat all that, I'll die," I said.

"Got to keep up the old strength."

"There are enough vitamins here for the whole room."

He ignored the complaint. "Vitamins do great things for the brain," he said.

Mazzola did vitamins like a speed freak does amphetamines. He was also fighting a losing battle with his hair. He spent an hour every morning weaving what few strands were left over a pate as bald as a kitchen table. To compensate he had grown a beard which made his dark Mediterranean looks and intense brown eyes more intimidating than usual. He slid a handful of vitamins across the table to me.

"These are yours," he said. "This stuff's from China. Incredible, has all kinds of—"

"Cisco, I'm not into vitamins, okay? I'm into coffee and a little booze, an occasional lay, rare steaks, wine, mashed potatoes and gravy . . ."

He looked like he was going to throw up.

"I'm not into vitamins and weird herbs."

"In two days you'll notice an improvement."

"If I got a good night's sleep I'd notice an improvement. I was up half the night thanks to the sudden departure of half the Tagliani clan."

"We'll get to that," he said, digging in to his breakfast, a plate of health food that looked like it had been dredged from the bottom of a swamp.

"Besides," I said, "I read where overdosing on vitamins makes your hair fall out."

He looked up, aghast.

"Where did you read that?"

"In the paper. One of those health columns. Rots out the roots of the hair."

I tried to keep the gag going but I started to laugh. He leaned back in his chair and narrowed his eyes.

"No more jokes about the hair, okay? Do I joke about your knee?"

"It's my ankle."

"See, you're touchy about that."

"I'm not touchy about it. I happen to have shitty ankles. Great wheels, shitty ankles; otherwise I wouldn't be here, I'd be a retired millionaire football player living in Tahiti. On the other hand, you only have about four strands of hair left, although I'll say the beard helps."

"Fuck you," he said. "Fill me in."

I gave him a fairly thorough walk-through of the events of Sunday night.

"You're the expert on the Triad—what the hell's going on here?" he asked.

"I'll tell you what I don't think's going on," I said. "I don't think it's an outside mob and I don't think it's an inside job."

"That's interesting," he said. "That just about rules out every-body. Who do you think did it, the tooth fairy?"

"It's logical. The last thing the Triad wanted to do was create attention. They uprooted their families and sneaked in here. If it had been a family feud, it makes more sense that it would have been done before they left Cincinnati. Besides, this thing just doesn't read like a Mafia hit. Salvatore agrees with me."

"Salvatore's an expert, huh?" he said, looking over his breakfast plate and raising his eyebrows.

"He knows their style. Hell, he ought to, his father was an LCN cannon in south Philly."

"I know that." He went back to his breakfast, waving a fork at my plate. "Talk and eat, it'll get cold."

"The only exception to that is that maybe it could be Chevos and Nance."

He looked up, surprised.

"I didn't know they were here."

"They're here somewhere."

"Oh, you're guessing again."

"It's logical."

"You and your logic," he said. "You can make any argument sound good. One minute you tell me you don't think it's internal and the next you tell me it is."

"Chevos and Nance are different."

"That's 'cause you want them to be," he said, pointing a finger at me. "This is department business, pal. I didn't bring you in here to carry out a personal vendetta."

"I'm just running the possibilities past you. Chevos is devious enough to try it and Nance is psychotic enough to do the work. So, if the shot fits . . ." I let the rest of the sentence dangle.

"It's 'if the shoe fits,'" he said.

"Not in this case."

"All right, tell me more."

"We have reason to believe whoever's in on this did time in Nam."

"How do you figure that?"

"Weapons, MO, style."

"Uh-huh."

"Nance was in Nam, right in the thick of it."

"Uh-huh. And so were you, Stick, and half of Dutch Morehead's bunch. Hell, even I was in Nam. That doesn't make Nance an assassin. Some people might even consider him a hero."

"The war's over," I said.

"I think maybe you're shagging flies," he said.

"Maybe," I said with a shrug.

"Anything else?"

"Well, uh . . ."

He leaned over the table and dropped his voice to a whisper.

"Before you go any further," he said, "let me remind you that you're not here to solve homicides. Just between us, I don't care if Yankee Doodle Dandy's doing it, unless it's relevant. I want the package on Tagliani."

He didn't wait for me to say anything.

"This used to be a nice, quiet, historical tourist trap," he said. "It's turning into Rotten City, U.S.A. I want to know how deep Tagliani had his hooks in. What did he own? Who did he buy? How did he pull it off? Hell, I don't have to give you the lecture, you know what the Freeze is all about."

"If you're interested in what I think," I said, "I think the homicides have to be relevant."

He pointed at me with his fork.

"Don't get lost on me, Jake. And don't lead Stick astray."

"Lead Stick astray! You got to be joking. And what's all this shit about him not being jaded?"

"What do you think of him?" he asked with a smile.

"He's as off the wall as the rest of Dutch Morehead's hooligans," I said.

"He's just like you were," he said. "Eager, tough, a lone wolf. You two can help each other. Working with Dutch and his boys'll give you both a sense of team play."

"I know all about team play, remember?"

"You been playing your own game for a while," Cisco said. "Now you got plenty of help. I want to nail the Cincinnati Triad. I think we got a giant washing machine here, Jake, and I want to see the inside of it. I want to know how it works. That's what this trip is all about, okay?" He paused for a moment and added, "And I'd like to find out while a few of them are still breathing. Seen the morning paper?"

Cisco could change the subject in midsentence. When he had said all he had to say on a subject, he just dropped it and moved on.

He laid the paper beside my plate. It was turned to page 12, where the Tagliani killing was reported quietly, under a one-column headline:

THREE DIE IN
HOUSE ROBBERY

I read the story, which was vague, inaccurate, and short. The police weren't saying anything except that they expected an arrest "shortly."

"They're expecting an arrest, I see," I commented.

"Keep reading," Cisco said. "It gets worse."

Tagliani was identified as Frank Turner, a Cincinnati businessman with interests in racehorses. Stinetto—Nat Sherman in the story—was listed as "a business associate of Mr. Turner's." Robbery was the suspected motive. Not a mention of the Molotov cocktail the killer had dropped on his way out. According to the story, the police believed that Turner and Sherman surprised the robbers and were killed in so doing. There was a very fuzzy picture of Tagliani and his wife getting into a car, obviously shot from somewhere in New Jersey and blown up until the grain was as big as the moon.

"Not a mention of Draganata."

"That's on page eighteen," Cisco said without looking up from his breakfast.

The Draganata story, identifying him as John Dempsey, a retired businessman, was even more ludicrous. It was three paragraphs long and said he died in his swimming pool. The police did not suspect foul play.

"Well," I said, "the police got the Draganata kill right. He certainly did die in his swimming pool."

"Point is, that's the kind of reporting you can expect here. Nobody's gonna dig for anything; they'll print what they're told to print."

"Dutch told me this would happen and I as much as laughed in his face."

"Yeah, well, he's got the last laugh. Just keep this in mind, pal, everybody supported the track. The press supported it and the businessmen's association and the chamber of commerce *and* the local politicians. Even the board of education endorsed it. Don't you get it? They don't want anything to make their town look sour. So they'll play it down, make it look like exactly what they want it to look like, and hope somebody will solve the case so they can cover it up. Let the killer cop a plea and keep his mouth shut."

"That's bullshit," I said.

"It's the way the world turns," he said. "That's why I don't want you spinning your wheels on the homicide angle. Just find out how the Tagliani clan got their foot in the door and how far in it is now, okay? Forget local politics. Things here haven't changed in two hundred years, and a little massacre isn't gonna make a bit of difference."

"These islands have been raped," I said bitterly.

"Maybe so," he went on, "but look around you. These are the people who pull the strings in Dunetown. When you talk about the rape of paradise, these are the people who are doing the raping. They're the ones making the big bucks. Tagliani didn't ruin the place. He just got in on the kill." Then he did another fast change-up. "Anything else for now?"

"Did you hear the tape of the Tagliani chill?" I said.

He nodded.

"Did you catch that, about a fix at the track?"

He gave me one of those "what do you think I am, stupid?" looks.

"So?" he said.

"So, if Tagliani knew about it, maybe the track's dirty too."

Cisco's dark brown eyes bored into me. "It's an illegal tape," he said. "Anyway, it's probably just some owner building up odds on one of his ponies. On the other hand . . ." He paused for a few moments and stared off into space.

"On the other hand what?" I asked.

"On the other hand, this commissioner, Harry Raines? He might be worth looking into. He's got more muscle than anyone else in the town."

Bingo, there it was. I felt a twinge of vindication.

"He controls gambling in the whole state," Cisco went on. "The racetrack commission is also the state gaming commission. It's the way the law was written."

"Interesting," I said.

"Yeah. If they want anything, Harry Raines is the man they need to deal with—or bypass."

"Maybe they bought him," I suggested.

"From what I hear, not likely, although always a possibility," said Cisco. "I'll give you some logic. Whether they bought him or not, the last thing anybody wants right now is a gang war. If Raines is in their pocket, it puts him on the dime and destroys his effectiveness. If they haven't bought him, this melee still hurts everybody, the Triad included. The bottom line is that Raines needs this kind of trouble like he needs a foot growing out of his forehead. He and his partner, Sam Donleavy, are both up the proverbial creek right now."

"Donleavy was in here last night," I said. "I saw Titan talking to him, and the old man didn't look like he was giving away any merit badges."

"They're all edgy," he said, sliding the bill across the table to me. "Here, put this on your tab. I've got to catch a plane."

He stood up and threw his napkin on the table. "It's time somebody put a turd in the Dunetown punch bowl," he said. "Glad you're here—I can't think of a better person to do it. Finish your breakfast and get to work. See you in about a week."

And with that he left.

I didn't have to leave the restaurant to get to work. Babs Thomas walked in as Cisco walked out. I decided it was time to find out whose shoes where under whose bed in Doomstown.

18

CHEAP TALK, RICH PEOPLE

The Thomas woman was tallish, honey blond, coiffured and manicured, dressed in printed silk, with a single strand of black pearls draped around a neck that looked like it had been made for them. Her sunglasses were rimmed in twenty-four-karat gold. An elegant lady, as chic as a pink poodle in a diamond collar.

I scratched out a note on my menu: "A gangster from Toronto would love to buy you breakfast," and sent it to her table by waiter. She read it, said something to the waiter, who pointed across the room at me; she lowered her glasses an inch or two, and peered over them. I gave her my fifty-dollar, Toronto-gangster smile. The waiter returned.

"Ms. Thomas said she'd be delighted if you'd join her," he said. I gave him a fin, dug through my wallet and found a card that identified me as a reporter for a fictional West Coast newspaper, and went to her table.

She looked me up and down. I was wearing unpressed corduroy

jeans, a blue Oxford shirt, open at the collar, and an old, scarred Windbreaker. Definitely not the latest mobster look.

"If you're a gangster from Toronto, I'm Lady Di," she said, in a crisp voice laced with magnolias, "and I've got a good ten years on her."

Closer to fifteen, I thought, but a very well-disguised fifteen.

"You don't look a day over twenty-six," I lied.

"Oh, I think we're going to get along," she said, pointing to a chair. "Sit."

I sat and slid the card across the table to her. It identified me as Wilbur Rasmussen from the Las Andreas *Gazette* in San Francisco. She looked at it, snorted, looked at the back, and slid it back across the table.

"Phooey, a visiting fireman," she said. "And here I thought I was going to be wooed by some dashing *mafioso*."

"Do I look like a dashing *mafioso*?"

"You look like an English professor with a hangover."

"You're half right."

"Try a screwdriver. At least the orange juice makes you feel like you're doing something decent for your body."

"I couldn't stand the vodka."

"It'll get your heart beating again. What can I do for you? I'll bet you're here about that mess last night." She leaned over the table and said quietly, "Everybody in town's talking about it," flagging down a waiter as she spoke and ordering me a screwdriver.

"No kidding?" I said, trying to act surprised.

"It was ghastly. I had calls before the maid even opened my drapes this morning. I hardly knew this Turner man, but he seemed like a charming old gentleman."

"Charming?" I said. Uncle Franco was probably smiling in his grave.

"Well, you know. He contributed to the ballet and the symphony. He was on the board of the children's hospital. And he was quite modest about it all."

"No pictures, no publicity, that sort of thing?"

"Mm-hmm. Why?"

"Just wondering. I always suspect modesty. It's unnatural."

"You're a cynic."

"Very possibly."

"I always suspect cynics," she said.

"Why's that?" I asked.

"There's security in cynicism," she said. "Usually it covers up a lot of loneliness."

"You the town philosopher?" I asked, although I had to agree with her thesis.

"Nope," she said rather sadly. "I'm the town cynic, so I know one when I see one."

"So what's the pipeline saying about all this?" I asked, changing the subject.

She lowered the glasses again, peering over them at me. "That he's a gangster from Toronto," she said with a smirk.

"Couldn't be, I never heard of him," I said.

"Just what is your angle?"

"I do travel pieces."

"Really."

"Yeah."

"And lie a lot?"

"That too."

"To gossip columnists?" she said.

"I don't discriminate."

"Thanks."

"Maybe I ought to try and get a job on the *Ledger*," I said, changing the subject.

"Why, for God's sake?"

"I don't know much about women's clothes but I can tell a silk designer dress when I see one. They must pay well over there."

She threw back her head and laughed hard. "Now that is a joke," she said. "Did you ever know any newspaper that paid well?"

The waiter brought my screwdriver. I took a swallow or two and it definitely got the blood flowing again.

"Actually my husband died young, the poor dear, and left me wonderfully provided for," Babs said.

"You don't sound real upset over losing him."

"He was a delight, but he drank himself to death."

"What did he do?" I asked, sipping at the screwdriver.

"Owned the hotel," she said casually, but with a glint in her eyes.

"What hotel?"

"This hotel."

"You own the Ponce?" I said.

"Every creaky inch of it. Actually I hired a very good man from

California to run it before Logan died. I love owning it but I dread the thought of having to run it."

"You live here?"

She nodded and pointed toward the ceiling. "Six flights up. The penthouse, darling. Owning the joint does have its percs. I have a beach place out on the Isle of Sighs but I don't go out there much anymore. It's a bit too solitary."

"I'm on the third floor," I said. "I don't have any percs."

"Is there something wrong with your accommodations?" she asked. "If there's a problem, I have a lot of pull with the management."

"The room's fine, thank you." I ordered coffee to chase the taste of vodka out of my mouth.

"What's your room number? I'll have them send up a basket of fruit."

"Three sixteen. I love fresh pineapple."

"I'll remember that. You were telling me what you're doing here."

"I was?"

"Mm-hmm."

"Actually I'm interested in doing a piece on the social order in Dunetown. Movers and shakers, that kind of thing."

"For the Los Aghast *Gazette* or whatever it was?"

I would have bet my underwear that she remembered the name of the paper and everything else I had said since joining her.

"Yeah, kind of a background piece."

She said "Mm-hmm" again and didn't mean a syllable of it. She lit a pink Sherman cigarette, leaned back in her chair, and blew smoke toward the ceiling. "Well, it was founded in 1733 by—"

"Not that far back."

"Just what do you want, Wilbur whatever-your-name-is, and I don't believe that for a minute, either."

"Who would make up a name like Wilbur Rasmussen?" I said.

She dipped her dark glasses at me again but made no comment.

"I hear it's an old town run by old money," I said.

"You're looking at some of it, darling."

"Accurate?"

"Fairly accurate."

"They making any money off the track?"

"Honey, *every*body's making money off the track. If you own a bicycle concession in this town you can get rich." She sighed. "I suppose we are going to have to talk about this, aren't we?"

"Sooner or later."

The waiter brought my coffee and as I was diluting it with cream and sugar she made an imperceptible little move with a finger toward the hostess, a pretty, trim young black woman, no more than nineteen or twenty, who, a second or two later, appeared at the table.

" 'Scuse me," she said. "You have a phone call, Ms. Babs."

"My public is after me," she said with mock irritation. "Excuse me for a moment, would you, darling?"

I watched her in the row of mirrors at the entrance to the restaurant. She picked up the phone at the hostess desk and punched out a number. That would be the desk she was calling, checking me out. She said a few words, waited, then hung up and came back to the table, still smiling, but a little colder than when I first sat down.

I smiled back.

"Jake Kilmer," she said.

"Nice trick with the hostess. I could see you calling the desk in the mirrors."

"That obvious, huh? Hmm. I wonder how many other people have caught me at it."

"Lots. The others were just too nice to mention it."

"Why do I know your name?"

"It's fairly common."

"Hmm. And you're a cop," she said.

"Kind of."

"How can you be kind of a cop?"

"Well, you know, I do statistical profiles, demographic studies, that kind of thing."

"You're much too cute to be that dull."

"Thanks. You're pretty nifty too."

"You're also an outrageous flirt."

"I am?" I said. "Nobody's ever complained about that before."

"Who's complaining?" she said, dipping her head again and staring at me with eyes as gray as a rainy day. I passed.

"So tell me who makes Dunetown click," I said.

"Persistent too," she said, then shrugged. "Why not, but it'll cost you a drink at the end of the day."

"Done."

She knew it all. Every pedigree, every scalawag, every bad leaf on every family tree in town. She talked about great-grandfathers and great-great-grandfathers who came over in the early 1800s and made a fortune in privateering, cotton, land, and shipping; who rose to become robber barons and worse, what Babs called "varmints," a word that seemed harmless somehow, the way she used it, but which I took to mean tough men who destroyed each other in power brawls. She talked about a onetime Irish highwayman named Larkin who escaped the noose by becoming an indentured servant to a Virginia tobacco man and then ran off, arriving in Dunetown, where, fifteen years later, he became its first banker; about Tim Clarke, the stevedore from Dublin who stowed away to Dunetown and ended up owning the shipyard; and an Irish collier named Findley who once killed a man in a duel over a runaway pig, and who went on to make a fortune in cotton and converted his millions to land before the bottom dropped out, and was the man who talked Sherman out of burning Dunetown because he owned most of the town and didn't want to see it torched like Atlanta. Doe's great-grandfather.

Hooligans, the bunch of them, the Findleys, Larkins, Clarkes, and the second generation, with names like Colonel and Chief, the ones who said yes, no, and maybe to every decision that affected the city for two centuries. And finally the third generation, the Bubbas and Chips and Juniors, so intimidated by their fathers that they were reduced to panderers, more interested in golf than empires.

Once she started, it was like turning on a tape recorder with no stop button. A twenty-minute dialogue, at the end of which I knew about every inbred mongoloid child, every lady of color who had married across the line, all the bastard and aborted children, the adulterers and adulteresses, the covered-up suicides, the drunks, gays, and feuding families, the banker's daughter who was a prostitute in L.A., and the two Junior Leaguers who ran off together and left two confused husbands and five children behind.

Routine for any small money town.

Three names stood out: Findley, Clarke, and Larkin.

The Findleys and the Larkins had been cautious partners through the years.

The Clarkes were their adversaries—in politics, business, even in love affairs.

"Jimmy Clarke would have died to marry Doe Findley," Babs said, "but Chief wouldn't hear of it. He picked an outsider for her. Not old money but respectable. His father was a lawyer and later a judge."

"Harry Raines?" I said. Funny, I couldn't remember Jimmy Clarke, although the name rang a bell.

"You do get around," Babs said.

"What about Raines?"

"What about him?"

"The way I get it, he married rich and got richer."

"My, my," she said caustically, "aren't we being a little catty?"

"No, I've been doing a lot of listening, that's all."

"Did they tell you Harry's going to be governor one of these days soon?"

"I keep hearing that. Has he been nominated yet?"

"Cute," she said.

"Well?"

"As well as, darling."

"Why?"

"Because he's Dunetown's golden boy. He's handsome, he's rich, he's young. He's a lawyer, married to a beautiful woman, and an ex–football star. His politics are moderate. His family's acceptable. And he's the state racing commissioner. Isn't that enough?"

"Sounds like he was born for the job."

"Besides, Dunetown's long overdue for a governor, particularly with the city growing so, and Harry's just perfect."

"Couldn't that be a hot spot?"

"Governor?" she said.

"Racing commissioner."

"Anything but, dear boy. Harry's brought a lot of money to the state. And a lot of tax money for the schools."

"I never trust a politician who was born with his mouth full of silver," I said.

"Ah, but he wasn't."

"So he married the money, that it?"

"Do you know Harry?" she asked. Her tone was turning cautious. I had the feeling I had stretched my luck a little thin.

"Nope," I said. "Just trying to get the feel of things. Obviously he's a man with a lot of drive. A lot of ambition."

"Is there something wrong with that?" she asked.

"Not necessarily. Depends on how much ambition and how big a drive. What you're willing to trade for success."

"He didn't have to trade anything for it, darling. He got all the prizes. The town's richest and most desirable young woman, her father's political clout. But he didn't sit on his little A-frame and drink it up the way a lot of them have. He made a name for himself."

"What's he like personally?"

She leaned back in her chair and eyed me suspiciously. I was beginning to sound a little too much like a man with an axe to grind and Babs Thomas was nobody's fool.

"Just what the hell is your game, Kilmer?" she said.

"Told you, I'm trying to get a line on the town."

"No, you're trying to get a line on Harry Raines."

"Well, he's part of the big picture," I said, trying to sound as casual as I could.

She leaned forward and said flippantly, "You don't have to like a man to vote for him. Personally I find him a bit cold, but he gets things done. The rest of the state is in a depression and Dunetown is in the middle of a boom. You can't have everything. If he was any better he'd probably be in the movies."

I laughed at her rationale. I'm sure most of the voters in the state would look at Harry Raines in the same way. Babs Thomas had a bit of Everywoman in her, although I'm sure she would have killed anyone who accused her of that.

"Anyway," she said, tossing her head, "the sheriff's on his side. That's reason enough to get elected."

"That would be this Titan fellow?"

"No, darling, not 'this Titan fellow.' *Mister* Stoney. God owes *him* favors."

"And he and Raines are buddies?"

I was coaxing information now.

"When Chief's son, Teddy, was killed in Vietnam," she said, "Chief almost died with him. Doe married Harry less than a year later. Chief faded out of the picture right after that."

"As soon as he was sure the keys to the kingdom were in the right pocket," I said. It was not a question. "And now Sam Donleavy's running the store for Raines, isn't that it?"

"Yes. They're inseparable friends."

Listening to her was like déjà vu.

"Is Donleavy one of the landed aristocracy?"

"No, he's just plain people. He's from New *Joisey*," she said playfully. "Nouveau riche. You'd like him."

I grimaced at her. "Thanks a lot."

"Just joking. Actually Sam's quite a charmer. His wife left him about a year ago. Ran off with her karate instructor. Sam took it quite hard at first, but he's over it now. In fact, right now I'd say he's the town's most eligible bachelor—and enjoying every minute of it."

"Is this Raines clean?" I asked.

"Clean? You mean does he bathe?" She wasn't joking; it was obvious she didn't understand me.

"No, you know—does he cheat on his wife, that sort of thing?"

"Harry, cheat? He wouldn't dare." She stared over my shoulder as she spoke and her eyes grew wide. "Speak of the devil," she said. "There's Doe Findley now."

LITTLE TONY LUKATIS

It's hard to be casual when every muscle in your body has turned to ice. I tried playing for time.

"Who?" I asked, in a voice that seemed to me to be at least an octave above normal.

"Doe Findley," Babs said impatiently, pointing over my shoulder. "Turn around!"

I turned in slow motion, still playing the charade, still acting like the whole thing was a bore. Doe was coming out of a small meeting room with a dozen other well-dressed women. She was wearing tan silk slacks and a dark green silk blouse and her golden hair was pulled back in a tight ponytail and tied with a red ribbon.

"That's the horsey set," Babs said. "Thoroughbred breeders."

But I wasn't paying any attention. I was remembering the first time I ever saw Doe. Her hair was tied back just like that, except she was only fifteen at the time. Teddy brought her into the dorm, where we shared a room. She was wearing tight white jeans and a red pullover and she didn't look any more like a fifteen-year-old than I look like Muhammad Ali. I had seen her pictures, of course; Teddy was big on family pictures. But she didn't look like that in pictures. No way. All I clearly remember was that she had an absolutely sensational rear end. I couldn't take my eyes off it.

I was embarrassed, but my eyes kept straying. It was like a magnet. I tried, I tried really hard, but it didn't do any good. I kept sneaking peeks. Then Teddy suddenly buried an elbow in my side.

"She's fifteen," he hissed under his breath.

"What's the matter with you?" I whispered back.

"Clicking eyeballs, Junior," he said. "Lay a finger on that behind before she's eighteen and I'll disengage your fucking clutch." Then he broke down and started laughing.

That was the fall of 1960, a couple of weeks after Teddy Findley and I met, became roommates, and began a friendship that would last far beyond college. He started calling me Junior the day we met. I don't know why, and he never explained it. I finally figured it was because he was taller than me. Two, three inches. Nobody else, not even Doe, shared that privilege.

Anyway, I waited until she was eighteen. Two and a half years; that's a lot of waiting. And during those two and a half years she kept getting better and better, blossoming from little sister to big sister to woman, while I watched it happen. Teddy didn't help. He became a verbal calendar, taunting me every week of the way.

"How about it, Junior," he'd say, "only four months to go." It never occurred to me until later that I was being sized up all that time: that waiting until she was eighteen had as much to do with me as it did with her.

"Jake! Jake Kilmer. Is that really you?"

She was standing a foot away. I could feel the fire starting in the small of my back and coursing up to my neck, like the fuse on a stick of dynamite.

Time seemed to have evaded her. No lines, no wrinkles. Just pale gray eyes staring straight at me and the warmth of her hand as she squeezed mine.

I stood up and said something totally inadequate like "Hi, Doe."

Then she put her arms around me and I was smothered by the warmth of her body pressing against mine, by the hard muscles in her back and the softness of the rest of her. I was consumed with wanting her.

Then she stepped back and looked up at my face, cocking her head to one side.

"Hardly a gray hair," she said. "And every line in the right place."

"Is that your way of saying I'm growing old gracefully?" I tried to joke.

"Oh, no," she said softly, "not that. You look beautiful." She stared hard at me for another second or two, and just as quickly turned her attention to Babs.

"I see you've cornered him already," she said playfully, and then back at me: "Call me . . . please. I have a private line. It's listed under D. F. Raines. Chief would love to see you."

I didn't buy that. To Chief I would just be bad news, a vague face from the past, a painful reminder that his son was dead. What she was really asking was, Are you coming to Windsong tonight?

"Sure," I said.

"Promise?"

"Promise."

She didn't just leave, she turned and fled.

I sat back down and looked across the table at Babs, whose mouth was dangling open. She reached up slowly and pushed it closed with a finger.

"You sly son of a bitch," she said.

"What're you talking about?"

"You know Doe Findley *that* well?" she said.

"What do you mean, *that* well?"

"I mean *that* well."

"We knew each other in college. Twenty years ago."

"Uh-uh, honey. That wasn't a 'gee it's nice to see you again after all these years' look. That was a 'where the hell have you been for the last twenty years' look."

"It was probably a shock seeing me again. I knew her brother."

"I don't care who you knew. These old eyes are not that bad yet. Twenty years, huh?"

"What are you raving about?" I said to her.

"So where did she fall in love with you? She didn't go to Georgia, she went to . . . oh, let's see, one of those snotty colleges up north."

Now she was doing the coaxing.

"Vassar," I said. "Real hard to remember."

"So you have kept track?"

"Through Teddy."

"Oh, right. And you just sat there, letting me jabber on about the Findleys and Harry Raines . . ."

"Trash it," I said.

"Trash it?"

"Trash it. There's nothing there."

She wasn't about to back off. She leaned back in her chair and appraised me through narrowed eyes.

"Jake Kilmer. That name ought to mean something to me," she said.

She sat there struggling with her memories, trying to sort me out of the hundreds of names and faces from her past. Then recognition slowly brightened her eyes.

"Of course," she said. "You played football for the Dogs."

"You have some memory," I said, wondering how often that interlude was going to keep haunting me. I doubt that it had been mentioned once in the last ten years, and now it seemed to pop up every time I said hello, or maybe it was just popping up in my mind.

"You and Teddy played on the same team, didn't you?"

"For a while."

"She's not a real happy woman, Kilmer."

"How would you know that?"

"I know *everything*, darling. It's what I do, remember? I'm the town snoop."

"I thought you said Raines had a wonderful family."

"I didn't say he had a happy one. Raines is married to politics and Doe doesn't play second fiddle well at all."

"People seem to think she married well."

"Tom Findley couldn't have picked a better man for the job."

"Christ, you are bitchy."

"I like Doe," she said, ignoring the slur. "She's very honest. Not too bright, though, do you think?"

"I don't remember. When I was in college I thought everybody was brilliant but me."

"She had an affair, you know."

I leaned over toward her. "I haven't heard a word about her since Teddy died, okay? I am not hooked into the Dunetown hot line."

"You're really not going to ask who she had the affair with?"

"Nope."

"It was Tony Lukatis."

"No kidding. Little old Tony, huh?"

"You're much too blasé to really be blasé, I know it. I know all the tricks. Listen, we have name entertainers coming out to the beach hotels now. I get some big-time gossip. They all try to act blasé, too, but it doesn't work—and they've been at it forever. Tony Lukatis was the guy. The golf pro at the country club. His father was the manager."

My memory jumped back to that summer like the ball bouncing over the lyrics of a song at an old-time movie matinee.

"Nick?"

"Ah, you do remember."

"I remember Nick. I don't remember Tony."

But then suddenly I did remember him, a little kid with incredibly curly hair who spent most of his time on the putting green when he wasn't caddying. He must have been fifteen or sixteen that summer.

"Aha, I see recognition in those green eyes."

"Yeah, he's younger than she is."

"The best kind, darling."

"He had a sister."

"Dierdre . . . DeeDee?" Babs pressed on.

"Skinny little kid, used to hang around the club?" I asked.

"Skinny little kid? I can tell you haven't seen *her* in a while."

"What's she doing these days?" I asked, trying to seem interested.

"She's Charlie Seaborn's secretary—Seacoast National Bank."

"Did Raines know about the affair?" I tried not to sound too interested.

"Not so you could tell."

"What happened?"

"Poor little Tony. Rumor has it he decided to get rich quick and got mixed up in some pot smuggling. He went to prison for five years. I've lost track of him since. It almost killed DeeDee."

The conversation was cutting close to the bone. I decided it was time to ease on out.

"You've been a lot of help," I said. "I've got to get moving but I owe you a drink."

"You better believe you do, dearie," she said. "You know how to get in touch. And if you don't, I will."

I headed out of the restaurant, feeling like I had barely averted disaster.

No such luck.

20

HIDE AND SEEK

Stick was hiding behind the morning paper in the lobby of the hotel when I left the restaurant. He flashed that crazy smile of his when I spotted him.

"Not bad, not bad at all," he said. "Doe Findley and Babs Thomas for breakfast. And I was afraid you'd get lonely."

"Strictly business," I said.

"Hey," he said, spreading his arms out at his sides, "I never doubted it for a minute."

"I'm sure you have my social calendar filled for the day," I said. "What's up?"

"A little war conference with the troops."

"You mean they're speaking to me?"

"They're thinking about it," he said, leading me out the door. His Black Maria was hunched down in the loading zone, like it was looking for trouble.

"Why don't I take my car?" I suggested. "In case we have to split up."

"No worry," he said, opening the door for me. "I'm your tour guide for the day. It was a raffle. I lost."

"Keep it under ninety, will you?" I asked as I got in.

"It stutters under ninety," he answered.

"Fine, let's listen to it stutter for a while."

He took me to a bright, airy place in a row house overlooking the river. It didn't look like a restaurant; it was more like having coffee in someone's living room. The place was about five minutes away, hardly time for the Maria to get up to speed, for which I was momentarily thankful. I was sure I wouldn't be that lucky for the entire day. Zapata, Salvatore, and Flowers were seated at a table in the back.

"Hey, Mildred," Salvatore yelled across the room as we entered, "two more javas."

They all stared at me as I approached their table.

"What's the matter, is my fly open?" I asked as I sat down.

"Sorry," Charlie One Ear said. "We haven't seen you in the daytime."

"What you see, gentlemen, is a ruin," I said. "Give me a couple of days to get some sun. I look much better with a decent night's sleep and a little color."

"It's the fluorescent lights in the Warehouse," Charlie One Ear joked. "They give everyone a ghastly pallor."

"Well," I said, smiling at everybody, "thanks for not judging me on first appearances."

"Yeah, you're welcome," said Salvatore.

"Y'see what it is, Kilmer, we decided to throw in with you," Zapata said. "On a temporary basis, see what happens."

"Gee whiz, I don't know what to say," I replied sarcastically.

" 'Thank you' will be fine," said Charlie One Ear.

"Thanks again."

"Our pleasure," Charlie One Ear replied. "Now, just what specifically is it we're looking for?"

"What I need," I said, "is connections."

"Like such as?" Chino Zapata asked.

"Like maybe a hooker who's been bending her heels in Louisville, suddenly shows up here. Chances are, she's on the circuit. The mob moves them around like that."

"How about pimps?" Charlie One Ear queried.

"Sure, the same thing. Maybe I can tie a pimp to some outfit in Cincy or Chicago. Next step is, who's he working for? How did he get here? Pimps don't move from town to town. What I mean is, they don't free-lance. They move when the heat's on. They usually work for the man. He tells them where to go."

"So what's different about Dunetown?" Salvatore said. "That's pretty common, isn't it?"

"What's different is that the Tagliani family is here," Stick threw in.

"Right," I said. "If I can make a connection between here and someplace else, that's the start of an interstate case. If I can tie it to Tagliani's mob, that's part two. If I can prove it, then I can take it to the Justice Department. That's three, and then it's their problem. Anything else I lay off on you guys. I'm not here to make collars, okay?"

"All that is by way of telling us you're looking for out-of-town talent, correct?" Charlie One Ear said.

"Right. I'd also like to know the names of companies owned by the Triad. Where they bank. Who they do business with. What kind of straight businesses they're into."

"That's a little outta our line," Zapata said.

"The key man is the accountant, Cohen," I said. "He's the bag-man. Unless he's changed his MO, he makes three or four pickups a day, never at the same spots. He carries a little black satchel, like one of those old-fashioned doctor's bags, and it's probably full of cash. That's the skim, the money they need to wash."

"The IGG," offered Charlie One Ear.

"Correct."

"This is street money, right?" Stick said, playing along with me. "Gambling, prostitution, dope, that kind of thing."

I nodded.

"So why don't we just grab the bag away from the little shit and take a look?" Zapata suggested.

"For one thing, he's probably got four or five cannons escorting him," I said.

"Yes," Charlie One Ear said snidely. "It's also against the law. It's called robbery. One to five for first offense, which might not be applicable in your case."

Zapata looked at him and laughed.

"They don't usually put their swag in the bank," Salvatore of-fered.

"I agree," I said. "But Cohen's a crafty son of a bitch. He may have something worked out at the bank."

"They're in cahoots?" Zapata asked.

"Not necessarily," I said. "He may be depositing in several dif-ferent accounts or putting it in a safe deposit box. The bank doesn't have to be involved."

I was trying to be honest about it, but I couldn't help wondering whether Charles Seaborn, president of that bank, and a member of the Committee, knew Cohen personally. And if so, whether Sam Donleavy knew that Seaborn knew Cohen. And whether Raines knew that Donleavy knew that Seaborn knew Cohen. It was time I faced up to the facts. I *wanted* Raines and Donleavy to be up to their necks in it, because if things had gone differently and Teddy were still alive, I would have been in Donleavy's boots. I didn't want to feel that way, but coming back to Dunetown had stirred old emotions that I thought were long dead, and the lies, the hurt, the resentments, were as visceral as fresh wounds. I could taste the blood. So there it was. What can a man do?

"We should maybe talk to Cowboy," said Salvatore, breaking

up my train of thought. "He shagged the little weed for a couple days."

"Good," I said. "If we can put together enough evidence to show cause, we might find a judge who'll let us look into their bank accounts or let us have some wiretaps."

"Kite Lange can handle that," said Zapata.

"He means *legal* wiretaps, el retardo," said Salvatore.

"In the meantime, I can throw a few crumbs your way," I offered.

"How's that?" said Zapata, slurping his coffee.

I decided to try Charlie One Ear out, to see if he was as good as everybody said he was.

"I spotted Spanish Eddie Fuereco on the way in," I said.

"At the airport, no doubt," Charlie One Ear piped up immediately.

Zapata stared over at him, obviously impressed.

"Right," I said.

"How'd you know that, Charlie?" asked Zapata, who appeared to be genuinely in awe of the one-eared detective.

"And in the bar," Charlie One Ear added.

"Right again," I said.

"Geez," Zapata said.

"The old coin trick," Charlie One Ear said. "Was he spinning heads and tails?"

"You got it," I said.

"What's the coin trick?" Zapata asked.

"He marks the top of a quarter, say on the heads side but along the ridges so you can't see it unless you're looking for it," said Charlie One Ear. "He lets the mark spin the coin. Spanish Eddie never touches it. The mark doesn't suspect anything, y'see, because he's controlling the spin and Eddie's calling whether it'll fall heads or tails. He can tell by the mark on the coin. He's also a sleight-of-hand artist. If the mark wants to switch coins, he always has another one ready."

"Geez," Zapata said again, his wonder still growing.

"He's very good," Charlie One Ear said. "On a real good night he can score enough to buy a new car."

"So how come you knew he was at the airport?"

"If the mark starts getting pushy," Charlie One Ear said, "Fuereco switches to a regular coin, plays on the mark's money for a few rounds, then has to catch a plane. That's why he does airports. Gives him an excuse to end the game."

"I'll be damned," Zapata said. He looked over at me. "Charlie knows every scumbag in the business," he said with great pride.

"Only the cream of the crop," Charlie One Ear threw in. "And Spanish Eddie Fuereco only by reputation. I'd love to go a few rounds with him, before I put the arm on him."

"He'll beatcha," Zapata said. "He can read the coin."

"I'm not too bad at sleight of hand myself," Charlie One Ear said proudly. "I'll mark two coins and switch them back and forth so he keeps reading them wrong. What a coup, beating Fuereco at his own game!"

"He's all yours," I said.

"I love con games," Zapata said. "Did you ever wonder who dreams them up?"

Charlie One Ear stared at Zapata for a moment or two, then said, "No, I never really thought about it before."

"I also saw Digit Dan out there," I said.

"Ah, now there's a man with talent," said Charlie One Ear. "Fastest hands I've ever seen. Nobody works the shoulder bump like Dan."

"The shoulder bump?" Zapata said, his sense of wonderment continuing to grow as Charlie One Ear showed off.

"He works crowds, bumps the shoulder of the mark. Usually the mark will touch his wallet to make sure he hasn't been boosted. That does two things for Digit. One, it tells him where the mark's wallet is. Two, the next time he bumps him, the mark is too embarrassed to check his belongings. Bingo! The wallet's gone and so is Dan."

"You don't miss a trick, there, Charlie," Zapata said, shaking his head.

"The thing about Digit Dan that's remarkable," said Charlie One Ear, "is that he always hits somebody who's well heeled. He has that talent. He can look at a mark and tell how much money he's got in his kick."

"Amazing," Zapata said, shaking his head.

"He'll be working the track tomorrow," Charlie One Ear said. "We'll nail him. Now, about your problem. Perhaps we can give you something there."

That didn't surprise me.

"A pimp named Mortimer Flitch, alias Mort Tanner," he continued. "A wimpy sort and not too flashy. Handles high-class clientele, usually four or five girls at most. He calls Saint Louis home. He also has a thing for ladies of means."

"Rich broads, you mean," Zapata said.

"Yes, Chino, rich broads."

"A gigolo, eh?" said Stick.

"I hate to give him that distinction," said Charlie One Ear.

"Where'd you see him at?" Zapata asked.

"Out on the Strip, a week or two ago. This Turner thing came up and I never followed through."

"It's Tagliani," said Salvatore.

"What's he look like?" Zapata asked.

"Tallish, a little under six feet. Slender. I'd say one forty, one forty-two. Wears three-piece suits. Lightweight for the climate. Goes in for colored shirts and has atrocious taste in ties. Flowers, lots of bad colors, that kind of thing. Brown hair and not a lot of it. Combs it over his forehead to stretch it out. Brown eyes. Always wears black boots."

"Quirks?" Zapata asked.

"Bites his fingernails."

Zapata turned to me. "You want this guy?"

I wasn't sure what I'd do with him, but I said, "Sure, it's a start."

"Thirty minutes," Zapata said. "Wait here. Come on, Salvatore, I need company," and they were gone.

"Zapata's amazing," Charlie One Ear said, watching them rush out the door. "Nose like a bloodhound."

"Looks more like a waffle iron," I said with a laugh.

"True," said Charlie One Ear. "But that doesn't impede his instinct for finding people. He's unerring."

I got the impression maybe Zapata had been hit one or two times too many on the soft part of his head. Later I learned that he was as streetwise as any cop I've ever known. He may have been short on Shakespeare, but he was long on smarts.

"He was a middleweight contender, you know," Charlie One Ear continued. "Got full of patriotism, volunteered for the army, and spent a year in Vietnam. Then he came back and joined the Hell's Angels. I've never quite understood why."

"You seem to have a nice team going," I said. "You spot them, Zapata finds them, and Salvatore sticks to them."

"Like flypaper," said Charlie One Ear.

Stick excused himself to go call the coroner and see if there were any autopsy reports yet. When he left, I leaned over the table toward Charlie One Ear.

"I've got to ask you something," I said. "It's a personal thing."

"Yes?"

"I heard your father was an English lord and your mother was a Ute Indian. Whenever your name comes up, somebody says that."

"Only partly correct. It was my grandparents and she was a Cree. I inherited my memory from my father and my instincts from my mother. Thank God it wasn't the other way around. I'm quite flattered you've heard of me."

"Charlie Flowers, the man who smashed the Wong Yang Fu opium ring in San Francisco almost single-handed! You're a legend in your time," I said with a smile.

"I really enjoy this, y'know," he said, grinning back. "I have an enormous ego."

"Is it true you once busted so many moonshiners in Georgia that they threw together and hired a couple of Philly shooters to do you in?"

"Actually it was four, including Dancing Rodney Shutz out of Chicago, who was reputed to have killed over sixty people, a lot of whom didn't deserve the honor."

"And you got 'em all?"

"Yes. Without a scratch, I might add. They made a mistake. They all took me on at once—I suppose they thought there was safety in numbers." He paused for a minute and then flashed a twenty-dollar smile. "Dancing Rodney was so aghast I don't think he realizes to this day that he's dead." We both broke out laughing.

"So what're you doing here?" I asked.

His smile stayed but got a little brittle. "Well, I don't share Dutch Morehead's consternation with condos. My wife and I enjoy ours quite a lot. Beautiful view. We're near the water. The climate's wonderful . . ." He paused. He could have let it drop there, but he went on. "Besides, I couldn't get a job anywhere else."

"What!"

He took out one of those long, thin Dutch cigars, lit it, and blew smoke rings at the ceiling. "I was working internal affairs for the state police out in Arizona a couple of years back. There had been a lot of killing and they suspected it was dope-related. The main suspect was a big-time dealer named Mizero. They sent me in, undercover, to check it out. It was Mizero's game all right, but he had an inside man, a narc named Burke, who was very highly situated. What they were doing, Mizero would make a big sale. Maybe a hundred pounds of grass. Then Burke would step in, bust the buyer, confiscate his money and goods, tell him get lost and he wouldn't press charges. If the buyer got antsy, Mizero would push him over. Then they'd re-sell the dope.

"I got too close to the bone and blew my cover. So Burke decided he had to get rid of Mizero. The trouble was, it went the other way. Mizero dropped Burke. The locals made a deal with the state to keep Burke out of it. It was an election year and this was a big case. Nobody wanted to deal with a bad-cop scandal.

"I was a key witness for the prosecution. They knew they couldn't muzzle Mizero, so they wanted me to testify that Burke was working undercover with me. I said no, I won't do that. Some things I'll do, but I won't perjure myself for anyone, particularly a bad cop. Next thing you know, they ship me out of state so the defense can't call me, and put out the word I'm a drinker, a big trouble-maker. And, get this, they put it out that I committed perjury! For over a year everybody in the business thought I was a drunken liar. And I don't even drink."

"How about the Feds?" I said.

"They didn't want me back. I was always too independent to suit the bureaucrats. Anyway, Dutch heard about it. I was living in Trenton working a security job and he showed up one day, didn't ask any questions, just offered me a job. After I took it, I said, 'I don't drink and I've never told a lie under oath in my life,' and he says, 'I know it,' and it's never come up since."

Then he leaned across the table toward me. "That's my excuse, what's yours?"

"I know the rest of the Cincinnati Triad is here. I just want to dig a hole under all of them. I don't care where they fall, but I want them to drop."

"Is it because you couldn't nail them up there?"

"That's part of it."

"And the rest of it's personal?" he said.

I nodded. "Absolutely."

He gave me another big smile. "Splendid," he said. "I truly admire a man who's strongly motivated." He offered me his hand. "I think Zapata and I will have a go at finding this Nance chap."

"I'd like that a lot," I said.

A minute or two later Stick came back to the table. "Zapata just called," he said. "They've already spotted Tanner. He's at the Breakers Hotel eating breakfast."

"See what I mean about Chino?" Charlie One Ear said with a grin, and we were on our way.

21

MEMORANDUM

Okay, Cisco, you're always complaining that I don't file reports. So I have a thing about that. I can't type and it takes me forever to peck out one lousy report. Also there are never enough lines on the forms and I can't get the stuff in between the lines that are there. If you want to know the truth, it's a royal pain in the ass. But if I were going to write a memorandum, it would probably go something like this:

I've been in Dunetown less than twenty-four hours. So far I've witnessed one death, seen three other victims, fresh on the slab, been treated like I got smallpox by Dutch Morehead and his bunch of hooligans, and seen just enough of Dunetown to understand why they call it Doomstown. It's an understatement.

Due process? Forget it. It went out the window about the time Dunetown got its first paved road. As far as the hooligans are concerned, due process is the notice you get when you forget to pay your phone bill. Most of them think *Miranda* is the president of a banana republic in Central America.

Stick understands the territory but he's kind of in the squeeze. He has to go along with the hooligans so they won't tumble that he's a Fed. On the other hand, he's smart enough to know that any evidence these guys might gather along the way would get stomped flat at the door to the courthouse.

What we're talking about, Cisco, is education. Stick is a smooth operator. The rest of Dutch Morehead's people would rather kick ass than eat dinner. Yesterday I tried to discuss the RICO statutes with them and Chino Zapata thought I was talking about a mobster he knows in Buffalo.

The only exception is Charlie "One Ear" Flowers, who knows the game but doesn't buy the rules. He's like the rest of these guys—they've been fucked over so much by the system that they walk with their legs crossed. I'm not making any value judgments, mind you. Maybe some of them deserved their lumps.

Take Salvatore, for instance. He was up on charges in New

York City when Dutch found him. The way I get it, Salvatore was on stakeout in one of those mom and pop stores in the Bronx. It had been robbed so often, the people who owned it took out the cash and put it on the counter every time somebody walked into the store. The old man had been shot twice. Classic case. It's the end of the year and Salvatore is behind two-way glass and this freak comes into the store and starts waving a Saturday night special around. Salvatore steps out from his hiding place, says, "Merry Christmas, motherfucker," and blows the guy into the middle of the street with an 870 riot gun loaded with rifle slugs. The police commissioner took issue with the way Salvatore did business. Now he's down here.

One thing about them, they don't complain. Between you and me, I'm glad they're here.

You can add this to everything else: every time I go around a corner I get another rude shock. Like going out to the beach today. I wasn't ready for that. The traffic should have been a clue. It got heavy about a quarter mile from where the boulevard terminates at Dune Road, which runs parallel to the ocean. See, the way I remember Dune Road, it was this kind of desolate macadam strip that merged with the dunes. It went out to the north end of the island and petered out at the sea; one of those old streets that go nowhere in particular.

Now it's four lanes wide with metered parking lots all over the place. There are three hotels that remind me a lot of Las Vegas, and shops and fast-food joints one on top of the other, and seawalls to protect the hotel guests from the common people. Two more going up and beyond them condos polluting the rest of the view. And the noise! It was a hurricane of sound. Stereos, honking horns, and hundreds of voices, all jabbering at once.

La Cote de Nightmare is what it is now.

See what I mean about rude shocks? The Strip, that's one rude shock.

Anyway, I'm on my way out there with Stick and Charlie One Ear followed in his car. Going anywhere with Stick is taking your life in your hands. He doesn't drive a car, he flies it. He can do anything in that Pontiac but a slow roll and I wouldn't challenge him on that. I ought to be getting combat pay.

Without boring you with details, Salvatore and Zapata made this St. Louis pimp named Mortimer Flitch and we went out to have a chat with him.

He was hanging out on the Strip and before I go any further

with that, let me tell you about the Strip. The first thing I noticed when we got there, the hotels are almost identical triplets. Take the Breakers, for instance. The lobby is the size of the Dallas stadium. It would take about five minutes to turn it into a casino. I could almost hear the cards ruffling and the roulette balls rattling and the gears cranking in the slot machines. When Raines pushed through the pari-mutuel law, he promised there would never be any casino gambling in Dunetown. Well, you can forget that, Cisco. They're ready. It's just a matter of time. I'll give them a year, two at the most. What we're looking at is Atlantic City, Junior. About fifteen minutes told me all I wanted to know about the Strip.

When we get there, the pimp, Mortimer, is sitting in a booth in the coffee shop looking like he just swallowed a 747. Salvatore is sitting across from him, kind of leaning over the table, grinning like he's running for mayor. One thing I left out: Salvatore carries a sawed-off pool cue in his shoulder holster. It's about eighteen inches long and it's always catching on things, which doesn't seem to bother him a bit. Zapata is standing by the door. That's their idea of backup.

When we arrived, Zapata split. He's on the prowl for Nance and Chevos. That makes me feel real fine, because if Chevos and Nance are within a hundred miles of here, Zapata will find them. I'll make book on it.

We join Salvatore and Mortimer at the table and then I see why this Mortimer Flitch has got that screwy look on his face. Salvatore has his pool cue between Mortimer's legs and every once in a while he gives the cue a little jerk and rings Mortimer's bells.

"Tell him what you told me there, Mort," Salvatore says, and bong! he rings the bells and Mortimer starts singing like the fat lady in the opera.

"I got in a little trouble in Louisville about two months ago and—"

Bong! "Tell 'em what for," says Salvatore.

"Beating up this chippie. She had it coming—"

Bong! "Forget the apologies," says Salvatore.

"Anyway, the DA was all over me and—"

Bong! "Tell 'em why," says Salvatore.

"It, uh, it—"

Bong!

"It was my fifth offense. Anyway, I give a call to a friend of mine, does a little street business in Cincy, and he says forget it out there, things are real hot, I should try calling Johnny O'Brian down here. So I did and he sends me the ticket."

Mortimer stopped to catch his breath and Salvatore gave him another little shot.

"Tell 'em about the hotel and all," he says.

"Look, O'Brian did me all right. I could get blitzed over this."

Bong! "Tell 'em about the fuckin' hotel, weed."

"He gets me a suite here in the Breakers, give me two G's, and says I got a couple of weeks to line up some ladies. It's a sixty-forty split. He gets the forty."

Salvatore looked over at me and smiled.

"What else you want to know?"

"Did you bring any ladies with you?" I asked.

"Uh—"

Bong!

"Yeah, yeah. Two."

"That's the Mann Act," I said.

"Look, could we maybe meet somewhere else if we're going to keep this up?" Mortimer pleaded. "I could take a boxcar ride just talking to you guys."

"How many pimps does O'Brian have working down here?" I asked.

Mortimer looks at Salvatore wild-eyed and says, "Swear to God, I don't know. I got the hotel, that's all I know."

"This is your territory exclusively?" Charlie One Ear asked, and Mortimer nodded vigorously.

"Okay," I said. "Finish your breakfast. We wanted information; we're not going to tell anybody about our chat. Don't screw up and leave town."

He shakes his head, Salvatore pockets the cue, and we split.

"Can we use this?" Charlie One Ear asks on the way out.

"No," I said, "but it's nice to know."

"Coercion, huh?"

"Yeah."

Now I know why Salvatore carries a pool cue. He calls it his sweet nutcracker.

See what I mean about due process, Cisco?

22
DRIVE-IN

Stick drove intelligently on the way back. Neither one of us had much to say. About halfway to town he wheeled into a drive-in and got us each a hamburger and a beer. He pulled around behind the place and parked under some palm trees in the parking lot and we opened the doors to let the breeze blow through.

"You okay?" he asked.

"Sure, why?"

"I figure maybe you got the blues."

"How come?"

"You got that look in your eye."

"I'm doing fine."

"I know the blues when I see them." He looked at me with that crazy sideways smile. "I just thought I'd let you know I'm a good listener and I got an awful memory."

"It's nothing you haven't heard before," I said.

"I'm only thirty-one," he replied. "You'd be surprised what I haven't heard yet."

"I'll keep that in mind."

There was a lot of activity in the parking lot; a lot of young girls wearing just about as little as the law allowed and young men with acne and cutoff jeans making awkward passes at them. The beer was ice cold and it tickled the tongue and made the mouth feel clean and fresh, and the hamburgers were real meat and cooked just right. So I hunkered down in the seat, bracing my knees on the dashboard, and took a long pull on my bottle. It had been a long time since I had spent lunch watching pretty young girls at play.

"Just look at that, would you," Stick said wistfully.

"I'm looking," I said, just as wistfully.

After a while two girls in a TR-3 pulled in and parked near us. One of them got out and threw something into the trash can. She was wearing thin white shorts that barely covered her bottom and a man's white shirt tied just under her breasts, which were firm and perilously close to popping out. She stood by the door of the TR-3 for a minute, flirting with Stick, and then she got in and leaned over and whispered something to her friend. When she did, the shorts tightened around every curve and into every crevice and you could see the lines of her skimpy bikinis through the cotton cloth and see the half-circles of her cheeks.

"Holy shit," Stick muttered, "that's damn near criminal."

"She's not a day over fifteen, Stick."

"I don't remember fifteen-year-olds being stacked like that when I was a kid," he said somewhat mournfully. "Do you remember them looking like that?"

I remembered Doe at fifteen, coming up to Athens with Chief for homecoming, flirting with me every time Teddy or Chief looked the other way. She definitely looked like that.

"Seems to me they were all flat-chested and giggled a lot," Stick went on.

"They're giggling," I pointed out.

"That's a different kind of giggling."

"They're just beginning to figure it out," I said.

"Figure what out?"

"How to drive a man up the wall."

"She's got the angle, all right," he said, drumming the fingers of one hand on his steering wheel and staring back at the little cutie, who lowered her sunglasses and stared back.

"Oh my," Stick moaned. "You just don't know where to draw the line."

"About three years older than that," I said.

"What a shame."

He took a long pull on his beer, smacked his lips, and sighed.

"I missed all that," he said. "They were little girls when I went to Nam and they were grown up and spoken for when I got back. What a fuckin' ripoff."

The girl in the TR-3 leaned her head way back and shook her long black hair across her face, and then she leaned forward and flipped it back and smoothed it out with her hands. The shirt came perilously close to falling completely open.

"She's doing that on purpose," Stick said, watching every move. He looked back over at me. "Fifteen, huh?"

"At the most."

"Shit. What a fuckin' ripoff."

The driver of the TR-3 cranked up and pulled around in a tight little arc so they drove past us.

"Love your hat," the girl in the white cotton shorts purred as they went by. Stick whipped the hat off and scaled it like a Frisbee in the wake of the TR-3. It hit the parking lot and skipped to a stop as the sports car vanished around the building. Stick retrieved his hat and got back behind the wheel.

"All bluff," he muttered, and then added, "I may have to take the night off."

"I wouldn't mind taking the rest of my life off," I said. "I been on this case too long. Almost six years. I'm sick and tired of the Taglianis. They're enough to give anybody the blues."

"Relax. The way things are going there won't be any of them left to be sick and tired of," he said almost jauntily, staring at another young girl in a bikini bathing suit who was sitting on the back of a convertible, her face turned up toward the sun. Her long, slender legs were stretched out in front of her and her breasts bubbled over the skimpy top. The driver, a skinny kid in surfing trunks and a cutoff T-shirt, stared dumbly at her in the rearview mirror.

"Look at that kid in the front seat," Stick said. "He doesn't know what the hell to do about all that."

"It'll come to him," I said.

"They're all over the place," Stick cried lasciviously. "You know what this is? It's a plague of young flesh. Do you get the feeling this is a plague of young flesh?"

"Yeah," I said. "God's throwing the big final at us. He's testing our mettle."

"Mettle, shmettle," Stick said. "If that little sweetie in the back of the convertible takes a deep breath, her top'll fly off and kill that kid up front." After a moment he added, "What a way to go."

He finished his beer and put the empty bottle on the floor between his legs. "That's all it is then? You're tired of the Tagliani case?"

I wondered whether he was fishing and what he was fishing for. Then I thought, who cares, so he's fishing. Suddenly I had this crazy thought that while Stick was younger than me and newer at the game, he was protecting me. It was a feeling I had known in the past and it scared me because it made me think about Teddy.

"I've been chasing Taglianis longer than anything else I've done in my whole life," I said. "Longer than college, longer than law school, longer than the army. I know everything there is to know about the fucking Taglianis."

"That's why you're here enjoying the land of sunshine and little honeys," Stick replied. "Think about it—you could be back in Cincinnati. Now that's something to get the blues over."

"I hope you're not gonna be one of those jerks who always look on the bright side," I said caustically.

In a crazy kind of way, I felt a strange sense of kinship with the Taglianis, as if I were the black sheep of the family. My life had been linked to theirs for nearly six years. I knew more about the Tagliani clan than I did about the Findleys or any of the hooligans. I knew what their wives and their girlfriends were like, what they liked to eat, how they dressed, what they watched on television, where they went on vacation, what they fought about, how often they made love. I even knew when their children were born.

"You want to hear something really nuts?" I said. "I almost sent one of the Tagliani kids a birthday card once."

"I knew a detective in D.C., used to send flowers to the funeral when he wasted somebody. He always signed the cards 'From a friend.' "

"That's sick," I said.

"You know what we oughta do, buddy? When this fiasco is all over we ought to take a month's leave, go down to the Keys. I got a couple of buddies live down there, sit around all day smoking dope and eating shrimp. That's the fuckin' life. Or maybe get the hell out of the country, hit the islands, Aruba, one of those. Sit around soaking up rays, getting laid, forget all this shit."

"Wouldn't that be nice?" I said.

"We'll do it," he said, slapping the steering wheel with the palm of his hand, and then he said suddenly, "Hey, you married?"

"No, are you?"

"Hell no. What woman in her right mind would spend more than a weekend at the Holiday Fuckin' Inn."

"That's where you're staying, the Holiday Inn?"

"Yeah. It's kind of like home, y'know. They're all exactly alike, no matter where you are. If you get one of the inside rooms overlooking the pool, the view doesn't even change."

"I had this little basement apartment when I was in Cincy," I said. "I took it by the month because I didn't think I'd be there that long. There weren't even any pictures on the wall. Finally I went out and bought some used books and a couple of cheap prints to try and doll the place up but it didn't work. It always seemed like I was visiting somebody else when I came home."

"Yeah, I know," he said. "It's been like that since Nam. We're disconnected."

That was the perfect word for it. Disconnected. For years I had worked with other partners but always at arm's length, like two people bumping each other in a crowd. I didn't know whether they were married, divorced; whether they had kids or hobbies. All I knew was whether they were good or bad cops and that we all suffered from the same anger, frustration, boredom, and loneliness.

"Don't you ever wonder why in hell you picked this lousy job?" I asked him.

"That's your trouble right there, Jake, you think too much. You get in trouble when you think too much."

"No shit?"

"No shit. Thinking can get you killed. You didn't make it through Nam thinking about it. Nobody did. The thinkers are still over there, doing their thinking on Boot Hill."

There was a lot of truth in what he said. I was thinking too much. There was this thing about Cisco telling me to forget murder unless it was relevant. That bothered me. Hell, I was a cop and murder is murder, and part of the job, like it or not, is to keep people alive, like them or not, and keeping them alive meant finding the killer, no matter what Cisco said. It was all part of the territory. And there was the lie about Teddy which I hadn't thought about for years, because I had stuffed it down deep, along with the rest of my memories. I had walked away from the past, or thought I had. I had even stopped dreaming, though dreams are an occupational hazard for anyone who has seen combat. Now the dreams had started again. You can't escape dreams. They sneak up on you in the quiet of the night, shadow and smoke, reminding you of what has been. You don't dream about the war, you dream about things that are far worse. You dream about what *might* have been.

"Hell, it's very complicated, Stick," I said finally. "I don't think I've got it sorted out enough to talk about. Sometimes I feel like I'm juggling with more balls than I can handle."

"Then throw a couple away."

"I don't know which ones to throw."

"That's what life's all about," he said. "A process of elimination."

"I thought I had it all worked out before I got here," I said. "It was very simple. Very uncomplicated."

"That's the trap," he replied. "Didn't Nam teach you anything,

Jake? Life is full of incoming mail. You get comfortable, you get dead."

"That's what it's all about, Alfie?"

"Sure. It's also the answer to your question. We're cops because we have to keep ducking the incoming. That's what keeps us alive."

Finally I said, "Yeah, that's what we'll do, go down to the islands, lay out, and forget it all."

"That's all that's bugging you, a little cabin fever then?"

"Right."

He flashed that crazy smile again.

"I don't believe that for a fuckin' minute," he said as he cranked up the Black Maria.

23

HEY, MR. BAGMAN

Cowboy Lewis was waiting in the Warehouse when we got back. The big, rawboned man was sitting at a desk, laboriously hunting and pecking out a report on a form supplied by the department. He didn't worry about the little lines or how many there were. He typed over them, under them, through them, and past them. Getting it down, that was his objective. There were a lot of words x'd out and in one or two places he had forgotten to hit the spacer, but I had to give him A for effort. At least he was doing it. His face lit up like the aurora borealis when he saw me.

"Hey, I was writing you a memo," he said, ripping it out of the Selectomatic in midword. "I'll just tell you."

I looked at the partially completed report and told him that would be just fine. The thought occurred to me that I could sign it myself and send it to Cisco. That would probably end his bitching about my reports, or lack thereof, forever.

"Salvatore says you're interested in that little weed, uh . . ." He paused, stymied temporarily because he had forgotten the name.

"Cohen?" I helped.

"Yeah. Little four-eyed wimp, got his head on a swivel?" he said, twisting his head furiously back and forth to illustrate what he meant.

"That's him," I replied. "Unless times have changed, he's the bagman for the outfit."

"Yeah," he said, which was his way of agreeing. "Carries one of those old-timey doctor's bags, black. Hangs on to that sucker like he's got the family jewels in there."

"That's about what it is," said Stick, "the family jewels."

"I shadowed him three days—Tuesday, Wednesday, Friday, last week—and got him cold." Lewis took out a small black notebook. "He stays real busy in the morning. Moves around a lot. Goes to the bank every day at two o'clock, just as it closes."

"Every day?" I asked.

"All three days he went to the bank there on the river." He nodded.

"This activity in the morning—does he always go to the same places?" Stick asked.

Lewis shook his head. "He's all over town. But he always seems to wind up on the Strip around noon. Leastwise he did these three days."

"Where does he bank?" I queried.

"Seacoast National, down there by the river like I said. Although sometimes he makes deposits at the branches."

The good-news worm nibbled at my stomach. That was Charles Seaborn's homeplate.

"Cash deposits?" I asked.

"Never got that close," Lewis said with a shrug. "Didn't wanna tip my hand, y'see. He travels first class. Big black Caddy limo with a white driver looks like he could carry the heap in his arms. Then there's another pug in the front seat and a souped-up Dodge Charger with a high-speed rear end following them. Usually two, three mutts in it."

"Like a little parade?" Stick suggested.

"Yeah," he said with a smile, "a little parade. Any one of 'em could win an ugly contest, hands down. The Charger is usually in pretty tight. Half a block behind at best."

"And he moves around a lot, you say?" I threw in.

"Uh-huh. But he always ends up there at the bank by the river, just before it closes."

He offered me his notebook, which had notations scrawled everywhere. Slantwise, up the sides of the pages, upside down. It was far worse than his typed report.

"What does all this mean?" I asked.

He looked a little hurt. "That's addresses and stuff," he said.

"See here, 102 Fraser, that's an address where he stopped. Here's Bay Br. That's the Bay branch of the bank. Uh, I don't know what this one is for sure, but I can figure it out."

"Any of these addresses mean anything to you?"

"Well, some of 'em do. See here where I wrote down 'Port?' That's the Porthole Restaurant on the way out to the Strip. He hit there two days, Tuesday and Friday. 'Bron,' that's Bronicata's joint. That was Wednesday."

"He sure eats a lot," I said.

"Naw. Never stays that long. Five minutes, sometimes ten. I ambled in behind him once at the Porthole. He has a cup of coffee at the corner of the bar, goes to the can, and leaves. Two guys from the Charger sit a few stools away, another grabs a table near the door. The other two stand by the car. He sure ain't lonely."

It was an excellent tail job, but it was impossible for me to decipher his notes.

"This is a great job," I told him, "but I need a big favor. Can you list the places he stopped with the dates and times for me? Nothing fancy, just write them down in a straight line on a sheet of paper."

"Can't read my writing, huh?" he said, looking hurt again.

I tried to ease the pain. "It's strictly my problem," I said. "I have a very linear mind."

His "Oh" told me that he didn't quite get my meaning but wasn't interested in pursuing it any further.

"Does Dutch have you shadowing Cohen anymore?" I asked.

"Tomorrow," he said. "I'm pulling a double. Logeto tonight, Cohen in the morning. Then I'm off a day."

"Maybe he ought to watch the car instead of Cohen," Stick suggested. "Some of his operators probably have a key to the trunk. He parks in a lot or on a side street somewhere, goes into a place, and while he's gone, the henchman makes a drop in the trunk."

"Excellent idea," I said. "Also you might switch cars with one of the other guys. These people are very nervous. They keep their eyes open; that's their job."

"That and cutting down anybody that gets near the family jewels," Stick said.

"Got it," Cowboy said. "I'll get right on this list." He returned to his desk.

I pulled Stick out of earshot. "When he gets finished," I said, "we need to pull a Link matrix on this stuff, just to see where these pickups overlap. The same with the rest of the gang. This Cohen is very particular. I'm sure he's smart enough to avoid any obvious patterns, but in the long run he's going to end up setting patterns whether he likes it or not."

"What's the significance of the restaurants?" Stick asked.

"I'd have to guess."

"So guess."

"Bronicata probably owns the Porthole, as well as his own place. Maybe some other eateries around town as well. That's probably dope money. The hotels is probably skim. I'm sure they have double-entry books to keep the Lepers off their ass."

Stick said, "We might have Salvatore pay Mortimer another visit and find out who he pays and when. That could give us a lead on the pros take."

He had learned his lessons well, the Stick. He was revealing himself as a first-class detective with a handle on how the mob operates and I told him so.

"Thanks, teacher," he said with that crooked smile of his. "Anything else?"

"Yeah. It wouldn't hurt to know who owns the businesses they frequent. We've got to start putting together some kind of profile on the whole Triad operation here."

"Charlie One Ear's the man for that. He knows all the tricks and you can't beat that computer he uses for a brain. I can help with the legwork."

"Good enough," I said.

"How about dinner tonight?" Stick asked. "Maybe hit a few hot spots afterward."

"I'm tied up tonight," I said. "Can we shoot for tomorrow night?"

Stick smiled. "I'll check my dance card," he said.

Charlie One Ear appeared from the back of the building with an expression that spelled trouble.

"You need to have a chat with Dutch, old man," he said to me.

"Trouble?"

"I think his feelings are hurt."

"Oh, splendid," I replied.

"I'll fill Charlie in," Stick said as I headed back toward the big man's office. Dutch operated out of a room the size of a walk-in closet. A desk, two chairs, one of which he occupied, and a window. The desk could have qualified for disaster aid. It was so littered with paper that he kept the phone, which he was using when I knocked, on the windowsill.

"Talk to ya later," he barked into the phone, and slammed it down. I decided to close the door.

"You don't have t'do that," he growled. "We ain't got any secrets here." He pointed to the other chair. "Take a load off."

I sat down. He cleared his throat and moved junk around on his desktop for a minute or so, then took off his glasses and leaned back in his chair, staring at the ceiling.

"I don't wanna sound unappreciative," he started, "but I got a way of doing things, okay? It may not be SOP, and it may not be to the Fed's liking, but that's the way it is. Now, it seems to me that all of a sudden you're kind of running this operation, got my people running errands all over town, doing little numbers on wayward pimps, like that, and I like to get things off my chest, so I'm speaking my piece right up front."

"Is that all that's bothering you?" I asked. I sensed that there was something else behind his annoyance but I wasn't sure exactly what.

"So far."

"Okay," I said. "Since it's your ballgame, maybe you better tell me the rules."

He opened a drawer and took out a sheet of paper.

"This here's my schedule sheet. I spend a lot of time workin' this out, make sure all the bases are covered, people have some time off when they need it. You go short-stoppin' me and it's goin' to get to be a big mess."

I don't like to be put on the defensive, nor do I like apologies and excuses. "That's fair enough," I said. "Can we work out a compromise?"

"Such as what?"

"Such as you and me sitting down and drawing up a list of priorities."

"I got a list of priorities."

"It would help if you explained them to me."

"When it comes up, I will."

"See here, Dutch, I didn't come here to screw up your operation. You've got a good bunch of people here. A little rough around the edges, but that may be good in the long pull. All I'm trying to do is give them a little direction."

"There's channels," he said brusquely.

"What channels? You? You're the channel, Dutch. I'm sorry if I stepped on your toes—"

"It ain't that," he said, cutting me off.

"Then what is it? Look here, if you want to keep boosting dips and hassling street pushers and hookers, that's your business. I didn't come here to kick ass, I came here to do a job, which is to dump the Tagliani outfit. I thought we saw eye to eye on that."

"Don't screw up my schedule!" he bellowed, slamming his fist on the desk.

I jumped to my feet.

"Fuck your schedule," I said quietly. "Maybe I better get some help in here from the field and go it alone. And don't raise your voice to me. This isn't high school."

It was a bluff but I decided to call his hand before the pot got too big to cover. Sometimes the best way to defuse a situation is to light the fuse. He didn't like it one bit. It caught him off guard. His eyes glittered dangerously and beads of sweat popped out in his mustache. I started for the door.

"You shoulda told me about you and Doe Raines," he said, before I could get to it.

So that was it. Titan had let the tiger loose.

"Why? It's personal business. Titan knows that."

"Titan didn't tell me."

"Nobody else knows about it," I said. "That was twenty years ago, damn it."

He leaned back and raised his eyebrows. "Babs Thomas" is all he said.

I felt like a fool. The last thing I needed to show Dutch at this point was misjudgment. We stared at each other for what seemed like an hour. Finally his shoulders loosened and he wiped his mouth with the back of his hand.

"*Sheiss,*" he growled, half under his breath, then waved at the chair. "Sit down. Let's start over."

I sat down. There was no point in pushing it any further. We both had made our points.

"Suppose you tell me how you want to run the show," I said.

The storm was over. "It ain't that," he said quietly. "I just got hot under the collar, see. I didn't like hearin' things about a man I'm workin' sock and shoe with from the local gossip."

"She's guessing," I said.

"Is she guessing right? Did you have an affair with Doe Raines?"

"Shit, Dutch, I had a college romance with Doe Findley. That was over and done with a long time ago. Besides, what's that got to do with the price of eggs?"

"Right now a scandal could really upset the apple cart."

I felt like getting righteously indignant except that he was cutting close to the bone. I wasn't sure how to deal with the situation without straight-out lying to the man.

"There's not going to be any scandal," I said finally.

"Is that a fact?" he asked seriously.

"That's a fact."

He nodded slowly. "Okay," he said. "I'm sorry I brought it up but I'm just as glad we got it out of the way. Anyway, I got run through the ringer this morning. Titan and Donleavy both shoved it up and broke it off."

"Does Donleavy know about Doe and me?"

"I doubt it. It didn't come up."

"So what's their beef?"

"No more'n you could expect," he moaned. "My job was to keep people like Tagliani outta here. Now they want the whole mess cleaned up. Titan's idea is to just run them out of town."

"That stuff went out with Buffalo Bill."

"Tell them that. So far, Raines hasn't figured it all out. The name of the game is sweep it under the rug."

"It's gone too far for that."

"You know it and I know it."

"But they don't, is that it?"

"Livin' in the past," he mused. "Donleavy doesn't know anything about the rackets. He's seen too many James Cagney movies."

"Unless I'm mistaken," I said, "Donleavy had a hand in all this. He was supposed to screen these people."

"I think it goes something like this: the buck stops here," he said, pointing to himself. "It doesn't go any higher."

"How did you get yourself in this fix?" I asked. "You're not the kind of man that kisses the ass of people like Donleavy."

I was thinking of what Charlie One Ear had told me, about the way Dutch hired him and Salvatore. I was sure Dutch had used the same kind of judgment in hiring all the hooligans.

"The rules changed on me," he said sadly. "Leadbetter was supposed to be the in-between man. When he went down, it fell to me. Up until now, I didn't have any bitch."

"Up to now it didn't matter," I said.

He looked over at me for a long time. I was putting the squeeze on him and he knew it. What he wanted was for me to let him off the hook, but I couldn't do that. I needed Dutch right where he was, standing between me and the damned Committee. And that meant he had to stand up to them, like it or not.

"You don't give a man much, do you, son?"

"I'm not telling you how to run your business, Dutch. I could ask you to trust me but you don't know me that well. What I will tell you is that this thing is going to blow and soon. The powder keg's in the fire."

"So what's the answer?" he said, holding his hands out like a man going down for the third time.

"Try to beat the explosion," I said. "I need to find the key that will put the Triad against the wall."

"What key?"

"I need to build a RICO case against these bastards."

"That could take years!" he cried.

"Except we have one edge," I said. "I already know the players and how they operate. It's not like we were starting from scratch. What I need is the local buy-out."

"Who do you suspect?" he asked.

"Hell, there's so many termites in this woodpile it's hard to say. Just give me free rein with your SOB's for a few days. We can work together. But if something pops, I don't want to have to run you down and explain it. Trust me that far. I may work your boys to death, but it'll be worth it in the long pull."

"I'll give you this—you already made believers outta Charlie One Ear, Salvatore, and Cowboy Lewis. Zapata's still on the fence but he's about to come around. That leaves only Kite Lange, the Mufalatta Kid, and Pancho Callahan to convince. I don't know how you did it, but you sure moved fast."

"I'm just a charming fellow," I said with a smile, trying to ease the pressure.

"You don't have any ideas?" he asked, pressing the question.

"It could be Raines. Maybe that's the reason he's so coy. He's keeping arm's length from the action. And Donleavy could be his front."

"That don't even make good sense, Jake. They got more to lose than anybody, particularly Harry."

"Harry Raines didn't get where he is by running on empty," I said. "He's ambitious and he's got more than his share of pride. The mob might be making him a bigger offer than just governor of the state. Their clout in Washington is scary."

He shook his head. "You got one helluva devious mind," he said.

I didn't say any more. I couldn't tell him that I wanted Raines to be in it. Or Donleavy. Or that my reasons were purely selfish because I was in love with Raines' wife. Hell, I'm only human.

24

DUE PROCESS

Charlie One Ear was killing time near the water fountain when I left Dutch's office. His expression asked the question. I made a circle with thumb and forefinger and winked.

"Just your basic lack of communication," I said.

"Good," he said. "He's a fine man, Dutch. There's not a man in the squad who wouldn't kill for him."

"He deserves it," I said. "He's got a mean job and right now the local hotshots have got him shoved against the wall."

"I just wanted to make sure you understood," said Charlie One Ear. "You're a nice chap and all that, but we're throwing in with you because it appears to be the only chance he's got."

It was obvious that Charlie One Ear was the spokesman for the SOB's, or perhaps chairman would be closer to it.

"I appreciate your honesty, Charlie. Just so there's no misunderstanding either way, I intend to take advantage of that loyalty every chance I get."

He smiled and put out his hand. "Thus far you seem to know what you're doing. Someday I hope to add a new chapter to the legend that seems to be growing around me. Busting the Triad with Jake Kilmer."

"Let's hope you can write it," I said. "We got the clock against us."

"I have already come to that conclusion," he said as we walked toward the door. "There seems to be a covert attempt in Dunetown to ignore the Tagliani kill-out."

"You noticed that, huh?"

"Yes. Obviously they're hoping for a break before they have to fess up," he continued. "I'm certain the powers that be are aware that the homicide division couldn't find their collective asses if they were all farting 'Dixie' in harmony."

"Did Stick talk to you about the information we need?"

"Yes," he said. "I'll start on it this afternoon. I just wanted to make sure everything was A-one with Dutch."

"He just wants me to stop fucking up his schedule," I said, laughing.

"He's been days behind on the bloody schedule since the first week we started," Charlie One Ear said with a grin.

"I think he just needed to blow off a little steam," I answered.

"By the way, just so you'll know. Cowboy may seem a bit dense at times, but he's really quite bright. He's on about a ten-second flash-to-bang delay."

"Okay," I said. "Has he always been like that?"

Charlie One Ear shook his head. "He got the back of his head blown off in Vietnam. Thre's a steel plate in there. That's why he wears that ridiculous baseball cap. It covers up the bald spot."

I didn't know how to respond to that. What do you say? Gee, that's tough? Everybody knows it's tough.

"Actually I mentioned that because Cowboy was a sheriff in Waco, Texas, before he went off to war. When he came back nobody would hire him. Dutch found him working on the docks in New Orleans."

"Thanks, Charlie, I'm glad to know that."

"I'm sure he'll have that list up for you by tomorrow, even if he has to work on it all night."

"Tell him I said thanks," I said.

"Tell him yourself," said Charlie One Ear. "I'm off for the hall of records."

Cowboy Lewis was right where I left him, laboring over his errant notebook.

"Cowboy, don't kill yourself on that, okay?"

"Tomorrow," he said, shoving the baseball cap back on his head. "I got to tail that Logeto tonight but I'll have it by tomorrow."

"Thanks."

"By the way, Zapata said to tell you he went out to find that creep that shot you."

"His name's Turk Nance," I said.

"Turk Nance, right." He smiled. "Zapata'll find him, you can put that in the bank."

"I'll thank him when I see him," I said.

"I think I'm going to have to take writing lessons," he said as I was leaving. "I can't read my own fuckin' writing."

As I headed for the door a new figure loomed in my path. It was the cop with the waffle-iron features.

"We didn't have a chance to get acquainted last night," he said. "I'm Kite Lange."

"Jake Kilmer."

"I'm a good wire man," he said. "You need anything wired, you call me, okay? I can bug a fly in motion right in front of your face, you wouldn't see me do it."

"Terrific."

"I'm not bragging," he said, and his battered features broke into a smile. "It's a God-given talent."

"And I'm sure you don't abuse it," I said.

"Not unless somebody asks me to," said Kite, then he added, "I hear you were in Nam."

"Yeah," I said.

"When was that?"

" '67, '68. I got held up coming home by Tet."

"What outfit?"

"Military intelligence. How about you?"

"Medevac chopper pilot," he said.

"How many missions did you fly?" I asked.

"You'd throw up if I told you."

I hesitated for a moment before asking him the next question, but I figured, what the hell. I was getting to be one of the boys.

"Mind if I ask you a personal question?" I said.

"Shoot."

"How did you fuck up and get in this squad?"

Lange's smashed face bunched up and he howled.

"Hey, that's getting right to the point," he said. "Well, I was flying helicopter traffic control for the Denver PD. Three guys heisted a bank and I was tailing them at about five hundred feet. A blue and white was closing in on them but he lost his car and went off the road. So I dropped right down on top of the getaway car. You know, a couple of feet. I was hanging right in there, radioing back his position, trying to force him off the road, when we came to a railroad bridge. At the last minute I had to pull up to get over it."

"Yeah?"

"I didn't see the freight train that was crossing the bridge at the time. Flew right into an open boxcar. It happened to be the mayor's favorite chopper. Had his name on the side and everything. You should of seen it, the chopper, I mean." He stopped a moment and chuckled. "It looked like the Jolly Green Giant had it for lunch."

"So you got the old heave-ho for breaking the mayor's toy, huh?"

"That, and the city had to buy a new boxcar for the train. They didn't even give me a going-away party."

I said, "You're lucky you lived through it."

"What d'ya think happened to my face?" Kite said, still grinning.

"What were you doing when Dutch found you?" I asked, expecting him to tell me he was selling used cars or something.

"A traffic gig in Roanoke, Virginia, with a lady reporter," he said. "It was kind of demeaning after doing police work, but it had its moments. She used to give me head on the way back from the afternoon rush every day."

It was my turn to laugh. "You must be some kind of pilot," I said.

"After Nam, it's all pie a la mode."

Then I got an idea. I still don't believe what I did next, Old Mr. Due Process, ex-lawyer, always-do-it-right Kilmer. Maybe the hooligans were beginning to rub off on me.

"I got an idea," I said.

"Shoot."

"You know the Seacoast Bank's main branch down near the river?"

"I can find it."

"I'd like to know who the president's doing business with. Who he talks to during the day, that kind of thing. His name's Charles Seaborn."

"How about the phone?" Lange asked. "You want it bugged, too? I got a two-for-one special on."

"No, they wouldn't be that dumb."

Lange spread another smile over his boxcarred face.

"Done."

25

LIGHTNING PEOPLE

All the way back to the hotel I was thinking she had probably called and left a message canceling out. It kept building up in my mind until I broke out in a sweat, the way you do when you want something so bad you're sure you won't get it. I started getting pissed and by the time I got to the hotel I had this dialogue between us worked out in my head. I would get it all off my chest, once and for all.

Then I got to the room and there were no phone calls or messages. It was almost a letdown.

I was still in a sweat so I peeled off my shirt and pants and sat down in front of the air conditioner in my shorts. I sat there until I got chilled. That took about fifteen minutes, which meant I had four more hours to go.

I kept waiting for the phone to ring, expecting her to call the whole thing off. The suspense was awful. I took the phone off the hook but it started screeching like bad brakes do and I hung it up. I sat on the bed and took it off the hook and waited until it screeched; then I'd depress the little bar and wait a minute and let it up again. I killed another fifteen minutes that way until my finger got tired.

About six o'clock I ordered a steak, potatoes, salad, and coffee. I had forgotten how bad room-service food is until I took the first bite. I wasn't hungry anyway. The coffee was in one of those ugly purple Thermos pitchers that always look dirty and it was lukewarm but I drank it because it was something to do.

I was killing time. Hell, who am I kidding, I was watching it crawl by on its hands and knees, checking the clock every five minutes. In desperation I started to read Cisco's report on Dunetown. It might just as well have been written by the chamber of commerce for all it told me. I dropped it in the wastebasket and stared at the television set for another thirty minutes.

At about seven I decided to take a bath, soak my tired muscles, and kill another half hour. I turned on the spigots and the radio. The water was so hot it took ten minutes of juggling and dipping before I settled in. A bath is great therapy, particularly when it's just about too hot to bear. It opens up the head, clears away the cobwebs, helps you sort the real stuff from the bullshit. Kind of like meditation.

About ten minutes after I got into the tub the muses began to whisper to me. They were saying things I didn't want to hear. The muses don't always cooperate.

Wake up, Kilmer, the voices said, you made Dutch a promise. No scandal, you told him, and he took you at your word, no questions asked.

Wake up, Kilmer, you can't erase twenty years with a kiss and a smile and a roll in the hay. 1963 is history. You had prospects then. What have you got now? Stick spelled it out, the Holiday Fucking Inn, that's what you've got. Now that would really give Doe a laugh—for about the first five minutes.

Wake up, Kilmer. You don't even know what's real and what's fantasy anymore.

I was getting pretty fed up with the muses, and the radio didn't help. It was set on one of those easy-listening stations and Eydie Gormé was singing "Who's Sorry Now?" Just what I needed, background music with a sob in every note.

I lifted my foot and turned on the hot water with my toes and waited until I had to grit my teeth to stand it. The water was reaching the boiling point when I turned it off. That killed another fifteen minutes.

I needed to get a little perspective on things, separate what was real and what I wanted to be real. I needed to be objective.

But that's not what I did. What I did was think about that place at the base of her throat, the soft spot, the one where you can see the pulse beating. I used to stare at it and count the beats. I could tell when she started getting excited.

I thought about the way she closed her eyes and parted her lips about a quarter of an inch when I was about to kiss her. She had the softest lips. You could get buried in those lips. I never felt her teeth. I don't know how she did it. Her lips were as soft as a down quilt.

Three years, that's how long I had waited, watching her grow from a fifteen-year-old tease to an eighteen-year-old woman, playing the brother-sister act when they came up to Athens for football weekends. That was to appease Chief. When she was about sixteen, her good-bye kisses started getting softer. And longer.

Talk about strung out.

Get off it, Kilmer. Think about something else. Details, concentrate on details. And events. Reality is what we're after here.

I concentrated on her eighteenth-birthday party. It came to me in flashes, like a movie when the film breaks and they lose a few frames.

She wouldn't let me see her all that day. The way she acted, you'd have thought it was her wedding day. About midmorning Chief, Teddy, and I went to the Findley office on Factors' Walk. It was part of the ritual when we came down for the weekend, going to the office on Saturday morning. We had to wear ties and sports jackets, setting an example so the workers wouldn't get the feeling that they could take it easy because it was the weekend. Chief was big on setting examples. The office was only open half a day, so the employees thought they were getting a break. "Gives us four hours' jump on the competition come Monday morning,"

Chief said with a wink. He winked a lot for emphasis, a habit Teddy had picked up.

He'd always pull off some kind of deal, usually on the phone, just to show us how it was done. When he was wheeler-dealing, his left eye would close about halfway. Teddy called it the Evil Eye. When the Eye started to narrow, watch out, he was on to something, closing in for the kill. It's one of the things the rich inherited, that predatory sense. I guess that's why they're rich—they have a built-in instinct for the jugular.

I never got a true handle on the business. They were into everything. Cotton, shipping, real estate, industry, farming, you name it. All it did was bedazzle the hell out of me. I don't think Teddy got into it either. He was more interested in hell-raising. And poon. That's what he called it, poon. "Let's go down to the beach, Junior, check out the poon."

I got another flash. On that particular morning the office was closed in honor of Doe's eighteenth birthday. When we got there, the janitor let us in and we went up to the third floor. I always loved that building. It was all brass and oak and everything was oiled and polished so it sparkled.

Chief stood in his office, which seems now like it was maybe half the top floor. He stood there and swept his hand around.

"I'm going to divide this room up into three rooms, boys," he said. "I'll take this corner. One of you can have the river view; the other one, the park." Then he flipped a coin.

"Call it, Jake," he cried. I don't remember what I called. He covered the coin with his hand and peeked under it, looked up very slowly, and smiled at me. "You win, Jake. Take your choice, river or park?" I figured Teddy wanted the river and he had a right to it because it was obviously the choice view, so I picked the park.

And I remember Chief looking at me and that left eye narrowing down for just an instant, and then he said, "That's very generous of you, Jake."

The Evil Eye. Looking back on it, I think Chief saw that move as a sign of weakness. To him, it was winner take all.

The more I got into it, the faster and faster the flashes came. The way the place looked. Daisies all over Windsong, hundreds of them. And candles—my God, there must have been ten thousand candles. It was a fire hazard there were so many candles.

And people. Three hundred maybe, the top of the list. Black tie, a live orchestra, champagne, the works. Chief had seen to that. It's what you call taste, another thing the born rich inherit.

"I got to give you credit, Junior," Teddy had said as I was straightening his black tie. "Three years, man, you really stick in there."

Was that it? Was it a test?

Before the guests arrived, Chief took the two of us out onto the porch and popped a bottle of champagne and we stood there watching the sun go down. We drank a toast to Doe and threw our glasses at the big oak tree at the corner of the house.

"One more year, boys," Chief said. "And you'll be off to law school. The time'll fly. You'll be back here in business before you know it."

That was another part of the trap, Chief laying it all out for us that way, planning our lives. Only then it felt good. When you're on the inside, it always feels good. When he put his hand on my shoulder, there was lightning in his fingers. That's the way Chief was. That's the way all three of them were. They were Lightning People. You could feel their aura crackling around them.

"It's a helluva night, lads," he said. He didn't know the half of it.

It was dark and all the candles were lit and the guests were all assembled when she made her entrance. I still have trouble breathing when I think about that moment. My mouth gets dry and my hands shake thinking about her walking into the eerie candlelight, dressed in white, with a scarlet sash that tightened her waist and molded every magnificent line of her body. Talk about lightning. Everybody applauded when she came in. She went straight to Chief and kissed him. Chief always came first. Then she came to us and that soft spot was twitching like crazy and it was all I could do to keep my hands off her. It was like that all night. I couldn't get close enough to her. I guess I never will.

The party ended about three in the morning and we were all a little drunk from champagne. Teddy had latched on to this kind of dippy girl and the four of us piled into the dune buggy and drove out to the beach. He threw me the keys. He was in the back, working up a little poon. When we got in the car it was all Doe and I could do to keep our hands off each other. Well, we didn't. She leaned over and put her hand down inside of my thigh and wrapped her fingers around my knee and squeezed it hard and the electricity started humming.

When we got out there we took some dunes and spun around a few times in the moonlight. Teddy popped a bottle of champagne, shook it up, and used his thumb to squeeze off a stream of it. We were all soaked with champagne and the dippy girl jumped out and ran down to the surf and jumped in, clothes and all, Teddy right behind her. We drove off and left them there, clawing at each other in the surf.

And I remember Doe saying, "Stop soon, Jake. Please!" I never heard that tone in her voice before. Husky, with a lot of breath behind it. I topped a dune and slammed on the brakes and we tumbled out before the buggy was fully stopped. It rolled down to the bottom of the hill and stalled.

We were like animals freed from a cage. Touching, feeling, pulling. I found the soft spot in her throat and when I kissed it I could feel her heart beating in my mouth and she cried out and pulled her dress down and her breasts jumped free and I slid my lips down to her and opened my mouth as wide as I could and sucked her up into it, feeling her nipple grow hard under my tongue. Then her hands reached down and found me and she turned me sideways and began stroking me. Finally I unzipped the dress and slid it down over her feet and she hooked her thumbs in the sides of her panties and slid them off too. Then she helped me undress and we lay back for a minute and just stared at each other. Then there was more touching and pulling and stroking until finally I felt her open under my fingertips and she pulled me over on top of her and guided me into her, enveloping me, crushing me, devouring me with her soft muscles . . .

Nice going, Kilmer. That's putting it all in the proper perspective. Objective, right?

Sure.

SILVER-DOLLAR WOMAN

Oh, Jesus, just keep it in me!
Take it, take it all, baby.
Oh, God, don't stop!
You're all alike, can't get enough, can you, baby?
Never!

There . . .
More . . . oh, yes, MORE!
There . . .
What are you doing?
There . . .
Come on, you bastard, fuck me!
Hereitcomes, hereitcomes . . .
OH . . . ohoh, nownow, ohoh, nownow . . .
Here comes the fuckin' freight train!
Now . . . yes, now . . .
ONE potato, TWO potato, THREE potato, FOUR . . .
Oh, you . . . fucking . . . m-m-machine . . .
GodDAMN!
Don't stop now, oh, sweet Jesus, don't stop now!
Gonna . . . fuck you . . . dead . . . l-a-a-a-d-e-e-e
Oh . . . God . . . NOW!
Yeah.
NOW!
YEAH!
NOW . . .

Later . . .
I'm going to be sore for a week, you damn crazy . . .
Hey, you're the one keeps cryin' for more.
Yes. More.
Not enough anything for you, is there?
Not that.
Not just cock, ANYthing.
After tonight we'll have it all.
No such thing as ALL, baby. And no such thing as enough.
Fuck me again.
Gotta save up some spunk, lady. It's gonna be a long night.
When it's over . . .
We'll celebrate. I'll fuck your head off . . .
Promise?
You got it.
Crazy doin' it tonight.
When'll he be here?
Fifteen minutes.
That's takin' it to the edge.
I love it. Gimme a kiss.

Sure. So long, babe.

He caressed her throat with his thumbs, running them, side by side, from her collarbone up along her carotid to her chin and back and then again, and this time he pressed harder and her face bunched up.

Too hard . . .

Too late. His thumbs suddenly seemed to spasm, digging deep into both sides of her Adam's apple.

Her eyes bulged, her tongue shot out, quivering obscenely.

He pressed deeper. Something cracked. She gagged, fought, tried to scratch.

He stopped suddenly, straightened up, struck her sharply with two fingers in the temple, and her life blinked out.

He rolled her over in the bed, arranged her as if sleeping, killed the light, and went to the window.

Ten minutes. Two black limousines pulled up. Four men jumped out of the first limo, perused the street. Two of them entered the apartment house while the other two waited at the door.

Footsteps on the stairs, some muffled talk. He moved silently across the room and entered the closet.

One of the men inside opened the front door of the apartment house and nodded to the two outside and one of them ran to the second car and opened the rear door. A tall, chunky man, whose face indicated that he had once been thinner, got out and hustled into the apartment. One of the goons checked the second floor hallway and waved him in. He was nattily dressed in a dark blue blazer, tan gabardine pants, a pale blue shirt, and a dark striped tie. He climbed the stairs, nodded to the man by the door of the apartment, who went back down. The chunky man took out his key and let himself in.

The four men gathered just inside the front door of the apartment and started pitching silver dollars against the wall in the carpeted hallway.

The chunky man stood inside the doorway, looking at the woman on the bed, sleeping on her side, the bed a mess. He started getting hard, thinking about it. What a wanton bitch she was. He smiled and walked to the end of the bed and began to shake it very easily.

The closet door opened without a sound. The chunky man never heard anything until the whirrr of the rope as it whipped around his throat, then the sudden, awful vise around his neck. He reacted almost instantly.

Almost.

A leg wrapped around both his legs and he lost his balance and fell forward on the bed. He was thrashing, trying to break loose, but the vise tightened.

He began to jerk . . .

And jerk . . .

And jerk . . .

Downstairs in the hall, the boys pitching dollars could hear the bed-springs squeaking.

That Tony, he didn't waste no time.

Fuckin' bull. Go on, Ricky, pitch.

The silver dollar twinkled as it soared down the hall and hit the carpet and bounced against the wall.

And the winner sang:

"Yuh kin t'row a silver dollar, across thu floor,
It'll roo-ool, 'cause it's ro-ound,
Woman never knows what a good man she's got,
Until she lets him down."

27

BUSINESS AS USUAL

After I got out of the tub and dried off, I went in and lay down naked on the bed to cool off. I stared at the ceiling fan for a long time. Objectivity is a painful enterprise at best, and I had avoided it for twenty years. Now, as it grew dark outside, shadows stretched across the room like accusing fingers pointing at me. In the loneliness of the dark, romance wore off and reality took over. Other memories started coming back to me. The past began to materialize again, unfettered by candlelight and daisies. One face emerged from the harsh shadows and began to taunt me. It was Stonewall Titan.

I remembered Titan the night of the party, a little man, a shade under five five, who chose not to wear a tux, opting instead for his usual dark, three-piece winter suit, and arriving just minutes before Doe made her entrance.

More than once during the evening I caught him staring across the room at me with those agate eyes glittering in the candlelight. I didn't pay any attention to it at the time; it didn't seem important.

Mr. Stoney never smiled much anyway; he was a quiet man, constantly introspective or contemplative or both, not an uncommon demeanor for short people. But now, reflecting on it, it strikes me that it was a hard look, almost angry, as if I had offended him in some way.

After Doe came over and officially welcomed Teddy and me to her party, after she had taken my hand and almost squeezed my fingers off and then drifted off to greet the rest of the guests, I worked my way across the room and greeted the taut little man. He stared up at me and said, "You really stick to it, don't you, boy? Been waiting a long time for tonight."

"What do you mean?" I asked with a smile.

"Just don't count your chickens," he said, and moved away.

That was the end of it. A caustic remark which he never repeated again during the summer I spent with the Findleys. I had forgotten it. Looking back on the moment, it occurred to me that the little man probably thought me unworthy of the Findley dowry. And since that night seemed to be the end of my probation period, he apparently had been overruled. After that, I was treated more like family than ever before. But Stonewall Titan never warmed up to me, I presume because I had offended him by going the distance.

Was I really being tested during those years or was it just my paranoia, an excuse to back away from another emotional commitment, to remain disconnected, as Stick called it? None of this had occurred to me at the time. When you're nineteen or twenty years old and it's all going your way, you don't think about such things.

But now in the darkness of the room, my suspicions were stirred.

Was that it? Was it all part of the Findley test? Were Doe and Teddy part of that three-year probation during which they sized me up and checked me out for longevity, consistency, durability, loyalty, all the *important* things? Perhaps I had never passed the test at all. Perhaps they had seen in me some fatal flaw that I myself did not perceive, something more ominous than bad ankles, something that did not prevent Teddy from accepting me as his best friend, but precluded my becoming one of the Findley inheritors. Perhaps my blood had never been blue enough.

Wake up, Kilmer.

Lying there, I began to feel like a piece of flux caught between two magnets. One drew me toward Doe and Chief and the sweet life that might still be there. The other, toward the Taglianis of the world, which was, ironically, a much safer place to be. In a funny way, I trusted the Taglianis precisely because I knew I *couldn't* trust them and there was safety in that knowledge.

A lot of raw ends were showing. It scared me. It clouded my judgment. Dunetown was dangerous for me. It was opening me up. My Achilles' heel was showing.

The magnets were drawing me out of my safe places.

I lay there, immobilized, staring at the lazy ceiling fan until the room was totally dark. At five after nine the phone rang. It rang for a long time. At twenty after, it rang again. I didn't move. I lay there like a statue. I couldn't talk to her, not right then. At nine thirty it rang twelve times; I counted them. After that, every five minutes. At five of ten I heard a scratching at the door. It sounded like a cockroach crawling across a kitchen cabinet. I raised up on one elbow and looked over. There was a slip of paper under the door.

I picked it up and sat on the edge of the bed for a few minutes before I turned on the light. It was a phone message from Dutch Morehead.

Tony Logeto had made the list.

THE SINGING ROPE

It didn't take me five minutes to get dressed. As I hurried through the lobby toward the garage, the Black Maria roared into the motor lobby and screeched to a stop. The front door swung open and I crawled in. Stick dropped it into first and left an inch of rubber in the drive.

"I hope to hell the place isn't far," I moaned.

"Ten minutes," he said, putting the red light on the top of the car and flicking on the siren. It was the longest ten minutes of my life. We boomed south along the river, where late-returning shrimp boats were reduced to streaks of light.

The place was near Back O'Town, a row house that had been converted into pleasant apartments facing the small river they called Hampton Run. Flat roof, fancy front door; a classy-looking place. There were a lot of police cars parked haphazardly in the narrow street in front.

Cowboy Lewis was standing by the door, looking very unhappy.

"I fucked up," he said tightly. "They got by me."

"Who got by you, Cowboy?" I asked.

"Whoever did them in," he said, looking at my feet.

"Them?" Stick said.

"There's two of 'em," he said, jabbing a thumb over his shoulder toward the building. "Second floor in the front."

"Who else?" I asked as we headed for the door.

"Della Norman," he said.

A new name!

"Should that mean something to me?" I asked.

"She was Longnose Graves' favorite lady," said Stick.

"Yeah, but she was in bed with Logeto when he got hit," Lewis added.

I whistled through my teeth.

The mess was in a second-floor bedroom.

"The singing rope," I said, looking at the man's neck.

Dutch's "Huh?" told me he had never heard of the trick.

"That's what the Vietnamese call it, the singing rope. A knock-off of the Thuggee knot."

It was also known among the British as the Bombay Burke—Bombay because the Thuggee stranglers operated in India, Burke being British slang for strangulation, named after an Englishman who tried to kill Queen Victoria, failed, and had his neck stretched for his trouble.

It had been more than a dozen years since I had last seen that particular kind of bruise. It was blood red and about the size of a half dollar, in the soft place at the base of Logeto's skull on the back of his neck. The deep, gnarled, bloody ring around his throat filled in the picture.

"Anybody else here?" Stick asked Dutch.

"Salvatore," Dutch answered. "He's out checking the neighborhood."

"I haven't seen a mark like that since Nam," I said.

"Beautiful. What in hell next?" said the weary lieutenant.

Cowboy Lewis filled the doorway, the handle of a Cobra .357 looming from the front of his pants, right over the fly.

"If that goes off accidentally, you're gonna have to change your name," Dutch said. Lewis didn't say anything. "Okay," said Dutch, "let's have the long and short of it."

"It's SOP, Logeto coming over here. It's every Monday night, rain or shine, six o'clock or close to it. He usually stays an hour, hour and a half. He had two limos and four shooters. He goes in, the four goons start pitching coins in the hall. Two hours later the mark's still there. About eight thirty I started getting nervous. Finally I decided to take the door, have a look."

"By yourself, with four gorillas between you and Logeto? That don't call for backup in your book?" Dutch demanded.

Cowboy shrugged. "I had buckshot loads in the Magnum. I go in, start up the stairs, get some shit, show the cannon. 'You wanna get picked up in a dustpan, fuck around' is all I told 'em. I put my ear against the door, give a call or two. Nothin'. So I kicked it in."

He swung his arm casually around the room, indicating what he had found.

The bed looked like a plowed field. Covers and sheets half on the floor, pillows on head and foot. The woman lay on her side naked, her hair sprawled across her face. Logeto was on his face, fully dressed, both fists clutching the sheets, his feet hanging off the bed but not quite touching the floor.

"So that's Della Norman," I said. Even in death, you could tell she was a dish.

"Apeshit," Stick said.

"He means Longnose ain't gonna handle this too well," Dutch said, and shook his head ruefully. "A new wrinkle," he went on. "What in hell was Tony Logeto doin', shacked up with the Nose's favorite lady?"

The arrival of Chess, the ME, broke his thought train. Chess was short and on the tubby side, wearing old pants and a pajama top stuffed half in and half out of his pants. He was not too happy about being there.

"And who do we have here?" he asked.

"Tagliani's son-in-law and Longnose Graves' girlfriend."

Chess looked up with a lascivious grin. "Isn't that interesting," he said. "It's the best part of the job, y'know, the inside stuff. I wonder how Longnose is going to take this."

"Badly," Stick chimed in.

Chess put down his black satchel. "Ladies first. Let's get some pictures before I mess things up."

The photographer appeared, shot the room top and bottom, and was gone in ten minutes. The doc stepped in and started his work, jabbering continually as he did.

"We got a simple strangulation here, on the woman. From the front I'd say. See the thumbprints here on her larynx. Death was quick. My guess's her carotid, jugular, the whole shooting match in her throat is crushed. Powerful set of hands at work here."

He kept probing, talking while studying the corpse.

"You gotta slow down there, Dutch. The freezer downtown is full and we don't have but five people in pathology and I got a vacation comin' up in three months. It would be nice to be finished by then."

"Ho, ho, ho," Dutch said, his sense of humor wearing thin, as was all of ours.

I looked around the apartment while the ME continued his work. It occupied the front side of the building. The living room, bedroom, and kitchen all faced the street. The place was decorated in early nothing. Expensive furniture that didn't go together. Her closet had enough clothes in it to start a salon.

The bathroom and several closets were adjacent to an alley that ran along the side of the building. There was only one door into the apartment, the one we had all come in through.

I ambled into the bathroom. It was large, with a double sink, commode, step-in tub, and stall shower.

The window over the commode was open and the curtains shifted idly in the breeze. I took a look out.

Straight up to the roof, straight down to the street.

I went back to the scene of the crime.

A new face had appeared. His name was Braun, out of homicide, a short, slender, hawk-faced man with age spots on the backs of his hands and dark hair turning white.

Braun said in a nasal voice, "I hear, Dutch, that you're planning to retire tomorra. There won't be anything left for you t'do."

Dutch said, "Don't make me laugh too hard, I'll wet my pants."

"How many is this between last night and tonight?" Braun asked, continuing to needle the big man. "Got enough for a football game yet?"

"Just do yer job, okay, Braun? Leave the comedy to Bob Hope."

The homicide cop looked down at Della Norman.

"Lookit that spook's tits. Bet there was some good pussy went through the window when she blinked out."

"You want maybe we should all step out in the hall for a minute or two while you get a little?" Dutch chided.

"Up yours," Braun said.

All class.

Chess finished his work on the woman and turned to Logeto.

"What've we got here?" Chess said. "Looks as though there's been a hangin'."

"Jake here says this job looks like an old Vietnam trick called the singin' string or something."

"D'they learn it on *The Lawrence Welk Show*?" Braun asked.

"It's called the singing rope," I corrected. "The way it works, you take a rope, tie a knot halfway down it, and tie a small stick in the end. The Arvies would come up behind their target, whip the rope around his throat, catch the stick, and twist. The knot pops the main nerve in the back of the neck and paralyzes the mark. After that, all it takes is about sixty seconds or so to finish the job."

"You like havin' the Feds do yer thinkin' fer yuh?" Braun asked.

Cowboy Lewis made a growling sound deep in his throat and balled up his fists. Dutch laid a gentle hand on the big man's shoulder.

"Anybody touch anything up here?" Chess asked.

The Cowboy shifted from one foot to the other.

"I used toilet paper when I phoned it in. No prints," Cowboy said.

"Excellent, m'boy. I see you teach them right," Chess said to Dutch.

"Yeah, all yuh gotta do now's teach 'em to talk," Braun said.

"Cowboy, g'downstairs, see what you can shake outta those dago coin-tossers," Dutch said, probably saving Braun a trip to intensive care. When Lewis was gone, Dutch said to Braun, "What's your problem, putz?"

"You and your special headquarters and shit," said Braun. "So far looks t'me like all you've done is fuck up."

"You make a lot of noise for somebody with six unsolved murders in his lap," Dutch said.

Braun said, "We got enough bodies downtown for one night."

"Braun, you cry too much. You can't see straight through all the tears," Dutch said.

"Fuck you," Braun said.

Tension crackled in the room. Chess broke up the witty repartee.

"Well," he said, "if you two Shirley Temples are tired of goosin' each other, I'd like to get this pair down on a slab and start work."

"It ain't my beat anymore," Dutch said. "I get 'em alive, putz here gets 'em dead."

"What's your guess about the time, Doc?" I interjected, hoping to ease things a little.

"I'd guess—and I'm guessing, remember, don't hold me to this—I'd guess they were both killed close together, the girl first. Three to four hours ago, give or take."

It was ten thirty-five.

The ME turned Logeto's body over and the dead mobster lay on his back, staring sightlessly at the ceiling with his tongue stretched out of his mouth. The corpse was nattily dressed. His tie wasn't even loose.

An idea or two began to brew in my head.

I ambled out into the hall, found the stairs to the roof, and climbed up them. The door to the roof was unlocked. I checked it out, looking down to the open bathroom window and giving the brick wall a close check. There were three grooves in the ledge above Della Norman's bathroom window.

As I came back down I saw the Stick talking to one of the four coin-tossers, a weasel-faced little hood who stood sideways, looking off down the street someplace as he spoke, as if the Stick were not there.

Stick finally nodded and left his stoolie, entering the building and joining me on the second floor.

"I got sidetracked," he said. "That little shit I was talking to, his brother's in the dock waiting to be sentenced for pushing. He's hoping I'll go to bat, get the bastard a reduced sentence. But he doesn't know shit about what happened and neither do the other three. What he says, Logeto came here at six fifteen. They saw him go into the girl's apartment, which is usual for Monday night. They heard some bedsprings rattling a coupla minutes later, figure Logeto was so horny he jumped right to it. They made a couple of jokes, then pitched dollars until Cowboy Lewis showed up and busted in."

"Go take a look inside."

We went back into the apartment together. Della Norman's body was already wrapped up and on a stretcher. The ambulance lads worked a body bag over Logeto's feet and wheeled both bodies out. Braun followed them into the hall and Dutch, Stick, and I were alone in the room.

"What's this bit about them getting Burked?" Dutch asked. "What's that all about?"

Stick said. "I saw this once downcountry. The CRIPS used it. Silent and quick."

"What's a CRIP?"

"Combined Recon and Intelligence Platoons. They were kind of the army's on-the-spot Green Berets. Only they didn't have the training. They recruited everybody. Guys in the brig, misfits, old French Legionnaires, mercenaries, people who didn't want to come back after their tour was up. Basically they were assassination squads. Send 'em out, kill a village leader or a tax collector, some rebel leader who's getting a little muscle. Like that."

Morehead shook his head. "Different kind of army," he said.

"You were in the army?" said Stick.

"Korea. Foot soldier. Sixteen months," the big German said. "You remember Korea, boys? Nowadays most people think Korea's the name of an all-night grocery stand."

"Poor old Della," the Stick said. "Why would anybody want to ice her?"

"What about her?" I asked.

He shrugged. "Della and I got along. I had occasion to bust her once. A pot charge. It was just a fishing expedition, see if maybe we could turn up something on Nose. She figured it out and took it like a sport."

"Wonder what Logeto was doing with her."

"Maybe she was just a good piece of ass," the Stick conjectured. "Wasn't he supposed to be the Taglianis' resident cocksman?"

"That's a simple enough explanation," Dutch said.

I was barely listening. I was too busy wondering how Logeto and Della Norman had been killed without being seen or heard by four goons at the foot of the stairs.

"I can think of one reason Della was killed," I said.

"We're holding our breath," said Dutch.

I did some verbal logic, to hear what the ideas sounded like:

"Logeto came here every Monday night. Whoever killed him knew that, knew what time he usually came, and he or she also knew that there was a lot of heat on. Getting past Logeto's bodyguards wouldn't be easy. So what's the answer? Come in first and kill the girl. Killer knew Logeto would come in alone; he's too macho to have his boys sweep the place first. So he or she killed the girl and then waited. When Logeto came in, the killer Burked him. Logeto never made a sound."

"Then he or she dusted off through the bathroom using a dropline," Stick finished.

"Except they went up, not down," I said. "And got away across to the roof next door so they wouldn't be seen from the ground."

"That's probably how he got in," Stick said. "Went down the line, killed them both, then went back up."

"Beautiful planning," I said.

Dutch chewed that over for a moment or two. "Yeah, I don't have a problem with that. Got a lot of guts, acing out a mobster with four of his handymen pitching coins in the hallway below."

"Yeah. Or desperate," I said.

"Desperate?"

"Yeah. Either somebody with more guts than Moses or somebody who can't afford *not* to get it done."

Dutch said, "In that case, if it's Nance doing this number for Chevos, that leaves only Costello, Bronicata, Stizano, O'Brian, and Cohen left."

"Five to go," said Stick.

Dutch was leaning against the wall of the apartment with his hands stuffed deep in his pockets.

"It's the full moon," he said woefully. "Pregnant women have babies, men go apeshit. What can I tell yuh."

"That's good," the Stick said. "That's what we'll tell the papers, that it was the full moon."

29

DISAWAY

I went back to the hotel and went to bed.

The phone rang several times during the night. How many times, I couldn't tell you. Finally I put it on the floor, threw a pillow over it, and died. The next thing I knew, someone was trying to knock down my door. I flicked on the lamp, struggled into a pair of pants, and found Pancho Callahan standing on the threshold.

"Change in plans" was all he said.

"Huh?" was all I could muster.

"Tried to call," he said.

"Appreciate it," I mumbled, and started back to bed.

"Going out to the track," he said in his abbreviated patois.

"What, now?"

"Yep."

"What time is it?"

"Five."

"In the morning!"

"Yep."

"Tuesday morning?"

"Tuesday morning."

I stared bleakly at him. He looked like a page out of *GQ* magazine. Gray cotton trousers, a tattersall vest under a blue linen blazer, pale blue shirt, a wine tie with delicate gray horses galloping aimlessly down its length, and a checkered cap, cocked jauntily over one eye.

He didn't look any more like a cop than John Dillinger looked like the Prince of Wales.

"Not on your life," I croaked.

He put his hand gently on the door.

"Gonna be a great day."

I was too tired to argue.

"Smashing."

At exactly 5:15 we were in a red sports car with more gadgets than an F104, heading out into a damp, musty morning. As we crossed the tall suspension bridge to the mainland, we picked up fog so thick I couldn't see the shoulder of the road. Callahan, a tall, muscular chap, with high cheekbones and a hard jaw that looked like it might have been drawn with a T-square, chose to ignore it. He drove like it was a sunny afternoon on the interstate. I was beginning to think the whole bunch was suicidal.

"Foggy" was the only word out of him during the twenty-minute trip. Not a mention of the previous night's events.

He eased back on the throttle when we reached the entrance to Palmetto Gardens, tossed a jaunty salute to the guard, who had to look twice to see him through the soup, and parked near the stables.

"Here, pin this on your jacket," he said, handing me a green badge that identified me as a track official. I did as I was told and followed him to the rail, which popped out of the damp haze so suddenly I bumped into it. So far, all I could tell about the track was that it was in Georgia and about twenty minutes from town, if you drove like Mario Andretti.

"Wait here," Callahan said, and disappeared for five minutes. I could hear, but not see, horses snorting, men coughing, laughter, and the clop of hoofs on the soft earth as I stood in fog so thick

I couldn't see my own feet. When Callahan returned, he brought black coffee in plastic foam cups and warm, freshly made sinkers. I could have kissed him.

"What the hell are we doing out here?" I asked, around a mouthful of doughnut.

"Workin' three-year-olds," he answered.

"That's it? That's what we're doing here in the middle of the night? Listening to them work the three-year-olds?"

"So far."

"Is this something special? How often do they do this?"

"Every morning."

"You're shitting me."

He looked at me through the fog and shook his head.

"You're not shitting me. Great. I got dragged out of bed for, uh . . . to stand around in this . . . this *gravy* listening . . . just *listening* . . . to a bunch of nags doing calisthenics."

Callahan turned to me and smiled for the first time. "Flow with it, pal. You're here, enjoy it. Put a little poetry back in your soul."

"What are you, some kind of guru, Callahan?"

"Horse sense. Besides, Dutch says you need to learn about the track."

"I can't even see the track. And don't call me pal. I'm not a dog, my name's Jake."

"Sure."

He moved down the rail and I followed. Dim shapes began to take form in the fog. The outriders were leading their riderless charges through an opening in the fence and out onto the track.

"This is the morning workout," Callahan said. "Gets the kinks out of the ponies." He pointed to a stately-looking cinnamon-brown gelding, frisky and hopping about at the end of its tether. "Keep your eye on that boy there," he advised.

"What about him?" I asked.

"That's one fine horse."

"Oh."

"If you don't mind my asking," he said, "just how much do you know about racing?"

I had been to the horse races twice in my life, both times out in California with Cisco Mazzola, who loved three things in life: his family, vitamins, and betting the ponies, and I'm not real sure in what order. Both times I had lost a couple of hundred dollars I couldn't afford to lose, making sucker bets. After that, Cisco stopped inviting me.

I said, "I know the head from the tail and that's about the size of it."

"That's okay," Callahan said, although he seemed surprised at my ignorance. "Keep your ears open, I will give you the course."

Before the day was out, I was to learn a lot about Pancho Callahan and a lot more about racing, for he talked to me constantly and it was like listening to a poet descibe a beautiful woman.

"First, I will tell you a little about Thoroughbreds," he said. "Thoroughbreds are different from all other animals. Thoroughbreds are handsome, hard, spooky, temperamental. They are independent and proud. And they are also conceited as hell because, see, they *know* how good they are. The jockey, if he is worth his weight, he takes his kid in tow and he talks to him and he disciplines him around the track. The trainer may tell the jock how he wants him to run the race, like maybe hold the pony in until the backstretch or let him loose at the five-eighths pole or the clubhouse turn, like that, but once that gate opens up, it is just the jock and the horse and that is what it's all about."

In the fog, with the sun just beginning to break behind the large water oaks nearby, we could hear the horses but not see them until they were on top of us. The three-year-old gelding was frisky and playful and the outrider was having trouble with him. He was snorting and throwing his long neck across the saddlehorn of the outrider and trying to bite his hand as they galloped past in the fog, which was eerily magenta in the rising sun's first light.

It was one hell of a sight. Callahan was right, there was poetry here.

The three-year-old was to become a lot more important than either Callahan or I realized then. His name was Disaway. And on this particular morning, he wanted to run.

"He is full of it," Callahan said. "A real Thoroughbred feeling frisky. Is that a sight?"

I allowed as how it was a sight.

"Thoroughbreds are trained to break fast out of the gate and open up and run quickly and flat away to the finish line, save up a little extra and put it on hard near the end, like a swimmer doing the two twenty," Callahan said. "This horse wants to go, so they have to calm him down a bit. Otherwise he will be too brash and spooky when the rider is up."

So they were not running hard and instead were trotting in and out of the cotton wads of fog, working out the early morning kinks. When they brought him in, he made one more halfhearted effort to bite the outrider and then, hopping slightly sideways, he kicked his heels a couple of times and settled down. The trainer led him to the tie-up to be saddled.

Disaway was a fine-looking animal with very strong front legs and a sweat-shiny chest, hard as concrete. The muscles were quivering and ready. Callahan walked close and stroked first one foreleg, then the other, then strolled back to the rail.

No comment.

The owner was a short, heavy man in a polo shirt with a stopwatch clutched in a fat fist and binoculars dangling around his neck. His name was Thibideau. He stood with his back to the jockey, chewing his lip. When he spoke, his voice was harsh and sounded like it was trapped deep in his throat.

"Okay," he said, without turning around or looking at the rider, "let's see what he can do. You open him up at the three-quarter post."

The exercise rider looked a little surprised and then said, "The three-quarter, yes, sir."

They threw the saddle over the gelding's back, all the time talking to him and gentling him, and got ready to let him out.

"All these characters are interested now," Callahan said. "The track handicappers, the owners, the trainers, the railbirds—all standing by to see just how much horse he is today."

The exercise rider led the gelding out onto the track, lined him up, and then, standing straight up in the stirrups and leaning far over the horse's mane, egged him on until he stretched out his long legs and took off down the track into the fog. Half a dozen stopwatches clicked in unison somewhere in the mist.

I could hear him coming long before he burst through the haze, snorting like an engine, his hoofs shaking the earth underfoot. Then, pow! he came out of it and thundered past us, his head up and his mane waving like a flag. The watches clicked again. Callahan looked at the chronograph on his wrist.

Still no comment.

"Let's get some breakfast," he said. "The jockeys'll be showing up about now."

I watched Disaway as they led him out to be hosed and squeegeed down and fed. His nostrils were flared open, his ears standing straight up and slightly forward, and there was a look of defiant madness in his eyes. I was beginning to understand why Pancho had a thing about Thoroughbreds.

"Well, what do you think?" I asked as we walked down the shedrows.

"About what?"

"What was all that about, feeling the horse's legs, the stopwatches, all the inside track stuff?"

"Well, he's not a bad kid," Callahan said as we walked through the dissipating fog. "He's strong, good bloodlines, has good legs, but he's a mudder. He just does okay on the fast track. If I were a betting man I'd put my money on him to show. He's about half a length short of a champion."

"You got all that from feeling his forelegs?"

"I got all that from reading the racing form."

As we walked past the shedrows and headed across a dirt road toward the jockeys' cafeteria, I saw a dark blue Mercedes, parked near the stables. It was empty. I looked around, trying not to be obvious, but the fog was still too heavy to see anybody farther away than twenty feet.

"Old Dracula's here," Callahan said.

"Dracula?"

"Raines. The commissioner."

"You don't like him?" I found myself hoping Callahan would say no.

"Runs a tight operation. Like him a lot better if he had blood in his veins. One cold piece of work. That's his wife right over there."

It caught me by surprise. I turned quickly, getting a glimpse of Doe through the fog, talking nose to nose with a horse in one of the stables. Then the mist swirled back around her and she vanished.

"Let's mosey to the commissary," Callahan said. "Grab some groceries. Listen to the jocks and trainers."

I didn't know Callahan well, but he was acting like a man who's on to something.

The fog had lifted enough for me to see the contours of the cafeteria, a long, low clapboard building. The dining room was a very pleasant, bright room that smelled of fresh coffee and breakfast. It was about half-filled with track people: jocks, trainers, owners, handicappers, exercise riders, stewards. The talk was all horses. Mention Tagliani to this group, they'd want to know what race he was in and who was riding him.

I stayed close to Callahan, ordered a breakfast that would have satisfied a stevedore, and listened. Callahan was as tight with these people as a fat man's hand in a small glove. He talked to the track people from one side of his mouth and me from the other:

"The little guy with the hawk nose and no eyes, that's Johnny Gavilan. Very promising jock until he took a bad spill at Delray a couple years ago. Turned trainer . . ."

Or:

"The little box in the coat and cap is Willie the Clock, the track handicapper. He works for the track and sets the beginning odds for each race. Knows more about horses than God and he's just as honest . . ."

Or:

"The guy in the red sweater, no hair, that's Charlie Entwhistle. A great horse breeder. Started out as a trainer, then won this horse called Justabout in a poker game. At first it was a joke because old Justabout was just about the ugliest animal God ever created. He had no teeth. He'd stand around the paddock munching away on his gums and from the front he looked bowlegged. People would come down to the paddock, stick their tongues out at him, throw things at him, laugh at him. The Toothless Terror they called him, and he didn't look like he could beat a fat man around the track.

"Everybody was laughing at Charlie Entwhistle.

"But it turns out there's only one thing Justabout was any good for, and that was running. He not only loved to run, he couldn't stand for anything to be in front of him. Brother, could that kid run. He was home in bed before the rest of the field got to the wire. He rewrote the record books, made Sunday school teachers out of a lot of horseplayers, and he made old Charlie Entwhistle rich."

Callahan looked at me and smiled.

"And that's what horse racing's all about."

We had finished breakfast, and he picked up his coffee. "Now let's go to work," he said, and we moved toward the other side of the room.

"Just listen," Callahan said as we drew fresh cups of coffee, though I hadn't so much as cleared my throat for the last thirty minutes.

"Every day of the season, Willie the Clock judges the top three horses in each race and sets the opening odds. His choice is printed in the program as a service to the bettors. No guarantees, of course, but that doesn't matter. The players are always pissed at him. He's maybe the best handicapper in the business, but it's a thankless damn job."

"Why?"

"Because favorites lose more than they win. They get a bad break out of the gate or get caught in a traffic jam in the backstretch and can't find a slot. Here comes a long shot paying thirty to one and the players yell 'boat race.' Everybody wants to lynch Willie."

We sat down next to the square little man, who was about sixty, had a face the texture of weatherbeaten wood, wore the same coat, rain or shine, winter or summer, and had a black cap pulled down hard over his eyes. His binoculars were as big as he was. He didn't talk much and was very cautious about his clipboard, which is where all his information was scribbled.

He peered suspiciously from under the peak of his cap, recognized Callahan, gave him what I assume passed for a smile for Willie, and scowled at me.

"This's Jake, Willie," said Callahan. "He's on our side." Willie grunted and returned to his breakfast.

"What's lookin' good?" Callahan asked.

The little man shrugged and ate awhile longer. We sipped coffee while Callahan eyeballed the room. He nudged me once and nodded toward a wiry little guy, obviously a jockey, who came into the restaurant and sat by himself in a corner. The newcomer didn't look a day over fifteen and wouldn't have weighed a hundred pounds in a diving suit.

"Ginny's Girl looks good in the fifth," Willie said finally, then closed up for another five minutes. Callahan didn't press but finally said, "How about Disaway?"

Willie looked at him from the corner of his eye.

"Something special?" he asked.

Callahan shrugged. "Just wondering, y'know, after he dozed off in the stretch Sunday."

"He's lookin' fair."

Another minute or so of silence, then:

"Not too crazy this morning; clocked out at 3:22. Not bad since they opened him up at the three-quarter and he's usually a stretch runner . . ."

He washed down a piece of dry toast with a gulp of black coffee, searched for something in the corner of his mouth with a forefinger, then added:

"Track gets a little harder later in the day, he may tiptoe around. Right now I'd say he's a toss-up to place behind Polka Dits, who was kinda wild at the workout."

"Talk at ya," Callahan said, and we moved on again.

"You get all that?" he asked when we were a respectable distance from Willie.

"I think so," I said. "If the track's hard, Disaway'll probably fold in the stretch again. If it stays soft, he could come in second."

"Very good. You're learning."

"The little guy you gave me the nudge on," I said. "What was that all about?"

"That's Scoot Impastato. Out of Louisiana. Started racing quarter horses when he was thirteen. Moved up to Thoroughbreds when he was sixteen, if you believe his birth certificate. He's a seasoned jockey, great legs, magic hands, and he's all of twenty, soakin' wet."

"Very impressive," I said. "So why the nudge?"

"He was riding Disaway on Sunday," Callahan said, and headed toward the little guy.

The jockey, Scoot Impastato, was a man in a child's body, with a voice that sounded like it was still trying to decide whether it was going to change or not. Right now it was kind of low choirboy. But the boy had hands made of stainless steel.

"Hey, Mr. Callahan," he said as we sat down.

"How they runnin', Scoot?" Callahan asked.

"So-so," the youngster answered. "You know how it goes—some days it don't pay to answer the call."

"Still upset about the race Sunday?" Callahan said. He was

fishing. I don't know much about horse racing but I know fishing when I hear it.

The kid chuckled. "Which one?" he asked. "I was up four times and I ran out of the money four times." He seemed to be taking it in stride.

"Well, maybe it was some little thing, y'know, maybe you handled them a little different than usual and they got pissed. You know Thoroughbreds."

He laughed aloud. "I oughta," he said. He poured half his cup of coffee into an empty water glass and filled the cup with cream until it looked like weak chocolate milk, the way New Orleanians like it.

He added some sugar and kept talking as he stirred it up. "Once at Belmont I was up on Fancy Dan, fifty wins in two seasons, the horse couldn't lose. He went off a three-to-two favorite. The bell rings, the gate pops, he just stands there! I'm whackin' him with the bat, I'm bootin' hell outta him, I'm cussin' him, I'm sweet-talkin' him. He ain't goin' nowhere, he just stands there lookin' at the crowd and smellin' the grass. For all I know, he's still standin' there."

"So what happened with Disaway?"

Definitely fishing.

"Crapped out," he said with an aimless shrug. "He came outta that three stall like Man O' War and led the pack all the way around the backstretch; then we come into the clubhouse and all of a sudden he starts fallin' asleep on me. Midnight Star comes by like we was stopped for gas, then half the field passes us. I guess he just decided to walk home. I was yellin' at him just to keep him awake."

"How'd he look in the morning workout?"

"Fine. Not too spooky. Ran good. Two-tenths ahead of his usual speed."

"Well," Callahan said, "at least he got out of the gate."

"Sunday was like that. Seems every horse I rode wanted to be someplace else for the day. Well, it's Thoroughbreds for you, like you said."

His breakfast came. Steak, three eggs, and grits, and he dove in. I wondered how he stayed so small. Callahan kept fishing.

"You up on Disaway today?"

"Nope. No more. Got me another ride. Chigger Bite."

"How come?"

"Me and Smokey had it out. After the race he starts chewin' my ass for lettin' Disaway out early. Finally I says, 'Hey, it wasn't me, it was Mr. Thibideau,' and he looks at me like he thinks maybe I'm lyin' or somethin'. Who needs that shit anyways? The owner says let him loose at the five-eighths, I let him loose at the five-eighths." And he laughed again. "Maybe he thought the seven-eighths pole was the wire." He kept talking while he ate. "It ain't like it was some big surprise. Hell, we been talkin' about it. Mr. Thibideau wanted to try a change-up, letting him out at the five-eighths 'stead of the stretch, maybe cut a coupla tenths off his time. He just didn't have anything left for the stretch. Anyways, I never argue with the owners."

"You didn't disagree with Thibideau, then?"

"Not out loud. Hell, he comes up just before post time, tells me boot him on the backstretch, and that's what I did. I just figure you want to try a change-up, why do it when you're the favorite? I'd rather wait until we're not on the board—nothin' to lose that way."

"Well, he probably had his reasons."

"Afterwards he comes up, says he's sorry, and gives me a double century, make up for the purse. 'I made a mistake' is all he says."

"He had the exercise boy break him out at the three-quarters again this morning," Callahan said casually over his coffee cup.

"Disaway's a marginal. Put him in a field with a bunch of heavyweights he might pull in third if he's feeling just right, it's been raining, track's soft, like that. Give him a little mud, a slow field, he takes the money."

"Thibideau ought to handicap him a little better."

"Mr. Thibideau, he keeps tryin', y'know, hopin' the horse'll show a little more stamina. You wanna know what I think, the pony's a stretch runner. He don't have it to run wide open them last three furlongs. Also he was favoring his left front gam. Anyways, I got another ride."

"When was he favoring the leg?"

"Just after the race. Probably got a pebble in his shoe. I told Smokey about it."

"Well, good luck today," Callahan said, and we moved outside. The fog had burned off and left behind a beautiful day, with a cool breeze under a cloudless sky.

Callahan said, "That was probably Greek to you."

"I followed it pretty well. I just don't understand the drift of it all."

As we walked around the corner of the cafeteria, I got my first good look at the track and whistled between my teeth.

"Impressive, huh?" Callahan said.

Impressive was an understatement.

It sprawled out in the morning sun, a white structure framed against a forest of trees. It was three tiers high with cupolas on each end and a glass clubhouse that stretched from one end of the top floor to the other. The designer had modeled the building after Saratoga and other venerable tracks. It looked like it had been there for fifty years. There were azalea gardens to give it color and giant oak trees standing sentinel at its corners. Great care had obviously been taken to remove only those trees necessary. The parking lot even had freestanding oaks and pines breaking up the blacktop. It was a stunning sight and, I had to admit, a tribute to Harry Raines' taste. The clubhouse windows sparkled in the morning sun, and in the infield the grass was the color of emeralds.

"Wow!" I said.

"Some nice operation," Callahan agreed.

The Mercedes was gone.

I decided to get back to the subject at hand.

"Why are you so interested in Disaway?" I asked.

"He was two horse in the third race Sunday."

"Is that good luck or something?"

"Remember the tape Sunday night?"

"How could anybody forget it?"

"You forgot something," Callahan said. "Tagliani told Stinetto it was a fix for the four horse in the third heat."

"I still don't get the point."

"The four horse was Midnight Star. He went off as place favorite, eight to one, won, paid a bundle. The favorite was Disaway. Wasn't set up for Midnight Star to win, was set up for Disaway to lose. No sense any other way. Sunday, everything was A-one for him, up against a weak field, track was soft, he went off a five-to-two favorite. Strolled in eighth."

"Eighth!"

"It can happen. We all have bad days."

"So the trick was to slow Disaway down?" I said.

Callahan nodded. "Midnight Star romped first, paid $46.80. You bet Midnight Star, you got $46.80 for every two bucks you put down. Figure it out, bet a thousand bucks, go home with $23,400 smackers—not a bad day's work. My way of thinking, Disaway wasn't just having a bad day Sunday."

"Supposing Midnight Star had a bad day?"

Callahan smiled. "That's horse racing," he said.

"How did they do it? Make him lose, I mean?"

"Lots of ways. Legal ways."

"You think the jockey was in on it?"

"Maybe, not likely. Scoot doesn't like Thibideau or the trainer. He's a straight-up kid; like to think it wasn't him."

"How about the trainer?"

"Smokey? Maybe again, but he was pissed because he thought the boy booted the horse early. Didn't know Thibideau told him to."

"So that makes it the owner?"

"Looks that way. Thing is, Tagliani knew about it. Tagliani got wasted couple of hours later. Maybe there's no connection, but got to think about the possibilities."

"So what do we do about it, go to Raines?"

"Can't. Illegal wiretap. Dutch can't afford to have anybody know about it. No tape, all we got's guesswork."

"So we forget it?"

"I don't forget it," he said ominously. "Happens once, it'll happen again."

INVITATION

I was tired of the track and anxious to get back to town. There were a lot of loose ends that needed tying up and I suddenly felt out of touch with things. It was pushing noon, so I told Callahan I needed to make a phone call or two and then I'd grab a cab back to town.

"Stick's on his way out," Callahan said. "Back gate, fifteen minutes."

"How do you know that?" I asked, wondering whether Callahan was psychic in addition to his other talents.

"Arranged it last night," he said, and added in his cryptic dialogue, "Due at the clubhouse. See ya."

"Thanks for the education," I said.

Callahan stood for a moment appraising me and then nodded. "Disaway runs again Thursday afternoon. Ought to be here."

"It's a date," I said.

He started to leave, then turned back around and offered me his hand. "You're okay," he said. "Like a guy who listens. Thought maybe you'd turn out to be a know-everything."

"What I don't know would fill the course."

"You know plenty," he said, turning and heading across the infield toward the clubhouse.

I went looking for a phone to check the hotel for messages. By daylight, I had started having second thoughts about the night before. I knew some of the phone calls had been from Dutch. I wondered whether any of them had been Doe calling.

I was walking past the stables when I heard her voice.

"Jake?"

The voice came from one of the stalls. I peered inside but saw nothing, so I went in cautiously. I could hear a horse grumbling and stomping his foot and the pungent odor of hay and manure tickled my nose, but my eyes were slow adjusting to the dark stable after leaving the bright sunlight.

"Are you going blind in your old age?" she said from behind me. I turned around and she was standing in the doorway, framed against the brash sunlight, like a ghost. My eyes gradually picked out details. She was all dolled up in jodhpurs, a Victorian blouse with a black bow tie, and a little black derby. Twenty years vanished, just like that. She looked eighteen again, standing there in that outfit, scratching her thigh with her riding crop. My knees started bending both ways. I felt as awkward as a schoolboy at his first dance.

"You could have called," she chided, as if she were scolding a kid for stealing cookies.

"I got tied up," I said.

She came over to me and ran the end of the riding crop very gently down the edge of my jaw and down my throat, stopping at that soft depression where the pulse hides.

"I can see your heart beating," she said.

"I don't doubt it for a moment."

"Can you forgive me?"

"For what?"

"Twenty years ago?"

"There's nothing to forgive," I lied. "Those things happen."

She shook her head slowly and moved closer. "No," she said, "there's a lot to forgive. A lot to forget, if you can forget that kind of thing."

"What kind of thing?"

"You know what I'm talking about," she said evasively.

"Look, Doe, I . . ."

She put the tip of the crop against my lips, cutting off the sentence.

"Please don't say anything. I'm afraid you're going to say something I don't want to hear."

I didn't know how to answer that, so I just stood there like a fool, grinning awkwardly, wondering if we could be seen from outside the stall. If we could, it didn't seem to concern her. She stepped even closer, put the riding crop behind my neck, and, holding it with both hands, drew me closer. Her mouth opened a hair, her eyes narrowed.

"Oh, God, I'm so sorry," she whispered. "I never wanted to hurt you. I didn't know Chief had written that letter until Teddy told me. You just stopped writing and calling, like you'd died."

"The phone works both ways," I heard myself say, and I thought, Shut up, you fool, play it out. Let her talk. You've been dreaming about this moment for twenty years; don't blow it now.

"Pride," she said. "We all have our faults. That's one of my worst. I wanted to write, then Teddy told me to leave you alone. He said you'd had enough. Please forgive me for being so foolish."

I wondered if she really thought we could puff off twenty years so easily. Say we're sorry and forget it. Was she that sure of my vulnerability? The armor started slipping around me but she moved closer, six inches away, and shaking her head gently, she breathed, "There will never be anyone like you for me. Never again. I've known it ever since I lost you, just as I knew you wouldn't come last night."

"How did you know that?" I said, my voice sounding hoarse and uncertain.

"Because I don't deserve it," she said, and her lips began to tremble. "Because I wanted you to come so much and—"

"Hey, easy," I said, putting a finger against that full, inviting mouth.

What's happening here? I thought. How about all the decisions I had silently made to myself the night before? Is this all it takes to break old Kilmer down?

Yeah, that's all it takes.

Then she closed her eyes, and her lips spread apart again, and she moved in and it was like the old days. I got lost in her mouth, felt her tentative tongue taking a chance, and responded with

169

mine. And then she was in my arms and it was all I could do to keep from crushing her. I felt her knee rubbing the outside of mine, heard the riding crop fall into the sawdust, felt her hands sliding down the small of my back, pressing me closer to her.

I forgot all the things I was going to say to her. The accusations, the questions that would clear up the dark corners of my mind. Whatever anger lurked inside me vanished at that moment. I slid my hands down and felt the rise of her buttocks and pressed her to me.

"Oh, Jake," she said huskily, "I wish it was that summer again. I wish the last twenty years never happened."

Don't we all, I thought; wouldn't that be nice. But I didn't say it.

"Forget all that," I mumbled without taking my lips away. "Nothing to forgive."

"Oh, Jake, I want it to be like it used to be," she said, with her lips still brushing mine. "Come tonight. Please come tonight. Don't stay away again."

And without thinking any more about it, I said, "Yes." And I knew I meant yes. I knew I would go and the hell with Dutch and the Taglianis and the hell with safety and distance and vulnerability. I would go because I wanted to and because it was my payoff for twenty years. I said it again. And again.

"Yes . . . yes . . . yes."

UP JUMPS THE DEVIL

When I left the stable, the first person I saw was Stick. He was leaning against the dreaded black Pontiac and was looking right at me when I came out. She was a couple of feet behind me, standing inside the stall but visible nevertheless. His expression never changed; he simply looked the other way as he took out a cigarette and lit up.

"Later," I said quietly, without turning, and walked straight to the car. Stick had traded in his slept-in seersucker for a pair of ratty chinos, dirty tennis shoes, and a black boatneck T-shirt, but the brown fedora was still perched on the back of his head.

"Sorry if I'm late," I said, staring out the windshield.

"First things first," he said, swinging around and heading back out the gate.

We drove a couple of minutes in silence and I finally said, "That wasn't what it looked like."

"I didn't see a thing."

"Look, I knew her a long time ago. It's no big thing."

"No big thing. Gotcha."

"It's no big thing!"

"Jake, it's nothing to me," he said. "See no evil, hear no evil, that's me."

"What do you mean, evil!"

"It's a saying. Hey, there's no need to be touchy, man." He drove a moment or two more and added, "I admire the hell out of the way you gather information." And he started to laugh. I started to get burned, then he looked over at me and winked. He reminded me of Teddy. I was waiting for him to add the "Junior" on the end of the sentence. I started laughing too.

"Shit," I said.

"Is it that important?"

"I don't know," I said with disgust. "It's one of the balls I've been juggling."

I was surprised at how easily it came out.

"Well, if you want an amateur's opinion, I sure wouldn't throw that one away."

"Her husband's the fucking racing commissioner," I said.

"I know who her fucking husband is," he said with a chuckle. "Anybody who's been in town for fifteen minutes knows who her husband is."

More driving. More silence. Then he started to chuckle again. "I got to tell you, Jake, I really do admire your style."

"It hasn't got anything to do with the job," I told him. "This is old, personal business. Something that was never finished properly."

"O-kay," he said, drawing out the "Oh" for about five minutes. "Well, I'm glad you're doing it up right this time."

"Don't be an asshole," I grumbled.

"Why don't you talk about it?"

"I don't want to talk about it."

"Okay." A long pause. "But I know you want to."

"I don't want to talk about anything!"

"It's just like the blues. I can tell."

"Damn it, Stick, drop it."

"Done," he said, and dropped it. I didn't. He was right—I had to get it off my chest.

"There was a time—in my . . . late-blooming youth—when I thought I was going to marry her. I took it for granted, one of my more spectacular mistakes."

"Marry her, huh. Shit, you do have a problem."

"It's no problem."

"Hey, this is the Stick, my friend. You can bullshit me about not finishing things properly and all that crap, but don't tell me it's no problem."

"It's no problem," I said emphatically. It sounded more like I was trying to convince myself than him.

"Jake, getting into it is never the problem. Getting out of it, that's the problem."

"I'm already out of it. What I'm trying to avoid is getting back in."

"Oh, that's what you're trying to do?"

"Yes!"

"You got a unique approach," he said, and after a few seconds he asked, "Are you still in love with her?"

"Shit."

"No shit."

I sighed. "Hell, I don't know. Maybe I'm in love with the idea of her. Maybe I never took the time to get out of love with her. I haven't worked it out."

"When are you going to see her again?"

I had a moment of panic, as though I'd told him too much already. The old paranoia.

"What time tonight are you going to see her?" he repeated.

"Who says I'm going to see her tonight?"

He shot me another crazy smile.

"Nine o'clock," I said.

"You need some backup?"

"Don't get funny."

"I don't mean that, Jake," he said seriously. "I mean do you want me to cover you? Keep an eye on the place, make sure nobody's hounddogging you? What I'm trying to say is, I'm for you. Whatever it means to you, I hope it comes out right."

I was moved by his concern. There was a lot of Teddy in Stick. But I was wary of him. I was wary of everybody. I had taken two steps, back to back. First opening up to Doe, and now Stick. I was moving farther away from my safe spots. It scared hell out of me.

"I shouldn't have come back to this fucking place," I snapped finally.

"Aw, c'mon," he said. "Then you wouldn't have met me. I'm the magic man, my friend. I can wave my hand and make the impossible come true."

"Where are we going?" I asked, deciding to change the subject.

"City docks."

"What's out there?"

"We got a surprise for you."

"Who's 'we'?"

"Me and Zapata."

"Well, try to keep it under ninety, will you?"

"The Bird here runs a little rough under ninety," he said, grinning as he patted the steering wheel.

"Too bad about the Bird," I said. "I run a little rough over ninety. What happens at the city docks?"

"The shrimpers unload there," he said, as if that explained everything. I decided to be surprised and said no more.

He turned right onto Front Street and drove slowly in the direction of the beach. In the first two blocks I saw six hookers, working in pairs. Two were chatting with a very friendly policeman, whose hands moved from one rear end to the other throughout the conversation; another pair was negotiating something with a middle-aged couple in a Winnebago wearing Iowa plates; and two more almost jumped in front of the car trying to get our attention. After that I lost interest.

"I took a detour. This is the scenic route," Stick said as I watched the strip joints, lingerie stores, and porno houses glide past the window. "I thought you'd like to see it in the daytime."

"So this is what America's all about," I said. "Fifty-year-old swingers in recreation vans are replacing Norman Rockwell, Stick. The Front Streets of America are replacing Bunker Hill. Whatever happened to Beaver Cleaver and the father who knew best and the days when a major crisis was whether Ricky was going to run out of gas in the Nelsons' Chevy?"

"Who's Beaver Cleaver?" he said, sarcastically.

When I'd seen enough, Stick turned off Front, went two blocks north, and turned east on Ocean Boulevard. There was very little traffic to disturb the palmettos, palm trees, and azaleas that lined the divided highway. It looked much better in the daylight, without benefit of Day-Glo streetlights.

The day had turned hot and humid and we drove with the

windows down, back over the bridge to Thunderhead Island. We were still an island away from the ocean, but I could feel the air getting cooler.

I was remembering Oglethorpe County twenty years ago, and riding the two-lane blacktop out to the beach on warm summer nights. The county spread out over ten or eleven islands and the people had a fierce kind of pride that all islanders seem to possess, an independence which, I suppose, comes from living in a place that is detached from the mainland. The islanders I knew didn't give a damn what anybody else thought or did. They did it their own way.

"Y'know, years before booze was legal in the state, drinks were sold openly across the bar in this county," I told him. "They called it the free state of Oglethorpe."

"Breaking the law in those days had a certain charm to it," he said. "That's probably where Titan's power started."

I had never thought about it before, but Stick was probably right. That's where the patronage had begun. God knows where it had spread.

"What do you think of Titan?" I asked.

"The toughest seventy-five-year-old man I ever met," he said emphatically.

Twenty years had transformed Thunderhead Island from a deserted, marshy wonderland to a nightmare of condos; stark, white, three-story monoliths that lined the river to the north, while to the south, the marsh had been dredged out, cleaned up, and concreted into a sprawling marina. There was hardly a tree in sight, just steel and stone, and the masts of dozens of sailboats, endlessly bobbing up and down, up and down, like toothpicks.

I wondered who got rich—or richer—when they plundered this piece of paradise.

The Stick interrupted my angst.

"I had the computer pull the military files on everybody in the Triad who was in Nam," he said. "Costello was in Saigon for about six weeks on some legal thing. The rest of the time he was in Washington. Adjutant general's office. Big shot. A couple of their musclemen did time too. But Harvey Nance—that's his real name, Harvey—he's another case entirely. He was in Nam for two years. He was in CRIP, operating out of Dau Tieng. You know about CRIP?"

"Headhunters," I said, with a nod.

"I know this is gonna sound strange," Stick said, "but I still have this funny feeling about guys from Nam. You know, the chemistry. After a while you get so used to a guy, he starts a sentence, you finish it. And when he's hurting, you know he's hurting. Like you are now."

I knew what he was talking about. Once, just after I came back from Nam, I was in San Francisco and I went to the movies and when I came out there was this topkick sitting on the stairs. He had hashmarks up to his shoulder and I don't think I ever saw so many decorations and he was sitting there crying so hard he was sobbing. People were walking by, looking at him like maybe he was unglued. Well, maybe he was, he probably had the right. Anyway, I sat down beside him and put my arm around him and he looked up and all he said was "Ah, Jesus," and we sat that way for a long time and finally he got over it and said thanks and we left the theater. He went that way and I went this, so I knew what Stick was talking about.

And he was right, I was hurting.

"You lose track of reality fast," I said. "When I first went into combat, the Hueys took us into U Minh Forest. It was a free-strike zone. The B-52's had done it in that afternoon, and there was this old man sitting against a wall and he was clutching his leg to his chest, like he was afraid somebody was going to steal it. He bled to death like that, just clutching that leg. This old man, probably, I don't know, maybe sixty, sixty-five, too old to do anything to anybody. I started thinking, Holy shit, there's some weird people over here. Whoever's running this war needs to get his head re-wired."

He was nodding along with me.

"It was the ultimate scam, Nam," he agreed. "Nam the scam, the big con. Shit, from the day we're born we get sold the big con about war and manhood. We get conned up for that all our lives. The big fuckin' war payoff. Be a hero—except there weren't any heroes in Nam. All it was was a giant fuck-up with a high body count."

"That's what you wanted, Stick? To be a hero and have a parade?"

Stick laughed. "Would have been nice if somebody had made the offer."

"I never did figure out what it was all about," I said. "That was the worst part of it."

"Guilt is what it's all about."

I knew about that. First you're exhilarated because you're still alive and others around you are dead. You don't want to admit it, but that's the way it is. The guilt sets in later. That's the way it was with Teddy.

"Anyway," I said, "you get over the thing about camaraderie the first time one of them takes a shot at you. That's part of the scam."

"I didn't mean to get off the subject," Stick said. "The thing is, the CRIPS were mean motherfuckers and Nance was one of them."

"Why all this interest in Nance?" I asked.

"I'm about to show you."

He peeled off Ocean Boulevard just before we reached the bridge to Oceanby Island and the beaches. The city docks were clean, well-kept, concrete wharves, stretching several hundred feet along the river. It was early for the shrimpers. There was one boat unloading. It was jet black, its nets draped from the outriggers like the wings of a bat. The strikers were shoveling shrimp from the hold onto a conveyor belt that carried it into a sheet-metal building that was little more than an elaborate icehouse.

Stick pulled into a large parking lot flyspecked with battered fishing cars and stopped near a beat-up Ford that looked vaguely familiar. Zapata peered out of the front seat and grinned.

"Hey, amigo," he said. "How's everything at the track?"

"I got an education," I answered.

"You're about to get another one," he said.

"How's that?"

He reached out between the cars and handed me a pair of binoculars.

"Check the belt."

I checked the belt running into the building. It appeared deserted.

"Nobody around," I said.

"Just keep watching for a minute," said Zapata.

Stick put lighter to cigarette and hunched down behind the wheel.

A man with a clipboard came out of the shrimp house. He was a short man with a white beard, rather benevolent looking, with a stomach that was used to too many beers. His bullet head was covered by a bright green fishing cap, and he was checking wooden crates piled against the back of the building. I watched him for a full minute before I realized it was Tuna Chevos. A new beard and dark glasses were my only excuses. I knew that face well.

"Son of a bitch," I said. "There he is, the missing link. I knew it! I knew that old bastard had to be around here. That means Nance can't be too far away. How did you tumble on to them?"

"Shit, this was easy," Zapata said. "You said Chevos ran barges on the Ohio River. Seemed logical he'd stick to the same trade, especially since shrimp boats move a lot of grass. So I got out the phone book, turned to shrimp companies. I got lucky. This is the third place I checked out."

"What's the name of this joint?" I asked.

"Jalisco Shrimp Company," Stick answered.

"Let's find out who owns it."

"Check."

Another man joined Chevos, a tall, lean, ferret of a man who walked on the balls of his feet, loose and rangy. His head moved constantly, as though he were stalking some unsuspecting prey. I could almost smell his feral odor three hundred yards away.

"There he is," I said, no longer trying to conceal my hatred of Turk Nance. "That's Nance."

"Yeah, I figured," Zapata said. He was grinning like the man in the moon.

"You did good, Chino," I said.

"Thanks. Piece of cake, this one."

"You really have a hard-on for Nance, don't you?" Stick said.

"I owe the son of a bitch."

"Well, maybe we can fix it so you'll be accommodated," Zapata said almost gleefully.

"That would be nice," I answered. "At least we know they're all here."

I watched them taking inventory of the shrimp boxes.

"They look like they're actually working for a living," I said.

"These are the real bad ones, huh?" asked Zapata.

I kept watching Nance, his snake eyes gleaming malevolently. Nance had killed a dozen men I could think of.

"The real badasses," I affirmed. "The way it is, if anybody in the Tagliani outfit is capable of wasting the whole family, it's Chevos, with Nance probably doing the batting.

"Twenty-four-hour surveillance on these two, okay?" I said to Zapata.

"I'll see to it personally," he said, obviously proud of his score.

"It also might help to know where the two of them were last night. Particularly Nance. But don't let them on to you."

"That may be a little tougher but I'll see what I can do. You want Nance, you got him."

I gave the glasses back to Zapata. "I'll tell you how I want Nance. I want Nance doing the full clock in the worst joint there is. I want him screaming in solitary for the rest of his natural life."

The Stick stared at me with surprise for several moments, then broke into his grin.

"We got the point," he said.

33

ISLE OF SIGHS

It was eight thirty when I started out to the Isle of Sighs and it was dusk by the time I had put Front Street and Dunetown behind me. Crab fishermen were standing hard against the railing of the two-lane bridge that connects the main island to Sea Oat Island. Below it, an elderly woman, as freckled as an Iowa corn picker, and wearing a battered white fishing hat with its brim folded down around her ears, fished from a flat-bottom skiff that drifted idly among the reeds in the backwater. The hyenas hadn't got this far yet.

Sea Oat was the buffer, a small, marshy islet that separated the whore-city from the wistful Isle of Sighs. There were few cars, the road was populated mostly by weathered natives on bikes. The islanders seemed to have prevailed here, stubbornly refusing to surrender to time or progress. I passed what seemed to be an abandoned city square, its weeds crowding the wreck of a building at its center, then half a mile farther on, a small settlement of restored tabby houses, surrounded by laughing children and barking dogs. Streets narrowed to lanes, oyster shells crackled beneath my tires, and the oaks, bowed with age, turned the roadways into living arches, their beards of gray Spanish moss *shushing* across the top of my car.

I was racing the sun, hoping to get to Windsong before dark, but as I got closer to the old, narrow, wooden bridge that ties the Isle of Sighs to Sea Oat, I unsuspectingly burst out of the trees for several hundred yards and the marsh spread out before me for miles, like an African plain. It was as if I had suddenly driven to the edge of the world.

I pulled over, got out of the car, and leaned against a fender. The sun, a scorched orb hanging an inch or two above the sprawling sea grass, lured birds and ducks and buzzing creatures aloft for one last flight before nightfall. I watched the sun sink to the horizon, merge with the flat tideland, and set it briefly afire. The sky turned brilliant scarlet and the color swept across the marsh like a forest fire. The world was red for a minute or so and then the sun dropped silently behind the sea oats and marsh grass.

Whoosh; just like that it was dark.

When I got back into the car, I had a momentary attack of guilt. My mind flashed on Dutch and the promise I had made to him. No scandal, I had told him. I thought about that for at least sixty seconds as I drove on through the oak archways and across the narrow bridge to the Isle of Sighs. Nothing here had changed. It was like driving into a time warp. Here and there, along the rutted lanes, hand-carved signs announced the names of houses hidden away among pine and palm. Once this had been the bastion of Dunetown, a fiefdom for the power brokers who took the gambles, claimed the spoils, divided them up, and ruled the town with indulgent authority. The homes were unique, each a masterpiece of casual grace.

Windsong was the fortress.

It stood at the edge of the woods and a mile from the main road, down a narrow dirt corridor, tortured by palmettos and dwarf palms, that was more path than lane; a stately, two-story frame house, ghost-white in the moonlight, surrounded by sweeping porches, with a cap of cedar shingles and dark oblong shutters framing its windows. Before it, a manicured lawn spread a hundred yards down to the ocean's edge. Beyond it, past the south point of Skidaway Island, a mile or so away, was the Atlantic Ocean. The gazebo, where bands had once played on summer nights, stood near the water like a pawn on an empty chessboard.

Memories stirred.

A lamp burned feebly in a corner room on the second floor and another spilled light from the main room to a corner of the porch. Otherwise the place was dark.

I stopped near a dark blue Mercedes sedan that was parked haphazardly on the grass near the end of the driveway, got out, and stood for a minute or two, letting my eyes deal with the darkness. Moon shadows were everywhere. A south wind drifted idly across the ocean and rattled the tree branches. Out beyond the house, a night bird sang a mournful love song and waited for an answer that never came. It was obvious why Chief had called it Windsong; no other name could possibly have fit.

I remembered Chief and Stonewall Titan, ending each day sipping whiskey on that porch. I opened the trunk and put my pistol under the spare tire and pressed the lid shut as quietly as I could. This was no place for sudden noises.

The boathouse was a dark square, jutting out into the ocean to the east of the house. I walked down toward it. The night bird started singing again and then, suddenly, flew off in a rustle of leaves. Then there was only the wind.

I knew what I was going to say; I had been rehearsing it in my head ever since I saw her.

Hang tough, Jake, don't let soft memories shake you. Get it said and get out.

I was ready.

She was standing in the boathouse, haloed by the moon, swinging on a twenty-five-foot Mako bow line clamped to a hook above her head. She didn't see me at first. Eyes closed, she was lost in the moonlight, stirring her own memories.

A small Sony tape deck was whispering on the dock beside her. And that summer came back, a riptide that erased whatever scenario I had planned. I recognized Phil Spector's breakaway guitar on the old Drifters version of "On Broadway." Twenty years ago I could whistle every note and break, right along with him. I didn't even think, I just started whistling softly between my teeth, amazed that I could still keep up with all the riffs and pauses.

She turned, startled, her fawnlike eyes fluttering as they tried to adjust to the darkness. The ocean was slapping the pilings beneath us and the Mako bumped easily against the rubber tires in the side of the dock.

Nothing else but the wind.

"Jake?" she said, a decibel above the night sounds.

"Yeah."

She moved away from the line.

"You can still do it," she said, and laughed.

"I'm a little rusty," I said.

"No. Not rusty at all."

There was an awkward pause, where you feel you should say something just to fill the silence. She did it for me.

"I'm so glad you came. I wanted it so bad it hurt."

"You haven't changed at all," I said huskily. "Time has passed you by."

"You always say the perfect thing, you always did." Another pause, then, "I didn't even hear you. I was lost for a minute."

"I can't think of a better place to be lost."

She eased toward me, a shimmering vision, still moving slightly with the music.

"Remember the night party? Dewey Simpson got drunk and tried to swim to the channel marker in his tuxedo . . ."

I remembered it and said so.

". . . and you kept egging him on . . ."

The moon silhouetted her, trim legs etched behind a white cotton skirt.

". . . and we kept playing that song, over and over, while Teddy swam out to pull him in . . ."

The brief triangle of her bikini panties, the swell of one of her breasts, tinted by a moonbeam.

"And my eighteenth birthday, when we took the dune buggy and left Teddy and that girl on the beach . . ."

Her blond hair was swirling in the wind, whipping the shadow of her face.

"We were at the very end, remember? Down at the point . . . the breakers were running so high."

She whisked her fingertips down her neck.

"It was so hot that night. Remember how hot it was?"

I began to feel the same heat, rising round my neck. She was some piece of work, make no mistake.

"It was just like tonight . . . the moon was full . . ."

She was close enough to smell.

". . . that was the first time I ever saw you naked . . ."

And now she was close enough to feel my heat.

"We were lying there in the dunes and you let the buggy roll down the hill . . ."

"Oh yes, I remember . . ."

"You were gorgeous . . ."

"You still are," I heard myself say. My voice was as shaky as a spinster's dream.

"I feel the same way now, Jake. I feel like I'm on fire inside . . ."

She moved against me, her breasts exploring my chest as tentatively as a butterfly exploring a blossom.

But it was not 1963 and we were not on the beach; it was now and here and she stepped back from me, her dress already unbuttoned, her breasts pushing out past the white bodice, and she lifted her shoulders so gracefully that she hardly moved, and the dress slipped away, hovering down to the dock at her feet, and she leaned forward, her hands sweeping swiftly down her thighs, and suddenly she was naked before me again.

If anything, time had improved her body.

She moved against me and I ran my hands slowly across the swell of her buttocks, pressing her hard against me. She began to rock back and forth, urging me to rise to her. I let the flat of my hand slip down along her thigh and then back up, and she urged herself against it. She was warm and moist and she clamped her legs together, trapping my hand, and began to rock harder. Her fingers moved nimbly to my belt, unfastening it, and then she slid her hand down and began to caress me and then we were moving together.

"Oh, God, Jake," she moaned, "where have you been?"

I lowered her slowly to the cushions in the boat and she stretched out before me, her hands over her head as I teased her, my hand barely touching her soft down, until suddenly she thrust up against my hand. She began to tremble under my touch, took my hand and pressed it harder, and began to move my hand with hers, showing me where to touch, what to explore, orchestrating her pleasure. Her hands groped for something to hang on to, found the edge of the seat and clutched it. Every muscle in her body seemed to be responding. She was moving back and forth as my fingers sought all her secret places.

She started to whimper and the whimper became a growl, deep in her throat, and she stiffened suddenly, wrapped her arms around me, buried her head in my shoulder, and her cries were muffled against my flesh. She reached down, searching with desperate fingers, and turning slightly, guided me into her. Then there was only the feel of her, her soft muscles engulfing me, urging me to come with her, and the rush of her mouth against mine.

There was nothing else.

No Ciscos, no Taglianis, no hooligans, no wounds or screams of grief. There were only our own cries of joy and relief, whisked to sea on the wind.

34

LATE CALL

The tape recorder had run its course and turned itself off and I had pulled my Windbreaker over us, although I didn't need it. Her warm body lay across mine like a blanket. We didn't say much, we just lay there holding each other. Half an hour crept by and then my beeper broke the spell, like a phone that's been left off the hook too long.

I shifted under her enough to reach up onto the dock and riffle through my clothes until I found it and turned it off. My watch said eleven fifteen.

She twisted back against me and sighed. "What was that?" she asked.

I was wondering who would be beeping me at this time of night.

"The beeper," I whispered. "I gotta call the office."

She rose up an inch or so, a tousled head peering through tangled hair with one half-open eye.

"Wha' time is it?"

"Past eleven."

"You have to call the office at this time of night?"

"I have terrible hours."

"Ridiculous. Besides, it's too early to leave."

"You've got a husband, remember?"

"I have a husband in Atlanta for the night," she said. She looked up at me and smiled. There wasn't a hint of remorse on her face. She looked as innocent as a five-year-old.

"He may call."

She snuggled up again.

"Uh-uh. Out of sight, out of mind. Besides, he trusts me."

I didn't feel like dealing with that. I didn't feel like dealing with any of it. Guilt gnawed at my stomach like an ulcer and it had nothing to do with Harry Raines. I kept lying to myself that it had been inevitable. I shifted again and reached for my clothes. She sat up, leaning naked against the bulkhead, her tawny form outlined by the dying moon.

"More," she whispered, and it was more of a demand than a plea.

A new fire ignited deep in my gut, but the old devils were creeping back: guilt, frustration, jealousy, distrust.

I threw the Windbreaker over her.

"Give me a break," I said, squeezing out a smile.

"You never asked for a break before," she said, putting a hand as soft as chamois on my chest.

"I was in training then."

"Please come back," she said as I started to dress.

"I never know about later. I could be on my way to Alaska an hour from now."

"No."

I laughed. "No? What do you mean, no?"

"I waited all these years for you to come back. You are not going to just up and leave, not again."

She closed her eyes and put her head back against the side of the boat. "I went crazy inside when I saw you at the restaurant yesterday and then at the track this morning," she said. "It all came rushing back at me. Like a tidal wave inside me." She opened her eyes and looked at me. "It happened, and it wasn't one of those things you question. Do you know what I mean?"

Instant replay: a rampant fantasy from the past. For months after Chief had written his good-bye letter, fantasies had infested my days. Uncontrollable, they were like panes of glass, separating me from reality. The fantasies were impossible dreams; that she would show up at my door in the middle of the night to tell me she couldn't live another instant without me; that I would find her waiting in the corner of some restaurant. I looked for her everywhere I went, in supermarkets, in the windows of other cars as I drove down the highway. I bought a pair of cheap binoculars so I could scan Chief's box at Sanford Stadium on football weekends. Even a glimpse, I thought, would help. Finally I accepted the danger of fantasies. They sour into nightmares and vanish, leaving scars on the soul. Tonight could not change that, even though the fantasy was becoming real again.

I could feel the armor, like a steel skin, slipping around me.

"Don't go away again," she said. "Not for a while, at least. Give it a chance."

I let some anger out, not much, just relieving the pressure for a moment.

"That isn't exactly the way it played," I said harshly.

"It was Chief. He never understood how we really felt about each other."

"He understood all right."

She looked away, fiddling with a strand of cotton raveling from her dress.

"Hell, Jake, you know Chief. He always made whatever he said sound so . . . so, right. Nobody ever argued with Chief."

"Maybe somebody should have."

She stared at me for several seconds before saying, "Why didn't you?"

I didn't know how to answer that properly.

What I said was "Pride," and let it go at that.

She nodded. "Beats us all, doesn't it."

"Well, it's a little hard, coming to grips with the feeling that you're a failure at twenty-one because you have bad ankles. It made me readjust some of my values."

"Jake," she said suddenly, changing the mood entirely. "I want to hear about Teddy."

"I wrote you all there is to know."

"I want to hear it from you."

"Why, for God's sake?"

"So I'll know it's true and I can forget it, once and for all."

"It's true, believe me. I won't replay it, Doe. It's not one of my favorite images."

It had been so long I had almost forgotten the lie. It was heroic, a real Greek tragedy, that much I remembered.

"Time you laid Teddy to rest," I said softly. "Forget the war. That wasn't reality, it was madness. Remember him the way he was the day you pushed him into the bay. That's what he'd want."

Then she started to cry, very softly so you would hardly notice it.

"He'd like it, that we're together here. He was all for us, Jake."

"I know it."

She went on, ignoring the tears. "When I think back, I think of all of us together. Such bright promises, and all of them broken. Everything seemed to go bad and stay bad. They kept taking things away from me. First you, then Teddy, then . . . oh, just everything."

"Then what? You started to say something, finish it."

"Lots of thens. I have this horse, a beautiful stallion, Georgiabred. He had real promise. Chief gave him to me when I turned thirty. He said Firefoot—it was a silly name but he had this white splash on one foot, jet black only he had this white streak, so I called him Firefoot—anyway, Chief said Firefoot and I would stay young together. I wanted to race him, oh, how I wanted that. But Harry got involved with this racetrack thing. I guess inheriting Dunetown from Chief wasn't enough. It wouldn't look right, he said, the racing commissioner's wife racing horses. So Firefoot's up for stud now. When I go out there, he runs across the meadow to me with his head up, so proud . . . he wanted to race; it's what Thoroughbreds are all about, Jake, they're born to run, to prove themselves. He really deserved the chance. He deserved that. An animal like that, it has rights."

She stopped and bit off another strand raveling from her dress, wiggled it off her fingers, then turned back to me.

"It's been that way ever since you left. Everything went bad."

"I'll buy that," I said bitterly.

"It just seems like nobody's what they appear to be," she went on angrily. "At first Harry reminded me of you. He was fun and he laughed a lot and he made me laugh. Then Chief decided to retire and Harry changed overnight. It was business, business, business!"

"That went with the territory."

"I didn't know he was so ambitious. Suddenly Findley Enterprises wasn't enough. Next it was politics and then the track. It's always something new. He's like a man on a roller coaster; he can't seem to stop. I didn't want that. There's no reason for it. We've got more than we'll ever need."

For a few moments I felt sorry for Raines, because I understood that drive. Harry Raines had to prove himself. He couldn't be satisfied with the role of Mr. Doe Findley, and for that I respected him. I wondered if I would have done the same thing. But I didn't say anything, I just listened. I had very little respect for his political aspirations. In my book, politicians usually rank one step above bank robbers and child molesters. That was my prejudice and my problem to deal with, of course, but I had met damn few of them I either liked or trusted.

"I love Harry," she said. "I'm just not *in* love with him anymore. He's not Harry anymore, he's already Governor Raines."

"Maybe he's got troubles," I said, buttoning my shirt.

"Tiger by the tail, that's all he keeps saying."

"More like a two-ton elephant on a piece of string."

"Is it that bad? Is he in trouble?" she asked.

"I don't know. Is he honest?"

"Chief believed . . . believes in him."

"Oh, so Chief picked him out," I said. It was a cruel comment. I was sorry I'd said it before all the words were out of my mouth.

She stood up, her back as straight as a slat, smoothing her dress. "*I* picked him out," she snapped.

"Sorry," I said. "Anyway, I'm not interested in what Chief thinks, Doe. What do you think?"

She pulled on the dress, but didn't button it, and gave me back my Windbreaker.

"I don't think he could be dishonest."

"That's a nice vote of confidence."

"I'm trying to be honest myself. Are you here because of something to do with the track?"

"Hell, I'm not sure of anything," I answered. "I'm new in town. Can I use the phone up at the house?"

She opened a metal box on the wall of the boathouse, reached in and took out a wall phone, handed me the receiver, and leaned back against the wall, staring at me.

I dialed the war room and Dutch answered.

"Where are you?" he bellowed.

"With friends," I said. "What's up?"

"You got a weird phone call about an hour ago. Kite fielded it. He says a guy wanted to talk to you real bad, but he hung up when Kite tried to press him. Thing is, Kite says the guy didn't exactly sound like Mary Poppins. The reason I'm calling, before Kite put it together he told this guy he might be able to reach you at the hotel. So you might want to keep your eyes open."

"Thanks. Maybe we ought to have breakfast and do a little catchup."

"I'll pick you up at nine," he said. I told him that was real civilized of him and hung up.

"More trouble?" Doe asked, anxiety in her voice.

"I don't think so."

"Please come back."

I played it tough. "Sure," I said, and leaned over and kissed her. As I started to leave I felt her hand on my sleeve.

"Jake?"

"Yeah?"

"What did they do to us?"

"The hyenas got us," I said. "The bastards never let up."

When I got back to the car, the light was still on in the upper bedroom. Then I remembered that that was Teddy's old room. I wondered if the light was left on permanently, like the eternal torch at Arlington.

I drove as fast I could back to reality.

35

WESTERN UNION

A gray Olds blundered on to me a couple of blocks before I got back to the hotel and followed at a respectable distance. The driver was pretty good. I did a couple of figure-eights, trying to throw him off, but he didn't panic and he didn't close the gap. He stayed a block or so behind me all the way to the hotel.

I parked in front and let the doorman take the car. The Olds pulled in half a block away and sat with the lights out. I checked the desk. Then I walked across the lobby and ducked behind a small forest of ferns and ficus trees near the elevators.

A medium-sized man got out of the Olds and drifted across Palm Drive, acting like he wasn't in a hurry. I got a better look at him in the light of the lobby. He was neither tall nor short, fat nor thin, old nor young. He was decked out in a nondescript gray business suit, no hat, and his chiseled features might have been handsome except for the deep acne scars that pitted his cheeks. Once he got inside, he picked up his pace, his deep-set eyes darting back and forth, perusing the lobby. He headed straight for the elevators and speared the up button with a forefinger.

I stepped in behind him, grabbed a handful of jacket and collar, slammed him face-forward against the wall, bent his left arm behind him, reached under his arm, and relieved him of a Smith & Wesson .38.

"Whad'ya think yer doin'?" he whined.

I leaned close to his ear and put a rasp in my voice.

"You just took the words right out of my mouth," I whispered. "You've been following me for the last ten minutes. I don't think you're attracted by my beautiful eyes."

"Lemme go," he continued to whine.

I shoved his gun between his shoulder blades.

"You got a name?" I asked.

He paused and I shoved harder. He turned his face sideways, glared at me through yellow-flecked snake eyes, and snarled, "Harry Nesbitt."

"Just why are you so attracted to me, Harry?"

"I came to talk. Lemme loose."

"You talk with your arm?"

"You got the gun, hotshot."

"Yeah, and I'm kind of jumpy, homicide being the hottest game in town right now. Talk first."

"Look, all I'm doin' is a Western Union. You wanna listen or not."

"I'm listening, Harry."

"Johnny O'Brian wants a meet."

"Is that a fact. And what's that to you?"

"I work for him."

"What do you do, carry his gun?"

"Very funny," he said, beginning to put an edge back into his voice. I let him go, slipped his gun into my belt, and backed away from the potted plants, out to the edge of the lobby.

"Do you mind," he said, his eyes beginning to dance around the room again. "O'Brian ain't anxious the whole fuckin' world should know we're talking."

"Uh-huh," I said.

He moved farther back among the plants.

"This joint is crawling with people," he said, although all I could see was one sleepy bellhop and a desk clerk who was busy sorting bills.

"Just speak your piece and shag," I said.

"O'Brian says he'll meet you anywhere you say, any time. One on one. Nobody knows but him and you."

"What about you? You going to get amnesia?"

"Cute." He chuckled. "Anyway, I already got it."

"And how do I contact O'Brian?"

"You don't. I do the go-between, okay? You tell me, I give it to the boss."

"And why should I trust you? Because I like your taste in ties?"

"Lookee here," said Nesbitt. "He wants to make a deal with you, okay? He ain't got nothing to do with this hit parade goin' down."

"Now how would I know that?"

"Look, it comes to O'Brian that you heated up Cincy real good. It comes to O'Brian that you burned Skeet Tagliani and gave Uncle Franco and the rest of them a hotfoot there. It also comes to him that you're a stand-up guy when it comes to your word. He wants to do business. What's the matter, you got something against free enterprise?"

"Am I supposed to be flattered by all this?" I asked.

"You wanna talk or you wanna audition for vaudeville? O'Brian ain't lookin' for trouble, okay? Am I drifting your way?"

"Getting scared, is he?"

"O'Brian don't scare," Nesbitt said matter-of-factly.

"Pigs don't lie in the mud, either."

"Look, my boss don't go to the party empty-handed, know what I mean? You wanna be the smartass, don't wanna listen, fuck off."

I thought about it for a moment or two—not about meeting O'Brian, that was a gimme—but about where and when to meet him. It could be a setup, except there was no reason to set me up. Was he representing the family? Or was he free-lancing? What was he willing to talk about that could interest me? I was still guessing that O'Brian was running scared, looking for an umbrella to hide under.

"Does he know who scratched Tagliani and the rest?" I asked.

Nesbitt shifted from one foot to the other and sighed. "Whyn't yuh ask him? I told yuh, I'm just doin' a Western Union. I don't know shit besides that and my orders are to forget it!"

"When?" I asked finally.

"Sooner the better."

"How's tomorrow morning sound?"

"Worse than now, better than later," he said with a shrug.

"It's too late to do anything now," I said. "It's got to be tomorrow, middle of the morning." I make a lot of bad decisions this late at night.

"That's the best you can do, that's the best you can do. You wanna pick the spot?"

I didn't know or remember the town well enough. I decided to test the water a little.

"Does O'Brian have a place in mind?"

"Yeah, but he don't want you should get nervous, him pickin' it out, I mean."

"Try me."

"He has this little fishing camp out on Skidaway. On the bay side, sits out over the water. It's private; his old lady don't even go out there. Also it has good sight lines; there ain't a blade of grass within twenty yards of the place."

I thought some more about it. It would have been smarter to leave then and follow Nesbitt to the meet, but I wanted to let somebody know where I was.

"Where is this place exactly?" I asked.

"You hang a right three blocks after you cross the bridge from Thunderhead to Oceanby. It's a mile or so down the road, on the bay, like I said. You can't miss it, the road ends there."

I studied him for a long minute, tugged my ear, and then nodded. "What's the name of the street?"

"Bayview."

"I have a breakfast appointment," I said. "It'll be about ten thirty."

"No problem, he's spending the night out there. Ten thirty." He smiled and held out his hand, palm up. "How about the piece?" he said.

I took out the revolver, loosened the retaining pin, dropped the cylinder into my palm, and handed him his gun.

"I'll give O'Brian the rest of it when I see him," I said.

His acne scars turned purple and pebbles of sweat began to ridge his forehead. He looked at me quizzically. "Why the badass act?" he said. "You don't have to prove how tough you are. Like I told ya, we know all about Cincy."

"I'm a cautious man," I said. "Too many people are dying in town right now."

"Did I lay any heat on you, Kilmer? No. I just come and delivered the message like I was supposed to. Y'know, I get caught in the middle on this thing, I'll end up in the bay, parley-vooin' with the fuckin' shrimps."

"That's your problem."

"So I come back with half a gun? It gets everything off on the wrong foot, know what I mean?"

I tossed him the cylinder for his .38 and he caught it without taking his yellow eyes off mine.

"You owe me one," I said.

"You talk to O'Brian, you'll be paid in spades," he said, and was gone, darting across the lobby like a dragonfly and out the nearest exit.

36

BREAKFAST TALK

There was a message in my box when I went down to meet Dutch the next morning. It was a handwritten note from Babs Thomas:

"Cocktails in the penthouse tomorrow at 6. I expect you there. Love and kisses, B.T."

She wasn't in the breakfast room but Dutch and Charlie One Ear were. I slid the note across the table to Dutch as I sat down. He read it and chuckled.

"You better be there," he said. "It's a felony in Doomstown to turn down a command performance from the duchess."

"Just what I need," I said, "a freaking cocktail party."

"Give you a chance to see how the other half lives," Charlie One Ear said without looking up from his fruit cocktail.

"I don't like crowds," I said.

He looked up and smiled. "Perhaps it'll be just the two of you," he suggested.

That earned him a dirty look from me and a bit of contemplation from Dutch.

"Well," Dutch said, "you could do worse."

"Let's forget cocktail parties for the moment," I said, ending the conjecture. "Something's come up. It could be our first real break."

"Oh?" Dutch retorted.

"Johnny O'Brian sent one of his gunmen to see me last night. He wants to have a powwow. Sounds like he could be running scared."

"Are you going to meet him?" Dutch asked.

"Yeah. At ten thirty. Do you have anybody on O'Brian's tail?" He nodded. "Salvatore's doing the honors today."

"Has he reported in?"

"Do any of these guys ever report in?" Dutch said. "I can check the Warehouse and see, but I can tell you what the chances are."

"We've got to raise him," I said. "My deal is that I go alone. If O'Brian tumbles onto Salvatore it could blow the whole deal."

"I'll see what I can do," Dutch said, heading for the phone.

"Is that real smart?" Charlie One Ear asked.

"You mean going alone?"

He nodded. The muscles in his face had tightened up. I knew what he was thinking.

"Don't worry," I said. "If this is some kind of a trap they wouldn't warn me first. They can't be that sure I won't have some kind of backup with me."

"You know this bunch better than I do," he answered, turning back to his breakfast. "But I wouldn't stray too far from the range, just in case."

"I appreciate your concern," I said. "The thing is, if O'Brian wants to make some kind of a deal, we can't afford to lose it. I've been down this road before, Charlie. I'll watch my step."

He shrugged. "You're a big boy now," he said. "I assume you know what you're doing."

I ordered a light breakfast and doctored my coffee. Dutch was gone about five minutes. He seemed concerned when he got back.

"Okay," he said. "Zapata was in the Warehouse and he beeped Salvatore. Zapata's going to call me back if he raises him."

"I thought Zapata was tailing Nance," I said.

Dutch was scowling. He lit a cigarette and blew smoke toward the ceiling.

"He lost him," Dutch said. "Followed him out to the docks at dawn. Nance went out on a shrimp boat and left Zapata at the altar."

I got a sudden chill, as if a cold breeze had blown across the back of my neck. Nance being on the loose was a wild card I hadn't counted on.

"An awful lot of people know about this gig," I mused.

"Are you worried about Salvatore and Zapata?" Dutch asked stiffly.

"No. But I don't want anybody screwing this thing up."

"Don't worry about it," Dutch replied. "We'll raise Salvatore and call him off, if you're sure that's the way you want to play it."

"That was my deal," I said as the waitress brought my breakfast.

"You want to tell us where you're going?" Charlie One Ear asked.

"Not really," I said. "You know how it is with these people, Charlie. They spook real easily."

I decided we had talked enough about O'Brian and changed the subject again.

"Anything new on the Logeto killing?" I asked.

Dutch shook his head. "We combed the neighborhood. Nobody saw anybody on the roof or coming down the walls. So far it's a blank. But I do have something for you." He took an envelope out of his pocket and handed it to me. "Here's that list of drops Cohen made. Cowboy finally got it together for you."

I opened it up and checked over the list. Most of the addresses didn't mean anything to me. The most significant note was that on two of the three days, Cohen had visited both a branch bank of the Seacoast National *and* made his usual two o'clock visit to the bank.

"Have you checked this over?" I asked Dutch.

He nodded. "I can give you chapter and verse on the drops if you want."

"I don't have time now," I said. "There's one thing that jumps out. I wonder why Cohen has been hitting the bank twice. On Wednesday and Friday he went to a branch *and* the main bank. Now why would he do that?"

"Maybe he doesn't like to carry a lot of cash around for too long," Charlie One Ear suggested.

"Maybe," I said, staring at the list. "But I don't think so. Unless things have changed, he's used to moving large sums of money."

"You got another idea?" asked Dutch.

"Yeah. Maybe he's skimming a little off the top for himself."

"If he is, he's got more guts than I give him credit for," said Dutch.

"Or he could be working it with Costello," I said.

"Wouldn't that be sweet, to catch them in the middle like that," Charlie thought aloud. "We could probably get a whole chorus of canaries out of it."

"That's *if* he's playing games," I said.

"Cowboy's on him again today," Dutch said. "Maybe he'll turn up something new." Then his eyebrows went up. "I'll be damned," he said. "Speak of the devil. See the two guys that just walked in? The one that looks like a football player and the jellyfish with him?"

The two men sat down at a corner table and immediately began to jabber like two spinsters gossiping. One was Donleavy. The other one was as tall, but slender, and older, probably in his mid-forties, with wavy, graying hair that framed a weak, flaccid face. His manicured hands jittered nervously as he talked, fiddling with the bits of toast on his plate the way a spider fiddles with a fly. Both of them looked like they spent a lot of time in the sun.

"The one on the left is Donleavy," said Dutch. "The bird in the navy blue suit is the banker, Charles Seaborn. From the looks of things, they're having a lovers' spat."

"I think I'll just stir the pot a little," I said.

"What are you going to do?" Dutch asked nervously.

"Just introduce myself," I said, patting his shoulder as I rose. "I'm not going to bite anybody."

I strolled across the restaurant toward the table where Donleavy and Seaborn were bickering over breakfast. Donleavy saw me from the corner of his eye. He kept talking, but it was obvious that he sensed I was heading their way and he didn't want to be disturbed. As I reached them, he looked up angrily, trouble clouding his brown eyes.

"I'm Jake Kilmer," I said before he had a chance to explode. "I think it's about time we met."

He wasn't sure what to do. The anger in his hard features was suddenly replaced by a wide grin, a car salesman's grin, the kind that makes you want to count your fingers after you've shaken hands.

"Yes, yes, yes," he suddenly babbled, and jumped up. "Of course." He pumped my hand and introduced me to Seaborn, who looked like he'd just bitten his tongue. Seaborn offered me a hand that was as clammy as it was insincere.

It was obvious that neither of them was overjoyed at meeting me.

"I'd like to have a talk with you," I said to Donleavy, "whenever it's convenient."

"Is it urgent?" he said. "Aren't we going to see you tomorrow night?"

"Tomorrow night?"

"At Babs' cocktail party," he said with a lame grin. "You better not forget—she's touting you as the guest of honor. She's got a short temper and a long memory."

"I'll be there," I said. "But I need a little time alone with you. It's nothing unpleasant. Information mostly."

He dug a small notebook from an inside pocket and leafed through it. "How about Friday around noon?" he asked. "I'll take the phone off the hook and send out for sandwiches."

"Sounds like a winner," I said. "I'll buy."

"Not in my town you won't," he said. His smile had grown more relaxed and genuine. "It's Warehouse Three, overlooking the Quadrangle. We have the whole top floor."

"I'm afraid I won't be seeing you tomorrow evening," Seaborn said. "I have the bank examiners in town. You know how that can be."

"By the way," I said to Seaborn. "I believe you have a customer I know from Cincinnati. His name's Cohen."

"Cohen?" he echoed, raising his eyebrows much too high. He looked like he had just swallowed something much too big for his throat, which was bobbing up and down like a fishing cork.

"Yes. Lou Cohen?"

"Oh, yes, I believe I've seen him in the bank from time to time."

"Give him my regards the next time you see him," I said.

I could almost hear their sighs of relief when I left the table. And I knew enough about human nature to know that Charles Seaborn had more than a casual acquaintance with Cohen.

Perhaps Cowboy Lewis would confirm my suspicions. In the meantime, I couldn't help wondering why tiny beads of sweat had been twinkling from Seaborn's upper lip. I usually don't make people *that* nervous.

When I got back to the table, Dutch still looked nervous.

"What'd you say to them?" he asked. "Seaborn looked like he swallowed a lemon."

"I just asked Seaborn if he knew my old friend Lou Cohen," I said with a smile.

"Verdammt," Dutch said, shaking his head. "You sure do play hard cheese."

"Is there any other way to play?" I replied.

On the way out Dutch was paged. He spoke into the lobby phone for a few moments and hung up.

"That was Zapata," he said. "Salvatore's screaming bloody murder, but he's giving up O'Brian. He thinks you're nuts."

"I've been accused of that before too," I said.

"Just so you'll know," Dutch added, "Salvatore knows where O'Brian is. If you're not back in two hours, we're going in with the marines, although I don't know why we should bother."

"We're just getting accustomed to that ugly pan of his," Charlie One Ear commented.

It was nice to know they cared.

The fat old pelican sat on a corner post of the deck surrounding the fishing shack, looking bored. He surveyed the broad expanse of bay which emptied into the Atlantic Ocean a mile away to the east at Thunder Point. A warm breeze ruffled in from the sound and the old bird stared, half-asleep, across the surface of the water, looking for the tell-tale signs of lunch. Then, spotting a school of mullet, he flapped his broad wings and soared off the post, climbing twenty feet or so above the water, wheeling over and diving straight in, hitting with a splat and bobbing back up with a fish flopping helplessly in his bucket of a beak.

The Irishman watched the pelican make his catch. He was making a fishing lure. He had set up a small vise on the edge of a table and was carefully twining and retwining nylon, hook, and feathers, weaving them into a shiny lure. He had stopped to watch the pelican, keeping the line taut so it would not ravel.

He was a big man with one of those florid Irish faces that would look fifteen years old until he was ninety. A few lines grooved its smooth surface, but not enough to mar his youthful, carefree expression.

There was very little traffic along the bay. A few shrimp boats had gone out against the rising tide and a weekend sailor was trying, without much success, to get a lackluster wind in the sails of his boat a couple of hundred yards away. Otherwise it was so quiet he could hear what little wind there was rattling the marsh grass.

This was the Irishman's love, his escape from a business he neither liked nor understood. He felt like a misfit, a Peter Principled gunman forced to act like a businessman. O'Brian liked to settle disputes his own way. Negotiating confused him. But here he was king; he was alone and free, master of himself and his tiny domain, for O'Brian had mastered the secrets of fishing. It was one of the few things he did well, and he loved the sport with a consummate passion.

When the phone rang, he snapped, "Damn!" under his breath and weighted down the loose end of the lure with a metal clamp before he went into the main room of the cabin to answer it.

"It's me, boss, Harry," the gravelly voice on the other end of the line

said. "He's through eating breakfast. You sure you don't want I should follow him out, make sure he isn't bringin' company?"

"I said alone."

"He could bring company."

"Naw, he won't do that."

"You never know with these Feds."

"He don't have nothin' on me," the Irishman said.

"He's pretty quick, this guy."

"Just camp out at Benny's down the road. I need ya, I holler."

"Want I should ring once and hang up when he leaves?"

"Good idea."

"Everything calm out there?"

"No problem. Coupla shrimp boats went by. Nobody's been down the road. There's some jerk out here trying to get his sailboat back to the city marina, which is kinda funny."

"What's so funny about it?"

"There ain't no wind."

"Well, don't take no chances."

"Don't worry. You just hang out there at Benny's, have a coupla beers, come on in when you see him leave.

"Gotcha."

They hung up and the Irishman switched on the radio and walked out onto the deck for a stretch. The sailboat had drifted four hundred feet or so west of the shack, toward the city, and the sailor was trying vainly to crank up his outboard, a typically sloppy weekend sailor in a floppy white hat, its brim pulled down around his ears. The putz, he thought, was probably out of gas. But he had learned one thing since discovering the sea—sailors helped each other.

He cupped his hands and yelled:

"See if you can get it over here, maybe I can help."

The sailor waved back. He shoved the submachine gun under his windbreaker near his feet, took an oar from the cockpit of the sailboat, and began to paddle toward the Irishman. . . .

FLASHBACK: NAM DIARY, THE FIRST SIX

The twelfth day: *Today I killed a man for the first time. I have a hard time talking about this. What happened, we're moving on this village, which was actually about a dozen hooches in this rice field seven or eight kliks downriver. This village was at the bottom of some foothills. There were rice paddies on both sides and a wide road lined with pepper trees and bamboo kind of dead-ending at it.*

Before we start down, Doc Ziegler, our medic, hands me a couple of buttons. "What are these for?" I ask. "Dex," he says. "Make you see better, hear better, move faster. Just do it." So I popped the speed. It took about twenty seconds to kick my ass. I've never had speed before. I felt like taking on the village all by myself. I mean, I was ready!

We go down toward it, two squads on each side in the rice paddies, because they make good cover, and we have the Three Squad backing us up in reserve. We go in on the left and the One Squad on the right. They take the first hit. The VC opens up with mortars and machine-gun fire and starts just chewing them up. One guy, the whole top of his head went off. The noise was horrendous; I couldn't believe the racket.

The lieutenant runs straight toward the village with his head down just below the edge of the ditch and I'm right behind him. The radio man is having trouble calling up the reserve platoon because we're in this little valley and the reception is for shit, so the lieutenant sends back a runner and then he says, "Fuckin' gooks are eating One Squad up, we got to take them," and he goes out of the paddy and runs for this stretch of bamboo which is maybe twenty yards from the gooks and me still right behind him.

That tips Charlie and they start cutting away at us. They're shooting the bamboo down all around us, just cutting it off. Then I see this VC in his black pajamas and he's got his head out just a little, checking it out, and I sight him in and, ping! he goes down, just throws his hands up in the air and goes over backward. Then another one comes running over and he's shooting as he comes, only he's aiming about ten meters to my left and I drop him. Then I see the machine gun, which is in the dirt out in front of the first hooch, and there's two of them and they're just cutting

One Squad to shit, so I run up through the bamboo and get in position and blitz them both, pow, pow, pow, pow, pow!

Next thing I know, the lieutenant and the rest of the squad are running past me and the One Squad breaks loose and then it's all over. Five minutes, maybe. I was thinking, Jesus, I did more in the last five minutes than I ever did in my whole life. I mean, it was such a high. And to still be in one piece!

There wasn't anybody left. Women, kids, old people, VC. The entire village was blitzed. Nobody seemed to pay any attention to that; it was just business as usual. Then they brought in a flamethrower and scorched the whole place. I didn't look at the civilians, I just looked the other way. I figure, this is the way it's done, but it doesn't change how I feel about it.

Otherwise we were all feeling pretty good because none of our guys was hurt.

"You okay?" the lieutenant says after he makes the body count, and I says, "Yeah, I feel good." And I did.

"You looked okay in there," he says.

I wasn't a virgin anymore and I was still alive. Jesus, I felt good.

It took me a long time to get used to it, that I had killed those people and it was okay, that it was what they expected me to do. For a while I kept dreaming they would come at night and arrest me.

The 38th day: *Doc Ziegler doesn't even believe in all this. He's a medic, doesn't carry any weapons. He says he would have gone to Canada but his old man had a bad heart and Doc figured it would kill him if Doc jumped the border. So he said "Fuck it!" when he got his notice. "I can put up with anything for a year," he says. Among other things, Doc supplies the speed. He doesn't do it himself, says he doesn't need it since he doesn't carry a weapon. But he smokes pot a lot. Morning, noon, and night. Hell, I don't think I've ever seen Doc unstoned. But when there's trouble he can move with the best of them. What the hell, if it makes it easier. He's been on the line a month longer than me and he acts like he was born here.*

Carmody is the best officer I ever knew. All he thinks about is what's out there. He never talks about home, his wife, nothing. Just business and his men. He was a green shavetail when he got to Nam ten months ago. He has a funny sense of humor, like no matter what you ask him, he's got a one-liner for you. I asked him once where he was from.

"My old man had the poorest farm in Oklahoma," he says. "Our hog was so skinny, if you put a dime on its nose, its back feet would rise up off the ground."

Then there's Jesse Hatch, who used to drive a truck all over the country, one of those big semis; and Donny Flagler, who's like me, just out of college. Both of them are black guys. And there's Jim Jordan, who was in law school; his old man was a senator and still couldn't get him deferred. Jordan is one pissed-off guy. He's a short-timer, has two months to go, a first-class pain in the ass. Hatch is the M-60 man; he can really handle that mother. Flagler is our radio. None of us are regulars, but after a month out here, I feel like one.

The 42nd day: *We get orders to take this knob for an LZ. Charlie is all over the place. He won't give it up. They have the high ground; they sit up there and lob mortars down on us all after-fuckin'-noon. Carmody gets on the radio and calls in the Hueys. He wants them to blitz the place so we can rush it, only it's raining and a little foggy, and they're giving him some stand-down shit and he starts yelling:*

"I want some air in here, now! Don't gimme any of that fog shit. Nobody's told us to go home because it's raining. Get me some goddamn air support fast!"

He slams the phone down.

"Listen, kid, if you can't get a chopper in when you fuckin' need one, forget it. That's the edge. You don't have the edge, you're in trouble. We can't beat these motherfuckers at this kind of game, for Christ sake, they been doing it for fifteen fuckin' years. When you need air, get nasty."

That's the way he was, always teaching me something.

About ten minutes later these two Hueys come over and really waste that knob. Carmody doesn't wait for shit, we're off up the hill while the Hueys are still chewing it up. Six or eight 50-millimeter and 20-millimeter cannons working. Good god, there were VC's flying all over the place in bits and pieces. A boot with a foot in it hit me in the shoulder and splashed blood down my side. I was getting sick. Then the gooks broke and ran and we took the knob and sat up there picking them off as they went down the other side. We must've shot ten, twelve of them in the back. After a while I stopped counting. It didn't seem right. Maybe I've seen too many cowboy movies, but shooting all those people in the back seemed to be pushing it. But then, I've only been on the line two months. I'm still learning.

The 56th day: *Last night a bunch of sappers jumped this airstrip eight or nine kliks north of here and pillaged two cargo planes. They got ahold of some of our own Bouncing Bettys. What you got there is a daisy cutter, a 60-millimeter mortar round, and it's rigged so it jumps up about waist* *high when you trip it, and it goes off there, at groin level, cuts you in half.*

We're always real careful about mines, but the motherfuckers have these Bettys all over the fucking place. A couple of places they rigged phony trip lines so you'd see the line and move out of the way and they'd have another trip line next to it and you'd nick that and it was all over.

I hear it go off. Nobody screams or anything, it just goes boomf! *and shakes some leaves off the trees where I am. I run back. It's maybe a hundred meters. Flagler's laying there and he's blown in* half. *Two parts of him. I can't believe it. I start shaking. I sit down and shake all over. Then Doc comes up and gives me a downer.*

Carmody is taking it the worst. He just keeps swearing over and over. Later in the day we catch up with a couple of VC. We don't know whether they rigged the Bouncing Bettys, but we tie the two of them to these two trees, side by side, and we set one of the mines between the trees and rig it and then we back off about a hundred feet and we keep shooting at the line and those two gooks are screaming bloody-fucking-murder. It was Jesse finally tripped it. We left them hanging in the trees.

Psychological warfare, that's what we call it.

39

DEAD MAN'S FLOAT

It took me twenty minutes to make the drive to Skidaway Island. Three blocks on the far side of the bridge I found Bayview, a deserted gravel lane, hardly two cars wide, that twisted through a living arch of oak trees heavy with Spanish moss. Here and there, ruts led to cabins hidden away among trees, palmettos, and underbrush. I passed a roadhouse called Benny's Barbecue, which looked closed except for a gray Olds parked at the side of the place that looked suspiciously like the car Harry Nesbitt was driving when he followed me the night before. After that there was nothing but foliage for almost a mile before I came to O'Brian's shack.

It wasn't much more than that, although it seemed a sturdy enough place. It was built on stilts about twenty yards off shore and was connected to land by a wooden bridge no more than three feet wide. The tide was in and the cabin, which looked about two rooms large with a deck surrounding it and a screened porch at one end, was perched barely three feet above the water. A small boat, tied to one end of the platform, rocked gently on the calm surface of the bay.

Nesbitt was right—there wasn't a blade of grass within twenty yards of the cabin.

The place was as still as a church at dawn.

A slate-gray Continental was parked under the trees near the water's edge. It had been there awhile; the hood was as cool as the rest of the car. I walked out to the edge of the clearing and held my hands out, prayer style, palms up.

"O'Brian? It's me, Kilmer."

A mockingbird cried back at me and darted off through the palmettos. Somewhere out near the shack a fish jumped in the water. Then, not a sound.

I waited a moment or two.

"It's Jake Kilmer," I yelled. "I'm coming on out."

Still nothing.

I tucked both sides of my jacket in the back of my belt to show him I wasn't wearing a gun and started walking out onto the platform, holding onto both railings so he could see my hands.

"O'Brian!"

A fish jumped underfoot and startled me. I could see why O'Brian had built his shack on this spot. He could drop a line out the window and fish without getting out of bed.

"O'Brian, it's Kilmer. You around?"

Still no answer.

I reached the cabin. The front door was locked, so I went around to the porch, held my face up against the screen, cupped my eyes, and peered inside. The place was as empty as a dead man's dream.

"O'Brian?"

Still no sounds, except the tie line of the boat, grinding against the wooden railing.

Worms began to nibble at my stomach.

"Hey, O'Brian, are you in there?" I yelled. I startled an old pelican sitting on a corner of the deck and he lumbered away, squawking as he went. There was no answer.

I tried the screen door and it was open. The cabin was empty; nobody was under the bed or stuffed in the shower. But the radio was on with the volume turned all the way down, and the beginnings of a fishing lure dangled from a vise on the porch table.

The worms stopped nibbling and started gnawing at my insides.

I went back outside and started around the deck. The boat was empty.

I might have missed the two bullet holes except for the blood. It was splattered around two small nicks in the rear wall of the cabin; crimson, baked almost brown in the hot sunlight, yet still sticky to the touch.

The worms in my stomach grew to coiled snakes.

"Oh, shit!" I heard myself whisper.

I knelt down on the deck and peered cautiously under the cabin. The first thing I saw was a foot in a red sweat sock jammed in the juncture of two support posts. The foot belonged to Jigs O'Brian. The rest of him was floating face down, hands straight out at his sides, as if he were trying to embrace the bay.

Fish were nibbling at the thin red strands that leaked from his head like the tentacles of a jellyfish.

I didn't need a medical degree to tell he was DOA.

SKEELER'S JOINT

Dutch almost swallowed the phone when I got him on the line. He was on his way before I hung up. The coroner reacted in much the same way.

Dutch arrived fifteen minutes later with Salvatore at the wheel, followed by an ambulance with the coroner and his forensics team close behind.

The big German lumbered out to the cabin with his hands in his pants pockets, an unlit Camel dangling from the corner of his mouth, and stared ruefully down at me through his thick glasses. Salvatore was behind him, glowering like a man looking for a fight.

"I take the full rap for this one," I said. "If you hadn't called Salvatore off, O'Brian might be alive now."

"I should have left Salvatore on his tail," Dutch said. "That was my mistake."

"You just did what I asked," I said. "I told O'Brian I'd be alone. Where are your pals from homicide?"

"On the way," he said with a roll of his eyes, adding, "What did it this time, a flamethrower?"

"Small caliber, very likely a submachine gun," I said.

"How do you figure that?"

"He's got a row of .22's from his forehead to his chin so perfect the line could've been drawn with a straightedge. My guess is, the first couple of shots knocked his head back. The gun was firing so fast it just drew a line right down his face, zip, like that."

I drew an invisible line from my forehead to my chin with a forefinger.

"Some gun," he said.

"Yeah," I said. "There's only one weapon I can think of that fits the bill."

"Well, don't keep us in suspense," said Dutch. Salvatore began to show signs of interest. He stopped staring into space long enough to give me the dead eye.

"The American 180. Fires thirty rounds a second. Sounds like a dentist's drill when it goes off."

"Like on the tape of the Tagliani job," Dutch said.

"Yeah, just like that. I figure whoever aced him came in by boat and whacked O'Brian when he came out of the cabin. Two of the slugs went through his head; they're in the back wall."

"So what does all that mean to us?" Dutch said.

While the coroner was studying the bloodstained holes in the back wall of the cabin, his men were shooting pictures of O'Brian's body from everywhere but underwater.

"Chevos owns boats," I said. "It's his thing. I've heard he lives at the Thunder Point Marina. Where would that be from here?"

Dutch pointed due east. Thunder Point was a mile away, a misty, low, white structure surrounded by miniature boats.

"You really want to pin this one on Nance, don't you?" Dutch asked.

"Maybe."

"Look, I got nothing against headhunting; sometimes it can get great results. You got something to settle with that *sheiss kopf* it's okay with me."

The coroner dug the two bullets out of the wall and went back across the bridge to shore.

"Maybe he's holed up on a boat," I said.

"That's assuming he knows we're looking for him."

"Well, hell, I make a lot of mistakes," I said.

Dutch put a paw on my shoulder. "Aw, don't we all," he said, putting that discussion to bed. He strolled up and down the deck of O'Brian's shack, berating himself, like an orator grading his own speech.

Salvatore stood in one place, staring back into space and grinding fist into palm, like a bomb looking for someplace to go off.

"We should've brought 'em all in, the whole damn bunch," Dutch said, "get it out in the open. I laid off because it's homicide's baby. Well, it's our baby too. The Red Sea'll turn kelly green before that bunch of *pfutzlükers* get their heads out far enough to see daylight. Ain't it just wonderful!" He stared off toward Thunder Point. "I'm gonna haul that bunch of *ash lochers* in and get some answers. If nothing else, maybe we can throw these killers off their stride."

His tirade brought only a grunt from Salvatore, who was glaring back into space.

Dutch sighed. "Okay, let's see who we got left."

He started counting them off on his fingers. "There's the Bobbsey Twins, Costello and Cohen. Then there's Stizano and the pasta king, Bronicata, and your pals, Chevos and Nance. I miss anybody?"

There wasn't anybody else. Like Christie's Ten Little Indians, the field was running out.

"One thing," I said. "If you start hauling these people in, you better have a lot of help. They come complete with pistoleros. And you'll also be dealing with Leo Costello. He's quick and a helluva lot smarter than you'd like him to be. The son of a bitch sleeps with a habeas corpus under his pillow."

"I'll keep that in mind," Dutch said.

Salvatore finally broke his silence. He looked at me and said, "What it is with me, see, I coulda followed that ugly fuckin' Mick into his bedroom and held his nuts while he balled his old lady and he still wouldn't know I was there. I got a talent for that kind of thing. Me and Zapata, we're the invisible men."

"I told him I'd be alone," I protested. "We took a chance, what can I tell you? Next time I'll know better."

He stared at me for a beat or two longer and suddenly said, "Ah, shit, let's forget it."

"What do you think O'Brian wanted?" Dutch asked.

"I don't know, but if anybody knows, Nesbitt does," I said. "Let's put him on the radio, find out his story."

"Done," said Dutch. "I'll add him to the list."

We walked back across the narrow pier to solid land, where the coroner flagged us down.

"Stoney Titan's on his way out," he said, and turned to me. "He says he wants a word or two with you."

"Looks like the old man's finally throwing his oar in," Dutch said.

I didn't feel up to my first round with Titan; I had something else on my mind. "I've got some things to do," I told Dutch. "You know as much about this mess as I do; you talk to the old man."

"He's not gonna like that even a little bit," the big man growled.

"Tough shit," I said, and drove off toward Benny's Barbecue. I was anxious to see if the gray Olds was still there. It wasn't, but as I turned into the place, Stonewall Titan's black limo passed me, going like he was late for the policemen's ball.

I pulled around to the back of Benny's, oyster shells crunching under my tires, and found a tallish, deeply tanned man with dishwater-blond hair that had seen too much sun and surf loading soft-drink crates through the back door of the place. He was wearing black denim shorts and dirty sneakers, no shirt, and could have been thirty, fifty, or anything between.

"We don't open until five," he said as I got out of the car.

"I'm looking for a pal of mine," I said, following him inside. The place was dark and there was the leftover chill of last night's air conditioning lingering in the air, which smelled of stale beer and shrimp. He looked at me over his shoulder.

"I don't know anybody," he said flatly. "Half the time I can't remember my kids' names."

"I saw his car here a little earlier," I said.

"No kidding. Maybe he had a flat."

"He wasn't around."

"Probably ran outta gas. Maybe he had to walk up to the boulevard, pick up a can."

"Could be. I kind of felt he was in here."

"Hmm," he said, stacking the soft drinks in the corner. "You know how long I been here in this spot?"

"No, but I bet you're going to tell me."

He drew two beers from the spigot behind the bar and slid one across the bar to me. It was colder than Christmas in the Yukon.

"Thirty-three years. Be thirty-four in September."

I sipped the beer and stared at him.

"You know why I been here this long?" he went on.

"You mind your own business," I said.

"Right on the button."

"This guy's name is Nesbitt. Little squirt with roving eyeballs."

"You ain't been listening to me," he said.

"Sure I have," I said, sipping my beer. "If a fellow looks like that should come back by, tell him Kilmer says we need to have a talk. Real bad."

"That you? Kilmer?"

"Uh-huh."

"A guy I knew once had a mark on him, thought he was safe in downtown Pittsburgh. Then a wheelbarrow full of cement fell off a six-story building right on his head."

The metaphor seemed a little vague to me, but I took a stab at retorting.

"Tell him I won't drop any cement on his head."

The bartender chuckled and held out a hand. "Ben Skeeler," he said. "The place used to be called Skeeler's but everybody kept sayin' 'Let's go to Benny's' so I finally changed the sign."

He shook hands like he meant it.

"Long as we're being so formal, maybe I could see some ID," the cautious man said.

"That's fair enough," I said, and showed him my buzzer.

He looked at it and nodded. "I hope you're straight. The way I get it, you're straight, but this town can bend an evangelist faster than he can say amen."

I waited for more.

"Tough, too. I heard you was tough."

"I talk a good game," I said finally.

"These days, you know, you never can be too sure."

"Uh-huh."

"County ambulance just went by actin' real serious," he said. "You wouldn't know anything about that, would you?"

"Man named O'Brian just got himself killed out on the bay," I said.

His eyes got startled for a moment and then he looked down into his beer glass. "That so" was all he said. He pulled on his ear, then took a folded-up paper napkin out of his pocket and handed it to me.

"Dab your lips," he said. "I gotta get back to work."

He went outside and I unfolded the napkin. The message was written hurriedly in ballpoint that had torn through the napkin in a couple of places and left several inkblots at the ends of words. It said: "Uncle Jolly's Fillup, route 14 south about 18 miles. Tonight, 9 p.m. Come alone."

No signature. Skeeler came back with another crate of soft drinks.

"You know a place called Jolly's Fillup, route fourteen south of town?"

"Sounds like a filling station, don't it?" he said.

"Now that you mention it."

"You'll know it when you get there," he said, and went back outside. I finished my beer and followed him.

"Thanks for the beer. Maybe I'll come back and try the shrimp," I said as I got into the car.

"You do that, hear?" he said. "Be sure to introduce yourself again. I'm bad on names." And he vanished back inside.

RELICS

I started back toward Dunetown but when I got to the boulevard I went east instead of going back toward town. I really didn't have anything to do after I left Skeeler's, but I had to put some distance between me and Dunetown. I needed a little time to myself, away from Stick, Dutch, and the hooligans. Away from Doe. Away from them all. I was tired of trying to make some sense out of a lot of disparate jigsaw pieces, pieces like Harry Raines, Chief, and Stoney Titan. Like Donleavy and his sweaty banking friend, Seaborn. Like Chevos and Nance, a bad-luck horse named Disaway, and a black gangster I didn't even know whom everybody called Nose, but not to his face. I suddenly had the feeling that using people had become a way of life for me and I didn't like the feeling and I needed some room to deal with that. I needed to get back to my safe places again, at least for a little while.

When I got to the Strip I headed south, putting the tall hotels that plundered the beach behind me. I drove south with the ocean at my left, not sure where I was going. I just smelled the sea air and kept driving. Finally I passed a decrepit old sign peering out from behind the weeds that told me I had reached some-place called East Beach. It was desolate. Progress had yet to discover it.

I parked my car in a deserted public lot. Weeds grew up through the cracks in the macadam, and small dunes of sand had been collected by the wind along its curbs. I sat looking out at the Atlantic for a while. The sea here was calm, a mere ripple in the bright sunlight, and the beach was broad and clean. It revived memories long buried, the good times of youth that age often taints with melancholy.

My mind was far from Dunetown. It was at a place called Beach Haven, a village on the Jersey coast where I had spent several summers living on a houseboat with the family of my best friend in grammar school. I couldn't remember his name but I did re-member that his father was Norwegian and spoke with a mar-velous accent and wore very thick glasses and that the family was not in the least modest and that he had a sister of high school age who thought nothing at all of taking a shower in front of us. Sitting there in the hot sedan with sweat dribbling off my chin, I also recalled that I had spent a good part of that summer trying to hide a persistent erection.

After a while I got out and took off shoes, socks, jacket, and tie and put them in the trunk. I slammed it shut, then opened it again, dropped my beeper in with them, and went down to the beach.

I rolled my pants legs to the knee and walked barefoot with the sand squeaking underfoot. I must have walked at least a mile when I came upon a small settlement of summer cottages, pro-tected by walls of granite rock that were meant to hold back the ocean. It had been a futile gesture. The houses were deserted. Several had already broken apart and lay lopsided and forlorn, awash with the debris of tides.

One of them, a small two-bedroom house of cypress and oak, was still perched tentatively over the rocks, its porch supported by six-by-sixes poised on the granite boulders. A faded sign, hang-ing crookedly from the porch rail, told me the place was for sale, and under that someone had added, with paint, the words "or rent." There was a phone number.

I went up over the big gray rocks, climbed the deck railing, and looked through the place, a forlorn and lonely house. The floor creaked and sagged uncertainly under each step and the wind, sighing through its broken windows, sounded like the ghost of a child's summer laughter.

I stripped down to my undershorts, went down to the deserted beach, and ran into the water, swimming hard and fast against the tide until arms and legs told me to turn back. I had to breast-stroke the last few yards and when I got out I was breathing heavily and my lungs hurt, but I felt clean and my skin tingled from the saltwater. I went back up to the house and stretched out on the deck in the sun.

I was dozing when the woman came around the corner of the house. She startled us both and as I scrambled for my pants she laughed and said, "Don't bother. Most of the gigolos hanging around the hotel pools wear far less than that."

She was an islander, I could tell; a lovely woman, delicate in structure, with sculptured features textured by wind and sun, tiny white squint-lines around her eyes, and amber hair coiffured by the wind. I couldn't guess how old she was; it didn't matter. She was carrying a seine net—two five-foot wooden poles with the net attached to each and topped by cork floats. The net was folded neatly around the poles.

"I was halfway expecting my friend. He sometimes waits up here for me," she said, peering inside without making a show of it. Then she added, "Are you flopping here?"

I laughed.

"No, but it's a thought."

She looked around the place.

"This was a very dear house once," she said. She said it openly and without disguising her sadness.

"Do you know the owners?" I asked.

"It once belonged to the Jackowitz family, but the bank has it now."

Her sad commentary told me all I needed to know of its history.

"What a shame. There's still some life left to it."

"Yes, but no heart," she said.

"Banks are like that. They have a blind appetite and no soul. They're the robots of our society."

"Well, I see my friend down on the beach. I'm glad you like the house."

A skinny young man in cutoffs with long blond hair that flirted with his shoulders was coming up the beach carrying a bucket. She went down over the boulders to the sand.

"Hey?" I said.

She turned and raised her eyebrows.

"Is your name Jackowitz?"

"It used to be," she said, and went on to join her friend.

I got dressed and walked back through the surf to the parking lot. I found a phone booth that still worked and called the number that was on the sign at the house. It turned out to be the Island Trust and Savings Bank. I managed, by being annoyingly persistent, to get hold of a disagreeable little moron named Ratcher who, I was told, was "in beach property."

"I'm interested in a piece of land on East Beach," I said. "It might have belonged to a family called Jackowitz."

I could hear papers rustling in the background.

"Oh, yes," he said, probably after turning up the foreclosure liens. "I know the place." I could tell he knew as much about that cottage as I know about Saudi Arabian oil leases.

"Are you in real estate?" he asked curtly.

"No, I thought I might just rent it for the rest of the summer," I told him.

"The place is condemned," he said nastily. "And this establishment prosecutes trespassers." He hung up. I stood there for a minute or two, then invested another quarter and got Ratcher back on the phone.

"Ratcher?"

"Yes!"

"You're a despicable little asshole," I said, and hung up.

I drove back down toward the beach and, by trial and error, found a neglected road that led to the house and sat there, watching the woman whose name was once Jackowitz and her young man with the long hair, dragging their seine nets slowly along the water's edge, picking the shrimp and mullet out after each drag and putting them in the bucket. After a while it started to rain and they quit. I waved to them as they walked off down the beach. I'm not sure they saw me but it would be nice to think they did and that they knew the house still meant something to someone. Finally I drove back toward town in the rain, feeling beach-tired but recharged.

I thought about that place a lot in the days that followed, but I never went back. I didn't have to. Driving back to Dunetown, I realized I had left the safe places behind forever.

42

FIGHT NIGHT AT THE WAREHOUSE

I drove back to the Warehouse, and into bedlam.

A dozen men, including a couple of brass buttons, were jammed in the doorway. There was a lot of shoving, pushing, cursing, threatening. The Stick was standing outside, back from the crowd, watching the melee with a smile.

"Be goddamned," he said as I rolled up. "Dutch's put the arm on Costello and all his merry men!"

I jumped out of the car and we ran into the building.

A lot of racket from the back.

A cop stopped the Stick long enough to tell him they had Costello; his number one bodyguard and shooter, Drack Moreno, who looked and talked like a moron but had a genius IQ; two of his top button men, Silo Murphy, a.k.a. the Weasel, because he looked like one, and Arthur Pravano, whose moniker was Sweetheart, for reasons I'll never understand; and two other musclemen. In addition, they also had Chevos and Bronicata on tap with their various gunsels. Nance was missing, as was Stizano.

A small army of twelve, all of them but Costello raising almighty hell.

We headed for the war room, which is exactly what it had turned into from the sound of things.

The hooligans were well represented: Pancho Callahan, Salvatore, Chino Zapata, Charlie One Ear, Cowboy Lewis, and Dutch Morehead. Everyone but Kite and Mufalatta, who seemed to have vanished from the earth. With the Stick and me, it kind of rounded the teams off at eight to eight.

The yelling, cursing, and threats had continued down through the Warehouse and into the war room, which was as chaotic as the floor of the stock exchange at the closing bell.

Dutch had separated the big shots and shoved them into one of the cubicles. The gunsels were all in the war room. Dutch was standing in front of the room bellowing like a wounded whale.

213

"Everybody ease off, y'hear me, or some heads are gonna get loosened!" he roared.

The room settled down to a low rumble.

With Costello's bunch and the hooligans, the room was full of the meanest-looking gang of cutthroats I've ever seen gathered in one place.

I was standing in the doorway, eyeballing Costello and Chevos. In all the years I had been bonded to this gang, I had never seen either of them closer than fleetingly and from across the street or through binoculars. Now they were both fifteen feet away. I made no attempt to conceal my contempt for them.

Costello alone seemed calm. He was a tall man and better looking than I would have liked, his sharp features and hard-set jaw deeply tanned, his longish black hair bronzed by a lot of sun, his lean body decked out in a blue blazer, a pale blue shirt open at the collar, white slacks, and white loafers. He was one of those people whose age is superfluous. There were a lot of reasons to dislike him. Only his brown eyes were a clue to his anger. They glittered with suppressed rage. My rage was open, my hatred obvious, but I kept my mouth shut for the time being.

Chevos stood stoically in a corner of the cubicle, alone, staring at the wall, and Bronicata was jabbering like a monkey in heat.

The rest of the Tagliani mob was dressed casually for the beach, looking like graduates of a Sing Sing cellblock disguised as the Harvard crew team.

The hooligans rounded out the scene. A novice would have had one hell of a time separating the good guys from the bad.

"Kick that door shut there, Pancho," Dutch said, and Callahan closed the door.

Everybody chose up sides and lined up against opposite walls of the room, hooligans near the door, Costello's gunsels against the far wall.

Cowboy Lewis, wearing aged jeans, a faded Levi's jacket, a Derringer-type cowboy hat, and a brilliant red sunburn, was carrying a large grocery sack.

"We dumped 'em comin' offa Costello's rowboat," Cowboy said, in a voice that sounded like he swabbed his throat with number four sandpaper. I was to learn that Costello's "rowboat," as Lewis had genteelly put it, was a sixty-foot yacht that slept ten.

Cowboy carried a brown paper bag to the front of the room and dumped its contents on Dutch's desk.

Eight pistols of every kind and caliber, slip knives, brass knucks, two rolls of quarters, and other assorted tools of the trade. "The heavyweights were all light," he said.

Dutch's eyebrows rose with the corners of his lips.

"Neat. Did you all hear the Russians are in Charleston or some such?" he asked nobody in particular. Nobody answered, but there was a lot of grumbling and grousing.

"Definitely concealed weapons," said Lewis, who was nursing a split lip.

"Where'd ya get the fat lip?" Dutch asked.

"The little asshole with the mouse clipped me when I wasn't looking," he said, jerking a thumb toward one of the goons, who was wearing a black eye the size of a pancake. "I had to use reasonable force to subdue him."

The little asshole with the mouse got very tense.

"Okay, let's start makin' a list'r two here," said Dutch. "First off, we got concealed weapons—"

"They's all registered," said one of Costello's rat pack, cutting Dutch off.

"Shut up," Sweetheart Pravano said quietly. "L.C. says we don't say nuthin' to these monkeys, period."

Salvatore's eyes narrowed to slits and his fists balled and unballed. Cowboy Lewis stared at a spot in the corner of the ceiling and looked bored. Callahan just chuckled, and Chino Zapata took the gold tooth out of the front of his bridgework, put it in the change pocket of his jeans, and shook out his hands. Charlie One Ear mumbled something that could have been "shithouse mouse," although I'm not sure.

The Stick and I ambled into a neutral corner on the opposite side of the room from Dutch and laid back, waiting for something to happen.

Callahan started it.

"Tag these and put 'em away," Dutch told him. The dapper cop found paper and pencil and went up to the desk to complete his chore. He picked up a palm-sized .25 with a pearl handle, a cute little weapon, accurate for maybe three feet if the wind isn't blowing.

"Which one of you girls belongs to this?" Callahan said with a snicker, holding it between thumb and forefinger, like a dead fish.

Sweetheart Pravano, well over six feet tall and built like a Russian weightlifter, stepped up and slapped the carnation out of Callahan's lapel.

"Whyn't ya eat that daisy, ya fuckin' fag," he said.

His comment was greeted with a right hook that hurt *my* jaw and sent Sweetheart soaring across the room, head over heels over a table.

All hell broke loose.

Dutch was so appalled, he just watched it, openmouthed.

Cowboy swept the artillery back into the paper bag and threw it in a desk drawer.

I held my corner of the room.

The Stick waded right in.

Makeshift weapons appeared from under jackets, armpits, pants legs.

Salvatore drew his sawed-off pool cue from his shoulder holster and whapped Weasel Murphy across the back of the head as if he were swinging at a fastball. A tuft of Murphy's hair lifted straight up and Murphy slid across a table, sweeping file folders, baskets, and other stenographic paraphernalia before him to the floor.

Callahan took the meanest-looking of Costello's mutts, squared off in a fighting stance, and as the goon closed in on him, kicked him in the jaw. The toe of his sneaker was loaded with ball bearings. It burst open like a squashed grapefruit, and steel marbles rattled all over the floor. Callahan's target destroyed a typing stand and landed in a corner, spitting out his front teeth.

The floor was covered with ball bearings. It looked like amateur night at the roller derby, everybody dilly-dancing on the things like three-year-olds at ballet school.

Charlie One Ear, who had seemed a little overweight to me and far too elegant to mix it up with this bunch, slid out of his tweed jacket, spun around on the ball of one foot, kicked a goon in the diaphragm with a perfectly aimed toe-shot, slashed him across the temple with the flat of his hand, and was back on both feet before the goon hit the floor. A lovely little *pas seul.*

Zapata relied on nothing more than his fists, waltzing across the ball-bearinged floor and hitting any and all targets of opportunity.

The Stick picked Drack Moreno and they went at it, Moreno outweighing him by twenty pounds and outreaching him by three inches, a condition Stick quickly remedied by first kicking Moreno in the kneecap, then pulling a handkerchief loaded with silver dollars from his pocket and swinging it around and around like a bolo. It caught Moreno more than once. Moreno's face bunched up in pain. The Stick hit him in the throat. Moreno's tongue almost hit the far wall. His eyes crossed. He gasped for air. Zapata stepped in and flattened Moreno with a lovely one-two, a short jab to the face, followed by a gorgeous right uppercut to the jaw.

The Stick's silver dollars and Salvatore's pool cue finished off Weasel Murphy, who made the mistake of trying to get up off the floor.

Charlie One Ear gave another of his brief karate demonstrations and put another one away.

Salvatore held the last of Costello's strongarms by the collar of his shirt at arm's length and was socking him, almost casually, in the face, over and over again, with his pool cue.

Dutch ended the melee with two shots into the ceiling.

All motion was suspended.

"*Verdammt,* Salvatore, drop that guy!" he boomed.

Salvatore opened his hand and let him go, the tough dropping face first into a typewriter that lay on the floor.

Weasel Murphy groaned and slid down the wall.

The asshole with the mouse now had a pair of mice and no front teeth.

Drack Moreno's face looked like Omaha Beach on June seventh.

To my knowledge, not one of the hooligans had suffered so much as a bruise, except for Cowboy Lewis' fat lip.

The entire gala had lasted maybe a full minute, no more.

Dutch stood in front of the room, gun in hand, dust drizzling down on his shoulders from two holes in the ceiling.

"What's the matter with everybody? You all comin' unwired? Book these punks here for resisting arrest."

The door opened cautiously and three uniformed cops peered in nervously before entering the room. There were a lot of clinking handcuffs and groans as they cleared out the Tagliani goons.

Lewis and the others helped Callahan clean up his ball bearings.

"Brand-new sneakers," he complained, surveying the split toe of his Nikes.

All clubs and other weapons had magically vanished back to their nesting places.

The Stick returned to my solitary corner. He was smiling. "I feel much better," he said.

"I thought maybe one of them stole your hat," I said.

43

DOG WITH A BAD COLD

With things back under control, we left the war room and went back to the front of the Warehouse.

Costello remained in his corner, still tense, like a big cat waiting to spring. He looked back at me and stared for a few seconds, as though not quite sure who I was, and then recognition swept over his features. I could feel the hatred across the room. I smiled at him and stared back. My turn was coming.

Our group had narrowed down to the Stick, Dutch, and me. Most of the aggravated tension moved into the other room with us.

"Excuse me," Costello said in a voice that was flat, harsh, and no less venomous than the bite of an asp. "Do you mind reading us our rights and telling us what we're charged with?"

Dutch said, "The rest of them I'm gonna charge with, let's see, how about assaulting an officer, resisting arrest, creating a riot, destroying city property—"

"All right, let's make it simple," Costello interrupted. "What the hell are we doing here?"

"Things were a little too quiet, we only had one murder so far today," Dutch said. "So I thought we'd have us all a little picnic."

"Look," Costello said to Dutch, "I realize you're a well-respected police officer, Morehouse, but you're pushing—"

Now it was Dutch's turn to do the interrupting.

"Morehead," Dutch said in a growl. "Lieutenant Morehead."

"All right, Morehead—"

"Lieutenant."

Costello glared a moment or two more. *"Lieutenant* Morehead, what the hell do you want from us? Why are we here?"

Dutch said, "Maybe you haven't noticed, but a lot of your relatives have dropped suddenly dead in the last couple of days."

"Is that why that bunch of beach bums of yours has been harassing us for the past few weeks?"

"Oh, I would hardly call that harassment, Mr. Costello," Dutch said. "I'll be glad to show you real harassment, if you'd like."

Throughout the exchange, Chevos never took his eyes off me. They glittered like the eyes of a night predator. It had suddenly occurred to him who I was, a man whose assassination he had once ordered. I looked back and for a moment we were eye to eye. A lot went on in that face in a couple of seconds: hate, fear, annoyance, curiosity, anger, frustration. He finally looked away.

I finally cut into the conversation. "So you're representing all these people, right, Costello?"

"That's right. I'm glad somebody finally remembered I'm an attorney."

"Then let's just you and us talk," I said, and I stepped back into the war room. Dutch ushered Costello in and the Stick followed.

I slammed the door and said, "Look, let's stop fucking around. You're just a mobster, Costello. We all know it, so let's stop the bullshit. Uncle Franco is dead and that makes you primo candidate for *capo di capi*—that's if you don't join the rest of your worthless ancestors, which wouldn't hurt my feelings at all."

He started to say something but I held my hand up and kept talking. "Now we figure two things, Costello; either some mob from up country has decided to muscle you out of Dunetown and take over, or somebody inside your clan has got a real bad beef going on."

"Are you implying that I engineered these killings?" he said angrily.

"You haven't got the guts," I said, letting my feelings hang out. "I'm telling you what we know and what we're guessing."

"It's our problem."

"Wrong again, asshole," I said. "We just made it our problem."

"Not likely," he said, very slowly and deliberately. "Whatever the problem is, it's our problem and we'll take care of it."

"Yeah," I said with a smile. "Just like you have so far?"

His face turned red. Dutch said, "Wrong, anyway. We're talking about homicide, lots of it. It's out of your hands, Costello. It's officially a police matter. As such, what we're suggesting is your cooperation."

"I'll tell it one more time," he said, holding up a forefinger. "I don't know who is doing this, or why. And that's all any of us will have to say on the matter."

"That's hardly what we call cooperation, counselor," Dutch said. Then he piped up, "Right now, I got you down as an A-number-one client for a hit *and* an A-number-one suspect. You could be in a lot of trouble, Mr. Costello. I could book you as a material witness for starters."

"I'd be out before the desk sergeant cleared his throat," Costello said.

"Where's Turk Nance?" I asked.

"I barely know Turk Nance. Why, is he missing?" Costello hissed, then, turning to Dutch, added, "I'm leaving now and I'm taking my people with me."

"I'm booking that bunch of muggers of yours for disorderly conduct," Dutch said. "Seventy-five bucks apiece."

"Don't be silly . . ."

"Disorderly conduct, period," Dutch said. "You want to argue, we'll see you all in court. Otherwise you can pay the night judge on your way out. It'll fix the holes in the ceiling." He jabbed a thumb toward the two bullet holes.

Costello turned back to me. "You, I know about. Your name came down from Cincy. I hear you're on the list, buddy boy. Way up. My wife's uncle Skeet had a lot of friends."

"I'm all torn up over your wife's uncle Skeet," I said. "I'll make you a promise, wimp. I'm going to send you up there with him. A Christmas present, so he doesn't get lonely."

"You know, you could work yourself to death, Kilmer."

"I doubt even you're stupid enough to knock over a Fed," the Stick said to Costello.

"Sure he is," I said. "He's real stupid."

"Maybe you ought to be on the list too," Costello said to Stick.

"Love it," said the Stick, and started laughing.

"You've been a flea bite to my family for a long time, Kilmer," Costello said.

"Sure, that's why you all ran out of Cincinnati," I said with a leer. "You couldn't stand the itch."

"I suggest you back off," he said coldly. "We've done nothing illegal here. This is none of your business."

"Everything you do's my business," I snarled. "I've made you my favorite charity."

There was one of those tense moments when nobody says anything. I decided to fill in the blanks.

"There's an African proverb, goes like this," I said. " 'When the skunk saw the lion run from him, he thought he was king of the jungle. And then he met a dog with a bad cold.' That's me, Costello, I'm your dog with a bad cold. I know all about your lily-white record and I don't care. I'm going to turn you up. Sooner or later this dog is going to bite. That's if you're still around."

"Oh, I'll be around," he said, and turned to leave. He hesitated at the door. "This is a family affair," he said. "Resolving it is a matter of honor to us."

"That explains the problem," I said. "If honor's concerned in this, you're dead already."

Costello turned and left. I followed him back out and went up to Chevos, standing so I was a few inches from his face. He looked like one of those Russian assassins that usually get elected to the Politburo.

I put on my toughest voice, almost a whisper with an edge like a carving knife.

"Where's Nance, old man?"

He stared at me, snake-eyed, his jaws shivering. He didn't answer and he couldn't look me in the eye; he just kept staring over my shoulder.

"Where's Nance, *old man?*" I snarled again, with as much menace as I could put in it.

Blood filled his face at the insult but he still didn't answer.

"Give him a message from me," I hissed angrily. "You tell that gutless back-shooter he fucked up when he missed me in Cincinnati that night. Tell him the next time he tries, I'm gonna take his gun away from him, stick it up his ass, and blow his brains out. Do you think you can remember that, or are you too senile?"

He was so angry his eyes started to water. His Adam's apple was bobbing like a bubble in the surf as he swallowed his spit.

"I know all about you, you disgusting freak," I went on, getting all the venom I could out of my system. "You make junkies out of children. You kill women. You're scum, Chevos, and you're on my list too."

It felt good. Damn, did it feel good. I may not have had ball bearings in my sneakers or a sawed-off pool cue in my holster, but I felt good.

I turned and went back into the war room, followed momentarily by Stick and Dutch.

"Well, that's throwing down the old gauntlet," Stick said.

"That was some touchy stuff bein' said in there," Dutch agreed.

"Blood feud," I said. "I put their patron saint in the place and sooner or later some punk asshole's gonna try to even the score and make a name for himself. I just decided to give it a nudge."

"That's a comforting thought," said the Stick. Then he turned to Dutch. "What the hell did all that accomplish, anyway?" he asked.

"Blew off a little steam. I figured you boys needed some close-up contact, see these guys eyeball to eyeball. Us too. It's good to see the enemy up close. Also to get it out in the open air, so there's no question about where everybody stands."

Stick's face curled up into that crazy-eyed smile and he shook his head. "You made it clear, all right."

At that point Dutch stared past us in surprise.

"Well, I'll be damned," he said. "Look who finally blew in with the wind."

I turned to check out the new arrival.

"You're about to meet the Mufalatta Kid, Jake," Dutch said.

The Mufalatta Kid was not what I expected. I had pictured a man smaller and leaner, almost emaciated. I suppose because the Stick had implied as much. The Mufalatta Kid was a shade under six feet tall and built like a swimmer. He walked loose, his hands dangling at his sides, fingers limp, shoulders sagging from side to side, only the balls of his feet touching. No jewelry. The Kid was dressed for yachting: a pale blue sailcloth shirt, jeans, and dirty, white, low-cut sneakers. All he needed was a rugby shirt and a pipe. But what surprised me most was that he didn't look a day over sixteen. Even his pencil-thin mustache didn't help. The Kid was well named—that's exactly what he looked like.

"Welcome home," Dutch growled. "I hope you had a nice trip."

The Kid didn't say anything, but he didn't look too concerned about anything, either.

"Okay," Dutch demanded, "what's your story? We got World War Three going on here, and you drop off the face of the earth."

"I've been shagging Mr. Badass since Sunday morning, eleven a.m." His voice was soft, dusty, confident. I assumed Mr. Badass was Longnose Graves.

"You eyeballed him that entire time?" Dutch said.

"Until about thirty minutes ago. He's been in a high-stakes poker game at the Breakers Hotel with two horseplayers from California, some asshole from Hot Springs, Texas, in a Stetson hat who insulted everybody at the table, a white pimp off Front Street, and a few fast losers. A Louisiana horse breeder came into the game late today and Nose stayed around to clean his tank also. Fucker dropped fifteen grand before he could wipe his nose."

"Graves was the big winner, then?" I asked.

"That's it. Who the hell are you, anyway?"

Dutch did the honors. Mufalatta had a handshake that almost crippled me for life. He stuck up his nose at me upon learning I was a Fed. Another one to educate.

"Do you know what's been happening?" Dutch asked.

"No details. Just that all these bozos are from points north and somebody has a hard-on for them." He paused and looked at me for the blink of an eye, then added, "All of a sudden."

Dutch said, "Kilmer was on the plane when Tagliani got wasted. I picked him up myself at the airport."

The Kid shrugged. "No offense," he said. "My mother sold me for six bucks to a Canal Street vegetable man when I was four years old. I ain't trusted anybody since."

"How the hell did you keep him in sight for thirty-six hours?" Dutch asked.

"Nose don't know me from a brick shithouse, so I bribed the bellhop who's got the room, give him a Franklin and all the tips I took in, he let me take the job. I handled the room, mixed drinks, kept the place tidy. Kept the ladies in the other room happy. Let me tell you, the only time that nigger left the table was to go to the growler. He didn't do so much as a Ma Bell the whole time."

"Was he by himself?" Dutch asked.

"Just him and his bodyguard. A Chinee called Song. Big Chinee," the Kid said, giving it a little vibrato for emphasis. "I mean, that fucker makes King Kong look like an organ grinder's monkey."

"Graves probably wouldn't be doing the dirty work himself, anyway," I offered.

"I'd want long odds if I made that bet," the Kid said, glaring at me.

"You think he would?" I asked.

"He did Cherry McGee in, personally. And in broad fuckin' daylight. We couldn't bend him for disturbing the peace. And he disturbed the hell out of McGee's peace."

"What do you know about McGee?" I asked.

"He's a dead fuckin' honky," the Kid said.

I had a wild hunch and I threw it at the Kid. "That Louisiana horse breeder that came in the game late, his name wasn't Thibideau, was it?"

He looked surprised. "Thibideau? Yeah, I think that was the name. Short guy, dark hair, built like a crate?"

"Close enough. How much did he drop?"

"Fifteen and change. How you know he was in the game?"

"I'm psychic," I said.

"No shit?" he said. "Maybe you should read my palm. I been told I got a life line shorter than a lovebird's pecker."

"I wouldn't know," I said. "I've never seen a lovebird's pecker."

"See what I mean," he said. Then he turned back to Dutch. "What the hell's goin' on here? Who are all these people fuckin' up the place?"

"Kid, it's a long, *long* story," Dutch said wearily. "You're about three days behind. I'll buy you a sandwich; maybe Kilmer here can fill you in."

He looked back at me. "A fuckin' Fed, huh," he said. "We ain't got enough trouble."

"You'll learn to love me," I said, and begged off dinner with some vague excuse. I had to meet Harry Nesbitt at Uncle Jolly's and this time I decided to keep the meeting to myself.

I headed back to the hotel to take a quick shower.

There were four phone messages in my box. Three of them were from Doe Findley. The fourth was from DeeDee Lukatis.

UNCLE JOLLY'S

I put on my oldest jeans, a faded cotton shirt, clodhopper boots, a nasty old Windbreaker from my narc days, put my .357 under my arm, and slipped a bob-nosed .22 into my boot. It was about eight o'clock when I headed out Highway 35 south.

I was thinking about Doe, and I was also thinking about DeeDee Lukatis. She had obviously left the message at the desk. It was handwritten.

Dear Jake:

You probably don't remember me. The last time I saw you I was barely 15. I need to talk to you about a matter of some urgency. My phone number is below. If we miss each other I'll be at Casablanca after ten tonight.

An old friend,
DEEDEE LUKATIS.

It was followed by a P.S. with her phone number. I had tried it but there was no answer. I might have ignored the message except for two things. DeeDee Lukatis was Tony Lukatis' sister, and Tony Lukatis had once been Doe's lover. That would have been enough to warrant a phone call. But Babs Thomas had also told me that DeeDee Lukatis was the personal secretary of my favorite Dunetown banker, Charles Seaborn. That made it very important. She might know a lot about Lou Cohen's relationship with Seaborn.

Then I started thinking about Doe. Her first two phone messages had been simple and to the point: "Please call Mrs. Raines about the stud fee." Nice and subtle. The last message informed me that she was out for the evening but I could call her after ten in the morning. That was to let me know Harry was back in town. I felt a sudden urgency to see her, knowing I couldn't, and I felt some sense of guilt at not calling her earlier in the day.

Uncle Jolly's Fillup ended that reverie. The place wasn't hard to find. It would have been harder not to find.

It looked like a Friday night football game. A country cop was directing traffic, most of which was going down the same dirt road I went down. I followed the crowd about two miles through pine trees and palmetto bushes to the parking lot. Through the cracks and peeling paint I could just make out the sign: PARK HERE FOR UNCLE JOLLY'S FILLUP.

A hundred cars in the space, at least.

I parked among dusty Chevys and Dodges, Pontiacs with high-lift rear ends, and pickup trucks with shotguns in the rear window gunracks, and drifted with the crowd. As I passed one of those big-wheel pickups, the kind with wheels about six feet high, the door opened and the Mufalatta Kid stuck his caramel-colored face out.

"You take a wrong turn someplace?" he asked.

"What're you doing here?" I asked.

"Just checkin' out the territory."

"Me too."

"Glide easy, babes. Strangers make these people real nervous."

"What's this all about, anyway?" I asked him.

"You mean you don't know why you came all the way out here?" he said incredulously. "Shit, man, I guess you are psychic. This is the dog fights, babes."

It jolted me.

Dog fighting was the last thing I expected. Bare-knuckle boxing, a porno show, a carnival, a lot of things had occurred to me when I saw the traffic jam, but dog fighting was the farthest thing from my mind.

"Dog fighting," he repeated. "Not your thing, huh?"

"Jesus, dog fighting. I didn't know they still did that kind of thing."

"Well, you do now, man, 'cause that's what it's all about."

"You going to bust this little picnic?"

"Me? All by myself? Shit. If I was that fucked up I wouldn't have *any* life line. These people take their sports real serious. You wanna die in a backwoods swamp in south fuckin' Georgia? If I was you, what I would do is, I would hightail my ass back up the road and be glad you're gone."

"I don't want to start a thing," I said lamely.

"So how the fuck did you wind up here?"

"I was invited," I said.

"You are a piece of work, all right. Stick was tellin' me about you. 'He's a real piece of work,' he said. He left off that you're nuts."

"Well, that's what happens when you're in a strange town," I said. "You'll do anything for a laugh."

We watched a lot of coming and going, a lot of lean men in felt hats, overalls, and galluses, a lot of weary women in Salvation Army duds dragging four- and five-year-olds with them, a few friendly arguments over the merits of the dogs, two freckle-bellied high school kids wandering off into the brush to settle a dispute over a cheerleader who looked thirteen years old except for a bosom you could set Thanksgiving dinner on, a woman nursing a child old enough to tackle a two-dollar steak, and a few blacks, all of whom were men and all face-creased, gaunt-looking, and smiling.

As it started getting dark, the visiting team rolled up, a group of edgy, sharp-faced badgers in polyester knits. Mug-book faces. Twenty in all and traveling in a herd. The Romans had arrived; time for the festivities to begin.

"Track dudes," Mufalatta said. "Always a bunch don't get enough action at the races. Look at those threads, man. Now there's a fuckin' crime."

Next the emperor arrived—in a silver and gray stretch Lincoln limo big enough to throw a Christmas party in. The chariot stopped for a chat with the guard at the road.

"That's Elroy Luther Graves in that car there," the Mufalatta Kid said. Now I knew what the Kid was doing there.

"Elroy Luther?"

"That's his name, babes, Elroy Luther Graves," he said.

"Nice to know," I said, and decided to get a peek at the man everybody seemed to have a healthy respect for. As I started toward the limo, I ran into the back of Mufalatta's hand. He never looked at you when he spoke; he was always staring off somewhere at nothing in particular.

"Uh-uh," he said.

"Uh-uh?" I said.

"Uh-uh. Not that way."

"Fuck him," I growled.

Mufalatta moved his hand. "Okay," he said, "but you're on his turf, man. No place to start trouble."

I thought about that for a minute. What Mufalatta was telling me was that it wasn't just Graves' turf, it was the Kid's too.

"I didn't know you had something going," I said. "Sorry."

"Don't be. It's the way things happen. You'll get the hang of it."

"Okay," I said, "so we do it your way."

"That's cool," he said. "For now, the Kid's way is to hang loose, don't splash the water, don't wave your face around a lot, lay back, see what comes along."

"Is there gonna be trouble here?"

"Anyplace Elroy Luther is, there could be trouble. It comes to him like flies to a two-holer."

"Well, are you *expecting* trouble?"

"I just answered that," the Kid said, and shut up.

"I'm going to mosey around," I said.

I followed the silver chariot a hundred yards down the road until it ended at an old frame roadhouse, a big place with a cone-shaped roof, boarded-up windows, and a lot of noise inside.

And there were the dogs. Mean dogs. Not yipping dogs. These were angry, snarling, growling, scarred, teeth-snapping, gum-showing, slobbering dogs, biting at their cages with yellow teeth. I could feel the gooseflesh on my arms rising like biscuits in a stove.

In all, I estimated three hundred fifty to four hundred people were packed inside, all of whom had paid ten dollars a head, man, woman, and child, to the giant at the door. He was bald and black-bearded, wore overalls and no shirt, had arms like a truck tire and curly hair on his shoulders. For those who were not impressed by his size, there was a .38 police special hanging haphazardly from his rear pocket.

When the crowd outside the arena had thinned to half a dozen, a tall, pole-thin black man got out of the front seat of the Lincoln. The rear window glided silently down and he reached in and drew out a wad of bills big enough to strangle Dumbo. I got a quick look at a handsome black face at the window. I had imagined Nose Graves to be ugly. If that was Nose Graves, and I was fairly sure it was, he was the lady-killer type. Older than I'd thought, probably forty-five or so, give or take a couple of years either way. His bushy hair was graying at the temples and he had a deep scar almost the width of one eyebrow, another over his ear that carried a gray streak with it. His nose was straight and no larger than mine. He was wearing gold-rimmed sunglasses. My guess was, Nose Graves probably wore those glasses to bed.

The window went back up without a sound and the skinny man headed for the rear door of Uncle Jolly's. So that was the pitch, then. Longnose Graves was the banker. It was his house.

I sauntered up to the gate. My sawbuck vanished into the keeper's fist. He cut me about six ways with his black eyes before jerking his head for me to go in.

Noise, heat, odor, hit me like a bucket of hot water. Tiers had been built up and away from a pit in the middle of the room. Fruit jars of moonshine were being passed back and forth. Some of the families had brought picnics and were wolfing down dinner, waiting for the tournament to start. Smoke swirled around half a dozen green-shaded two-hundred-watt bulbs that hung from the ceiling over the plywood rink.

Most of the crowd could have been dirt farmers living on food stamps—until the betting started. That's when the U.S. Grants and Ben Franklins appeared.

The place suddenly sounded like a tobacco auction. Graves' man stood in the ring and handled it with the bored finesse of a maitre d'. A wizened, mean-looking little creep, with a flimsy white beard, whom I took to be Uncle Jolly, stood behind him with a large roll of movie tickets over one wrist, handing out chits as the bets were made, after scribbling what I assumed to be the size of the bet and the number of the dog on the back.

A lot of money was going down, big money. And this was only the first fight. Clyde Barrow could have knocked over this soiree and retired.

DOUBLE FEATURE

It had seen better days, the South Longbeach Cinema, a movie palace once long ago, when Garbo and Taylor were the stars and glamour and double features eased the pain of the Depression. Its flamingo-painted walls were chipped and faded now, and the art deco curves around its marquee were terminally spattered by pigeons and sea birds.

It stood alone, consuming, with its adjacent parking lot, an entire block, facing a small park. Behind it, looming up like some extinct prehistoric creature, was the tattered skeleton of a roller coaster, stirring bleak memories of a time when the world was a little more innocent and South Longbeach was the playground of the city's middle class.

Now the theater was an ethnic showplace, specializing in foreign films shown in their original language. It attracted enough trade to stay open, but not enough to be cared for properly. The park across the street was rundown too. Its nests of palm trees dry and dusty, the small lake polluted, most of its lights broken or burned out. At night nobody went near the place but drunks, hoboes, and predators.

The ocean was hidden from the area by an abutment, the foot of one of the many towering dunes from which the city had taken its name. The road that wound around it to the beach was pockmarked by weather and strewn with broken bottles and beer cans.

A long black limousine was parked in the "no stand' zone in front of the theater. The double feature was Roma *and* La Strada. *Stizano and his bunch had come only for the last feature,* La Strada. *Stizano, an inveterate movie buff, had dropped his wife off, and come back to the movies with his number one button and two other gunsels. It was his way of relaxing.*

They were still dressed in black. First came the shooters, both of whom looked like beach bums in mourning, their necks bulging over tight collars. They studied the street, then one of them stepped back and opened the theater doors and the number one button exited, a thin, sickly-looking man, the color of wet cement. He shrugged and summoned his boss.

Stizano was portly, with white hair that flowed down over his ears, and looked more like the town poet than a mobster. He walked with an ebony cane, his fingers glittering with rings.

The chauffeur walked around the back of the car to open the door.

Suddenly they were marionettes, dancing to the tune of a silent drummer. Tufts flew from their clothes; popcorn boxes were tossed in the air.

The only sound was the thunk of bullets tearing into the five of them, then the shattering of glass as bullets ripped into the show windows of the theater and an explosion of shards as the box office was obliterated, then the popping of the bulbs in the marquee.

Poppoppoppop . . . poppoppoppop . . .

Poppoppoppoppoppop . . .

Broken bulbs showered down on the street.

Five people lay in the outer lobby, on the sidewalk, in the gutter.

It had happened so fast there were no screams.

Nor the sound of gunfire.

Nor the flash from a weapon.

Nothing.

Nothing but five puppets dancing on the string of death.

Then, just like that, it was all over. Silence descended over the park. There was only the wind, rattling the dried-out palms.

A bird crying.

Somewhere, far on the other side of the park, a car driving lazily past on the way to the beach.

And the sizzling wires dangling in front of the theater.

DOGS

Harry Nesbitt was sitting up in the back of the arena, in a corner under a burned-out light. I stopped a couple of rows below him and checked out the crowd. Nobody was interested in us; they were concentrating on the two dogs getting ready for the first fight. One was a dirty gray pug, its lacerated face seamed with the red scars of other battles. The other, a white mutt, part bull-dog, was fresh and unscathed and an obvious virgin to the pit.

Two men, obviously the owners of the dogs, were on opposite sides of the pit but not in it, and they seemed to be washing the dogs down with a white substance. One of the men reached over and nipped the bulldog's neck.

I moved up and sat down next to Nesbitt.

"I wasn't sure you'd show," he said.

"I'm a real curious fellow," I said. "Besides, I like your pal Benny Skeeler."

"Yeah, what a guy."

"What are they doing?" I asked, nodding toward the arena.

"Checking out each other's dogs. That white stuff there, that's warm milk. They're checking for toxics in the dog."

"Why's that one guy biting it on the neck?"

"Tastin' the skin. Some claim they can taste it if the dog's been juiced up."

He pointed down at the small bulldog.

"Lookit there, see that little no-hair mutt down there, looks like a bulldog only uglier."

"I really don't like dog fights, Nesbitt."

"Call me Harry. Makes me feel secure, okay?"

"Sure, Harry."

"Anyways, that ugly little bowser, that's called a hog dog. You know why? Because they use them kind of mutts to hunt wild boars. The dog grabs the boar by the ear, see, and he just hangs on for dear life, pulls that fuckin' hog's head right down to the ground and holds him there. Tough motherfuckers. I got a hundred down on that one."

"You do this often?"

"Every week. Better than horse racing. The reason I picked the place, nobody'll ever go with me. So I know I ain't meetin' unexpected company, see what I mean?"

The owners retrieved their animals and took them into the pit. For the first time the two animals were aware of each other, although they were tail to tail across the arena. Hackles rose like stalks of wheat down the back of the scarred old warrior. The bulldog hunkered down, sleeked out, his lips peeled back to show gum and tooth.

Neither of the dogs made a sound, no growling, no barking. It was eerie.

The betting was done. The crowd grew quiet, leaning forward on the benches.

The referee, a lean man with a warty face and a jaw full of

chewing tobacco, whistled between his teeth and the place was silent.

"Gentlemen," warty-face said, "face yer dogs."

I turned away, looking over at Nesbitt, who was wide-eyed, waiting for two dogs to tear each other to pieces.

"So let's get on with it," I said.

I heard the referee cry, "Pit!"

The crowd went crazy. The dogs still did not bark. I was to learn later that they are trained to fight without a sound. It conserves energy.

My companion was really into it. He was on his feet. "Get 'im, ya little pissant!" he screamed.

"So let's get on with it," I yelled to Nesbitt. "This isn't one of my favorite things here, with the dogs."

"You know what's goin' down, man. Do I look like I wanna end up a chopped liver sandwich?" he said, without taking his eyes off the pit. He was almost yelling so I could hear him above the crowd.

"Okay, speak your piece," I said.

"Look, Kilmer, I din't have nothin' to do with Jigs gettin' pushed across."

"What are you telling me for?"

His speech came in a rush. He was talking so fast he almost stuttered.

"I'll tell you why, see. Because I was eyeballin' you in the restaurant up until you left. You had breakfast with a couple of guys, then you talked with a couple of other guys, then you went down and got your own car, okay? I drive on out the highway ahead of you, see, wait at the place, at Benny's. You pass it goin' in. I was there when you come by. It was exactly five to eleven."

"So?"

"So I couldn't of killed him. Shit, I talked to him on the phone right after you finished breakfast."

"Why?"

"Why what?"

"Why did you talk to him?"

"Look, I don't trust none of this, okay? I mean, O'Brian says he wants to bullshit with you. Lay off, he says, I promised him I'd be alone. It's one on one, he says. So I keep an eye on you when you come down in the morning, I call to tell him where everything's at, he says go to Benny's and wait until you leave. I din't have *time* to nix him, fer Chrissakes."

One of the dogs let out the damnedest sound I ever heard. It was a cry of agony that seemed to go on forever. My eyes were drawn to the pit.

The old fighter had the little hog dog by the thigh and was shaking his head while the newcomer was trying desperately to back away.

"He's got my boy fanged," Nesbitt said.

"What's fanged?"

"Bit right through his thigh and impaled his own lip. He can't let go, that ugly one can't."

The referee cautiously approached the fighting animals and took a stick and started prying the old warrior's jaws lose. I'd seen enough.

"Look, can we go outside and talk? This definitely is not my thing."

"Weak stomach?"

"Yeah, right."

"They take a little time out here, when the ref has to use the breaking stick like that."

"So what'd O'Brian say when you called him?" I asked.

"Nothin'. Nobody was around. Some shrimpers, a guy trying to make city marina in a sailboat. That was it."

"What time was that?"

"You left at ten-oh-five."

"You'd be up shit creek if I turned the time around a little, wouldn't you?"

"Where you think I am right now? Up shit creek without the proverbial, no less, is where I'm at. Everybody's on my ass, okay? The locals, the Fed, the Tagliani family, what's left of them. I mean, I got everybody on my ass but the fuckin' marines . . ."

"Somebody threaten you?"

"I don't have to hear from the pope, pal. I was O'Brian's chief button. My job was keepin' him alive. I fucked up. You think I'm gonna get a second chance? O'Brian was family, he was son-in-law to old man Franco."

"Maybe that's what they wanted."

"What the hell's that mean?"

"I'm talking about supposing somebody wanted Jigs out of the way, somebody big in the family. Supposing they put it to somebody to ice Jigs. And this somebody rigs the whole thing to provide himself with a perfect alibi—like me, for instance. Shit, Harry, what do you take me for—"

"Hey, you think I done O'Brian in? You think I done that thing?

C'mon. And the family put my nose to it? Come *on*. Shit, you need help, dreamin' up a story like that. The whole fuckin' family's getting aced one on top of the other, you think it's one of *them* behind it?"

"Why not? This is quite a plum, Doomstown. Be a nice place to control."

"Shit, you think this is an inside job, you're on the wrong trolley."

"How about Chevos? Or Nance?"

"That's family!"

"Not really."

"There ain't any bad blood there. Everybody was happy until the Tagliani knockover. Everybody had their thing."

"It's happened before, y'know. Somebody gets greedy. Like that."

"Not this time, pal. I mean, that Nance, he's a badass and all that, but I don't see him and Chevos doin' that. Look, I'm tellin' you, except for that local nigger there wasn't any problems."

"I still don't trust you, Harry," I said. "You could've dragged me all the way out to this pasture to try to get me to fix yourself up an alibi."

He was sweating. The dogs were at it again but he had lost interest. He was mine for now. He wiped his forehead with the back of his hand and leaned closer to me, whispering over the bellowing crowd.

"What d'ya want to know? Uh, the guys with you, one was the size of a semi, the other one was missing an ear . . . uh, you had a feast would choke a fuckin' hippopotamus. Then you went over and talked to two other birds . . ."

He rambled on, filling in details as they came to him, things nobody would have thought to tell him. He was a very observant man.

"Okay," I said, cutting him off, "so maybe for now I choose to believe you. You got something to trade? This is your party, so I assume you want something, and since Christmas is long gone, I figure you got something to throw in the pot. Otherwise we wouldn't be out here in this shithouse."

"Look, I know I'm probably on the shit list. I can't take a chance on leaving town if I'm gonna get busted. The Triad has got people all over the state on the payroll, man. I get busted, the boys'll hear about it, y'know, like yesterday. I won't make it to the South Carolina border, fer Chrissakes."

"That's what you want, a guarantee the law'll let you out of town without a hassle?" I asked with surprise.

"Once I'm loose, I'm okay," he said. "I got some friends in Phoenix. I'll take a moniker. But I can't take a chance, see, some dumb flatfoot, pardon the French, turns me up down here."

"Why don't you drive?"

"It's their car, their credit cards. I left the car in a downtown parking lot with the cards locked in the dash, sent them the keys. I'm breaking as clean as I can. Hell, I was even afraid to tap my bank account, y'know? It's all set up by the company."

"So you're tapped out, too?"

"I got a small stash, get me where I'm goin'. Look, I'm not askin' for anything except a ride and some company to Jacksonville. They can put me on the plane, that's it. Am I on the suspect list, Kilmer?"

"Hell, I think I'm even on the suspect list."

"I need some cover, man, to break out. Whad'ya say?"

The crowd noise surged and I was compelled to look down in the pit. The little dog, the hog dog, had the old warrior by one ear and was dragging it across the pit.

"See what I mean," Harry cried, forgetting his troubles for the moment.

"What's to trade?" I asked.

"You sure got a one-track mind."

"Yeah, and right now I'd like to get on that track and get the hell out of here."

"Like I said, what d'ya wanna know?" he asked.

"Everything you know."

"It ain't that much."

"How about narcotics?"

"I don't have nothin' to do with dope."

"How about Chevos?"

"Look, what do you want? All I'm askin' is a fuckin' ride out of town. This ain't the Inquisition. I can't turn anybody up. That ain't what this is about."

"Did I ask you to turn anybody up, Harry? You're making me play twenty questions here, that's all. We've never done business before. What's the game?"

"Look, I don't know what you want to know. One thing I *don't know* is who iced these people."

"Start from the beginning. The first time you came down here from Cincy."

He thought about it while I watched the activity in the ring. Finally he said, "I come down here four years ago. It was Tagliani,

Costello, Cohen, that's all. I was one of the old man's soldiers at the time."

"What happened?"

"Nothin'. We was gonna stay at this old hotel out where the Strip is now, but it was rundown. We ended up on this guy's yacht."

"What guy?"

"I don't remember his name."

"Was he local?"

"Yeah. A Doomstown johnny. I think he was in the banking business, like a big shot. Look, you wanna know the truth, it was the two guys you were talkin' to at breakfast."

"Seaborn and Donleavy?"

"I just don't remember that, I ain't good on names."

"Did you hear what they were talking about?"

"I never did that. It was none of my business. On the way back, though, Tagliani tells Costello he thinks this guy is gone around."

"You mean they made some kind of a deal with him?"

"That's the impression I got. In fact, I know it. We all got accounts in his bank."

"What bank?"

"Seacoast National."

"You *all* have accounts in the same bank?"

"Sure. We get paid automatically. Every Friday, you can book on it. It goes in automatically."

"And that's the whole family?"

"Anybody I know about."

"Did you come down again with Franco?"

"One other time. We stayed on the same yacht. That time it was only the older guy, not the one looks like a wrestler, and he brought this other bozo with him. Short fellow, skinny. Looked to be maybe thirty-five to forty."

I felt like kicking myself for not knowing anything about Sutter and Logan. They were the two members of the Committee I was still in the dark about. I didn't know what they looked like, how old they were, nothing except their names and what they did. Logan was the media man and Sutter was the lawyer.

"Could his name have been either Logan or Sutter?" I asked.

"His name coulda been Mussolini for all I know," Harry whined.

"And you didn't overhear any of their conversations."

"I couldn't listen to that stuff, Kilmer, you know that. It's see nothin', hear nothin'. Besides, at the time I didn't have no idea what was going down. Hell, I still don't for that matter."

The fact that Seaborn entertained Tagliani on his yacht was still not an indication of any wrong-doing. It was his job as a member of the Committee to size up big investors. But if Seaborn was washing money for Lou Cohen, that was a different ball game. Then the meetings on the yacht became pertinent testimony.

I decided to change the subject.

"What do you know about Cherry McGee?" I asked.

"He's dead," Harry said.

"I know he's dead. Before that."

"He was a pistol over in Covington, did free-lance work for Draganata back when Bannion tried to elbow in."

"So McGee was working for the Triad when he came down here?"

"I don't know that for sure. Nobody seemed too upset when he got blown away, though."

"When did you move down here?"

"With O'Brian. I was one of the kid's wedding presents. So I came with them. Nine months ago, maybe."

"The house was already bought?"

"Yeah, that was also a wedding present."

"So what was the reaction when Tagliani was iced?"

"Well, you know I been through a couple wars. When somebody in the family takes one, the first thing happens, everybody gets together, tries to figure out the who and the why. They did it at Franco's place the next day, the day of the wake."

"What happened?"

"It ended up nothin'. It didn't make sense. Both Franco and Draganata had got it by then. Everybody else was freakin' out. They din't think anybody even knew who they were. They started talkin' about you."

"What about me?"

"That you're sweet on Raines' old lady."

"Who said that?"

"Costello, maybe."

"So . . ."

"Costello says you're bad luck. There's a big hate on for you over there. It's why I was nervous for O'Brian to meet with you. They say you took down Skeet and then set fire under them in Cincy, which is true."

"So?"

"So Chevos says maybe he should take care of it and Costello says no, no Fed killing and besides, Nance fucked it up once before and Nance gets really pissed, like bad enough, he could have taken

Costello's head off. Couple of us, we had to take them apart. Anyway, it blew over. Later Costello tells Nance he's sorry, it's all blown over, and Chevos says maybe they can use this thing with the Raines broad to bring you down."

"What'd Costello say?"

"He says he'll think about it and Chevos says you're a jinx. He says, 'A black cat runs across your path, you kill it, one way or another.' That's his exact words and Costello repeats himself. 'I'll think about it,' he says."

"Is there paper on me?"

"Not that I heard, just the beef is all. Jesus would you look at that."

The two dogs were locked together in the center of the pit. Blood was splashed on the pit walls, the dirt floor, everywhere. The hog dog was no longer a pit virgin. Its face was shredded. I wanted to get out of there.

"Anybody in the mob got a beef against the Taglianis?"

"Not that I heard."

"Anybody inside got a hard-on for them?"

"Hey, it ain't like that, man. I told ya, everybody's happy."

"Anything else?" I asked.

"Well . . . there's one more thing I can give you. I heard something about a big coke shipment that's coming in. Mucho kilos."

"Well, what about it?" I demanded.

"All I know, there was some stuff comin' in from down south. Out of the country. I know this because some of our girls are into snow and it's been short."

"And . . ."

"And the boat's late. Not to worry, is the word. Could be a storm or something. If it got busted, we'd already know. You guys brag about shit like that."

"Maybe that's where Nance went, to bring the load in."

"What about Nance?"

"He's gone underground. We've been looking for him since Monday."

"I don't know anything about that," Harry Nesbitt said.

Down below, the fight had gone against the hog dog. The old warrior had it by the throat and was snarling for the first time. You could tell it was almost over for the little pit virgin. His one leg was dangling like it was broken and his throat was spilling blood.

"I'm leaving," I said to Nesbitt. "When do you want to leave town?"

"An hour ago."

"Okay, I'll see what I can do. I mean, I'll do the best I can. I don't know what the hell you gave me for this, but I'll talk to somebody and that somebody'll talk to somebody else and we'll get it together. It may be tomorrow morning before I can swing it. You got a place to flop?"

"Yeah. Early tomorrow, huh?"

"You call me first thing."

"Seven be okay?"

"Doesn't anybody in this town sleep past dawn?" I said.

But his attention was already back on the dogs. As I started down the tiers toward the door, the referee stepped in and ended the fight.

The little hog dog was finished. He dragged himself by one good leg toward his master and collapsed in the dirt, his tail wagging feebly. He looked up pitifully at his owner.

I turned away again and didn't see the owner take a .38 out of his belt and hold it down between the hog dog's eyes.

The shot startled me. I whirled around and drew my Magnum without thinking. It took me a second or two before I got the gun back out of sight.

Too late.

The giant at the door saw the move. As I got outside I heard his deep voice drawl, "Hey, boy."

I kept walking. I walked straight toward Longnose Graves' limo.

"Hey, you with that hotshot pistol. Talkin' to you, boy."

I stopped a few feet from the limo and turned around. Two friends had joined him. Just as big and just as ugly.

"Want something?" I asked in the toughest voice I could dredge up.

"That was some kind of move there inside," the giant said. "Like the old O.K. Corral."

"It's a nervous tic," I said. "Happens all the time."

"You needa get it fixed."

"I'll keep it in mind."

He moved closer.

"The only firearms we 'low hereabouts go with the house," he said.

"I was just leaving."

"You goin' the wrong way."

Behind me, I heard a car window whirring. I turned. Graves was a shadow in the back seat, a pair of eyes eager for trouble. The bad end of a .38 peeking over the windowsill took my attention away from his eyes.

A voice as soft as baby skin said, "Let him do his move."

They thought I was going for a heist.

Before I could say anything, the Mufalatta Kid's pickup roared out of the parking lot and skidded up beside me, raising a small dust storm. When it cleared, Zapata and Mufalatta were there. I wondered where the hell Zapata came from!

Zapata had his wallet in one hand and a police special in the other. The wallet was hanging open and his buzzer was gleaming for all to see. Mufalatta was behind the door of the pickup, aiming his Cobra at the limo.

"You sure know how to pep up a party," said the Kid.

47

TITAN DEALS A HAND

The tension was broken by the appearance of another limo. This one was black and I had seen it before, in front of the Ponce Hotel after Draganata was killed. I even remembered the license plate, ST-1. It pulled slowly toward us until its headlights were shining between us and Uncle Jolly's goon squad. All weapons magically vanished. I heard Graves' window glide quietly back up.

"A lot of limos here tonight," I said.

"Either one of these is a lot of limos," the Mufalatta Kid said.

The driver's door opened and a tall, rangy man in a county uniform got out. He wasn't an inch over six six and probably didn't weigh more than two hundred fifty pounds. He walked with a decided limp and there was about him a bug-eyed, almost haunted look. It was a look I had seen many times before, eyes full of fear of what they might see next—or had already seen. He limped toward the front of the car and leaned against the hood. He didn't do or say anything, just leaned against the hood.

The goon squad turned like robots and marched back inside the arena.

"Luke Burger, the sheriff's man," said Zapata. "He's only got one good leg but he can kick the shit out of a rhino with it."

"What happened to him?" I asked.

"What I heard," said Mufalatta, "he was chasing a bootlegger on his hog, lost it going over South River Bridge, took a header over the railing, and went through the roof of some public housing two stories down. I hear it took them six months to glue him back together. One of his legs ended up three inches shorter than the other."

Zapata said, "I also heard Titan covered all the bills his insurance didn't take care of."

Graves' man sauntered back to his boss's Lincoln and passed a roll of bills through the window.

All of a sudden it was business as usual.

"I had enough of this party for one night," Zapata said. "I think I'll just haul my ass outta here. You comin', Kilmer?"

"I think it's time for me to have a chat with Mr. Stoney," I said.

"I'll stick around," the Kid said. "I get a bang outta surprises. Take the pickup. I'll go back with Kilmer."

I walked toward the black Cadillac. Behind me, I heard the big-wheel scratch off in the sand. As I neared Titan's car, his man opened the back door.

"Get in," Titan's crusty voice said from the back seat.

I got in.

"You got more guts than a slaughterhouse floor, doughboy," he said, "but a sparrow's got more brains."

He sat forward, almost on the edge of the seat, his legs tucked close to the black cane, his gimlet eyes glittering like diamonds. When he wanted, his voice had the lilt of Irish flavored with molasses, a voice you listened to and wanted to believe. It could also be as tough as a cowhand's behind.

"I've heard you're a smart cop," he said quietly. "Very savvy, they say. I can believe that. You were a helluva good ballplayer. Too bad about the foot."

"It was my ankle."

"Foot, ankle, what's the difference? So you remember me, eh?"

"Hell, Mr. Stoney, who could forget you? I remember everything. That was one hell of a summer."

"It's a dead and buried summer. Best you forget it or move on."

I didn't respond to his veiled threat, I just listened.

"I know everything that happens in this town, this county. If a cow farts, I know it. I've had my eye on you since you got off the plane. You been havin' quite a time for yourself."

"Just doing my job," I said.

"I could get you recalled with a phone call, doughboy. You got yourself way off base."

"Seems to me that's my business."

"Don't be a dreamer. Best you forget the past and get on with your work. In the first place, you don't even have the credentials. Besides, she's a happy woman, just gets a little lonely."

"Did Chief send you to—"

"Chief doesn't know you're here. If he did, I doubt he'd remember you. He's still livin' in 1969. Teddy's death destroyed him."

"It didn't do a helluva lot for Teddy either."

"You gonna turn out to be a smartass?"

"I was with him when he died. That kind of thing stays with you."

"I saw the letter," he said. He was staring straight ahead, not looking at me or anything else in particular.

I gave him my hardest stare. "You never did like me, did you, Mr. Stoney? You never thought I was good enough for her."

"I told you what I thought," he said. "You were a good halfback until you got busted up. After that . . ."

He let the sentence dwindle away. Fill in the blanks.

"It was all part of watching out for Dunetown, right? Like you're doing now. Sticking your nose in my business again."

He looked at me and his lip curled up on one side.

"You found your level, doughboy," he said.

"Just like you, right?"

He sat for a few beats more and then, without looking at me, he said, "Harry Raines has a brilliant future. It wouldn't do for his wife to be caught screwin' around with a cop."

"Or anybody else," I added.

"There ain't anybody else, doughboy."

"How about Tony Lukatis?"

His eyes narrowed. "You sure been busy prying into things that don't matter."

"That makes two of us. Besides, you brought the subject up," I said. "Seems to me everybody's awfully concerned about Harry Raines' future and nobody particularly gives a damn about his wife."

"She ain't runnin' for office."

"That's all it's about, running for office?"

"Look, don't go making a monkey of yourself. She's vulnerable right now. I'd hate to think you were takin' advantage of the situation."

"You've got a lot of time invested in him, don't you?" I pressed on.

His eyes continued to twinkle, even in the subdued interior of the limo. He nodded his head sharply.

"Bet your ass I do," he said.

"I can understand your concern."

"Hasn't a damn thing to do with that. Chief and Doe are family to me. I won't stand by and see either of them hurt."

"I wasn't planning on it."

"Anything else would be tomfoolery," he snapped. The molasses in his tone had changed to flint.

"Could be there's more to it than that," I suggested.

"Now what the hell's that supposed to mean?"

"How long do you think you can keep this under the table? How long can Harry Raines play dumb?"

"He ain't *playing* nothin'," the sheriff snapped vehemently. "If Morehead was doin' his job, none of this would've happened."

"That's bullshit and you know it. If the *Committee* had done its job, none of this would've happened."

At my mention of the Committee, he reared back as if I had slapped him. I went on before he could say anything.

"That makes you as much to blame for what's happening here as anybody. I could understand Donleavy and Seaborn being naive enough to swallow Tagliani's line. You're the sheriff, Mr. Stoney, lord high protector of Dunetown and all its peasants and all its kings. You should have tumbled to them. Why dump it off on somebody else?"

"Doughboy, I'm beginning to think you're suicidal," he said softly, and with enough menace that it made me pucker a little.

"Okay," I said, "I'll put it on the table. How clean *is* Raines?"

"Don't be silly," he snapped. "You think Harry Raines had anything to do with this?"

I said, "If anybody local sold out to the Taglianis, they're looking down the throat of a RICO case. And that means you, Harry Raines, or anybody else."

"You have to prove racketeering on the Taglianis," he said. "From what I hear, you ain't got doodly-shit on any of them.

You're gonna bust out here, just like you did up north. They got you buffaloed, doughboy. Admit it."

I wanted to tell the crafty old bastard more, but I decided not to. Instead, I said:

"If he's dirty, he's going to get turned up."

"I said, don't be silly, boy. Harry Raines is as honest as a Swiss pocket watch. You're dreamin' if you think different. Dangerous dreamin'. Harry, Sam Donleavy, me, we all did our best to keep Dunetown clean. Sounds to me like you may be tryin' to put a size two shoe on a size ten foot."

"On the other hand, if the shoe fits . . ."

I let the rest of the sentence dangle.

"Let me put it to you straight, doughboy," he said with unmistakable authority. "You stay away from Doe Raines."

I didn't answer him. We sat and stared through the shadows for several moments. His jaw was flinching.

"This isn't going anywhere," I said finally. "I owe you my thanks. I don't know what you're doing out here, but I'm glad you showed up. A little law never hurt anybody."

"A *little* law ain't worth a damn," he said. "Either you got muscle or you got numbers. You didn't have either."

I asked it suddenly. I wasn't planning on it, it just popped out, kind of like my gun popping out at the dog fights.

"Is this your game, Mr. Stoney?"

He chuckled to himself, a mischievous chuckle, a tsk-tsk chuckle, which made me feel like a wahoo, which is exactly what he wanted.

"I'm gonna give you a little advice, us being in the same game, so to speak. I been at it forty-five years. How about you?"

"Almost ten."

"People are gonna gamble, doughboy, it's natural. The reason it's natural is because most people are losers and they see themselves as losers and they don't think they'll ever amount to a goddamn, so they gamble because in their eyes it's their shot at changin' their luck. So people'll gamble, and a lot of hardass law ain't gonna change it. The same thing can be said of whorin'. Always gonna be whorin' goin' on, doughboy. A man wants to get laid, he's gonna get laid. Now, my job isn't to teach 'em not to gamble or not to get laid; that's a job for a preacher. No, my job is to make sure they don't get hurt bad at it. We all know gamblin' and whorin' can attract some unsavory characters around it, so for that reason I keep my finger on things. I like to know who's doin' what. That way I keep things from gettin' outta line, my folks from gettin' hurt."

"That didn't answer my question," I said.

"The answer to your question is yes and no. I own quite a few fightin' dogs. It's kind of a tradition in my family. Been fightin' dogs all my life, just like my pap and his pap before him. The Titans've raised pit dogs since before Georgia was a colony. But I don't run the game, Mr. Kilmer. That's gaming and that's felonious, and while I can tolerate it and my conscience doesn't have a problem with misdemeanors, it balks when it comes to felonies."

It was my turn to laugh.

"That's the damnedest bit of rationalization I've ever heard," I said.

"Call it what you will, it's the way I keep law and I haven't had a lot of trouble doin' it and I been at it for longer than you've been alive, so that ought to tell you something. Besides, this ain't Cincinnati or Chicago or New York, it's south Georgia."

"You want to tell me what happened between Nose Graves and Cherry McGee? There was a definite touch of the Bronx to that."

"Why are you interested?"

"Because Cherry McGee had done dirty laundry for Tagliani in the past. I don't believe in coincidence, Mr. Stoney."

"Mm-hmm. So finish it."

"So I think Cherry McGee was sent in here by Tagliani to test the waters, find out if there was any local problem. Graves turned out to be a permanent problem for McGee. Then Uncle Franco decided to cool it. Now why do you think he backed off? It wasn't his style."

"It's your story, boy, why don't you tell me."

"Maybe he didn't want to attract any more attention. That's a possibility."

"Obviously not one you favor," he said sarcastically.

"No."

"And what's your notion, doughboy?"

"Maybe he was told to back off."

Titan never changed his expression but his knuckles got a little whiter over the cane.

"Now, who might do a thing like that?" he asked.

"I thought you could tell me."

"Until this very minute, I never thought to connect the two together."

"It's just a thought," I said. "If Franco had been in bed with somebody in Dunetown, that somebody might have told him to cool it before the whole deal went sour."

"You got a hell of an imagination."

"Not really. I can't imagine why the man that did McGee in is sitting over in that other limo and he's counting the take from the first fight, and the sheriff is sitting thirty feet away discussing modern romances."

"I've known Luther Graves since he was a bulge in his mama's belly. What he does, he does honestly. He's like a snake—he only gets mean when you step on him. Like I told you, this is still a small town and it's still my job to keep an eye on it. If it's gonna happen anyway, I like to deal with people who are predictable."

"You telling me he runs a straight game? Is that what you're saying?"

"However you care to put it."

"Well, Mr. Stoney, it's been your county for so long I guess you can run it any way you want to."

He looked over at me finally, a smile flirting with the corners of his mouth, his eyes still gleaming under shaggy white brows.

"You probably got a little more brains than I gave you credit for," Titan said. "Now I'll ask you a question. Did *you* kill 'em, doughboy?"

"Did *I* kill them?"

I had to laugh at that one. But I stopped when I realized he wasn't kidding. It was definitely something he had considered.

"I can get off right down there," I said. "That blue Ford."

Titan's man was still leaning on the hood.

"You avoidin' my question?"

"It's an insulting question, Sheriff. Besides, I was with half a dozen other cops when two of the slayings took place and I was on an airplane flying down here when Tagliani and his party got iced. And besides that, I'm not in the killing business. Thanks for calling off the dogs, if you'll pardon the pun."

I started to get out of the car.

"Just don't go around here actin' like Buffalo Bill or Pat Garrett or something. I got enough problems on my hands."

I got out of the limo and leaned back in and offered him my hand. He kept his folded over the gold handle of his cane.

"Thanks for the ride," I said.

"Take my advice about Doe Raines, one law officer to another," he said, without looking at me. He pressed a button and the window slid up. The conversation was over.

48

SO...LONG...

The Kid was sitting in the front seat when I got in my car. As I was about to find out, he was the philosopher of the outfit.

"Okay I hop a ride back to town with you?" he said. "We don't want you to get lost or something."

"Where's your pickup?" I asked.

"I gave it to Zapata," he answered. "He put his bike in the back."

"My pleasure," I said, cranking up.

"Well," he said, "I din't hear no shootin' so I guess you two got along."

"More or less," I said.

"You sure don't volunteer much," the Kid said.

"It was kind of a personal thing," I said. "I used to know Titan, a long time ago."

"Oh."

"How come you showed up out here?" I asked.

"It was Dutch's idea for Zapata to come out. He said you get in trouble when you're out alone. I was following Graves."

"Very astute of Dutch."

"No sweat. Is it any of my business what the fuck you were doin' out here?"

"O'Brian's button is running scared. He wants an escort out of town."

"Did he give up anything for it?"

I laughed. "I'm not really sure," I said. "According to him it's just one big happy family out there."

"You believe that?" the Kid asked.

"Sure. I also believe in the tooth fairy and the Easter Bunny."

"Must burn your ass, puttin' in all that work on this bunch and they get wasted all over the place."

"I don't like murder," I said, "no matter who the victims are."

He was quiet for a moment, then he said:

"My stepfather told me once, you take two violins which are

perfectly tuned, okay, and you play one, the other one also plays."

"No kidding," I said, wondering what in hell violins had to do with anything.

"The old fart was full of caca," the Kid went on, "but he played the violin. Not good, but he at least played the fuckin' thing. I couldn't do it, man. Me and the violin, it was war at first sight. Anyways, I figure he's probably right on that score."

"Uh-huh," I said, wondering what he was leading up to. Then he told me.

"He only told me one other thing in my whole life that I re-member, and that didn't make any sense to me at the time. Shit, I was just a kid; it was later on I figured it out, what he meant, I mean. Anyways, what it was, I was pissed off, see, because my best friend at the time din't always see things exactly the way I did. The old man says, 'Trouble with you, Fry'—he called me Fry 'cause I was small as a kid; that always pissed me off too—'trouble with you, Fry, you think everybody sees things the same as you.' Then he reaches down, scratches his ankle. 'My foot itches. That's reality to me. Yours don't. That's reality to you.' That's it; he goes back to the sports page.

"So, y'know, I'm maybe eight, nine, at the time, what do I know from reality and itching feet. I figure the old man's temporarily unwired. Twenty years later I'm after this creep in the French Quarter, a three-time loser facing a felony; I get him, he's down for the full clock, right? Son of a bitch is always one step a-fuckin'-way, I can't quite lay my hand on him. I'm thinkin' I know this guy better than anybody, why can't I nail his ass? Then one night I remember what the old fart told me. What I come to realize is that maybe I know this guy's MO, front and back, but I'm not *thinking* like him, instead I'm thinking like *me* thinking like him, see what I mean?"

"So did you catch him?" I asked.

"I would have but the dumb son of a bitch shot himself cleaning his .38. Really burned my ass. But I would've had him. So what I been tryin' to do, see, I been thinking like whoever's icing all these people here."

"And what've you come up with?"

"Not a fuckin' thing," he said.

I sighed. For a moment I thought the Kid had come up with something important. But he wasn't finished yet. "I don't know the why, see," he went on. "If I had a handle on the why, I would nail his ass. Or hers. Y'know, it could be a fancy, ever think of that?"

"Well," I said, rather pompously, "once we establish motive—"

He cut me off. "We're not talkin' motive, man. We're not talkin' about motive, we're talkin' about where that fucker's head's at. *Why* he's doin' it. Y'see, life ain't logical. That's the myth. Truth is, nothing is real, it's all what we make it out to be. It's the same thing—when his foot itches and we scratch ours, that's when we nail his ass."

"Okay," I said, "if my foot starts itching I'll let you know."

He chuckled. "Think about it," he said.

"And thanks for the backup."

"It's what it's all about," he said.

Five minutes down the road my headlights picked up Zapata. The pickup was idling on the shoulder and he was waving at us with a light. I pulled over.

"Kid, you know where South Longbeach Park is, down at the end of Oceanby?"

"No."

"Then follow me. Don't drag ass."

"What the hell's going on?" I yelled at him as he crawled back into the pickup.

"There's been a massacre out there," he yelled back, and roared out onto the highway in front of me. He had a red light on the roof and a siren screaming under the hood. I haven't driven like that since I was in high school. Most of the time I was just hanging on to the steering wheel.

It took us thirty minutes to get to South Longbeach. We came in behind the theater, a grim and foreboding specter in the darkness, even knowing as little as we did.

This one had drawn the biggest crowd yet, at least a dozen cop cars, red and blue lights flashing everywhere.

The brass buttons were in a semicircle about fifty yards in diameter around the front of the theater. Nobody got inside the circle, including them. Several men from homicide were stretching a yellow crime scene banner around the perimeter of the movie house and car.

Nick Salvatore, smoking a cherry cigar, was sitting on the fender of his car, looking as sad as a basset hound. Dutch was sitting sideways on the front seat of his car, his legs stretched out into the street.

"It's getting funny," he said, to nobody at all. Then he looked around and said, "Is this whole thing getting funny to anybody else or is it just me?"

"What the hell happened?" I asked.

"Somebody tried to top the Saint Valentine's Day Massacre," Dutch said.

"Right in front of my fuckin' eyes," Salvatore said, shaking his head.

Dutch was shaking his head too. "The last four days, that's a year's work for the geniuses in homicide. If we're real lucky, they might turn up a clue by the next census."

"Who is it this time?" I asked.

"The family man," said Dutch. "That's what I remember you saying about him. A big family man."

"Stizano?"

"And a rather large party of friends. Salvatore saw it go down. He's an eyeball witness, can you believe that? Doesn't anybody see the humor in all this?"

Salvatore ignored Dutch. He was anxious to tell his story again.

"You won't believe this," he said, speaking very slowly and deliberately, as though he were being recorded, and pointing out little scenes of interest as he described the massacre. "Stizano, when he comes outta the show, I'm maybe a hundred yards from him, all of sudden it's like . . . like somebody started shaking the ground. They fuckin' keeled over. Now here's where it really gets weird, man. I don't hear nothin', I don't see nothin'. The loudest noise was the slugs, thumpin' into them. Then the glass started going, the box office, marquee. Sweet Jesus, it got fuckin' surreal."

There were five bodies lying helter-skelter in front of the theater. Glass and debris everywhere. Several slugs had whacked the car.

"Looks like a bomb went off in front of the place," I said.

"It was fuckin' surreal, is what it was," Salvatore intoned.

"Who're the rest of these people?" I asked, pointing at the massacre.

"Coupla shooters, the driver, and another guy I've seen with Stizano more often than not," Salvatore said.

"Pasty-faced little runt, looks like he died of malnutrition?" I asked.

"That's the one."

"Name's Moriarty. He's Stizano's number one button."

"Not anymore," Salvatore said. His tone was changing, becoming almost gleeful.

The scene was as bizarre as any Fellini film.

Stizano lay on his back, staring at the underside of the marquee with a smile on his face and a cigar still clamped between his teeth. His black suit was full of bullet holes. It looked like a rabid dog had chewed up his chest. One of his shooters was five feet away, huddled against the box office on his side in an almost fetal position. His Borsalino hat was knocked down over the side of his face, somewhat rakishly. The bodyguard, whom I had pegged as a onetime Chicago hoodlum named Manny Moriarity, a.k.a. Dead Pan Moriarity, was leaning against the side of the theater on his knees, his right hand under his coat, and the only expression he ever had, on his face. Two slugs in the forehead, one under the right eye, and his chest was open for inspection. The other gunman, who looked like a body builder, lay face down with his hands buried beneath him, clutching the family fortune. The chauffeur had managed to get around the side of the car and had sat down, made a little cup in his lap with his hands, and tried to stop his insides from spilling out. He hadn't been very successful but it didn't make any difference. He was as dead as the rest of them.

As the little Italian completed his story, the Stick arrived in front of a trail of blue smoke that wound like an eel back down the dark street and, looking at the scene of the crime, said, "They giving away free dishes?"

"You're very sick," Dutch said. "There're five people dead over there."

"Bank night," Stick said.

Salvatore repeated his story to the Stick and then pointed across the street to the park.

"Had to be from over there. And, uh, uh . . ."

"Yeah?" Dutch said.

"This is gonna sound a little crazy."

"I'd feel there was something wrong if it didn't," Dutch said wearily.

"Okay . . . I don't think—judging from the way these people went down, okay—I don't think . . . or what I think is, it was one gun."

"One gun did all this?" said Dutch. "This looks like the Battle of the Bulge here."

"I know it. But, see, uh, they went down just bim, bam, boom, right in a row, like they was ducks in a shootin' gallery, starting with the driver, there, swingin' straight across. Next it was the two gunners, then the button—what was his name?"

"Dead Pan Moriarity," I coached.

"Dead Pan Moriarity," Dutch repeated, and smothered a giggle.

"Yeah, him, and finally Stizano. I mean, Dutch, it was *some* kind of fuckin' weapon. Took 'em all out in like . . . ten seconds!"

The Stick was leaning over Stizano, pointing his finger and counting to himself. He stood up, shaking his head.

"I make it eight slugs in Stizano, could be more. Look at him; he didn't know it was coming. Fucker's still smoking his cigar and smiling."

Stick giggled, a kind of uncontrollable, quirky little giggle, which got Dutch started, only he didn't giggle, he laughed, and the laugh grew to a roar. Then Salvatore broke down and started in and before I knew it, I was laughing along with the rest of them. The harder we tried to stop, the harder we laughed. We were standing there in hysterics when the chief of police arrived.

Chief Walters was fifty pounds overweight and had bloodshot eyes, a nose full of broken blood vessels, and a neck that was two sizes too big for his collar. He looked like a man who sweats easily.

"I must have missed something," he said, in a fat man's labored voice, heavy with bourbon. "What the hell's so funny?"

"You had to be here, Herb," said Dutch.

"Obviously you weren't," Walters said. "Maybe we better talk about this in the morning."

"We can talk about it right now," Dutch said with more than a touch of irritation as his smile faded.

"Right now I think I'd better join my people," Walters said, leaning on the "my."

Dutch defused the situation by introducing Walters to me, earning me a damp, insecure handshake.

"Dutch can obviously use all the help you can give him, right, Dutch?" he said.

"Why don't you go over and give the boys in homicide a pep talk," Dutch said.

"If I can help you in any way, Kilmer, just pick up the phone. I answer all my calls personally."

"That's wonderful," I said.

As he walked away he added somewhat jovially, "At least you can't say we've got a dull town here, right, Kilmer?"

I began to wonder if the whole damn police force had been recruited from some funny farm for old cops.

"Well, you've met the chief," Dutch said, "now you can forget him."

"Twelve in Stizano and this guy with the hat," the Stick cried out, returning to his self-appointed task of counting bullet holes in dead people.

Callahan was last to arrive, wearing a three-piece gray suit with a rose in his lapel. He got out of his car and looked around. No comment. While we were counting bullet holes and scratching our heads, Callahan vanished into the park and returned five minutes later with a whiskered, filthy relic wearing the dirtiest trench coat I've ever seen. You could smell his breath from across the street.

"Don't anybody light a match," Salvatore said as they approached.

"Saw something," Callahan said, explaining the bum in tow.

The drunk sniffed a few times, then wiped his nose with the back of his hand.

"D'wanno trouble," he mumbled.

Dutch leaned over him, his hands stuffed in his pants pockets and an unlit Camel bobbing in his mouth. "I'll tell you what," he said. "You don't spit it out, you'll have more trouble than a constipated goose."

The bum looked offended at first, until it dawned on him that he was, for the moment, the center of attraction. Suddenly he started singing like a magpie.

"I was down in the park near the pond, see, grabbing forty on a bench, and, uh, first thing I know, see, I hear a lotsa like clicks. Sounded like, uh, m'teeth." He hesitated and laughed but the laugh turned into the worst cough I've ever heard.

"Keep talkin', pops," Dutch said. "You're doin' fine. Just don't cough up a lung before you're through is all I ask."

The bum's Sterno eyes glittered feebly. "What's in it fer me?" he demanded. Then, looking around, he said, "Got a butt?" to everybody in earshot.

The Stick gave him a cigarette, steadying the old man's hand while he lit it.

"What's your name?" he asked.

"J. W. Guttman," he said proudly. "My friends call me Socks." He grinned and pointed to his feet. He wore no shoes but his toes wiggled through holes in a pair of rancid, once-white sweat socks.

"Okay, Socks, so you were on your favorite bench down there, you heard somebody's teeth clicking," Dutch said.

"That's what it sounded like." He flicked his uppers loose with his tongue and rattled them sharply against his lower plate. "*Tic-tic-tic-tic*, like that."

"Fine," Dutch said, rolling his eyes.

"And then all them lights down to the movie start blowin' up. Sounded like the Fourth of Julahrrgh." He coughed again, cutting off the end of the sentence.

"Did you *see* anything?" Dutch asked him.

He gathered his breath together and sighed. "Been tryin' to tell yuh—seen, uh, this car."

"Where?"

"On Pelican Avenue, goin' toward the beach."

"What kind of car?" Dutch demanded.

"Just a car. They all look alike."

"Did it have a color?" Dutch asked.

"Uh, well, it was a dark car."

"Verdammt," Dutch said.

"Black?" the Stick asked. "Two-door, four-door?"

"Tol' ya, it was dark. Coulda been—" He stopped and thought hard for several seconds. "Blue, right? Sure enough, in the dark there, see, coulda been blue. Dark green, maybe . . ."

He hunched up his shoulders, coughed, shivered, and did a little jig. Something under the stack of rags he was wearing was gnawing on him.

"Anybody know what's he talking about?" Dutch said.

"Maybe he thinks it's a test," Salvatore said.

"Somethin' else," J. W. Guttman said, when he had regained his breath.

"Don't make me beg," Dutch said.

"Had funny wheels."

"Funny wheels," Dutch said.

Guttman nodded vigorously. "That's right."

"What kind of funny wheels?" Dutch asked, and, turning to me, said under his breath, "I'm beginning to feel like a straight man for this old fart."

"Big floppy wheels. I could hear them . . . flop, flop, flop, up there on Pelican."

"What the hell's he talkin' about?" the Stick asked.

"Beats me," said Dutch. "Floppy wheels, huh, J.W.?"

"Popeta, popeta, popeta. That's what it sounded like."

"Maybe somebody had a flat," I suggested.

Socks smiled grandly, a man suddenly thrust into the limelight by *tic-tic-tic* and *popeta, popeta, popeta.*

"That's it?" said Dutch.

"It was dark," J. W. Guttman whined.

"I know it was dark," Dutch snapped.

The little man cowered.

"Five people get blown away and the best witness we can muster up is a whacked-out dipso," Dutch said, shaking his head. "Go back to your bench, Mr. Guttman."

"Socks."

"Socks." Dutch started to walk away and Socks grabbed his sleeve. "Look, Cap'n, how 'bout takin' me in, maybe you could, uh, book me for like a material witness. Cap, I ain't had a square meal since Saint Patrick's Day."

Dutch took out a tenspot and motioned one of the patrolmen over.

"Take Socks here over to the lunch counter, buy him a decent meal, and stay with him until he eats it," Dutch said.

"Me?" the cop said in disbelief.

"Who d'ya think I'm talkin' to, God?" Dutch growled. "Just do it."

"Right."

He started to lead Guttman away.

"Cap'n?"

"What is it now?"

"Can I get a pack o' butts, too?"

"Get him a pack of butts, too," Dutch said to the policeman.

"Yes, sir."

"God bless ya," Socks said, and stuck out his hand. Dutch recoiled in horror. "Take that thing away from me," he said to Socks, and to the cop: "Make him wash his damn hands before he eats; he's liable to poison himself."

Salvatore and Callahan returned to the fold with half a dozen brass buttons in tow.

"Just did the park. Nothin'," Callahan said, in his Western Union parlance.

"Had to be the car," said Salvatore.

The Stick was standing across the street, near the entrance to the park, looking back at the marquee. He waved us over and pointed at the front of the theater. Light bulbs had been blown out across the front of it. Wires hung down, spitting at each other. Several of the letters were blown out.

What was left of the sign spelled SO— LONG—— ——.

49

WHO'S NEXT?

The shootout at South Longbeach had attracted most of the SOB's and others were on the way. Only Kite Lange and Cowboy Lewis failed to show up for the festivities. While the hooligans were gathering, I grabbed a minute with Stick.

"Anything new on Nance and Chevos?" I asked.

"Nothing on Nance yet," he said apologetically. "No, nothing new but Kite Lange is still staked out at the marina where Chevos lives."

"I wonder how come Stizano didn't make the wake?"

"He did. He and his entourage left early, I guess to catch the flicks."

As far as I was concerned that still left Nance in the picture. I wasn't kidding myself or trying to conceal my joy.

Charlie One Ear was next to appear, as dapper as ever in tweeds although he had replaced shirt and tie with a turtleneck sweater.

"God, what a mess!" was Charlie One Ear's reaction.

Callahan said, "Take a look, other end of the park."

"Why?" asked Charlie One Ear. "Is it worse down there?"

"Line of fire," said Callahan, in his abbreviated English.

"Also we got a witness, thinks he saw a car," Salvatore added.

Charlie turned his back on the police gala in front of the theater and said, "Let's get off the firing line, shall we, gentlemen? I've got a bit of news I'd rather not share with the masses."

Dutch led us to the hot dog stand, where he ordered two dogs suffocated by chili, kraut, mustard, and raw onions. The rest of us settled for coffee, which was strong enough to poison a whale. Charlie One Ear ordered tea. We moved down the street for a powwow.

"So far it's a goose egg," he began. "Nobody knows anything, nobody's heard anything. I cruised the hotels out on the Strip, spent the afternoon at the track, and didn't see a face that worried me. I got on the horn, checked the network . . ."

He counted them off on his fingers.

"New Orleans, New York, Cincy, Detroit, Saint Looey, Chi, Vegas, L.A. What I got from that was bupkus. As of this minute, I'll stake my pension there aren't any outside guns in this town. At least none I can connect to this little hurrah."

"Maybe we should just sit back and wait a day or two more," Salvatore said. "There won't be anybody left and we can forget it."

"If this was an outside mob moving in, somebody would know about it," Charlie One Ear said. "That kind of information moves faster than a dirty joke at a wedding reception."

"Any of these insiders of yours try a guess as to the why of it?" Dutch asked.

Charlie One Ear shook his head. "No, but the word is about. The Taglianis, or what's left of them, are very nervous. Apparently they haven't got the foggiest either."

Dutch moved away from the group and stood on the curb, shaking his head, then turned suddenly and threw his cup at the wall. Coffee showered all over the sidewalk.

"What a bunch of *sheiss kopfes*," he growled to himself, "and I lead the parade. Twelve people! We had eyeballs on them all, they still get shot right out from under us!"

Frustration shimmered around him like an aura. He turned and looked down at me, his blue eyes burning fiercely behind his glasses.

"I'm goddamned embarrassed, if you want to know the truth," he said. It was one of the few times I heard him use profanity in English.

"Don't take it personally," I said. "These people have much more experience taking care of each other than you or I. If they can't keep themselves alive, it's not our fault."

"Look, I'm really sorry, old man," Charlie One Ear said, "but I may have a consolation prize for you. I'm not sure whether it ties in or not, but a chap I know is carrying a rather large snow monkey. He says the coke market's been dry for more than a month, but the local snowbirds are dancing in the street. The word is, the drought is about to end."

"Harry Nesbitt mentioned that," I said.

"When's this snowstorm going to happen?" asked Dutch.

"Imminently."

"Does this snitch know who the importer is?"

"I wish you'd refrain from calling them snitches," Charlie One Ear said. "Some of these people take a great deal of pride in working for me. It's rather like a public service for them."

257

"Charlie, all canaries sing alike. Does he know who the distributor is or not?"

"He only knows his own street connection."

"Want a guess?" I said. "Bronicata. It's his game."

"That makes sense," Stick said. "Unless maybe it's Longnose Graves."

The Mufalatta Kid broke his silence. "Nose don't touch hard stuff," he said.

"Times are changing," I countered. "This place is ripe for toot; it's wallowing in heavy rollers."

"I ain't stickin' up for the dinge," the Kid said. "On the line, he ain't nothin' but a shanty-ass, nickel-dime nigger, say. He just don't fuck with heavy drugs, man. Ain't his style."

Dutch stepped in. "Any idea how much coke we're talking about here?"

"Rumors vary. I would say fifty kilos, pure."

"Gemütlich!" Dutch rumbled under his breath.

Salvatore whistled softly through his teeth. "We're talking bucks here," he said.

Charlie One Ear took a thin, flat calculator from his shirt pocket and started adding it up.

"Let's see. A hundred and ten pounds of stuff, which they'll likely kick at least six, perhaps eight, to one. Let's say roughly eight hundred pounds, which is roughly thirteen thousand ounces, which is roughly three hundred thousand grams. At eighty dollars a gram, that would come to twenty-four million dollars along the Strand. Roughly."

That stopped conversation for almost a minute. Stick broke the silence.

"Well, that'll cover the old car payment," he said.

Dutch turned to me again. "You're the one knows these people," he said. "Do you think they'd snuff each other over twenty-four million bucks?"

"Hell, *I* might kill them for twenty-four million bucks, Dutch. The question is, does it make sense? My answer is no, it doesn't. They deal in bigger numbers than that every week."

Salvatore added his thoughts:

"I agree. It could happen if there was some rhubarb over territory, somebody in the family got his feelings jacked off, personal shit like that. Then, maybe. I don't see them cuttin' each other up over some dope deal either." He shook his head vigorously. "That don't come across as a possibility."

"So we're back to square one, and we got five more corpus delictis on our hands," Dutch said.

"I'll keep digging, of course," Charlie One Ear said, and went off to the other side of the park with Salvatore and Callahan to look for car tracks.

They returned ten minutes later. Charlie stood with his hands stuffed in his jacket pockets, rocking on his heels. After a proper dramatic pause he said, "It's highly likely the damage was done from the other end of the park. We found what could be tire tracks. Actually it looks like someone may have wrapped burlap or some other heavy material around the wheels so they wouldn't leave any identifying tracks."

"How far is it from back there to the theater?" Dutch asked.

"About a furlong," Callahan said, and when we all stared dumbly at him, he added, "Two hundred yards, give or take a few feet."

"An M-16 with a good scope could handle that," said the Stick.

"Isn't that comforting," Dutch said.

I took Callahan aside and told him about the game at the Breakers Hotel and Thibideau dropping over fifteen grand.

"Interesting," said Callahan. "Disaway'll go off, twenty, thirty to one tomorrow. It rains, pony wins, Thibideau can buy the Breakers."

"Maybe I'll come to the races tomorrow afternoon," I said.

"Back gate, one o'clock. I'll wait ten minutes." And he drifted back with the gang.

Dutch walked over and joined me.

"Twelve people blown out from under us," he said, "and all we've done so far is provide airtight alibis for every good suspect we got . . . at least the ones that are still alive."

"All but one," I said.

"Who's that?" Dutch asked.

"Turk Nance."

"You sure got a one-track mind," he said, drifting off to talk to the Kid and Zapata. I checked the time. It was half past twelve. I sought out Stick.

"How about a nightcap?" I suggested.

"Sure. Want to meet at the hotel?"

"Ever been to a place called Casablanca?" I asked.

His eyes widened. "I've been to almost every place in town at least once," he said. "Once was enough for that place."

"We'll take my car," I said, ignoring his comment.

"Done," he said with a shrug. As we headed for my rented Ford, Stick tossed his car keys to Zapata.

"Take my heap back to the Warehouse, will you, Chino?" he asked. "And keep it in second under forty, otherwise it'll stall out on you." And then to me, "Let's go to the zoo."

I was about to find out what he meant.

50

CASABLANCA

I didn't talk a lot on the way to the place. I was thinking about the Kid's itching-foot story, which led me to murder, which led me back to the Kid.

Maybe I was wrong about Nance. Maybe the killer was closer to home. Could it have been Salvatore? or Charlie One Ear? Callahan?

Almost any one of the hooligans could have done the jobs, except Dutch, who was with me when Draganata was slain, and Mufalatta and Zapata, who were at Uncle Jolly's when Stizano got his.

Of the group, Salvatore might have a reason, perhaps something related to his *mafioso* father and Philadelphia. I was thinking about the *why*, not the motive. The itching foot.

I let it pass. I didn't like the idea.

Casablanca was on the downtown waterfront, a scant fifteen minutes from the scene of the crime. I parked on the promenade overlooking the river and we walked down a circular iron staircase to the river level. The Stick and I were quite a pair, me in my narc Windbreaker and boots, Stick in a suit that looked at least a decade old, a tie that defied time, and his felt hat balanced on the back of his head.

The nightclub was perched on the edge of a pier. The windows had been taken out for the summer and replaced by shutters, all of which were open. A rush of music and heat hit us as we entered it.

"Welcome to Mondo Bizarro," said the Stick.

The place looked like it had been designed by an interior decorator on LSD.

None of the tables and chairs matched.

Gigantic stills from the Bogart film covered most of the walls. Towering up one was a gigantic blowup of Bogart, with cigarette and snarling lip, standing in front of Rick's nightclub in his white tux. Nearby, Peter Lorre leered frog-eyed at a fezzed and arrogant Sydney Greenstreet, while on another wall Claude Raines, dapper in his uniform and peaked cap, peered arrogantly at Conrad Veidt, who looked like he had just swallowed some bad caviar.

And, of course, Bergman. The eternal virgin stared mystically from under the sweeping brim of her hat on the wall opposite Bogie.

It wasn't the movie posters that gave the place its macabre charm, it was the animal heads, mounted like hunters' trophies between the blowups; psychedelic papier-mâché animal heads painted in nightmare colors. There was an enormous purple elephant with pink polka dots and a giant red hippo with mauve eyes. An orange snake speckled with blue dots curled around one of the posts that held up the ceiling, and a lapis lazuli parrot swung idly on a brass ring under a ceiling fan.

The waitresses were poured into tan leather pants tucked into lizard-skin cowboy boots and wore matching leather halters, which just barely earned the name, and safari hats.

Mondo Bizarro was a conservative appraisal.

The crowd was as eclectic as the decor: tourists, college kids, pimps, gigolos, gays, straights, local drugstore cowboys, and what looked like every woman in town, eligible or otherwise.

We took a table opposite the entrance and settled down to watch the Circus Maximus. I wondered if I could even see DeeDee Lukatis in the mob, or whether I would recognize her if I did see her.

It didn't take five minutes for the action to start.

I felt the eyes staring at me first. It started at the nape of my neck and crept up around my ears. I let it simmer for a while and finally I had to grab a peek.

I saw her in quick takes, a tawny lioness, glimpsed between sweaty dancers weaving to a thunderous beat that was decibels beyond human endurance, and through smoke thick enough to be cancerous.

Her sun-honeyed hair looked like it had been combed for hours by someone else's fingers; long hair, tumbling haphazardly around sleek, broad shoulders. Her gauzy white cotton blouse was open to the waist and held that way by that kind of dazzling superstructure that makes some women angry and others dash for the cosmetic surgeon. There wasn't a bikini streak anywhere on her bronze skin, at least anywhere that I could see. Her long thin fingers were stroking the rounded lines of the purple elephant's trunk. Her other hand held a margarita in its palm, the stem of the glass tucked neatly between her fingers.

I watched her glide through the frenetic dancers without touching a soul. Did she practice her moves in front of a mirror, or did they come naturally? Not that it mattered.

Could this be DeeDee Lukatis? I wondered. The way things were going, my ego needed a boost.

It took her a long time to get to our table.

She slid into the chair opposite me and became part of it, stroking the stem of her margarita glass with a forefinger as though she could feel every molecule of it.

"Hi," I said, dragging out my smoothest line.

That's when I found out she wasn't interested in me.

She had eyes for the Stick, who was leaning back in his chair with his hands in his pockets, a cigarette dangling from a lopsided smile.

"Well, what d'ya know," he said. "The place has a touch of class after all."

Her voice, which started somewhere near her navel, was part velvet and part vodka. "Wow, it can talk, too," she purred.

Class dismissed. Suddenly I was an eavesdropper.

The Stick had an audacious approach.

"The joint's full of younger, better-looking, richer guys. Why me?" he asked, certainly one of the great horse's mouth lines of all time.

Her smile never strayed.

"I love your tie," she said. "I like old, rotten ties with the lining falling out. The suit, too. I didn't think they made seersucker suits like that anymore."

"They don't. It's older than the tie," the Stick said.

"Are you going to be difficult?" she asked. "God, I love a challenge."

I leaned over to the Stick and said, "This is some kind of routine, isn't it? I mean, you two have been practicing, right?" My wounded ego was looking for an out.

"Never saw her before," he mumbled, without taking his eyes off her. "Who are you?" he asked her.

"Lark," she said.

"That your name or your attitude?"

That earned him a big laugh. Her gray-green eyes seemed to blink in slow motion. Her look would have melted the icecap.

"Wonderful," she said. "Let's go."

Just like that. Disgusting.

He jabbed a thumb at me.

"He's got the car."

She looked at me. Flap, flap with the slow-motion eyelids, then back at him.

"How about a cab?" she suggested.

"Do we call it or can we grab one outside?" he asked.

"No, I meant him with the cab." And she pointed at me.

"Nifty," I said. "Played like a champion."

"I knew you'd understand," she said, and slowly opened her hand toward me.

I dropped the car keys in her palm.

I glared at the Stick.

"Be in by one," I said.

His smile got a little broader. "Nothing personal," he said.

"Naw."

"Next time I'll loan you the suit."

She was on her feet already. The Stick followed. He walked to the door; she augered her way out.

I snagged one of the safari maidens and ordered a Bombay gin and soda with lime, no ice, and looked for someone who might be DeeDee Lukatis. The place had grown more and more obscure. It wasn't smoke, it was fog. A cold wind had sneaked across the marsh and invaded the warm river air. All of a sudden Casablanca seemed wrapped in gauze.

I was beginning to think it was all a bad idea when I felt a hand on my shoulder. I turned and looked up at a very pretty young woman. She had a model's figure, tall and slender, topped by long, straight ebony hair. Her angular features were as perfect as fine porcelain and required very little makeup. Gray, faraway eyes.

"Hi, Jake," she said. "Remember me? DeeDee Lukatis?"

51

A LITTLE R AND R

"I was about to abandon hope," I said. She sat down. She was wearing a kind of bunched-up-looking khaki jumpsuit with a lot of pockets and a First Cav patch on the shoulder. The full-length zipper was pulled about halfway down to her waist, which for Casablanca was conservative.

"I hope you don't mind the little subterfuge with Lark," she said.

"She's a friend of yours?"

"She works in the bank with me."

"I'm developing a healthy respect for Mr. Seaborn," I said.

"Mr. Seaborn's all right. A little stuffy maybe."

"There's nothing wrong with his taste."

"Thank you. I told Lark I wanted to talk to you alone. She agreed to try and lure away anybody who might be with you."

"Try?"

She laughed. "Actually, she thought your friend was cute."

"If that was an act, she ought to get out of the banking business."

"She's a free spirit. Lark does whatever makes her feel good. I wish I could. I come here twice a week. Lark says it's a good way to get rid of my inhibitions. This isn't even my outfit; I borrowed it from her."

"You have a problem with your inhibitions?"

She rolled her eyes. "You don't know what a trauma it was to write that note to you."

"Well, I'm glad you did."

She had to lean closer to hear me. The music seemed to be getting louder by the minute.

"I . . . I feel a little dishonest about this," she said.

"About what?"

"Asking you to meet me. Actually I want to ask a favor."

"I didn't think you were going to propose."

She laughed and began to relax.

"I've thought about you often over the years," she said. "I was so jealous of you and Doe and Teddy Findley that summer. The three of you were so happy all the time; you just seemed to have everything. I was fourteen; all I had was acne and a terrible crush on you."

"On me!"

"Crazy isn't it?" she said, lowering her eyes. "I guess in a way I still do. You never quite get over the early ones."

I thought about that for a moment or two and shook my head. "No, I guess you don't," I said. Then I began to get that feeling on the back of my neck again, only this time it wasn't pleasant. I shifted slightly in my chair and looked around the room, what I could see of it, but this time there was no tawny lioness skulking through the dancers. I saw no faces I recognized.

I gave my attention back to DeeDee.

"So what's the favor?" I asked, to make it easier for her.

"I've heard you're a detective now," she said.

"Well, not exactly. I'm a government investigator."

"The FBI?" She sounded startled.

"No, why? The possibility seems to worry you."

"I don't know." She hesitated before she went on. "It's about my brother Tony. I'm very worried about him but I can't go to the police."

"Why not?"

"Because," she said, "he may be involved in something wrong."

"You mean against the law, that kind of wrong?"

She nodded.

The din in Casablanca had become hazardous to the health. The music kept getting louder, the dancers more frenetic, and the special effects more surreal. The lights went out, strobes reflected off smoke and fog, lasers crackled from one side of the room to the other.

I got that weird feeling in the back of my neck again. This time when I turned I thought I saw someone, but it was a momentary flash through light spasms and haze.

DeeDee shrugged her shoulders as though a cold wind had blown by her.

"I'm sorry," she said. "I guess all the noise and—"

"Why don't we get out of here," I suggested. "I'll call a cab. We can go someplace and talk over coffee."

"I have my car," she said. "That was part of the deal. Lark would get your buddy and the car, I'd get you and keep mine."

265

"Did you rehearse this act long?"

She laughed. The idea of leaving seemed to brighten her. I paid the bill and we elbowed through the crowd and left.

The street was empty except for the eerie gas lamps flickering along the river's edge through the mist.

The hazy figure of a man stepped briefly through one of the halos, half a block away.

Barely audible over the din from Casablanca, a car door opened and closed.

We started toward the circular iron stairway that led up to the promenade. The street echoed with the throbbing of the music. The damp fog settled over us. Our footsteps sounded like horse's hoofs on the cobblestones.

I heard the car start. Then the stick dropped into place. It started to move, slowly at first.

No headlights.

Through the mist I could see the mouth of an alley thirty feet away.

I said to DeeDee, "Listen to me carefully. When we get to that alley, I'm going to shove you in. Start running. I'll be right behind you."

"What—" she started, but the tires behind us bit into the cobblestone street and squealed to life.

"Let's go!" I yelled, and started running, pulling her beside me.

Headlights pierced the gray swirling world around us. The car was beading in on us. I was almost dragging her as we reached the narrow passageway between two old warehouses. I shoved her in. There were half a dozen garbage pails piled up at the mouth of the alley.

"Down!" I yelled, and shoved her behind the cans.

The car, a black Pontiac, swept by a moment later, its brakes squealed, and there were three shots. I didn't hear them; they exploded against the cans and the wall behind us.

I clawed for my .357 and gave them three back. They smacked into the side of the car and it suddenly backed away from the mouth of the alley.

I looked behind us. The alley was about a car and a half wide, two hundred feet long. No doorways, although there was a loading platform and alcove about halfway down. The loading platform lip jutted three feet into the alley. There was dim light at the other end.

"We're going to run for it, " I said. "I'll be behind you. If you hear any shooting, keep running. If they come after us in the car, keep running."

She looked at me, terrified.

"Go, now!" I gave her a shove.

She pulled off her shoes and took off. I went after her. She could move, I'll give her that, even in stocking feet on cobblestones. We were almost to the end of the alley when I heard the rumble of the sedan.

The car had gone around the warehouse and was in front of us. Its headlights burst back on, turning the swirling fog into dancing halos.

"Damn," I cried, spinning her around. We dashed back the way we had come. The car screamed around the corner behind us. I heard a pop, heard the slug wheeze past my ear, heard rubber tearing at cobblestones. Light flooded the alley.

We ran to the loading platform and I dove up onto the lip, pulled her on top of me, and rolled over against a metal door at the back of the loading alcove.

The driver of the car swerved toward our side of the alley, saw the platform lip too late. Metal screamed against wood. The corner of the platform pierced a headlight, ripped through it, and tore part of a fender away. The sedan lurched sideways, its tires trying to get a grip on the cobblestones as it skidded sideways and raked the opposite wall with its rear end. Sparks showered from its tortured rear end.

The gunner was undaunted by all the action. Three more shots spanged off the metal door behind us.

Among other things, I'm a rotten shot. But my .357 was equipped with phosphorescent T-sights and I swung the heavy pistol with the car, steadied my hand, lined up the little green button on the end of the barrel with the notch in the back sight, and started shooting at the face leering in the rear window. Three slugs splattered the rear windshield.

They were playing hardball. The sedan slammed to a stop and I could hear the driver slapping it into reverse. Before he could let out the clutch I heard a cannon explode at the other end of the alley. It exploded three times. Two shots blew out the rest of the rear glass. The third one streaked off the rear bumper, an inch above the gas tank.

Stick's voice yelled down the alley:

"Go for the tires!"

Followed by another blast that sparked off the cobblestones barely an inch off target.

That whiskey-troubled voice was the sweetest sound I have ever heard.

"It's okay," I told DeeDee. "It's Stick. We're home free."

I lined up my little green sights and put two slugs into the left rear. The tire blew like a hand grenade going off. The driver shifted gears and roared off in retreat, the deflating tire peeling off the rim and the steel hub shrieking along the street. The hubcap spun off and clattered loudly against one wall.

The ruined sedan plowed into the garbage cans, showered them into street and river, screeched around the corner, and was swallowed by the fog.

I turned back to DeeDee, who was leaning against the metal door. Her eyes were the size of full moons.

"Okay?" I asked.

She stared at me for several seconds and then nodded furiously.

"Are you good on numbers?"

"I w-w-work in a b-b-bank, remember," she stammered.

"B-G-O 3-9-6," I said.

She repeated it. "Is that the license?" she asked.

"Right."

A moment later the Stick came running up, his .357 in hand.

"You two okay?" he asked breathlessly.

I threw my arms around him.

"Yeah, and damn am I glad to see you," I said, bear-hugging him. "Where the hell did you come from?"

"When we left the place there was a joker standing up the street under a light," Stick answered. "So we stopped at the edge of the park for a couple of minutes, just in case."

"So that's what that was all about," Lark pouted as she brought up the rear. "I thought it was love."

Stick gave her that crazy look of his. "It was both, darlin'," he said. "I doubled up."

"Whatever that means," she said.

"It means we're still alive," I said, "for which we'll be eternally grateful."

"Just part of our twenty-four-hour service," he said gleefully. "Keeps us on our toes."

I helped DeeDee off the platform and she sighed and fell up against me. I could feel her heart thumping against my chest.

"C'mon, we'll follow you pal," Stick said, pulling me up the alley by the arm. "Dutch is right. You're dangerous when you're out alone."

52

DEEDEE

At DeeDee's suggestion, she and I went back to her place. It was ten minutes away, in the restored section of town not far from where Della Norman and Tony Logeto had died a few days ago.

On the way she asked, "Shouldn't we report this to somebody?"

"I'm one of the somebodys you report it to," I said. "Besides, the car's probably registered to some nonentity. By now they've either dumped it in the river or dropped it at some body shop. We'll never see it again."

"You seem to know an awful lot about these things."

"It's what I do."

"I thought you just did investigative work."

"Sometimes it upsets people."

"*Upsets* people!" she cried. "Is that what you call it?"

The house was tucked among shaggy oaks, a two-hundred-year-old Revolutionary house that had been meticulously restored, as had the others on the street. It was like stepping into the eighteenth century. The inside was just as authentic. It was a museum piece, filled with bric-a-brac, old etchings and maps, and antique furniture that was as authentic as it was uncomfortable. There wasn't a cushion in the living room.

"This was my inheritance," she said. "Dad didn't have much, but he bought this house for a song when it was a falling-down wreck. He and Tony did most of the restoration work themselves. It took them years."

"Does Tony live here with you?"

"Sometimes," she said vaguely. We made small talk for ten or fifteen minutes, trying to talk past the awkwardness of the situation. Finally I got Lark's phone number and she went off to make coffee.

Lark answered the phone after eight or nine rings. Her voice was still sultry, but not quite as pleasant as earlier in the evening.

"Hello?" she said tentatively.

"I'm sorry to bother you," I said. "DeeDee gave me your number. I need to talk to the Stick. It's very important."

"Who?"

"Mickey."

"You could have waited just about two minutes more, you know," she said, "just two little minutes."

"This'll take about thirty seconds."

"Trash. The spell is broken."

A moment later Stick's whiskey tenor rasped its hello.

"Sorry to bother you," I said, "but there's something I didn't tell you back there."

"Yeah?" His interest was lukewarm.

"I got a good look at the shooter in the car. It was Turk Nance."

"Is that supposed to be a surprise?" he replied.

"Just thought you'd like to know," I said.

"Breakfast," he said. "I'll meet you at the hotel at nine. We'll grab some groceries and go hunting."

"You sound out of breath. Have you been jogging?"

"Fuck off, Kilmer."

Click.

DeeDee returned with the coffee. We sat on matching highback deacon's benches, facing each other across a rock maple serving table.

"Okay," I said. "Where were we?"

She stirred cream into her coffee and tasted it before she answered my question.

"I haven't seen or heard from Tony since Saturday. It's really uncommon for him to go more than a day or two without a call."

"Maybe he's out of town," I suggested.

"He said he'd be back Sunday night or early Monday."

"That's only a couple of days."

"I have this dreadful feeling something's wrong," she said, then after a moment of thought, added, "Maybe I should start from the beginning."

"That would help."

"Tony's been in trouble before."

"Oh?"

"Three years ago. He and this friend of his, who's a shrimper, were caught smuggling marijuana."

"How much?"

"A lot. Two or three hundred pounds."

"That's a lot."

"He was sentenced to two to five years. It could have been worse, but it was his first offense."

"How much time did he do?"

"Almost a year."

"Has he been clean since then?"

"Clean?"

"Out of trouble?"

She nodded.

"Why did he do it? I mean, was there anything other than the money?"

She toyed with her coffee, thinking about the question.

"He wanted something he couldn't afford," she said finally. "All the money in the world couldn't buy it."

"Doe Findley?"

"Raines."

"Right, Raines."

"So you know about that?"

"That's all I know."

"It was the same with Tony and Doe as it was with you and me, except you never gave me a second look. I was always the care-taker's ugly little kid."

"You don't know that," I said. "I happen to be a one-woman man."

"Still?" It was a gentle pass and I passed it gently.

"Still."

"That was my ego talking. Anyway, I think Tony's been in love with Doe since the first time he ever saw her. I don't blame her for what happened. Harry Raines was busy running around the state politicking for the gambling laws. She was lonely and Tony was always around. It just happened."

"So he decided to make a quick killing and take her away from all that?"

"No, it was over before he got in trouble. But in his mind, I think Tony feels if he has a decent car and money in the bank . . . oh, I don't know. Maybe he was just rebelling against the whole system, getting even for things he never had. He never really talked about it. When he went to prison, all he said was that he was glad Dad died before it happened."

"And you think he's mixed up in dope again?"

"That's what I'm afraid of. He left Saturday morning. We went

271

to dinner Friday night and he told me he had this job to do, that it was absolutely safe. 'Not to worry,' he told me, 'I'll be back for Sunday brunch.' I haven't heard from him since."

"He didn't say what the job was?"

She shook her head. "Things have been rough for him this past year. I offered to help, but he turned me down. I think he was desperate."

"Did he say anything about narcotics?"

"All he said was 'After this, we'll be as good as the rest of them.' He wouldn't say any more."

"Did he drive when he left?"

She nodded. "A white Mustang. I think it's a '79. But it looks brand-new."

"How about the license?"

"I'll get it for you."

She got up and rooted through a large mahogany desk, leafing through papers until she found a duplicate of the car registration. She handed it to me, along with a photograph from her wallet. It was a color Polaroid of a tallish, dark man, handsome, but a bit too intense, who looked to be in his early thirties and was built like a lifeguard. He was sitting on the edge of a swimming pool with his legs in the water.

"I remember him now," I said.

"I thought perhaps you might check around. Maybe somebody knows or has heard something," she said. "I don't want to do anything official. Do you understand?" It was more of a plea than a request.

I nodded. "Sure, I can do that. Is that all?"

"I'd just like to know he isn't . . ."

She didn't finish the sentence. She began to tremble. I moved over beside her and put an arm around her. The more she tried to stop trembling, the worse it got.

"I'll check around first thing," I said, trying to comfort her. "Don't worry, I'm sure he's all right. It's been five days. If anything had happened to him, you'd know it by now."

I wasn't sure that was true, but it sounded good and she bought it. She was suffering a delayed reaction to both her brother's disappearance and the action in the alley. I gently massaged her neck with two fingers, stroking the tight muscles that ran from the base of her skull to her shoulders. After a while she loosened up. She shifted, turning toward me, and curled up.

I massaged her neck until my fingers got stiff, and she

talked about a time that linked us to the past, but in different ways.

"It's funny, the things I remember about Doe from our school days," she said, and giggled. "Did you know," she went on, as if sharing a secret, "that the maids used to iron Doe's underwear? I know that sounds silly, to remember something like that. But when I heard it, I thought, That's the way it should be. That's the way a princess gets treated. That's what she is, a princess. Her father is the king and she lives in a castle on the ocean and nothing bad ever happens to her. I know that's not true, though. She lost Teddy." She paused and then added, "She lost you."

"That's not quite accurate," I said. "She didn't lose me."

"Oh, yes," she said with a nod, "she lost you."

I didn't disagree. There wasn't anything to disagree with. We had different points of view.

"I used to dream of being Doe," she said. "When we had a picnic, Doe always carried the flag and the rest of us cleaned up the trash. It's just the way it was. She never asked to be treated special; nice things just happened to her. I suppose it's always that way with the rich."

She said it almost wistfully and without malice, like it was an undeniable fact of life, and I suppose it was, until life inevitably caught up with even the rich. For the flash of a second I considered telling her what really happened to Teddy, but I didn't want to bust her pretty balloon. She seemed to have control of her memories. Perhaps that's why she recalled them with such innocence and without angst. She had learned the difference between memories and dreams.

She dozed off that way. It felt good there, with her curled up in my lap. I thought I might relax for a few minutes before going back to the hotel, to make sure she was sleeping soundly. I leaned back and thought about Tony and DeeDee Lukatis, always on the outside looking in, close enough to savor the sweet life, but never close enough to taste it. I thought about Tony Lukatis, who tried to make the dream come true and ended up in jail instead, and DeeDee, harboring a futile high school dream for all those years. I fell asleep thinking about them and realizing that in the end, DeeDee, Tony, and I were not that much different.

I had the same old dream again that night, only this time Tony Lukatis was running on the ridge.

53

NUMBERS GAMES

I awoke to soft sunlight, filtering through gauze drapes, and the smell of fresh coffee. Sometime during the night DeeDee had slipped a pillow under my head and draped a blanket over me, but I still felt like I'd been stretched on the rack.

She was wearing a plain black silk dress and her long hair was gathered in a bun at the back of her head, quite a departure from the previous night. Either way, she was a knockout. She put a tray with orange juice, toast, and coffee on the table in front of me.

"Thanks," I said. "What time is it?"

"A little after eight. This should give you enough strength to go back to the hotel and clean up before you meet . . . what's his name?"

"Mickey Parver. Everybody calls him Stick but don't ask why, it's too early to talk."

The juice was ice cold, the coffee strong and hot, and the toast wasn't burned. I wolfed it down while she sat across from me and had her second cup.

"I want to thank you for last night," she said. She sounded almost embarrassed.

"For what, almost getting you killed?"

"I mean later, after that. It's the first time I've slept in days. And thanks, too, for . . . listening to me ramble."

"Better watch out," I said. "Your inhibitions are showing again."

"I only wish there was some way I could repay you."

There it was, the perfect opening. It was time to play cop again. I sipped a little more coffee. It was tough coming out with it.

"Maybe there is," I said finally.

She was pleased at the prospect. "Really?" she cried. "What? Anything!"

I sipped at my coffee for a moment or two, trying to phrase it just right, but that never works. No matter how I put it, it was going to come out wrong in the end.

"You might want to think about this," I said.

"Think about what?"

"What I'm about to ask you."

Her smile started to fade.

"You know a man named Cohen who banks at the Seacoast?" I asked.

"Yes. Not personally, just as a customer of the bank."

"Does he come in often?"

"Usually every day. Why?"

"Do you handle his account?"

She cocked her head like a puppy hearing an unfamiliar sound.

"No," she said. "Mr. Seaborn handles it personally."

There it was. The connection. My pulse picked up but it still didn't prove anything. "Is that customary? I mean for the president of the bank to handle an account personally?"

"He does it on several major accounts, if that's what the customer wants. What's this about, Jake?"

"I need some information," I said. "It will be kept totally confidential, I promise you that. There's no danger of anyone ever finding out where it came from. It will only be used by me to dig up some background information."

Her forehead furrowed into a deep frown.

"What is it? What do you want?" she asked. Her tone was becoming more formal.

"I need the access number for the bank's computer, and Cohen's account number or numbers."

She was shocked. For two full minutes she stared at me in disbelief, then she lowered her eyes to the floor.

"So," she said, "we both wanted something."

There was no response to that. It was true.

"If it's at all risky . . ." I said, but her stare killed the sentence while it was still in my mouth.

"Isn't giving out that information a felony?" she asked.

"Only if you're caught."

"Seems to me somebody said that to Tony once."

I was prepared to take whatever abuse she might throw my way. It was a rotten thing to ask, a rotten position to put her in. Had it not been for her concern over Tony and my promise to try and help, I could never have broached the subject. I'm sure all of that was racing through her mind.

"Look," I said, "if you don't trust me, forget it. I'm still going to get a line on Tony for you, if it's possible."

"Thanks for telling me that, anyway," she said. She stared at the floor some more. I decided to push it.

"There are laws that make it possible to put people away," I said, "people who deserve to be put away, if we can prove their money is earned illegally. I believe Cohen is a money man for the Mafia. That's who tried to kill us last night."

She looked up sharply, her concern tempered by curiosity.

"It isn't the first time they've tried to put me away," I said. "I have a bullet hole in my side as a memento from their last try."

She kept staring without comment, making me work for it.

"Would you like to hear how they make their money? Or what they do to people who get in their way?"

"I got a hint of that last night," she said, getting up and taking the tray back to the kitchen. When she returned, she said, "Come on, I'll take you to the hotel."

She didn't say anything else. She got her things together and checked the door to make sure it was locked when we left. Just a couple of normal folks heading off for the daily grind. In the daylight her street was like a picture from an eighteenth-century history book. I almost expected to see Ben Franklin strolling by with a kite or Thomas Paine ranting on the street corner. It didn't seem possible that Front Street was only a few blocks away.

DeeDee didn't say a word on the way to the Ponce. When we got there she turned to me, her face tortured with anguish and anxiety.

"I know how to reach you," I said. "I'll call, even if I don't hear anything definite." I started to leave the car.

"Jake?"

"Yeah?"

She sat for a minute longer, then shook her head. "I can't do it," she said. "I owe a lot to Charles Seaborn, and somehow what you're asking seems like an affront to him. When Tony got in all that trouble, some of the directors at the bank wanted Mr. Seaborn to fire me. They felt it gave the bank a bad image. He stuck by me through it all, never said a word or asked anything more of me than I usually gave. I didn't even know about it for months. Lark found out and told me. I'm sorry, but what you're asking . . . I'd feel as if I'd done something to him personally."

"My mistake," I said. "I never should have asked."

"I'm glad you did," she said. "I'm glad you felt comfortable enough to ask me. I'm just sorry I feel this way."

"Loyalty's a rare commodity, don't apologize for it," I said. "I'll be talking to you."

"Thanks again," she mumbled as I got out of the car. I watched her drive away and went into the hotel. The Stick was sitting in the lobby reading the morning paper.

"This is a terrible hour to be getting in," he said drolly. "What'll the neighbors think?"

"You know what you can do with the neighbors," I snapped.

"Uh-oh. Get out on the wrong side of the bed?"

"I never got into bed."

"Ah, that's the problem."

I glared at him and suggested breakfast in the room to save time. "I need a shower," I growled.

We went to the room and I ordered food. I needed more than the toast and coffee DeeDee had provided. Then I got Dutch on the phone and gave him a quick report on the night's activities, not wanting him to hear it from anybody else. In the excitement at the movie theater I had forgotten to tell him about my meeting with Harry Nesbitt. I started off with that, finishing with the shoot-out at Casablanca.

The latter got him fuming.

"I'll have Kite pick up that son of a bitch Nance now," he growled.

"Won't do any good. He's probably got a dozen people who'll swear he was six other places at the time."

"So what do we do, ignore it?"

"For the time being," I said. "When we get him, I want to get him good—and I want it to stick."

"What do you want to do about Nesbitt?" Dutch asked. "It doesn't sound like his info on Nance was too swift."

"Maybe Nance went around the bend," I said. "I can't imagine Costello or Chevos pulling a stunt that stupid the way things are."

"Why not?" the Stick cut in. "If he'd nailed you, they could've written you off as another victim."

"I made a promise to Nesbitt and I'd like to keep it," I told Dutch. "Can we find a couple of honest cops who'll smuggle him down to Jax and stick with him until his plane leaves?"

"I'll take care of it," Dutch said. "Let me know when you hear from him."

"Thanks. Stick and I are working on some other things. I'll catch up with you later."

He rang off and I gave Stick the license number of the black Pontiac. He called the DMV while I showered and shaved.

The license plates were hot, stolen a few hours before Nance and company came calling on me.

"Shit," I growled, "the way this day is starting maybe I ought to go back to bed and start over."

A bellhop who didn't look a day over fifteen showed up with breakfast. The phone rang and I answered it, trying to eat, talk, and put fresh clothes on at the same time.

"Good morning, darling." Doe's voice was as soft as lambskin and husky with sleep. "Sleep late?"

I looked over at Stick, who was back into his newspaper, then turned my back to him and dropped my voice an octave.

"Yeah. A late night. A lot happened."

"I thought about you all day and all night."

"Me too," I mumbled.

"It was torturous being with Harry after the other night."

I made a dive for the safe spots, but stopped before I got there. I thought, Why does it scare me when it's what I want to hear?

"That's understandable," I answered.

"Are you under the covers? I can hardly hear you."

"My partner just stopped by for breakfast," I half whispered.

"Ah, so that's it," she purred. "Well, I'll let you go. I just wanted to hear your lovely voice before I got up. I want to lie here and think about you. Please make it happen again soon. God, how I miss you."

"Well, that's good," I said awkwardly.

She laughed. "What a silly thing to say," she replied. "I'll be staying at Windsong for a week or so, alone. Harry's staying at the townhouse. I'm coming out here after the party tonight."

"Party?"

"Babs' cocktail party, you goose. If you miss it, she'll kill you— that's if I don't do it first. See you at six. Thank you for coming back, Jake. I love you, my sweet."

"Uh, yeah, me too."

She hung up.

I cradled the phone and turned around to finish dressing. A minute crept by before Stick said, without looking up from his paper, "You really got it bad. You can hardly talk to the woman." Before I could protest, he held his hand up and closed his eyes. "Please, don't insult me by telling me that was your insurance man."

"That's right, it was my insurance man," I said with mock irritation.

"She wants to crawl all over your bones, right? It's always like that the morning after."

"How come you reduce *every*thing to a cliché? Maybe this is different."

"It's different, all right. I'll give you that in spades, friend. It is unique. Her old man owns the town, her husband runs the town, you'd like to put him in jail, at least for murder if nothing better pops up, and you tell me it's different! That's the understatement of the year."

"It's only a problem if I make it a problem."

"You've *already* made it a problem, putz! What in the fuck do you call a problem if this isn't one?"

"Dunetown. There's a problem."

I finished dressing and ate another piece of soggy toast.

"Okay," I blurted, "it's a problem. She's rooted too deep, man. I haven't been able to get her out of my mind for twenty years. I keep thinking it was the best shot I ever had. I want another crack at it. I'm stuck on what could have been instead of what is."

"Aren't we all," Stick said, with surprising bitterness. There was another pause before he added, "I think I missed something. The part about the price you have to pay. Or did you leave that out?"

"I don't know the price. That's the big question."

"I don't know what could have been," Stick said. "Want to run that by me?"

Now there was a rueful occupation—thinking about what could have been. But if I couldn't trust Stick, who the hell could I trust? Suddenly I heard myself laying it all out for him, starting from the day Teddy and I became football roommates at Georgia and ending on the day I got the kiss-off from Chief. I didn't leave out anything; I threw it all in—heart, soul, anger, hurt, all the feelings that my returning to Dunetown had dredged up from the past.

"Jesus, man, these people really fucked you over!" was his response.

"I've never quite admitted that to myself," I said. "I look at Raines, I think, that could have been me. I look at Donleavy, I think, if Teddy were still alive, that could be me. Every time I turn around the past kicks me in the ass."

"You're one of the ones that can't stay disconnected," he said seriously. "It's not your nature. But you've been at it so long you can't break training, you're afraid to take a chance. Like in Nam, when you're afraid to get too close to the guy next to you because you know he may not be around an hour later. It's an easy way to avoid the guilt that comes later, being disconnected is."

"Is that all it is, Stick? Guilt?"

"Like I told you the other day, it's guilt that gets you in the end. Shit, you're overloading your circuits with it. You got guilt over the girl, you got guilt because you want to pin something on her husband, guilt because you're losing your sense of objectivity, guilt because of her brother. What is it about Teddy? You keep circling that issue. You talk about him all the time, but you never pin it down."

I finally told him the story. It was easy to talk to him; he'd been there, he knew about the madness, he understood the way of things.

There were days when time dulled the sharp image of that night, but they were rare. A lot of images were still with me, but that one was the most vivid of all. It was a three-dimensional nightmare, as persistent as my memories of Doe had been. The truth of it was that Teddy Findley didn't die in combat or anywhere near it. He might have. There you have it again, what might have been. Teddy and I didn't have a very rough time in Nam until a few weeks before we were scheduled to come back to the World. Until Tet, when the whole country blew up under us. Hundreds of guerrilla raids at once. Pure madness. They pulled us out into Indian country and for the next six weeks we found out what Nam was all about. We got out of it as whole as you can get out of it and finally got back to Saigon. Teddy was a little screwy. He scored a couple of dozen Thai sticks and stayed stoned for days on end. He started talking about the black hats and the white hats.

"I got this war all figured out, Junior," he said one night. "What it is, see, we've always been the white hats before. We're supposed to be the good guys. But over here, nobody's figured out what we are yet. Are we the white hats or the black hats?" He said it the way the good witch in *The Wizard of Oz* said, "Are you a *good* witch or a *bad* witch?"

There was this compound in Saigon run by the military. They called it Dodge City because the man in charge was a major named Dillon. It looked like Dodge City, a hell-raisers' paradise, a place to blow off steam; a couple of blocks of whorehouses and bars controlled by the military for our protection. But the MP's couldn't be everywhere. Sometimes things went a little sour. One night we smoked enough dope to get paralyzed and we headed down to Dodge and we ended up in a whorehouse. It was nothing but a hooch divided up by screens. You could hear GI's humping all over the place.

"Let's get about five or six of 'em," Teddy said. "Have a little gang bang." It wasn't for me. I wasn't that stoned and I still had a little Catholic left in me. So he went behind one screen and went into the next stall. He started kidding me; it was like being in the same room.

"How's the foreplay going, Junior?"

"Will you shut up!"

"Having a problem?"

"Yeah, *you!*"

He started to laugh and then the laugh turned into a scream and the scream turned into a muffled cry that sounded as though he were underwater. I jumped up and smashed through the screen.

The girl was gone already. It was a fairly common trick. She had a single-edge razor blade held between her teeth when she kissed him, cut off his tongue with the razor and, while he was gagging in his own blood, slit his throat for closers. He died in my arms before I could even yell for help. I don't remember what the girl looked like; all I remember is that it could have just as easily been me instead of Teddy.

"I knew what it would do to Doe and Chief Findley, finding out he died like that," I told Stick, finishing the story. "I forged a set of records saying he was killed in action and I forged a recommendation for a Silver Star and the Purple Heart for him. The captain didn't give a shit. He acted like he didn't even notice it.

"Then I wrote the letter telling them how Teddy had died in action, that it was quick, no pain. I don't know which is worse anymore, Teddy's death or the lie. Reducing it all down to a fucking piece of paper like that."

Stick sat there for a long time after I finished, smoking and staring at his feet. It was not a shocker; that kind of thing was common. Just another day in paradise.

Finally he started shaking his head. "Man, you have really done a number on yourself, haven't you? What's the big issue here? You told a lie and made your best friend a hero. Big fuckin' deal."

"It's what it represents. Somehow Nam should be more important than that."

"Nam was a fuck-up. It's like a scar on your belly. You cover it up and forget it; you don't paint it red, white, and blue. You're one of those steel-covered marshmallows, Kilmer old buddy. You're a sitting duck for the vultures. You know what I say? Forget the lie part. Stick to the story; nobody wants to hear the truth anyway. Shit, pal, I say fuck the obstacles, go for it. Could be your last chance."

He lit a cigarette and went back to his newspaper, and then threw in, "Just put her old man in the joint, that'll solve all your problems."

"That's a shit thing to say."

He dropped the paper on the floor and looked up at me. "I'm just being honest. The perfect solution for you is to have Raines turn out to be the brains behind the killing and Nance the actual shooter. That way you nail 'em both in one whack. You get even and you get the girl. It's the perfect ending."

"Incredible," I said. "Those are great options."

"You just figured out the price," he told me.

"Yeah, business as usual," I said, and there was a lot of acid in my tone.

"If it's business like last night," Stick said, "count me in every time." It was obvious that he had said all he had to say about my personal problems.

"Thanks for sparing me your tales of conquest," I said.

"Speaking of business, I got a little for you. Let's get to the number one problem, okay? I don't like to brag, anyway. I was up and at the Warehouse by eight. We got good news, we got bad news, and we got some in-between news."

"Gimme the good news first," I said.

"The good news is that Kite's finally got Nance in view. The bad news is that he didn't make contact until about three a.m. Otherwise he might have been a witness to your little party over there on the waterfront."

"It'd be nice to know what he's been doing for the past two days," I said.

"Kite's working on it. Also Charlie One Ear has some information on who owns what in town and Cowboy Lewis is hot on Cohen's trail this morning. So what got your day off to such a lousy start, besides the fact that your head's not screwed on right?"

"First of all, I hurt a very nice lady," I said.

"What'd you do, turn her down?"

"Worse, I asked her to break the law."

"Oh, is that all? Murder, bank robbery, what?"

"The bank's computer code and Cohen's bank account numbers," I said.

He didn't bat an eye. I might have said I asked her to get me a glass of water, for all he seemed to care.

"Did she do it?"

I shook my head. "The lady has more integrity than I have," I said.

"Well, Lark hasn't got any such notions," Stick said, with that strange smile of his. "Here's the rest of the good news." He reached into his shirt pocket, took out a slip of paper, and handed it to me. There were two numbers written on it. Lark had drawn a smiling face behind the second one.

"Are these the bank's computer access numbers?" I asked excitedly.

"And the numbers for the Tagliani account."

"This is incredible! Are you sure they're correct?"

"I trust the lady all the way."

"The lady's got one hell of a memory," I said.

"There's a little more to it than that. Guess who the computer operator at the bank is."

"You'rc kidding!"

"She has a master's degree in mathematics and computer technology from Emory University. I may be in love. A dame looks like that with all those smarts, shit, I might even think about early retirement."

I was impressed with the information, but even more impressed that he had asked for it.

"How the hell did you know I was after these numbers?" I asked him.

"Lark told me you went to Casablanca to meet DeeDee, so I figured you must be after something," he said. "It wasn't hard to figure out what it was. Hell, I can put one and one together and get two almost every time."

"Now that I've got them, I'm not sure what to do with them," I said.

"Have you forgotten I spent six months slaving over a computer when I joined the Freeze? I know what to do with them."

"Can you access the code and get into the bank's main terminal?"

"I can hack into anything," he said with a grin. "I'm the magic man, remember?"

My palms got sweaty thinking about what we could come up with. For the first time since arriving in Dunetown, I felt we were getting close to something important. The information wouldn't stand up in court, but it could lead us straight to the bad seeds.

"You want to tell me what you want, specifically?"

"I'm not sure. But I am sure Cohen's the bagman and he deals only with Seaborn at the bank. DeeDee did tell me that. They're using the bank for a washing machine, I know it. That bank account should tell us something."

"I agree with you about Cohen. Lark says he usually makes cash deposits once a day. Big ones."

"Does she know how much?"

"No, but she checked the daily deposit tape once out of curiosity and it was in six figures."

"What! Jesus, Stick, we're on to something. Just maybe we can get them this time."

I whistled through my teeth and we laughed and slapped each other on the back and acted like a couple of high school kids. If Lark was right, Cohen could be moving as much as half a million dollars a week or more through the Tagliani accounts.

"It had to be shielded in some way," Stick said. "That kind of money activity attracts the Lepers like a petunia attracts a hummingbird."

I said, "It also means Seaborn has to be involved."

"So you want me to go fishing?"

"Yeah. What I'm really looking for is a Hollywood box, some kind of payoff account."

"That the tax boys won't tumble on to?" the Stick said.

"Right."

"That's been tried before by experts."

"Well," I said, "there's always somebody who thinks he has a better mousetrap."

54

FLOTSAM AND JETSAM

Dutch Morehead had a hunch.

When we arrived at the Warehouse, he was sitting with his feet on the desk under the two holes he had put in the ceiling the night before.

"Did y'see this?" he asked, tossing us the morning paper.

The article was on page 7, circled with a ballpoint pen:

MAN BELIEVED VICTIM
OF SHIPWRECK

The story, datelined Jacksonville, went on to say that an un-identified white male had washed ashore twenty miles north of the resort town the night before. Local police speculated that he was aboard a trawler believed to have burned at sea three days earlier. Charred wreckage of the boat had been floating up along the coast for two days. An autopsy was planned and there were no other details. The item was about three inches long.

"Don't we have enough trouble?" the Stick said.

"I already talked to the boys down there" was Dutch's answer.

"I guess we don't," the Stick replied.

"I got this hunch," the Dutchman said. It was obvious he was feeling proud of himself.

"Shit!" the Stick said. "Now what?"

"The Coast Guard got the name of the ship off some of the wreckage. It sailed out of Maracaibo nine days ago with a crew of four. Maracaibo is right around the corner from Colombia, and Colombia spells cocaine to me. The Department of Natural Resource boys have been picking up bits and pieces of it since Monday morning. Then this morning another stiff floated up. This new one is a black guy. Both of them are full of bullets, Jake. Twenty-twos."

"What's that got to do with—"

"I'm not finished yet," he said. "The labels in this black dude's shirt and pants say he's from Doomstown. Designer jeans, a two-hundred-dollar shirt, five-hundred-dollar boots. And one other thing—he has a shiv mark, from here to here." He drew a line with a thumb from ear to mouth.

"I'll be damned," Stick said. "Stitch Harper?"

"Fits him like homemade pajamas. He also had an empty holster on his belt," said the Dutchman. "Now what sailor do you know dresses like that and packs heat?"

"Who's Stitch Harper?" I asked.

"One of Longnose Graves' top honchos."

"If it's Stitch Harper," Dutch said, "we just might have us a whole new scenario working. And I'll know in an hour or so. I got photos of both victims comin' in on the telex."

"Okay, let's hear the theory," I said.

The way Dutch had it figured, Longnose Graves was bringing several kilos of coke by boat from Colombia to Doomstown. Graves bragged the information to Della Norman and she bragged it to her new boyfriend, Tony Logeto, who, in turn, passed it on to the rest of the Taglianis. Somewhere east of Jacksonville Beach, someone from the Tagliani clan hijacked the shipment, killed the crew, and burned the boat. If that's the way it happened, it was a clever scheme. It did Graves out of several million dollars' worth of snow and at the same time made him a loser to his people.

"I think," Dutch concluded, "that Graves is on the warpath. Add to all this his old lady gettin' snuffed in bed with Logeto, you got to have one angry mobster on your hands."

The idea had a lot of merit and I told him so. If Dutch's theory was true, the most likely person to have pulled off the hijacking was Turk Nance, which could account for Nance's whereabouts for the past few days.

"The way I see it," Dutch said, "it's either Costello or Graves who's behind all the killing. And right now Graves is the only one with a motive."

"We don't have anything to move on," Stick said.

It was true—it was all ifs and maybes. I decided to play devil's advocate.

"Supposing that Costello is *real* greedy," I said. "Maybe he decided to scratch out everybody except the ones he needed, which would be Tuna Chevos, who controls the waterways, Lou Cohen, his financial wizard, and Bronicata, who's the narcotics pipeline to the street. Maybe they got together, made a front-end deal to waste all the rest of the family, ruin Graves' credibility, and split the town up three ways."

"It's not as strong as the case against Graves," Dutch said. "He's fighting for his life and he's got a revenge motive to boot."

"Either way, we need that dope," the Stick said. "Without the coke, all we got is speculation."

One thing we all agreed on: If the dead black man wasn't Stitch Harper, or somebody from Graves' gang, Dutch's hunch would be colder than an Alaskan picnic. We decided to table all further discussion until the pictures arrived.

While we were waiting, I went looking for Charlie One Ear. He was sitting in his cubicle, dressed in his best with a cigarette bobbing at the end of a fancy holder, touch-typing a report at about a hundred and twenty words a minute.

"You do that like you know what you're doing," I said.

"My mother believed in the broadest kind of education," he said.

"Do me a favor, will you?" I asked. "I'm trying to get a line on a Tony Lukatis, thirty years old, dark . . ."

"I know Lukatis," he said. "Did time in Little Q. Pot smuggling." "That's him."

"Is he in trouble again?" Charlie One Ear asked.

"His sister's a friend of mine," I said. "She thinks he may be involved in another—"

I stopped in midsentence. My stomach was doing slow rolls.

"My God," I said, and ran back to the telex room with Charlie a few steps behind me. Dutch was sitting beside the machine, leafing through some reports.

"These things are embarrassing," he said as we entered the room. "If anybody else read them, they'd swear Salvatore and Zapata were illiterate." Then he looked up at me and said, "What's wrong with you?"

I handed him the Polaroid of Tony Lukatis.

"Know him?" I asked.

He took a look. "Sure, that's Tony Lukatis. He did a deuce for smuggling grass. Titan nailed him."

"Titan? I got the impression he more or less tolerated pot."

"Smoking, not smuggling," Charlie One Ear said. "What's this all about?"

"The white guy that floated up with Stitch Harper, it could be Lukatis," I said.

"Why?" asked Dutch.

"Hunch," I said. "He's been missing since Sunday. His sister thinks he may have been involved in smuggling."

The first photo rolled off the tube twenty minutes later.

"Stitch," Dutch said, "or what's left of him."

Crabs or sharks or both had done a lot of damage to the black man's face but there was enough left to tell who he was. The white man was not as lucky. He was missing a foot, his face was nibbled to bits, and he was badly bloated. I hoped the dead man would be someone else, anybody else. I remembered DeeDee's picture of Tony, pleasant, dark, good-looking kid. And I was thinking about DeeDee, to whom life so far had been one bottom deal after another. First her father, now the brother she adored, warts and all. I didn't hope for long.

"It's Lukatis," Dutch said.

"You're sure?" I asked.

He nodded. "There isn't much, but there's enough."

I turned away from the photo. I knew I would be the one to tell DeeDee. And now something new was gnawing at me.

Who had Tony Lukatis been working for? Longnose Graves or the hijackers?

OBIT

The Quadrangle was a grassy square formed on three sides by old brick warehouses that dated back to the Federalist period, and bordered on the fourth by the river. Cobblestone walks criss-crossed the park; a sundial at its center gleamed under a broiling, bronze sky. In one corner of the green oasis was a large oak tree, knobby with age, that shed what little shade there was, although nobody had sought its comforting shadows yet. There was hardly a breath of wind.

It was five to twelve when I got there. The park was beginning to fill up with pretty young girls in cotton summer dresses and men who looked awkward and uncomfortable in their business suits, most of them with their jackets tossed over their shoulders. A hot dog stand was doing record business. It was a pleasant enough place to enjoy lunch, despite the heat.

The Seacoast National was on the ground floor of one of the

buildings. Facing it on the other side of the Quadrangle was Ware-house Three, where I was to break bread with Sam Donleavy the next day. The third building, which ran lengthwise between them, facing park and river, turned out to be an old, one-story counting house that was now a maritime museum.

I sat on a concrete bench near the corner of the bank, so I could watch both entrances, and waited for DeeDee. I didn't have to wait long. At about five after, she and Lark came out, a striking pair that turned heads like waves as they walked by.

She eyed me uncertainly as they came toward me, as if she wasn't sure whether we were still speaking. I broke the ice.

"I thought maybe we could get back to being friends and forget business," I said.

Lark took the hint.

"Hot dogs and Cokes, anybody?" she asked brightly. "I'm buying."

DeeDee and I both ordered one of each and Lark slithered off toward the hot dog stand, stopping conversation all along the way.

"You were right this morning," I said. "It would've been a dishonest thing for you to do and I'm sorry I asked."

"What's the difference," she said, still edgy. "You got the num-bers anyway. Your friend convinced Lark it was the patriotic thing to do."

"Obviously he has more of a way with women than I do," I said jokingly.

"Oh, I wouldn't say that," she said, without looking at me.

We started walking and I took her by the arm and guided her under the large oak, away from the noonday sun worshippers. She turned suddenly and faced me, looking up straight into my eyes and sensing my anxiety.

"There's something wrong," she said. "I can tell." And then after a moment she added, "It's Tony. Something's happened to Tony!"

I nodded and said awkwardly, "I'm afraid it's bad news."

Her eyes instantly glazed over with tears. Funny how people know before you ever tell them.

"Oh my God," she said. "He's dead, isn't he?"

I nodded dumbly, trying to think of something to say, some gentle way of putting it when there wasn't any.

"Oh no," she said. Her voice was a tiny, faraway whimper.

She sagged against me like a rag doll with the stuffing punched out of it. I put my arms around her and stood under the tree for a long time, just holding her. I could feel her body tightening in ripples as she tried to control the sobs; then the ripples became waves of grief that overwhelmed her and suddenly she started to cry uncontrollably. I lowered her to the grass and sat beside her, clutching her to me, rocking her back and forth, as if she were a child who had just lost her first puppy dog.

I saw Lark walking back across the square, engrossed in a hot dog. When she saw us, I waved her over. She knew what had happened before she got to us. She stared at me, her eyebrows bunching up into question marks. She didn't say anything, just sat down next to DeeDee and began to rub her back, trying to fight the tears captured in the corners of her own eyes.

As we sat there I looked over at the bank and caught a glimpse of Charles Seaborn staring out the window. He stepped back into the shadows when he realized I had seen him. I looked back at the third-floor windows of Warehouse Three. I don't know what I expected, perhaps Donleavy sending semaphore messages across the park to the banker. The windows were empty, like blind eyes staring sightlessly out of the old building. All the power that had once ruled Dunetown seemed focused on this grassy flat, only now it seemed to be replaced by fear.

We sat under the tree for fifteen minutes, trying to console DeeDee. Finally she got the courage to ask what had happened.

"A boating accident," I lied. I didn't seem to have the guts for the truth at that moment. For the first time since Nam, I felt desperately sorry for someone on the bad side of the law.

Regardless of what Tony Lukatis had done, I knew what demons had taunted him to his death. Doe, the promise of Windsong, the easy life, the same demons that had taunted me, distorted my values, left me emotionally barren after Nam. I remembered the day I wrote the letter to Doe and Chief. It was like history repeating itself, except this time I couldn't escape behind a letter. DeeDee was here and I had to face her grief, to touch it, to feel her tears against my face.

Finally she started asking the inevitable questions, questions for which I didn't have answers yet.

Where? When? Did he drown? Probably. Was he doing something wrong when it happened? I wasn't sure. Where was his body now? I didn't know. Was it terribly painful? No, I said honestly, I didn't think so, it was very quick.

"Look," I said. "There's something I have to do. I'll tell Seaborn what happened. Take her home, Lark. Call the doctor and get her a sedative. I'll be over as soon as I can get there."

We took her to her car and Lark got behind the wheel. DeeDee sat motionless beside her, staring through her tears at nothing.

"Damn, damn, *damn!*" she cried vehemently, her anger suddenly spilling over. "Damn them all!" And she covered her face with her hands as Lark pulled away.

Seaborn's spidery fingers were dancing along the edge of a barren desk the size of a soccer field. He was trying to look busy when I tapped on the door and entered the room without being invited. He was startled, his eyes widening like a frightened fawn's.

The office was big enough to comfortably accommodate the enormous desk and was as barren as the desktop. Behind the highback desk chair, facing the door, was an oil portrait of a stern-looking man with devilish eyebrows that curved up at the ends and unsympathetic eyes. I guessed from his dress that the man in the painting was Seaborn's old man. There was one other picture in the office which I assumed to be of Seaborn's family. Otherwise, the room was as sterile as a spayed bitch. He started to object when I entered but I cut him off.

"DeeDee Lukatis' brother has been killed," I said. "Lark is taking her home. I told them I'd tell you."

"My God," he said, "how frightful. What happened?"

"Boating accident," I said, perpetuating the new lie. "He was in the water for a couple of days. The predators made quite a mess of things."

His face turned gray contemplating what I had just told him.

"What can I do?" he said, half-aloud, as though asking himself the question.

"Well," I said, "a little tenderness and understanding would help."

"Of course, of course," he said. Seaborn seemed to have trouble saying anything once. After a moment he cautiously asked, "Did this have anything to do with . . . uh, the, uh . . ."

"Murders?" I said. He winced at the word. "Why would you think that?" I asked.

"Her brother's been in trouble before, you know," he said, as though letting me in on a secret.

"I've heard," I said. "I can't answer that question. Right now I'm more concerned about DeeDee than why her brother died."

"Of course, of course," he repeated. And then, "What is she to you?"

"Just a friend," I said. "We all need them, you know." I left him sitting in his vast, sterile office, wiping the thin line of sweat off his upper lip.

As I left the bank, a frenetic little man with sparse black hair and hyperactive eyes scurried past me, hugging his briefcase to his side. Lou Cohen, making his daily deposit. Death didn't change anything in Doomstown.

56

DEAD HEAT

Driving out to the track, I kept thinking that it seemed like an awfully festive thing to be doing after the events of the morning. For the first time in years I felt connected to someone else's pain. I could feel DeeDee's, like psychic agony, but there was little I could do about it.

A cloud as dark as Tony's future followed me most of the way to the track, then obliterated the sun and dumped half an inch of rain in about thirty seconds. It was one of those quick, drenching summer showers that come and go quickly, but it made a mess of the traffic at the racetrack gate and made me a few minutes late arriving.

Callahan was waiting at the back gate, with his customary flower decorating a tan silk suit and his cap cocked jauntily over one eye. Here was a man who dressed for the occasion.

"What's the latest body count?" he asked dryly as we headed for the grandstand.

"I've lost count," I said, not wishing to get into the Tony Lukatis thing. "What's happening today?"

"Disaway's going to win," he said matter-of-factly. "Little storm drenched the track down just enough."

"Will it bring down his odds?" I asked.

"Doubt it. Hasn't shown anything his last two times at bat. Players don't trust him."

"Are you going to put some money on him?" I asked.

"Never bet the ponies," he said. "Rather give my money away."

The stadium and grounds were exquisite. The grandstand, with its gabled roof and tall cupolas at the corners, was Old South to the core. It could have been a hundred and fifty years old. Callahan led me on a quick walk through the premises.

The place was jammed. The parking lot was almost full and people were milling about the betting windows, worrying over their racing forms, studying the electronic totalizator boards, which showed Disaway paying $33.05 to win, almost fifteen to one.

"He has to beat Ixnay," said Callahan. Ixnay was the favorite, paying only $3.40 to win. "The eight horse," he continued. "Two horse, Johnny's Girl, is favored to place. Then it's nip and tuck among the field."

We went from the betting rooms to the paddock. Disaway and the rest of the horses in the first race were on display. He was showing good temper, standing with his legs slightly apart, his nostrils flared, checking out the crowd. Judging on looks, I would have had my money on Disaway. The other horses in the first race didn't look like they could carry his feed bag.

"Good-looking horse," said Callahan. "Too bad he's got such tender feet."

"Who's riding him today?" I asked.

"Scoot Impastato's up," Callahan said.

"I thought he was through with Thibideau," I said.

"Who knows," Callahan answered vaguely. "Maybe he needed a ride."

"Why would he do that?" I asked. "He seemed so dead against him the other day."

Callahan looked at me like I had just spit on his shoe.

"How would I know? Why do you do what you do? Why do jockeys jock? Hell, they get fifty bucks a ride, a piece of the purse if they win. Rainy days, when the track's muddy, it's easy for a horse to go down doing forty miles an hour. Jock can get trampled to death."

"You mean like today," I said.

"Not too bad out there now," Callahan said. "Sun'll cook off most of the standing water. When it's real muddy, shit! I'll tell you, racing in the mud is one piss-poor way to make fifty bucks. But it's a ride, what they do. Thibideau probably said, 'I'm sorry, kid, here's an extra fifty,' old Magic Hands is up. Kid knows the horse, Thibideau wants a winner. He made peace."

After the paddock we went to the top tier and he walked me

through the private club section, a posh series of tiered rooms protected from wind, rain, and sun by tinted glass, with royal-blue velveteen sofas, low-cut mahogany tables for drinks and snacks, and TV monitors to provide close-ups of the race for the privileged. Red-jacketed waiters, all of whom seemed to be elderly black men, solemnly served refreshments. The place seemed to brag of its elegance, a fact I mentioned to Callahan.

"The sport of kings," he said. "These are the aristocrats. Owners, breeders, money people. All part of it, all part of the show."

From the elite of the club we went down among the commoners at the rail. The crowd was already four deep. Callahan, I learned, had a box in the club section, courtesy of the track, but he preferred to be as close to the horses as he could get.

"Like to feel 'em go by," he said, adjusting his field glasses, checking out the infield, then the gate. "When betting starts, we can get next to the wood."

He handed me a program and I checked out the charts. There was a list of the stewards, headed by Harry Raines, and some track information that surprised me. According to the program, taxes took fourteen percent of the pari-mutuel's first ten million, eight percent of the next ten mil, six percent on the next fifty, and five percent on everything over that. Obviously the state was getting fat, a fact which certainly vindicated Raines.

The infield was as impressive as the stadium. A large pond with a fountain in the center had attracted herons and other water birds to it. Gardens surrounded the pond and there was a granite obelisk at one end.

"What's that?" I asked, pointing to the large marker.

"Remember me telling you about Justabout at chow the other morning?"

"You mean the ugly horse?"

Callahan nodded. "First big winner to come off this track. Ran his first heat here, ran here most of the next season. First two years he won forty-two races. Ugly as he was, he was so good he once got a standing ovation for coming in second. The crowd figured he'd been racing so much he was tired. Just before the season ended last year, he got trapped against the rail going into the far turn, tried to break out, bumped another kid, went down. They had to destroy him, so the board of stewards decided to bury him out there."

At exactly ten minutes before post time a horseman in a red cutaway and a black hunter's cap led the horses out onto the dirt, parading them around the track and in front of the stands. There was a ripple of applause, now and then, and a lot of chitchat among the horseplayers as the Thoroughbreds went by. Disaway was acting a little frisky, jogging sideways and shaking his head.

Callahan was right about the railbirds. Ten minutes before the first race, half of the crowd around us seemed to rush off en masse, waiting until the last minute to get their bets down. We moved up against the rail and across from the finish line, a perfect position.

The odds on Disaway changed very little, as Callahan had predicted. Five minutes before post time they dropped from $33.05 to $26.20, still a hefty long shot as far as the bettors were concerned.

As they started putting the horses in the gate, Callahan gave me the binoculars.

"Watch Disaway, the four horse. He's acting up a little but I don't think he's nervous. Anxious to run. Looks good, lots of energy."

I could see him jogging sideways and throwing his head about as the handler tried to lead him into the chute. Magic Hands was leaning over his shoulder, talking into his ear. A moment later the horse settled down and strolled into the gate.

I turned around and appraised the clubhouse with the glasses. Raines was in the center box, alone, looking stern, like Patton leading his tanks into combat.

"There's Raines," I said, "center stage."

Callahan gave him an unsolicited compliment. "Raines is a tough administrator. Built a rep for the track; well run, clean, profitable."

"Aren't they all?" I suggested.

"Hah! I got out of college," said Callahan, "got a job working for the vet at a little track. Florida. Assistant track doctor. Track was dirty. Shit, they switched blood samples, dosed horses . . . crazy. Saw two horses die that summer, one with heaves. Terrible. Pony just lies down, gags for air. Like watching him suffocate, only takes hours. Don't want to kill him because you keep hoping he'll turn around, make it. I decided to make a stink how bad it was. Got me fired. Told me I'd never work at a racetrack again. So I became a cop, went back, cleaned their tank. Heads up, they're coming out."

I gave him back his glasses just as the bell rang. I could see the horses charging out of the stalls, a blur of horseflesh and wild colors; mauve, pink, orange, bright blues and greens seemed to blend together in a streak of color, then the line began to stretch out as the field moved for position. The crowd was already going so crazy as the eight horses pounded toward the first turn, I couldn't hear the announcer giving the positions.

"How's he doing?" I yelled, unable to make one horse from the other on the backstretch.

"Off the rail and fourth going into the turn," Callahan yelled. "Got a bad break coming out of the gate . . . making up for it . . . Scoot's laying it on . . . on the outside now, moving into third. Scoot isn't letting him out full yet . . . passing the three-quarter post . . . Scoot still holding him back . . . running him to win, all right. Not gonna let him out until the stretch . . . there he goes into third place . . . he's moving for the inside now . . ."

I could see the horses clearly as they came around the clubhouse turn. Disaway was running hard, challenging the two horse, Johnny's Girl. I could feel the excitement of the crowd as they started down the last five hundred yards.

Callahan continued his running commentary.

"He's on the rail now . . . pushing for second. He's a nose out of second place now . . . and Scoot's letting him out! Look at that horse go! Damn, does he like that mud . . ."

Disaway nosed past the two horse and challenged the leader. I could feel the thunder of their hoofs as they stormed toward the finish line, the jockeys' livid colors splattered with mud.

Callahan's voice began to rise as he, too, was caught up in the excitement of the finish.

"Disaway's going for it. They're neck and neck coming down the stretch, and there he goes, he's pulling away, he's got the lead by a head and romping."

Suddenly Callahan stopped for a second, and then he cried out, "Jesus!"

As they approached the wire, Disaway suddenly swerved away from the rail and headed diagonally across the track, his left front leg dangling crazily as he made the erratic move. The two horse behind him tried to cut inside but it was too late. They collided, hard, neck on neck. Disaway was thrown back toward the rail as the two horse went down, chin into dirt, rolling over its hapless jockey. Disaway was totally out of control and Impastato was trying vainly to keep him on his feet, but the three horse was charging for the wire and they hit with a sickening thud. Scoot Impastato was vaulted from the saddle, spinning end over end into the rail, followed immediately by Disaway. The rail shattered and Disaway, Impastato, the three horse and jockey, and the horse behind it all went down in a horrifying jumble of legs and torsos and racing colors and mud.

The crowd shrieked in horror.

Then, just as suddenly, it was deathly still.

From the infield I heard a voice cry out, "Get him off me, please get him off me!"

One of the horses was trying to get up, its legs scrambling in the dirt.

One of the three jocks was on his knees, clawing at his safety helmet.

The two horse and rider were as still as death in midtrack.

Sirens. An ambulance. People running across the infield.

The place was chaotic.

"Let's get the hell over there," Callahan said, and we jumped the rail and headed for the infield.

57

RAINES GETS TOUGH

It was a bizarre sight: Disaway was spread out on an enormous metal table, three legs askew, his head dangling awkwardly over one side, his bulging eyes terrified in death, his foreleg split wide open and its muscles and tendons clamped back, revealing the shattered bone. The vet, whose name was Shuster and who was younger than I had pictured him, a short man in his midthirties who had lost most of his hair, was leaning over the leg with a magnifying glass, and Callahan, dressed in a white gown, was leaning right along with him. Both gowns were amply bloodstained. I walked to within three or four feet and watched and listened, keeping my mouth shut and my eyes and ears open.

So far, two horses were dead, a third might have to be destroyed, and two jockeys were in the hospital, Scoot Impastato with a fractured skull and a broken leg.

"I've never seen a break quite this bad," Shuster was saying.

"The other horses could've done some damage when they ran over him," Callahan answered.

"I think not. The pastern bone broke inward here . . . and here. No chips or other evidence of impact. This is what interests me. See? Right here and then down here, at the bottom of the break."

Callahan leaned closer and nodded.

"Yeah. Maybe it splintered when the bone broke."

"Maybe . . ."

Shuster took a pair of micrometers and leaned back over the carcass.

"Less than half a millimeter," he said. He took a scalpel and scraped something from the edge of the fractured bone into a test tube.

"Calcium?" Callahan said.

"We'll see."

"Butes did this," Callahan said.

"I'd have to agree. The horse was coming up lame. He should have been scratched."

"What was the trainer's excuse for dosing him?"

"Runny nose."

"Yeah, ran all the way down his leg."

"I couldn't argue," Shuster said apologetically. "It's a perfectly legitimate excuse."

"Nobody's blaming you. This isn't the first time a pony with a bad leg has been Buted up."

The door opened behind me and Harry Raines came in. His kelly-green steward's jacket seemed out of place in the sterile white room, but my rumpled sports jacket didn't add anything either.

A barrage of emotions hit me the instant he entered the room. In forty-one years I had never made love to another man's wife, and suddenly I was standing ten feet away from a man whom I had dishonored and toward whom I felt resentment and anger. I wanted to disappear, I felt that uncomfortable when he entered.

I had a fleeting thought that perhaps he knew about Doe and me, that maybe one of the Tagliani gang had anonymously informed on us. Too many people either knew or had guessed about us, Harry Nesbitt had made that clear to me. I almost expected Raines to point an accusing finger at me, perhaps draw an "A" on my forehead with his fountain pen. I could feel sweat popping out of my neck around my collar and for an instant I blamed Doe for my discomfort, transferring my anger and jealousy to her because she had married him.

All that in just a moment, and then the feelings vanished when I got a good look at him. I was shocked at what I saw. He seemed not as tall as when I had seen him at the track two days earlier, as if he were being crushed by an invisible weight. His face was drawn and haggard, his office pallor had changed to a pasty gray. Dark circles underlined his eyes. The man seemed to have aged a dozen years in two days.

Is he really the success-driven robot others have made him out to be? I wondered. He looked more like a man hanging over a cliff, waiting for the rope to break.

Quite suddenly he no longer threatened me.

My fears were unfounded. He didn't pay any attention to me at first. He was more concerned with the dead horse. When he did notice me, he was simply annoyed and somewhat perplexed by my presence.

"What are you doing here?" he asked, looking at Callahan as he said it, as if he didn't think I knew the answer.

"That's Jake Kilmer. We're working on this thing together" was all the big cop told him.

"Jake, this is Harry Raines." That seemed to satisfy Raines who dismissed it from his mind. If he recognized my name he didn't show it. He turned his attention back to the business at hand. "I don't mean to push you, Doc. Did he just break a leg?"

"Two places. He was also on Butes."

"What!"

"He had a cold."

"According to who?"

"Thibideau."

"Damn it!" Raines snapped, and his vehemence startled me.

"Uh, there could be something else," Callahan said. He came over to us and took off the gown. "There's a crack in the pastern leading out of the fracture. It appears to be slightly calcified, which means it's been there a while. A few days, at least."

"So it wasn't a cold."

"I'm telling you this because Doc here can't say anything until he finishes his tests. But I'd say this animal was on Butazolidin because he was gimpy after the race on Sunday."

"Where did you get that information?"

"The jock, Impastato. But he didn't have anything to do with this I don't think. He quit Thibideau Sunday because he'd been made to break the horse out at the five-eighths and the horse was strictly a stretch runner, which is another reason he lost Sunday."

"The trainer's Smokey Barton, right?"

Callahan nodded.

"He'll go to the wall for this."

"It's done a lot," Callahan said.

"Not at this track," Raines growled. "Not anymore."

Shuster went back to work and Callahan nodded for me to follow him out of the room. We went outside and leaned against the side of the building in the hot afternoon sun. Callahan didn't say anything. A few moments later Raines came out.

Callahan said, "Mr. Raines, I think we need to talk."

Raines cocked his head to one side for a beat or two and then said, "Here?"

"Preferably not."

"My office then. We'll go in my car."

He drove around the track without saying a word and parked in his marked stall. We took the elevator to the top floor of the stadium, then headed down a broad, cool hallway to his office.

It was a large room, dark-paneled and decorated completely in antiques, down to the leatherbound volumes in its recessed bookcases. Ordinarily the room would have been dark and rather oppressive, except that the entire wall facing us as we walked in was of tinted glass and overlooked the track. The effect was both startling and elegant.

His desk was a genuine something-or-other and was big enough to play basketball on. Executives in Doomstown seemed to have a penchant for big desks. This one was covered with memorabilia. It sat to one side and was angled so that Raines could see the track and conduct business at the same time. The view was breathtaking.

There were three paintings on the walls, two Remingtons and a Degas, all originals. There were only two photographs in the room, both on his desk. One was a black-and-white snapshot of an older couple I guessed were his mother and father. The other one was a color photograph of Doe, cheek to cheek with a black horse who must have been Firefoot.

I had a hard time keeping my eyes off her.

"Is this going to call for a drink?" Raines asked.

Callahan hesitated for a moment or two and then said, "I could do with a bit of brandy, thanks."

"Kilmer?"

"Sounds good to me," I said.

The wet bar was hidden behind mahogany shutters that swung away with a touch. Raines took down three snifters that looked as fragile as dewdrops and poured generous shots from a bottle that was old enough to have served the czar. The brandy burned the toes off my socks.

"Have a seat and tell me what's on your mind," he said in a flat, no-nonsense voice.

The leather sofa was softer than any bed I'd been in lately. He sat behind his desk with a sigh and rubbed his eyes.

I was beginning to like him in spite of myself. I had remembered him as just another football jock, but Raines had about him the charisma of authority, even as weary as he seemed to be. He dominated the office, not an easy thing to do considering the view.

"This thing with Disaway," said Callahan, "it goes a little deeper than splitting a foreleg because of Butes."

Raines swirled his brandy around, took a whiff, then a sip, and waited.

"Disaway was favored to win a race this past Sunday—"

"He dragged in eighth," Raines said, cutting him off.

"Yeah, right, well, we have what I would call very reliable information that the race was fixed for Disaway to lose. Would you say the information is good, Jake?"

"I'd say it's irrefutable," I said.

The muscles in Raines' jaws got the jitters.

"I can't tell you exactly how it was done," Callahan went on. "Probably cut back his feed for a couple of days and overworked him a little, raced him a little too much, then probably gave him a bag of oats and a bucket of water a couple of hours before the race and he was lucky to make the finish line. But there's no doubt that he was meant to lose. Money was made on it."

"By who?" Raines demanded.

Callahan hesitated for several moments. He was in a tight spot. To tell Raines about the recording was to admit that there was an illegal tape in Tagliani's house.

"I'm sorry, sir," Callahan said, firmly but pleasantly, "I can't tell you that. Not right now. The thing is, it worked as a double. He lost so big Sunday, his odds were way up for today's race."

"He went off at about fifteen to one," Raines said. He took another sip of brandy but his dark eyes never left Callahan's face.

"That's right, but he was posting $33.05 until a few minutes before post time. According to your man at the hundred-dollar window, a bundle was laid off on him just before the bell and his odds dipped to $26.00 and change."

"Do you know who placed the bundle?" Raines asked.

Callahan shook his head. "It was several people, spread across both windows."

"Who was responsible?"

"Could've been anybody from the groom to the owner. Thing is, sir, we can't prove any of this. Except we know the loss on Sunday was fixed."

"We can prove the horse was dosed with Butes," Raines said angrily.

"Yeah," said Callahan, "except it isn't against the law in this state."

"Well, it's going to be," stormed Raines. "I've always been against the use of Butazolidin on any horse up to forty-eight hours before a race. I know horses, Callahan."

"I know that," the big man answered.

"But I don't know the kind of people that fix horse races and you do. I need some proof to use on Thibideau so this won't happen again."

I decided to break in at this point. Callahan was playing it too close to the vest.

"Mr. Raines, Pancho here's reluctant to discuss this because it involves some illegal evidence-gathering. I trust you'll keep this confidential, but the fact is, we *know* the race was fixed, but we are powerless to say anything about it. The proof is on a tape which is nonadmissible."

He stared at both of us for a few moments, toyed with a pipe on his desk, finally scratched his chin with the stem.

"Can you tell me who was involved?"

"A man named Tagliani," I said. If he knew the name, he had either forgotten it or was one of the better actors I had ever seen in action. There was not a hint of recognition.

"I don't think I'm familiar with—"

"How about Frank Turner?" I said. "That's the name he was using here."

I could see Callahan's startled look from the side of my eye but I ignored it.

The question brought a verbal response from Raines.

"Good God!" he said. "Is this fix tied up in some way with the homicides in town?"

It was obvious that he had bought the soft-pedal from the press just as everyone else in town had. Just as obviously, he was totally in the dark about who Tagliani really was and the ramifications of the assassinations.

"Not exactly," Callahan answered, still trying to be cautious.

I decided it was time to let the skeleton out of the closet. I told him the whole Tagliani story, starting in Ohio and ending in the Dunetown morgue. I told him about Chevos, the friendly dope runner, his assassin, Nance, and their front man, Bronicata. I told him about the Cherry McGee–Longnose Graves war, a harbinger of what was to come. The more I talked, the more surprised Callahan looked.

Surprised was hardly the word to describe Raines. He was appalled.

I was like a crap shooter on a roll. The more aghast they got, the more I unloaded. I watched Raines' every muscle, trying to decide whether he had truly been misled by Titan and the others, or whether he was one of the greatest actors of all time. I decided he had been duped. Whatever had been weighing on his mind earlier in the day probably seemed insignificant compared to what I was telling him. I saved my best shot until last.

"I'm surprised Titan, Seaborn, Donleavy, or the fellow who owns the newspaper and TV station—what's his name . . . ?"

"Sutter," he said hoarsely.

"Yeah. He's handling the cover-up. I'm surprised one of your associates didn't tell you before this," I said.

Pause.

"They've known about it for several weeks."

Callahan looked like he had swallowed his tongue.

Raines got another five years older in ten seconds.

I'm not sure to this day whether I was venting my anger toward the Committee, Chief, and the rest of the Dunetown crowd, or telling the man something he should know, whether it was a petty move on my part because I wanted his wife, or a keen piece of strategy. That's what I wrote it off as, even though it was still a reckless thing to do. Whatever my motives were, I knew one thing for sure: A lot of hell was going to be raised. Some rocks would certainly be overturned. I was anxious to see who came running out.

By the time I was finished, he knew I knew who was on the Committee and the extent of its power, and I did it all by innuendo, a casual mention of Titan here, of Seaborn there, none of it incriminating. I stopped short of that.

I was having a hell of a time. It was the Irish in me: don't get mad, get even. I was doing both.

"Anyway," I said, summing it all up, "the fix wasn't part of this other mess, it's just indicative of what was happening here. Uh . . ."

I tried to think of a delicate way of putting it. ". . . A change of values in the city since the old days."

His cold dark eyes shifted to me and he stared at me for several seconds although his mind still seemed to be wandering. Then he nodded very slowly.

"Yes," he said sadly. "That's well put, Kilmer. A change of values."

It was then that I realized how deeply hurt he was. Bad enough to find out you have been lied to by your best friends, but to get the information from your wife's old boyfriend went a little beyond insulting. I stopped having a good time and started feeling sorry for him. A lot of Harry Raines' dreams had been destroyed in a very few minutes.

Pancho Callahan stared out the window at the racetrack. He had less to say than usual—nothing.

Raines got up, poured another round of brandy, and slumped on the corner of his desk.

"I appreciate your candor," he said, stopping to clear his voice halfway through the sentence. "I understand about your . . . previous ties to Dunetown. All this is probably difficult for you, too."

He wasn't doing bad at the innuendo himself. A lot of information was bouncing back and forth between us, a lot of it tacitly. I almost asked him what had been troubling him.

Instead, I dug it in a little deeper.

"It hasn't got anything to do with old ties, Mr. Raines," I said. "I'm an investigator for the government. I came to help clean up your town. I've been here five days and I only know one thing for sure. Everybody of importance I turn to for help, kicks me in the shins instead. Callahan wouldn't have told you all this. He wouldn't be that inconsiderate. I, on the other hand, have never scored too well in diplomacy. It doesn't work in my job."

I stopped talking. The dialogue was beginning to sound defensive.

Raines looked at Callahan. "Can you confirm this?" he asked quietly.

Callahan nodded slowly.

"My God," Raines said again. And then suddenly he turned his attention back to Pancho Callahan.

"The blame rests squarely with the trainer," Raines snapped, almost as if he had forgotten the conversation moments before. It was as if it had given him some inner strength. The weight seemed to be gone. Fire and steel slowly replaced it, as if he'd made a final judgment and it was time to move on. "I'll have Barton's ass. I'll get him out of here along with that damn Butazolidin."

Callahan chimed in: "Seems to me, sir, we're talking about two different things here. Buting up the horse today and fixing the race on Sunday. They're connected this time, but they're two different problems."

"Yes, I understand that," he said. He braced his shoulders like a marine on parade and ground his fist into the palm of his other hand.

"We talked to the jockey . . ."

"Impastato," Raines said, letting us know he knew his track.

"Right. Impastato got chewed out by Smokey Barton for letting Disaway out at the five-furlong post—he usually goes at the three-quarter. Anyway, it was Thibideau who told him to run the race that way."

"That happens; it's not uncommon," Raines said, attempting to be fair.

"No. But it's usually not done in a race where the horse is favored and the track is right for him."

"I agree," said Raines, who was turning out to be nobody's fool, "but it's not enough to prove the race was a fix."

"No, but there's something else. The last race Disaway ran, Impastato says the horse was shying to the left going out of the backstretch. Started running wide."

"Look, I'm sorry, Callahan," Raines said impatiently, "but I need to know where you got this thing about the race being fixed. I can't go to the stewards and tell them I heard it around the track."

"You can't take it to the stewards at all . . . or the Jockey Club," Callahan said, looking to me for support.

"And why not?"

"We can't prove any of it," I said. "You're a lawyer. All of this is expert conjecture. You could get your tail in as big a crack as ours would be."

"My tail's already in a crack," he growled.

Callahan said, "What Jake means is, we can't prove the horse was burned out so he wouldn't run well. We can't prove Thibideau put the final touch on it by opening him up too early. We can't even prove it was Thibideau. Fact is, we can't even prove for sure the horse has been running with a hairline crack in his foreleg."

Raines' anger was turning to frustration.

"Why don't you just spell it out for me," he said.

"Okay," said Callahan. "The way I see it, they couldn't Bute him on Sunday because there's a little kick to Butes; the horse might just have done the job anyway, and he was favored. The fix was for Disaway to lose. They had to Bute him today because he was going lame after the workouts, and today was his day to win. So Disaway ran like a cheetah, couldn't feel the pain in his foreleg until he went down. What I think is that Thibideau set up the loss on Sunday. Smokey's only sin was not pulling the pony because he was going lame. Hell, you could run a lot of trainers off the track for doing that."

"Then I'll run 'em off," Raines said angrily. He finished his second brandy and stood with his back to us, staring down at the track. "An owner's greed, a trainer's stupidity, and two horses are dead. One jockey may never ride again, and another is lying in pain in the hospital." He turned back to face us.

"To my knowledge, there's never been a fix at this track, not in almost three years."

"Well," Callahan said, "it was well thought out and impossible to prove. Would've worked like a Turkish charm, too, except the leg was weaker than they thought, which is always the case when a horse breaks a leg in a race."

"Then just what the hell *can* I do?" Raines roared, and for a moment he sounded like Chief Findley.

Callahan finished his drink and stood up.

"About this one? Nothing. Thibideau lost his horse; he's paid a price. The other two horses and jockeys? Don't know what to say. It'll go down in the books, just another accident. I don't think—see, the reason we told you this, it isn't the last time it's going to be tried. I know how you feel about the track and the horses. It's something you needed to know."

Raines sighed and sat back in his chair and pinched his lower lip.

"I appreciate it, thanks," he said. But he was distracted. His gaze once again was focused somewhere far away.

"Mr. Raines, it wouldn't help us—Callahan here, myself, and the rest of Morehead's people—for you to talk about this fix business. Not for just now. Maybe in a day or two, okay?"

He could hardly refuse the request and didn't.

"I respect your confidence," he said, without looking at either of us. "Will forty-eight hours be enough?"

Callahan looked at me and I shrugged. "Sure," I said, "that'll be fine. We'll be checking with you."

We left him sitting there, staring out at the track he had created and which he obviously loved and cherished and felt protective of, the same way Chief felt about Dunetown. I felt sorry for him; he was like a schoolboy who had just discovered some ugly fact of life. Callahan didn't say anything until we were outside the building and walking back around the infield to the car.

"You were pretty tough in there," he said.

"Callahan, do you ever get tired of dealing with pussyfooters?" I asked with a sigh.

"All the time," he said, looking down the track, where they were repairing the infield fence.

"That's what just happened to me. I got the feeling Raines is anything but. But he's surrounded by a bunch of pussies."

"It's your business to tell him?"

"Nobody else was going to do it. Time somebody played honest with the man."

"Did that all right," he said. "Just wonder what Dutch is going to say."

"I wouldn't worry about Dutch," I replied. "I'd worry about Stoney Titan."

After a moment Callahan said, "Yeah . . ." and seemed awed at the prospect.

I didn't tell him what else had happened, that I was measuring the man to see what kind of stuff he was made of.

I wasn't sure I liked the answer.

FLASHBACK: NAM DIARY, THE SECOND SIX

The 182nd day: We know this village is a VC hideout. We go by the place, there's this pot of rice cooking, enough for maybe a hundred people, and there's some old folks around, a dozen kids, two or three younger women, that's all.

"They sure are skinny, to eat that much," Jesse Hatch says as we walk by.

Flagler's replacement is this kid from Pennsylvania, handles a .60 caliber like it was part of his arm. He learns fast too. We call him Gunner. He says he used to hunt all the time, poaching and everything, summer and winter, since he was maybe eight, nine years old. Nothing scares him. He achieved "aw fuck it" status before he ever got to Nam.

Anyway, we go back tonight to see if maybe the village is a gook shelter and there was activity all over the place. What we got is Gook City. We flare the place and hit it from both sides, only there's a stream on the back side of the village and they get on the other side and we are pinned down. There are green tracers going all over the place, rounds bouncing off shit, kicking around us.

We're pouring stuff into the hooches, just shooting the shit out of them, and all of a sudden one of them goes off. They must've had all their ammo stored inside because it was the Fourth of July—squared. Grenades, mortars, tracers, mines. Everybody's freaking out, running around. Then Hatch catches one in the leg from the other side of the stream and he goes over the side into the water and he panics and starts yelling that he can't swim and Carmody is yelling, "Shut up, for Christ sakes" only it's too late and Jesse catches a couple in the head. Carmody and me, we go over the side and drag him back. But I knew he was finished. It was like trying to lift a house.

Carmody keeps saying, over and over, "Why did he yell, why the fuck did he yell. Fuckin' stream was only three feet deep."

But it was dark and everything had gone wrong and Jesse couldn't swim. Hell, I don't know why I'm apologizing for old Hatch, look what it cost him.

The 198th day: *The lieutenant's beginning to act weird. It started a couple of weeks ago when we lost Jesse Hatch. It's like he has a hard time making up his mind about anything.*

Last night I go by his hooch and I say, "C'mon, Lieutenant, let's have a beer." And he just sits there, looking at me, and then he says, "Let me think about it." Think about having a beer?

Today he says, "My luck's going bad. I shouldn't have lost Flagler and Hatch."

"You can't blame yourself," I say to him.

"Who'm I going to blame, Nixon?" he says, only he says it with bitterness. He's lost his sense of humor, too.

The 215th day: *We got separated from our outfit and we were two days out in the boonies. We come up on this handful of gooks. Ten of them, maybe. We just break through some brush and there they are, twenty feet away plus change.*

Everybody goes to the deck but the lieutenant. I don't know what happened. He just pulls a short circuit and stands there. This one VC has his AK-47 over his shoulder, he rolls backward and gets one burst off. Carmody takes three hits. He's lying there, a few feet away from me, jerking real hard in the dirt.

It's the shortest firefight I ever saw. It's over in about ten seconds. Everybody is shooting at once. We are on top of these people and Carmody is the only one gets hit. One of the gooks jumps in the river and Gunner just goes right in after him, takes him out with his K-bar. Just keeps stabbing him until he's too tired to stab anymore.

I take the lieutenant in my arms and hold him as tight as I can and keep telling him it's going to be all right. I hold him that way until he stops shaking and I feel him go stiff on me.

It doesn't seem possible. A month to go, that's all he had. I don't know why I thought the lieutenant was invincible. You'd think I'd know better after six months out here.

The 254th day: *It's almost six weeks since Carmody took it. I wish the hell I would have time to thank the lieutenant. If he had just come around for a minute or two. Shit, you just take too much for granted out here.*

I've been acting squad leader ever since. They made me a sergeant. Doc, Gunner, me, we're the only old-timers left. Jordan beat the rap and rotated back to the World. The night before he left we got him so drunk, shit, he was out cold. So we tie him to the back of this PT-boat and drag him back up to the base, which is about eight or nine kliks. He almost drowned. By the time we got to the base, he was sober. So we got him drunk all over again. He was a wreck when he got on the chopper to Cam Ranh. I'll bet he's still got a hangover. Something to remember us by.

Can you beat that, six months and I'm an old-timer.

I never even told the lieutenant I liked him.

The 268th day: *I got called down to Dau Tieng today, which is division HQ, and I talked with this captain who seems to run the whole show in this sector. He tells me I'm recommended for a Silver Star for this thing up at Hi Pien. It was a rescue mission and I guess I looked pretty good that day.*

He asks me how I feel about the war. Can you imagine? How does anybody feel about the war, for Christ sakes.

"I've had better times," I said. "Like the time I had my appendix out."

The captain has real dark eyes, like he needs sleep and could use a week or two in the sun, and he got a kick out of that.

"I mean, how do you feel about the war politically," he says.

"I don't know about that," I say to him. "I'm not interested in political bullshit. I'm here because I was sent here. I don't even know what the hell we're doing over here, Captain. Right now it looks like all we're doing is getting our ass kicked."

"Does that concern you? I mean, that we seem to be getting our ass whipped?"

"You some kind of shrink or something?" I ask him.

He laughs again and says no, he's not a shrink.

So I say to him, "Nobody's over here to lose."

Then he asks me how old I am and I tell him I'm twenty-one and he says to me, "You're a damn good line soldier."

"I'll tell you, Captain, I'm almost a short-timer. I got six months left to pull and I got two objectives in life. Get me back whole, get my men back whole. I don't think about anything past that. There isn't anything past that. You start thinking about what's past that and you're a dead man."

"I'm going to field-commission you," he says, just like that.

"Shit no," I says. "Don't do that to me, Captain. Gimme a break. What do you want from me?"

"I need a lieutenant on that squad and you're the best man for the job."

"Look, gimme six stripes, okay, that way I outrank anybody else on the squad. I'll stay right there, do the same shit I been doing, but I don't want a goddamn bar, man. Bars get you killed. I'm walking away from this, Captain. I'm not dying in this swamp. You hand a bar on me, it's like a fuckin' hex."

So he gives me six stripes and a night on the town, which is kind of a joke, and the next day I'm back at Hi Pien and nothing is changed. It's the same old shit.

The 287th day: *We had this nut colonel who came up on the line. He was an old campaigner, you could tell. He knew all the tricks and he just ignored them. He didn't even make a lot of sense when he talked. I don't think he was wrapped real tight anymore.*

Later in the day he was going to grab a medevac out and we're standing on the LZ on top of this knoll and he takes a leak right down the side of the hill, and just like that the VC start popping away at us. I don't know where they came from, and he's laughing, and I'm telling him, "Colonel, you better watch out, we seem to have Charlie all over the place."

"Piss on 'em," he says.

All of a sudden 9-millimeters were busting all around us. They must've busted fifty caps and the ground around his feet was churning up like little fountains. He finished, zipped up, and shot them a bird. Then the Huey comes in and he climbs aboard and they dust off. I thought, There's a guy needs to get off the line, bad.

"That crazy son of a bitch'll get somebody killed," Doc says. "He doesn't give a shit anymore."

"What the hell're they gonna do with him?" I say. "He's too crazy to send back to the World."

"I don't know, send him to the crazy colonel place," Doc says, and we all laugh about that.

The 306th day: *Gunner was over in Saigon for a week of R and R and he meets this ordnance guy and they hang out and get drunk and raise some hell. Anyway, the ordnance guy shows Gunner how to take the timer out of a hand grenade and when Gunner comes back, he sits around every night, taking the timers out of M-4's and then loading them into ammo packs. He puts five or six to each bag.*

A couple of nights later we're sitting on this LZ and the VC jump us. Gunner says follow him. He leaves the bags behind, we give them about thirty meters, hole in, and when they take the position we start a counter. Next thing I know there's hand grenades going off all over the place, gooks screaming, all this chaos. Then we went back and jumped them and took the position back. We wasted about twenty. Half of them only had one arm.

We did this a couple of times, moving off LZ's and what have you. Gunner keeps a couple of bags of these grenades around all the time now. Every time we move out we leave a couple behind. It's like our trademark. Fuckin' monkeys never learn. It works like a charm every time.

The 332nd day: *We had this ARVN assigned to us. I don't trust Vietnamese, not even the southerners. They have a tendency to run when things get hot. I know that's a generalization, but over here, sometimes generalizing keeps you alive. Anyway, this ARVN scout was on point and he runs into a sniper. One lousy sniper but this crud leaves the point and comes running back to report. What it was, he didn't have the guts to cream the fucking gook.*

So he comes running back and the sniper pops off three men, one, two, three, just like that. We get up there and I get around behind the sniper and I empty half a clip into him.

When we get back to base I radio upriver and tell them I'm sending this creep ARVN back to them, I can't use him.

"Keep him," they say. "It's politics."

Poli-fuckin'-tics. Jesus! Politics my ass.

Tonight we're camped out in the bush, he heads back into town to see his lady friend. I take off my shoes and follow him. He's going to the river to hop a ride and I jump him before he gets to the dock and slit him ear to ear with my K-bar, just drop him in the fucking river.

That's one son of a bitch isn't getting any more of my people killed.

The 338th day: *This time when I went down to Dau Tieng, it was the captain and this lieutenant named Harris, who looked like he didn't take shit from anybody, and we met in this bar which everybody jokingly calls the Café Society. I figure it's about the ARVN. They probably found him, he's some asshole's brother or something. It doesn't even come up.*

"You know the trouble with this war," the captain says. "We get these people for a year. Just when they're getting good enough to stay alive and take a few tricks, they go home."

And I says to myself, Uh-oh.

The lieutenant says to me, "You got a real handle on what it's all about, Sergeant."

And I laugh. I don't know what's happening two miles away and I say so.

"I mean out on the line," the lieutenant says.

"Oh, that," I says.

"Ever hear of CRIP?" he asks me.

I had heard some vague stories about a mixed outfit made up of North Viets who had defected to our side and called themselves Kit Carson scouts, plus infantry guys, some leftover French Legionnaires, and, some said, even some CIA, although you could hear that about anything. What I heard was that they were pretty much assassination squads. Our own guerrillas, like the Green Berets and the SEALS, which is like the Navy berets. Anyway I said no, because what I heard was mostly scuttlebutt.

"It's Combined Recon and Intelligence Platoons. Special teams. We keep them small, four or five people. You know how that goes, everybody

gets so they think like one person. You move around pretty much on your own, targets of opportunity, that sort of thing. I think it would be just up your alley."

"I got ten weeks left," I said, and I said it like You must be nuts.

But it was funny, I was interested in what he was saying. I mean, this lieutenant was recruiting me, asking me to do another tour, and I was listening to the son of a bitch. And he went right on.

"We have a low casualty rate because everybody knows what they're doing. You go out, you do your thing, you come back, everybody leaves you alone."

"That's about what I'm doing now," I said.

"That's what I mean, you're perfect for CRIP. We need people like you."

I'm getting a little pissed. "What's in this for me, Lieutenant? Just sticking my ass out there to get whacked off for twelve more months? Shit!"

He says, "So what's back home? You work eight hours, sleep eight hours. Shit, Sergeant, all you got left is eight hours a day to live. Tell me this isn't better than bowling."

I told him I'd think about it and I got shacked up for two days and went back down to the squad.

The 347th day: *We had this kid, a replacement, his first time on the line. I don't even remember his name. Anyway, we're rushing this hooch and there's a lot of caps going off and the kid twists his ankle and down he goes and he starts screaming. We all just stay down and all I'm thinking, as many times as I told this kid, "You go down, keep your mouth shut no matter how bad you're hurt," and he's losing it all.*

They zero in on him but Doc gets to him first and he's dragging this kid by the feet, trying to get him behind something, away from the fire.

I hear the round hit. It goes phunk, *like that.*

I was hoping it was the kid but no such luck. Doc took one round, dead center.

Then the kid freaks out and runs for it and they just cut him to pieces too.

What a waste, what a goddamn awful fucking waste.

Later on, the GR's come in with their body bags. Doc is lying beside a tree. He looks like he's taking a nap and I'm sitting beside him and this guy comes up with the bag and plops it down beside Doc and zips it open.

God, how I hate that sound. I hate zippers.

"Don't put that on him," I say, and I grab that goddamn green garbage bag. "Don't put that fuckin' bag on him."

"Hey, easy, pal, okay," the Gunner says. "He's gone. We lost him. Let them take him back."

You can't cry, you know. Nobody cries up here. You cry, everybody thinks you're losing it. Doc had eight days. Eight fucking days to go. All that time, all that experience. All stuffed in a fucking garbage bag.

The 353rd day: *Ever since, I been thinking a lot about Carmody and Flagler and Jesse Hatch. Doc Ziegler. Some of the others. The lieutenant's right; it is kind of a waste, spending a year on the line and then leaving it just when you really get so you know what you're doing. I've never been a pro before at anything. But I know how to fight these motherfuckers. I feel like I'm doing something positive, accomplishing something. You know, in my own way, doing something to turn this thing around, getting even for Jesse and Doc and the lieutenant, all the rest of them.*

And one more thing. I wouldn't want to tell them this, or anybody else. I like it. I'm going to miss it . . . getting a gook in my sights, squeezing off, watching the fucker go down. Shit, man, that's a jolt. That's a real jolt. There's not another jolt in the world like it.

59

PYRAMIDS

I took a couple of wrong turns before I found DeeDee's street. A red Datsun Z sat in the driveway and there were kids playing hide-and-seek in the yard next door. From the outside of the house, everything appeared normal. Obviously death had not made its presence known to the neighborhood yet.

Lark answered the door and ushered me inside. The house was dark, oppressive, silent. The rituals of passage had not yet begun. There were no flowers, no covered food dishes from the neighbors, no mourners sitting silently, trying not to stare at the casket.

Lark sat on one of the hard, uncomfortable antiques, her hands folded in her lap, looking at the floor, unsure of how to act in the presence of tragedy. I could tell it was a role uncommon for her, that she was accustomed only to the good things in life. Tragedy thus far had passed her by.

"Dee's sleeping," she said, after moments of strained silence. "The doctor gave her two shots before she quieted down. I don't know how long she'll be under. A couple of hours, at least." She paused, fiddling with the hem of her skirt. "Mr. Seaborn called. Thanks for telling him. He seemed to be honestly concerned."

"I'm sure he is," I said, trying to think of something more significant to say. "I just came by to see how she's holding up."

"Hard to say," Lark said. "I don't know what's going to happen when she wakes up. She was in shock when the doctor got here." She looked up at me suddenly and asked, almost with desperation, "Was Tony breaking the law when it happened? I think Dee's more worried about that than anything. Not for herself. She doesn't want people to remember him . . . badly."

"I can't say for sure," I said, "but it's possible."

"How did he die?"

"I'm not sure about that either," I said, and trying to avoid telling her a bald-faced lie, I added, "He could've drowned. Apparently he was in the water for some time. He washed up near Saint Somethings Island, wherever that is."

"Saint Simons," she said. "It's south of here, about fifty miles."

"They're doing the autopsy there," I said.

She shuddered when I said the word. Then she looked up suddenly. "I almost forgot," she said. "Mickey was by. He said if I saw you to tell you he needs to get in touch. He says it's very important."

"Do you have my number?" I asked, getting up to leave. I had really wanted to see DeeDee and had little else to say to Lark. She nodded. "I'm staying at the Ponce." And she nodded again. "Well," I said, "if I can do anything . . ."

"You did the toughest thing of all," Lark said. "It was nice of you, telling her that way instead of . . ."

The sentence seemed to die in her mouth, as if she were unsure how to finish it. I put my arm around her and hugged her until I felt the tension begin to ease. It was a hug I could use, too, just feeling someone close to me, to share a moment of caring with.

"You ought to have somebody here with you," I said.

"No, not yet. Dee wouldn't want that."

I left and drove back to the Warehouse. The Stick's black Pontiac was lurking in front. Inside the converted supermarket Stick was reading a computer printout.

"You're back early," he said. "Did'ya get my message?"

Obviously he had not heard about the events at the track and

I wasn't in the mood for details. It was only midafternoon but I felt like my cork had been pulled for the day.

"I'm dead," I said casually.

"A lot of people are having that trouble these days," he drawled. "How are things at the track?"

"There was an accident," I said. "Three horses went down."

"What!"

"One of the horses split a foreleg in the stretch and took two other nags down with it."

"Are the jockeys okay?" he asked.

"Busted up but they'll live. Lost two of the horses."

He whistled through his teeth, but that seemed to be the extent of his interest.

"And how are things at the bank?"

"I thought you'd never ask," Stick answered with a smile. "I tumbled on to how they're using the bank to wash their money. The bad news is, as far as I know, what they're doing is legal."

"Impossible!" I snapped.

"Well, to some extent it's legal," he said, amending his original comment. "The account Cohen uses is in the name of the Abaca Corporation. According to Charlie One Ear, Abaca owns Thunder Point Marina, Bronicata's restaurant, the Porthole, the Jalisco Shrimp Company, etcetera. I checked the account and there are daily deposits, but never more than a couple thousand dollars."

"That's inconsistent with what Lark told you."

"Hang on," he said, "I'm not through yet. I only had that one account number, so I decided to check the daily tape. That's a chronological list of all the deposits made at the bank each day. Lo and behold, there're ten deposits for ten grand each, all within seconds of each other." He made a grand gesture with his hands and smiled. "Pyramids," he said.

"Pyramids?"

"Cohen has this thing for pyramids."

"I don't understand."

"It's simple, once you tumble on to it. Cohen puts a hundred G's in, Abaca shows a deposit of only ten grand. It only gets complex when you start trying to decipher the whole system."

"Well, try, 'cause you've lost me," I said.

"First, let's assume that Seaborn is in collusion with Cohen. Cohen is using the bank as a washing machine. The whole point is to move a lot of cash through the bank without making the IRS suspicious, right?"

"Uh-huh."

"That's where the pyramids come in. What happens, let's say Cohen makes his daily deposit . . . ten grand, for the sake of discussion. The deposit goes into the Abaca Corporation. That's the base company, okay? But the computer is programmed to immediately dispense that money, by percentage, into several other accounts. It never appears as a ten-grand deposit because the computer spreads it over ten other accounts *before* making the deposit."

"Does it always go into the same accounts?" I asked.

He shook his head. "There's a code designation on the account number that tells the computer what set of accounts the money goes into and what percentage goes into each. Then each of those accounts is spread over five or ten other accounts. So what they got is pyramids."

"So every dollar that goes into the bank is diverted into so many other accounts, you don't see any big sums going anywhere and it doesn't wave any red flags at the Lepers," I said.

"Exactly," he said. "If you weren't looking for something, you'd never tumble over it. Thing is, they seem to be using these accounts for legitimate purposes. Payrolls for Triad employees, accounts payable and receivable for the Bom Dia restaurant, Jalisco Shrimp Company, Thunder Point Marina . . . the Seaview Company, Hojan and Rajah, whatever that may be . . . hell, there could be a couple of hundred accounts. This Cohen is a genius. If he had to, he could probably legitimately account for most of the money going into these pyramids."

"There's got to be a reason for going to all that trouble," I said. "There's got to be some skimming accounts, or payoff accounts."

"Yeah, I agree," he said. "But what are they? We're looking at one pyramid off another here. Creative bookkeeping compounded by creative computer technology. So maybe some of these accounts are payoff accounts or skim accounts; there's no way to tell which ones."

Stick was right. The system, although devious, was not illegal. What was illegal was using the bank to channel illegal monies from gambling, prostitution, narcotics, and whatever else, into legitimate accounts and then siphoning off some of those accounts without reporting the income to the IRS. The big question was how they were doing it.

"We'll never unravel it all without a key list of *all* their accounts," said the Stick.

I said, "Stick, we're close to nailing them. Cohen must have this defined somewhere. It's far too complex to keep in his head."

"Probably in a computer of his own," said Stick. "And there's no way we can access a private terminal."

"Then one damn thing is for sure," I said. "We've got to keep Cohen alive. He's got the key to the puzzle."

"Wanna put 'em under protective custody?" Stick said. "I can't think of anything else to do. We're baby-sitting 'em around the clock now."

"Yeah, and so far it hasn't helped any of them," I said.

There was one other possible answer. We could offer to put Cohen in the witness protection program if he would cooperate with us. And I know what my answer to that proposal would be if I were Cohen. I'd tell me to get stuffed.

60

THE COCKTAIL HOUR

I suppose the most spectacular view in town comes with the tallest building—that's if you have the money to make the view worth-while. Babs Thomas had them both and the taste to do it right. The penthouse was like a glass box surrounded by gardens. Glass walls everywhere: the living room, bedrooms, kitchen, even the bathrooms. Floor-to-ceiling drapes provided whatever privacy was necessary, although the only danger of eavesdroppers seemed to be from low-flying aircraft.

The penthouse was lit by slender tapers, an effect both unusual and stunning, since the glass walls reflected every flickering pin-point and then re-reflected it, over and over, bathing the rooms in a soft, yellow glow.

There were at least thirty couples there, Babs' idea of a few friends, all of them old-monied and well pedigreed. I assume only a death in the family would have been a suitable excuse for missing the soiree. That or, as in the case of Charles Seaborn, the bank examiners.

Babs, a vision in yellow silk wearing a white hat with a brim wide enough to roller-skate around, swept over to me as I entered, pulled me into a neutral corner, and filled in my dance card for me, advising me on who was worth talking to and whom to skip.

My top priority was to meet the remaining members of the infamous Committee.

Arthur Logan, the lawyer, was forty and looked sixty. Poor posture made him appear almost humpbacked, his face was pinched into a perpetual frown, and his eyes were paranoiacally intense and busy, like a man who expects to hear bad news at every turn. Ten minutes of conversation proved him to be as senile in mind as in body, a man so fanatically conservative that even Calvin Coolidge would have found him an anachronism. His wife, also singularly unattractive, appeared to have lost her chin somewhere along the way. She complemented him by smiling and keeping her mouth shut.

On the other hand, Roger Sutter, the big-shot journalist, was just the opposite, the epitome of the young man on the go. His handshake was painfully sincere, his gaze intense, his attitude open. He talked to me for five minutes before he figured out I wasn't there to invest money in Dunetown, then his gaze became less intense and began to wander from one female rear end to the other. His wife, who let me know she was the best tennis player at the club thirty seconds after we met, was busy flirting with the men in the room.

Charming.

No wonder the city had fallen prey to Tagliani. Dutch had said it the night I arrived. Dunetown had been entrusted to wimps. Were they involved with Seaborn and Cohen?

Doe caught me by surprise. I was ordering a drink when I felt a hand on my shoulder. I turned and she was standing there. My knees started to wobble again.

The big surprise was that Chief was with her.

He sat tall and erect in his wheelchair, and while time seemed to have taken its toll, the old man still looked like everybody's grandfather ought to look, his white hair cresting a craggy face that was indomitable.

I knew the Findley background well. I should have, it was a story I had heard repeated often enough. Chief's grandfather, Sean, an Irish collier, had emigrated to Dunetown, won a water-front tavern in a card game and parlayed that into the city's first million. After that it was cotton, banking, real estate, God knows what else. The same flint that had fired old man Sean had also struck wit and wisdom in every crevice of Chief's face and his eyes were as fiery and intense as ever. Only his body seemed to be failing him.

"Hello, Chief," I said. "Been a long time."

"Yes," he said, "and a sad one."

I knew the breed well enough to know that Chief would not mention Teddy or my unanswered letter. Apologies come hard and infrequently to men like that; they're not prone to admitting mistakes. Or maybe Chief just didn't see it the way I did; maybe he had just closed the book on that chapter.

"Doe tells me you're in government service," he said, with obvious sincerity. "That's quite admirable."

That was the end of our conversation. A moment later someone pushed past me to pay homage to the old warrior, and then someone else, and someone else, until I was gradually edged out of the circle. Doe eased her way to my side. I could feel the sexual electricity humming around her. Time had not changed one thing—they were still the lightning people.

"Where's Harry?" I asked.

"He canceled out at the last minute. There was an accident at the track. Some horses were killed."

"I know, I was there."

"It must've been just horrible," she said, then added hurriedly, "Albert's coming in ten minutes to take Chief home. I'll meet you out on the terrace after he leaves." She turned abruptly and wormed her way back into the circle of sycophants.

Suddenly I was alone and staring across the room at Sam Donleavy. I shouldered my way toward him through the crowd, catching snippets of conversation along the way. The women cheeped like sparrows, while the men sounded more like trumpeting elephants. Donleavy seemed relieved by my company.

"It's hot in here. Let's step out on the terrace and get some air," he suggested.

Lightning was playing in the clouds south of the city and the wind was jangling a delicate glass wind chime near the door. You could feel rain in the air.

"We still on for lunch tomorrow?" I asked, by way of starting the conversation.

"Looking forward to it," he said. "I heard about the Lukatis boy. A damn shame."

"Yeah," I said. "A tough break for his sister."

"Do you think it's tied in to these other deaths?"

"I wouldn't know. The body's down south of here. The autopsy will be done there."

"I see. Look, I want you to know that any help you give us in cleaning up this mess will be greatly appreciated. Things have been happening so fast it's hard to assimilate them."

"Yeah," I said, "the pace has been breezy."

"I suppose you're accustomed to such things."

"Not really. Murder is always ugly, no matter where it happens or who the victim is."

"Yes, I suppose. At any rate, if you need any help at all from me, just ask."

"Thanks," I said. After a decent pause I asked, "Did you know Tagliani?" I tried to make it sound casual.

"Yes. But as Frank Turner."

"Were you social friends?"

"Not at all. I met with Turner on a couple of occasions to help him get oriented, but that was some time ago."

"And to size him up?" I suggested.

He stared at me intently for a few seconds, then nodded slowly. "That, too."

"So you knew him personally?"

"Not really; it was all business. I haven't seen him to talk to since he moved here."

"When was that?"

"I couldn't say accurately. About three years ago."

"Did you meet here in Dunetown?"

He nodded. "The first time we were supposed to meet at the old Beach Hotel, but it didn't suit him, so we switched the meeting to Charlie Seaborn's yacht. The second time he had his own boat down here."

"What did you talk about?"

"Development ideas, other money interests. Later he put us on to"—he waved a hand vaguely in the air—"several others . . ."

"Bronicata, Chevos," I said.

"Yes, only not by those names. You've got to remember, he came very highly recommended. He had development resources, excellent credit references, all in the name of Frank Turner."

"And you never suspected who he really was?"

His face clouded up. "Of course not," he said. There was a touch of indignation in his tone but he tempered it quickly. "Look," he went on, "we were looking for developers here. It was obvious the track was going to change things, and Turner talked an excellent game. He seemed very civic-minded. His development ideas were sound. We had no reason to doubt him."

"I wasn't accusing you of anything," I said.

"I know that. I just want you to understand, this is all very new to us. At worst we were guilty of naiveté."

Babs Thomas appeared in the doorway, tapping her foot.

"The party's in here," she said sternly. "You two can talk football, or whatever you've found so damned interesting, some other time. And you, Sam, have a phone call. I think it's Charlie. You can take it in the bedroom."

"Damn!" Donleavy said. "I'm sorry. We can finish this over lunch tomorrow."

"Just one other thing," I said. "Do you happen to remember the date Tagliani came here the first time?"

He thought about it for several seconds, then took out a business card and scrambled a number on the back.

"No, but I've got an old date book at home," he said. "Here's my number. Give me a call about quarter to eight and I can give it to you precisely. Don't wait until eight or you'll be out of luck. Dutch Morehead usually calls me then. We talk once a week, keeps me in touch. He's very prompt and we've been known to talk for an hour or more."

I thanked him, pocketed the card, and we started back inside. As Donleavy hurried off to take his call, Stonewall Titan materialized from behind a potted plant.

"Hello, doughboy," he said. "Don't miss a trick, do you? Just pop up everywhere."

"I was thinking the same thing about you," I said.

Titan looked at me, the candles igniting sparks in his narrowed eyes.

"You've done it again, raised more hell, ain't you, son?"

"What do you mean?" I asked.

"I mean your conversation with Harry at the track. That was a damn fool thing to do."

"Time somebody leveled with him."

"You're a bad penny, doughboy," he growled. "You show up back here and within four days we got somethin' akin to twelve homicides."

He slashed at a potted plant with his cane.

"I haven't had *two* unsolved goddamn homicides at the same time in this county in forty damn years. Now I got twelve!"

Donleavy came out of the bedroom, made his apologies, and

left to await Dutch's weekly call, waving good-bye as he did. It was seven fifteen. In another thirty minutes we could all leave.

"I'll give it to you again," I said. "I didn't cause the homicides and murder isn't my game. It's not why I came here and it isn't why I'm staying."

"I mean *altogether* I haven't had twelve unsolved homicides since I been sheriff," he said, ignoring my comments. "You understand my concern when we have twelve in the space of a couple of days?"

"Sure."

"Sure? What do you mean, sure?"

"I mean sure, I understand your consternation."

"Hot damn, college boy. Consternation. Well, listen close, because my consternation tells me you know one helluva lot more about what the hell's goin' on than I do, and since this is my county, I think it's time we shared whatever information you might have."

I smiled. "And what would I get out of it?" I asked.

"Your ass, in one piece," he said flatly.

I laughed. "What're you going to do, Mr. Stoney, put out a contract on me?"

"It may be funny to you, doughboy—"

"That's not what I'm laughing about," I said, cutting him off. "I've been under the impression we were both on the same side."

He ignored my comment and went right on making his point. "I'm not without considerable influence where it means something," he said. "I could have your tail bent till it hurts by just raisin' a question or two about your conduct of this investigation."

"I'm sure you could."

"What the hell's goin' on? What are you after, Kilmer?"

"I'm looking for RICO violations, Mr. Stoney. You know that. Now, I could be wrong. Tagliani may very well have inched in here without anybody knowing who he really was. But I've got to know that for sure."

"No matter who gets hurt, that it?"

"I don't give a damn whose tombstones I have to kick over to get to the truth."

"Or whose bed you sleep in?"

"Who are you really worried about, Mr. Stoney? Who are you trying to cover?"

"The integrity of my county," he snapped.

I shook my head with disbelief. "You mean what's left of it, don't you?"

"You can be an irritatin' son of a bitch."

"Probably. I didn't come here to run for Queen of the May."

His tone became more condescending.

"I don't wanna see things blown out of proportion, okay, dough-boy? People make mistakes. It's natural. We ain't all perfect."

"I'll buy that," I said. "I just want to make sure that's what they were—mistakes."

"I'm tellin' you they were."

"Sheriff, I'll tell you everything I think. Not what I know, be-cause I don't know that much. I think the same gun killed Tagliani, Stinetto, and O'Brian, possibly an American 180. I think the same gun was used to kill Stizano and his bunch and Draganata, prob-ably an M-16 equipped with a grenade launcher. Whoever used them has a military background and killed Logeto and Graves' girlfriend, Della Norman, using a garotte that was fairly common in Vietnam. I think it was all done by one person."

Titan pursed his lips and cocked his head to one side. "Not bad for someone who's game ain't murder," he said. "Why?"

"If I knew that, I could give you the killer."

"Humph," he snorted.

"Now I've got a question to ask you. Who busted Tony Lukatis on the pot charge?"

"Why?"

"He's dead, that's why."

"I know that. They're doing an autopsy down in Glynn County right now. So what does Tony's previous record have to do with anything?"

"Just curious."

"The drug enforcement boys nailed Lukatis and his buddy."

"Did they both do time?"

He paused for a second or two and shook his head. "The shrimper turned state's and got a suspended sentence."

"Was Lukatis running marijuana for Longnose Graves?"

Titan looked shocked. "Hell no," he stormed. "Graves doesn't run dope. He may have a lot of faults but that ain't one of them. Far as I know, Lukatis and his friend were free-lancin'."

"Where were they caught?"

"On Buccaneer Island, where the South River empties into Buccaneer Bay. Why are you so interested in Lukatis?"

"Just trying to keep all the lines straight," I said. "He and at least one of Graves' men were killed at the same time. Don't you wonder why?"

He leaned forward and said, "I'll find out why when it's necessary."

"You know what I think, Mr. Stoney?" I said. "I think you want to neutralize me and I'm not sure why. Like I said, I thought we were both on the same side."

"I told you last night, I enforce the law my own way," he said. "Be advised." He turned abruptly, elbowed his way through the chitchat, paid his respects to Babs, and left. She breezed back over.

"You're just the life of the party," she said. "So far you've talked to Chief Findley, Stoney, and Sam Donleavy, and all three of them have left the party."

"I do seem to have that effect on people, don't I?"

"Well, darling, Doe is still here. All is not lost."

"I keep telling you—"

"And I don't believe a word of it," she said, finishing the sentence, and went off to attend to something.

I stepped out onto the terrace but the rain had started, its first big drops splattering me, so I stood under an awning, watched the thunderclouds gather around the penthouse, and listened to the wind give the chimes a nervous breakdown and the rain grow to a steady downpour.

Doe moved on me slowly, stopping here and there to chat as she came through the room. Finally she stepped outside and stood there, staring up at me.

"I've called you and called you today," she said, somewhat sternly.

"I don't spend a lot of time around the hotel," I said.

"Come back to Windsong with me tonight," she said in a half-whisper.

"You're crazy. What do you plan to do about Harry? He's—"

"He won't come out there. He stays at the townhouse during the racing season. He doesn't like to make that long drive twice a day. Are you going to make me beg you, Jake?"

"Don't be silly."

"I'm spoiled, Jake," she said with a laugh. "Nobody's ever denied that."

"Nobody ever complained either."

"I want to make love to you again. I want it tonight. I don't want to wait a minute longer."

"It's getting too touchy," I told her. "Even Titan knows all—"

"I don't care about Stoney. He's my godfather; he should want what's best for me and if he doesn't, the hell with him. We're talking about you and me and tonight. That's all I care about. I want you. I want to make up for twenty years."

"In one night?"

She laughed again. "Well, it's a start."

Bolts of lightning were dueling around us and the full fury of the storm lashed rain under the awning.

"Let's get inside," I said.

"Not till you promise."

"Promise what?"

"When you leave here you'll come out to Windsong."

"I have to make a stop on the way," I said, thinking about DeeDee Lukatis. I wondered whether Doe knew that her ex-lover was dead. If she did, she was handling it very well. I decided that if she didn't know, somebody else could tell her.

"How long?" she demanded.

"An hour."

"Don't be late," she said, wheeled away, and dodged back inside.

I waited for a minute or two before going back in. It was a futile gesture. Babs was watching intently from across the room, like the linesman at a tennis match. I nodded and smiled my way back to her.

"It's not what you think," I said.

"Please," she said, rolling her eyes, "you don't have to tell me a thing. I have two perfectly good eyes in my head."

"Don't make it sound like some damn intrigue," I said.

"Darling, I just love intrigue. It's what makes life worth all the trouble."

61

MIRROR TRICKS

Before I left the hotel, I stopped by my room and called Sam Donleavy. He was pushed for time, he explained, since Dutch would be calling shortly, but he assured me that he would locate the book and bring it to lunch the next day. I said that was just fine. Then I dug the company car out of the hotel garage.

A familiar black Pontiac was crouched under the trees in front of DeeDee's house when I got there. The Stick answered my ring.

"Just the two of you here?" I asked.

"Yeah, I brought over some dinner. Lark needed a little relief. She's stretched out there taking a nap."

"That bench is worse than the rack," I said.

"She was too tired to notice."

"How's DeeDee?"

"Still out. The doctor must've given her enough Sec to knock an elephant on its ass."

"Good, the more sleep she gets, the better. I'm afraid she's going to be in for it from the homicide cops, once they finish the autopsy."

"She doesn't know shit."

"You know it and I know it," I said. "But the turkeys from the murder division also don't know shit."

"I'll handle them," he snapped.

"Stop acting like Humphrey Bogart. They'd be dumber than I think they are if they didn't talk to her."

"What do we do about the pictures that came in on the telex? They'll be out here flashing them around."

"Burn them. She can't ever see him, Stick, not the way he looks now. She'd have nightmares for the rest of her life."

"You're beginning to sound like a concerned friend."

"I'm trying. This is one tombstone I'm sorry I kicked over. Besides, Tony's death isn't going to be handled by the local cops. It's out of their jurisdiction."

"Where'd he wash up?"

"Saint Solomons Island."

"That's Saint *Simons* Island."

"Well, they've got him down there, and it's their problem."

"Five gets you ten they dump it up here anyway."

"If it relates."

"*If?*" Stick said.

"Let's wait and see on that one," I said.

"There's something else bothering me," the Stick said.

"What's that?"

"Nance," he said. "He's moving around like a wolf on the prowl. Lange and Zapata are taking turns with him."

"I've been keeping my eyes open," I said.

"Why don't we lean on him? We can bust his ass—at least, let the fucker know he can't go around taking potshots at federal agents."

"He'd be on the street in thirty seconds. Costello'd see to that. I want the full clock on that son of a bitch when he goes. Life with no parole. There's no percentage bringing him in and then having him walk. All that is, is frustrating. Besides, I don't think he was ordered to put me on ice, I think he got a wild hair up his ass and decided to just do it. Nesbitt told me he took a lot of shit because he missed me that time in Cincinnati."

"Well, Zapata and Lange are all over him. He can't go to the john without Chino washing his hands when he's finished. Hopefully, he tries for you again, they'll clean his pipes."

"As long as he's in view, we're okay."

I changed the subject to the cocktail party and gave Stick a brief rundown on my talks with both Donleavy and Titan.

"Donleavy says the Committee passed on Tagliani because they're all naive," I said, summing it up.

"It's possible," he said. "What's the problem with Titan?"

I didn't want to discuss Doe Raines, so I shrugged. "Beats the hell out of me," I said.

"I almost forgot," Stick said, taking a sheet of paper from his pocket. "I did a little more work on the computer." He unfolded a readout sheet and handed it to me. "Here's a rundown on the eight main accounts and their subaccounts. There's eighty-six different accounts there, Jake. And that's like the tip of the pyramid, man."

"Thanks."

"So what do we do with them?" he asked.

I looked over the printout. About a third of the accounts were corporate.

"Can you access corporate information on that gadget?"

"Sure."

"I'd like you to check all the corporate names on this list and see if any of them were incorporated in Panama."

"Panama? The country Panama?"

"The country Panama."

"Do I get to know why?"

"Ever heard of the Mirror Rule?"

He shook his head.

"You haven't been doing your homework, Stick. Panama, the country, will not divulge any information about Panamanian corporations; not to anyone for any reason. You can't even get a list of officers or stockholders unless the company wants you to have it. So a Panamanian corporation is automatically indemnified from any kind of examination or investigation except by authorities of Panama itself."

"That's real interesting," the Stick said.

"It is if you incorporate in Panama. Because then you can have funds from an American bank transferred to a bank in the Virgin Islands."

"Where does the Virgin Islands fit into all this?"

"The Virgin Islands, although it's a U.S. territory, has its own revenue service. They don't like the Lepers, so they don't co-operate with them."

"The IRS can't get the info on Virgin Island bank accounts, that it?" Stick asked.

"Exactly. And the bank account in the Virgin Islands is a mirror account of the corporate account in Panama. So it's possible to transfer money from a U.S. bank to a bank in the Virgin Islands and then into a Panamanian corporation without the IRS knowing about it."

"You think that's what Tagliani was doing?"

"It could explain how the payoff accounts work. If there's a Panamanian corporation on this list, it could be a transfer account."

"And the payoff would go straight through the computer and into the Panamanian bank account, without ever showing up as a deposit," Stick said, with a touch of wonder.

"And so could their skim," I said.

"You think Seaborn knows about this Mirror Rule?" Stick asked.

"If he doesn't we ought to have him jailed for incompetence. It's international banking law."

"Which means Seaborn's involved."

"That's a little touchy right now. There's nothing illegal about transferring money to Panama. But there is if it's IGG."

Stick smiled. "The old ill-gotten gains. What would we do without them?"

"The question is, does Seaborn *know* it's a scheme to wash dirty money? Maybe not. He could be that naive."

"Well, if he didn't know, he probably does now."

"Right. And since we haven't heard from him, we can at least assume that he might be withholding information."

"Where the hell did you find all this out?"

"I may not file reports, pal, but I sure as hell read them. This dodge is used a lot by the Mafia. Using the bank's computer to pyramid their accounts, now that's a new wrinkle."

A phone rang somewhere in the back of the house. Stick bolted, trying to catch it before it woke someone up. He was too late. Lark stirred on the wooden bench, opened one eye, saw me, waved a limp hand in my direction, and managed a feeble smile.

"Go back to sleep," I said. "Stick and I will hold the fort a while longer."

Wrong again, Kilmer.

Stick came out of the kitchen with a crazy look in his eyes.

"What's the matter with you?" I asked.

"You're not gonna believe this, Jake," he said.

"Try me."

"Somebody just put a bullet in Harry Raines' head."

62

G-A-L-A-V-A-N-T-I

It took us fifteen minutes through heavy fog to get to the scene of the crime, and a familiar scene it was. Harry Raines had been shot down in the center of the Quadrangle, no more than a hundred yards from Charlie Seaborn's bank.

It looked like every police car in Dunetown was there. Red and blue lights flashed eerily through the thick fog, like silent fireworks. A small crowd had wandered up from the riverfront clubs and restaurants to see what all the fuss was about.

It took a couple of minutes to locate Dutch in the mist. He was standing with a couple of plainclothesmen, studying a chalk form drawn on the cobblestone walk. Yellow police-scene ribbons had been suspended around the area. Dutch informed us that the ambulance had come and gone already.

"He's still alive!" I said.

"Yeah, but not by enough to matter much. One shot, right here." He tapped his forehead an inch above the right eyelid. "Bullet's still in there."

"My God," a hoarse voice whispered, and it was a second or two before I realized it was mine.

"We got a couple of ear witnesses," Dutch said, leading us away from the chalk-marked form on the walkway.

"Ear witnesses?" the Stick said.

Their names were Harriet and Alexander, although, for reasons that elude me, Alexander preferred to be called Chip. They were in their midtwenties and two weeks away from their wedding day and she had lost his engagement present to her. The girl was as fancy as a plain girl can make herself. The boyfriend, short and stubby, with a badly trimmed mustache, seemed far more concerned over the missing necklace than the shooting.

"We stopped off here on the way to dinner because, see, this is where we met," he babbled, probably for the fifth or sixth time. "But it was so foggy, we went on down to the Porthole to meet our friends for dinner . . ."

"You couldn't see your hand in front of your face," Harriet said, nodding vigorously.

I was getting edgy, listening to their routine.

"Like it is now," Chip said. "This wasn't half an hour ago."

"Yes," I said. "I got that—go on!"

Harriet continued her extravagant nod. "Like it is now," she repeated.

He glowered at her and continued his story.

"And that's when her necklace was gone," Chip said. "It was a cluster of diamonds on a gold chain. Eight diamonds. They added up to a full carat."

"Can you please get on to the details!" I demanded.

"We're sorry about the necklace," Dutch said tersely. "Can you finish your story."

"Yes, well," he said, "so we excused ourselves and came back up here, hoping maybe we could find it."

"That's when the man got shot," Harriet said, nodding even more exuberantly as she got in the big one. Chip's bubbly cheeks turned scarlet at being upstaged.

"Did you see anybody?" I interjected.

They both shook their heads.

"Did you hear them? Did they say anything?"

"I'm not sure," Chip said firmly.

"Well, they did say something," Harriet piped up again, "or at least one of them did. He said, 'You're finished.' "

"You're not sure, Harriet," Chip said curtly.

She nodded her head vigorously.

"Would you recognize the voice if you heard it again?" the Stick asked.

Chip said, "We weren't paying much attention. We heard somebody on the walk, the footsteps stopped—"

Harriet jumped in, stealing his thunder again. "And there was 'You're finished' and *bang*!" Big nod.

Chip's face twisted in anger. "Harriet! May I please tell the story?" he said.

"What else is there?" I asked.

"Harriet screamed and the killer ran away," he said, glaring at his future wife to keep her quiet.

"Nobody's dead yet," Dutch growled.

"Well, you know what I mean," the kid said nervously.

"Which way did this person run?" I asked.

"We couldn't tell," Chip said. "You can't really tell because of the buildings, uh, the sound . . ."

"Acoustics, is that what you're talking about?" Stick asked.

"Exactly," Chip said, and he started the nodding routine.

It was true. With fog so thick you could hardly see your feet, and with the three buildings forming a kind of box, it was impossible to tell where sound was coming from.

"Did you find the body?" I asked.

They shook their heads in unison.

"No way," Chip said. "We ran back over to the bank because there were some lights on in the back, but nobody came to the door, so I went to the phone booth and called the police."

I asked, "This person who ran away after the shooting, could you guess whether it was a man or a woman?"

"Man," they said simultaneously.

That was all they had. It was too foggy to waste any more time there. Stick and I left our cars in the parking lot and headed for the hospital with Dutch. The lights in the back of the bank were out when we left.

There were a couple of blue and whites parked at the hospital emergency entrance and one car that could have been an unmarked police vehicle. The long, beige hallway inside the emergency doors was empty, as was the emergency operating room. Raines was in ICU, which was on the second floor.

Four uniformed cops and two plainclothes detectives held the unit captive.

"You taking this one on?" one of them asked Dutch.

"It's personal" was all the big Dutchman said in return.

The chief surgeon and the resident were there but noncommunicative. They were waiting for Raines' personal physician. An intern with the trauma unit, however, confirmed what we already knew and added a few details: that Harry Raines had been shot once in the left forehead by a large-caliber weapon, that it had been held close enough to cause heavy powder burning, that he was beyond critical and, as far as the intern was concerned, was moribund.

"He's a lot more dead than alive," the young doctor said. "If he lives another hour, the Catholics'll probably sanctify the whole wing."

"How's that?" Dutch asked.

"Because it would be a miracle," the young doctor said.

"Any idea what kind of gun did it?" I asked.

"I don't know about things like that," he said. "That's police work."

The intensive care unit was a fairly small room with curtained cubicles around its perimeter for patients and a control bank of machines and monitors at its core. Every cubicle was monitored by closed-circuit TV. There were three nurses on duty, all of whom seemed very busy. The two doctors retired to an empty cubicle and pulled the curtain behind them.

I could see Raines, in the tiny black-and-white TV screen, half his face bound up in bandages, muttering to himself.

"Do you have a tape recorder in that war wagon of yours?" I asked the Stick.

"Yeah, minicorder. A Pearl with a voice activator."

"Get it fast," I whispered, and he was gone, returning in less than five minutes with a recorder no bigger than the palm of my hand.

"Fresh batteries and a fresh tape," he said. "You gonna try and tape Raines?"

"Yeah. Keep the jokers at the door busy for a minute or two."

When I could, I slipped behind the curtain into Raines' cubicle and hung the tape recorder over the retaining bar by his head. His lips were moving but his words were jumbled. He was the color of clay, his unbandaged eye partially open and rolling crazily under the lid.

As I came back out of the cubicle, a small whirlwind of a woman in a dark gray business suit burst into the room. She was about five one, on the good side of forty, could have dropped ten or fifteen pounds without missing it, looked colder than a nun's kiss, and was meaner than Attila the Hun. She took over like the storm-troopers in Paris, snapping orders in a voice an octave deeper than nature had intended, punctuating every word with a thin, manicured spear of a finger. I could hear the arctic air whistling through her veins as she snapped orders to the four men with her. I stood back and watched the performance.

"You two get into hospital blues," she said. "You, get on the door. Nobody gets in unless I say so. And you, sit by that control desk."

Then she saw me.

"Who are you?" she snapped icily, jabbing the spear under my nose.

"I could be the doctor," I snapped back.

She looked me up and down. "Not a chance," she said.

"The name's Kilmer. Federal Racket Squad."

"Out," she barked, tossing her thumb over her shoulder like an umpire at home plate. "He's mine."

"And who the hell are you?" I demanded.

She stuck her tiny, bulldog face as close to mine as she could get it without standing on her toes and said, "Galavanti. Honorée Galavanti, G-a-l-a-v-a-n-t-i. Oglethorpe County DA. I've got my own people with me. I don't need you, so out."

"Not so fast," I challenged.

"Listen, here, uh, what was your name again?"

An act. This was a tough lady, but then she would have to be. It would take a tough lady to get elected DA in Stonewall Titan's macho court.

"Kilmer. K-i-l-m-e-r."

"Oh, yeah. Scram."

"Aren't you pushing this DA thing a little far?" I said.

She glared at me for several moments and said, "They told me you'd be trouble."

"Who's they?" I asked.

"Everybody that's met you," she snapped back.

Then she saw the tape recorder on the retaining bar beside Raines' head.

"What's that?" she demanded, spearing the air with her finger again.

"That is a tape recorder."

"Listen to me—"

I pulled her to one corner, away from the nurses, who were trying not to listen, and said, "Won't you step into my private office? I think maybe we should talk."

I led her into another empty cubicle and sat her down on the bed.

"Leave the recorder where it is. Anything that's on it is yours. All I want to do is hear it. If he says anything before he checks out, we share."

"You sound like his checking out is a fait accompli," she said.

"He's got a bullet in his brain."

"His doctor should be here any minute."

"The man's the color of wet cement, his fever's rising like fresh bread, and his blood pressure's about two over two. Unless God's on his way here, forget it. You've got a hot potato on your hands, lady, any way you cut it. That's the most powerful man in town dying in there. Somebody's gonna go to the dock before it's over and your case is going to rely on a homicide squad which, if I'm any judge at all, collectively couldn't put their socks on in the dark. Offhand I'd say you need all the help you can get."

That slowed her down a little. I could almost hear the gears clicking inside her brain.

"What have you got to offer?" she said after a minute or two of hard thought.

"Some ideas, a few hunches. All I need is a day or two to see if they wash."

"So what do you need me for, Kilmer?"

"Look, Gavalanti—"

"It's Galavanti," she said. "The 'l' comes before the 'v,' like in 'gal.' "

"Sorry . . . Galavanti. You've got twelve homicides on your hands. Thirteen if we lose Raines. Sooner or later you're going to have to deal with all these cases."

"What're you driving at?" she demanded.

"Maybe I can put them right in your lap."

"You know who's behind all this?"

"I'm getting close," I bluffed.

She laughed. "God, have I heard *that* line before," she said. "That the first thing they teach you at the police academy?"

"What have you got without me?" I asked.

"Zero-zero at this point," she admitted.

"Ms. Galavanti, I haven't laid eyes on you before tonight. Twelve homicides and this is the first time you show your face."

"Don't be naive. That man over there's being touted for governor."

"I think if you're smart enough to be DA of this county, you're smart enough not to pay any attention to what the newspapers are saying. You keep in touch with Titan and Morehead and everybody else in town that counts. You know all about the Tagliani connection."

"You think this shooting is connected to the others?" she asked cautiously.

"Seems likely, doesn't it?"

She pursed her heart-shaped mouth while she mulled over what I'd said.

"I'm also smart enough to know you Feds are after something

and murder's not it," she said finally. "Whatever happens, the villains in this piece will go to federal court before I get a crack at them."

"Maybe not . . ." I said and let her fill in the rest of the sentence.

"All right, Kilmer, what's your offer?"

"Before this is over, some RICO cases could be coming down. Between you and me, if murder's involved, too, I'd be glad to turn the culprits over to you on the homicide charges before I take them to federal court."

"Why are you being so good to me?"

"Two reasons. Murder puts them away for a lot longer than racketeering and we can always go after them after you get finished."

"And the other reason?"

"I want a little straight talk in return."

Suspicion put a frown on her face. "About what?" she asked.

"Tony Lukatis," I said.

"What about him?"

"Did you prosecute his case?"

"Yes," she said with a shrug, "although it's nothing to brag about."

"How come?"

"It was open and shut. We had a corroborative witness."

"His partner?"

"That's right. Gil Winslow."

"I heard the DEA made the arrest. Wouldn't that make it federal?" I asked.

"Titan's people were there. They took the credit."

"So Titan turned the case over to you for prosecution?"

"That's right. Listen, if you're looking to make trouble for Mr. Stoney . . ."

"I'm not looking to make trouble for anybody who doesn't deserve it," I said, and hurried on. "So Stoney took credit for the bust and put the case together. And he provided the turncoat witness."

She nodded suspiciously. "If you want to call Winslow that."

"I don't mean this to be insulting, but didn't the boat belong to Winslow?"

"Mm-hmm . . ."

"Wouldn't it make more sense to lay it on him, confiscate his boat, take him off the water?"

"None of my concern," she snapped. "Look, Kilmer, what

happened, the case came to me with Winslow. His testimony was that Lukatis had the scheme and the financing. Lukatis knew where a ton of pot was hung up in the Bahamas. He offered Winslow fifty thousand dollars' guarantee against a split if Winslow went over there and brought the stuff in."

"On Winslow's boat?"

"That's right."

"How much?"

"One ton."

"Whose idea was it to land on Buccaneer Island?"

"I don't know," she said earnestly.

"What was the other side of the coin? Lukatis must've had a story."

"Yes. He claimed it was Winslow who approached him."

"And the front-end financing?"

"Lukatis' story was that Winslow did it all; he just went along to help," she said; then her mood became hostile and suspicious. "How come you're so interested in this? Are you going to do something stupid—like try to overturn the verdict in the Lukatis case?"

"Hardly," I said. "Tony Lukatis is dead."

Her reaction told me she didn't know about Tony Lukatis yet. That made sense, since the homicide was being investigated outside her jurisdiction.

"What happened?" she asked.

"We're not sure yet," I said. "Our guess is that he tried another dope run and it went sour."

"Where?"

"South of here. We should have the autopsy report by now. He may have been in it with Longnose Graves."

"What? Never!"

"How come you're so sure he wasn't?"

She held up one finger and said, "Graves isn't in the trade," and then a second, "and if he were, he wouldn't go near Tony Lukatis."

"Why?"

"Because Mr. Stoney wouldn't like it."

"And Graves and Titan get along, that it?"

"An uneasy peace, but it seems to work for the sheriff. That's not my business, anyway, Kilmer."

"You could make it your business."

"Not and stay in office. We're getting off the subject, anyway."

"If Lukatis financed the Winslow run, I'd like to know where he got the hundred grand or so in front money it took. That's what we're talking about, hot off the boat."

"He was financed by his connection," she said with a shrug.

"Did you prove that in court?"

"It's what Winslow testified."

"So he was the main witness?"

"Yes. And the arresting officers."

"Do you think Lukatis was really the guilty one?"

It was an insult, a question I was sorry I asked as the words were coming out of my mouth. Her expression said how big the insult was. She looked shocked and angry.

"I'm sorry," I said hurriedly. "I withdraw the question."

"It was a strong case and a good one and I did the best I could with it, which is how I handle every case, Mr. Kilmer. I talked at length with Tony Lukatis. He was arrogant and uncooperative."

"Which is the way anyone might react if they felt they were being double-dealt," I said.

She hesitated for a moment and then shrugged. "I suppose so," she said. "Anyway, all this is a matter of public record."

I said, "With any luck, I'm going to make you a hero."

"I've heard that song before."

"Not in my lovely alto," I said.

She hesitated a moment longer. "God, would I like to trust you," she said, half-aloud.

"What've you got to lose? Besides, we've got a deal. You told me what I wanted to know."

We started to leave and a new face appeared in the ICU. He was tall and so painfully thin that he looked anorectic. He was wearing a tuxedo and there was a panicked expression on his face. He stared at us and at the cop sitting at the control unit.

"Who are all these people?" he asked, motioning to us, but looking at the nurses.

"I'm District Attorney Galavanti," she said, and pointing to me, "This is one of my people."

"Can we please clear the area," he said, taking command again. "I'm Dr. George Hanson, Mr. Raines' personal physician."

"Yes, sir," she said. "There's just one thing. I have a small tape recorder on the bar near Mr. Raines' head, in case he should say something . . ."

"Thanks," I said on the way out. "We may end up with zip, but we could score."

"Like I said, Kilmer, I'll believe it when it happens."

We stepped out into the hall and came face to face with Stone-wall Titan and Doe Raines.

63

DEATHWATCH

She looked like one of those wide-eyed French mimes you see on the stage. Tiny, fragile, vulnerable, terrified, and none of it an act, if I was any judge. This was a woman who was running out of control. A stone in the road could throw her over the edge.

The DA excused herself and got out of the line of fire. Dutch and the Stick had moved back down the hall, out of earshot.

"How is he is he all right?" she babbled, making one question out of two. Titan looked at me as if I had bubonic plague. His nostrils flared like an angry mule's.

"Don't you ever light anyplace?" he growled.

"Jake, how is Harry?" Doe demanded, ignoring Titan.

I steered her into a small waiting room adjacent to the ICU. Titan scurried along behind us, his cane tapping along the linoleum floor like a blind man's. I pushed the door shut behind him. She stared at me with her saucer eyes, waiting.

"He's dead, isn't he?" she said.

"No, but there's very little hope," I said.

"Oh, God," she cried out. "Oh, God, I did this to him."

"What are you talking about?" I said.

"That's pound foolish," Titan added.

She started to sag. I took her by the shoulders and put her in a chair. She sat there with her hands between her knees and began to shake.

"Better get a doctor in here," I said to Titan, and he left to look for one.

"What did you mean, Doe?" I asked, kneeling in front of her.

"I do love Harry, I do. He's a fine person and he's been a good husband," she said in a whimper.

"I know it."

"Maybe if I'd been more honest . . ."

"You had nothing to do with it, Doe. Don't go off on some guilt tangent."

"Why did this happen?" she asked as tears burst from her eyes.

"I don't know."

"Was it something to do with the horses?"

"I doubt it," I said. "Did he tell you where he was going tonight when he canceled out of the party?"

She shook her head. "He called me from the track, told me about the accident, and said he was staying in town."

"He didn't say why?"

"No. It was fairly common—not the accident, his staying in town."

"Look, we'll find out who did this, I promise you."

She nodded but she was close to shock. Nothing was getting through to her.

"Where was he shot?" she asked.

"Down at the waterfront, in the Quadrangle."

"Oh," she sobbed, "his favorite place in the world." She stared around as if expecting some psychic cloud to drift into the room and erase her pain. "It was his idea. We donated the land for it."

I took her hands between mine and rubbed some warmth into them.

"Jake, I feel so . . . rotten."

"Titan's right, that's pound foolish. Nothing good can come from that kind of thinking."

But she wasn't listening. She began to rock back and forth and moan like an injured animal.

"How did Harry sound when he called you?" I pressed on. "Was he angry? Sad? Confused?"

"He just sounded like Harry. He was funny about keeping things from me if he thought they would be upsetting. My God, listen to me, I'm talking like he's dead already. Oh, Jake, I'm so sorry."

She lowered her head into her lap and started sobbing. A moment later Dr. Hanson and Titan came in. Sam Donleavy was with them. She jumped up and rushed over to him.

"I'm sorry. I just heard," Donleavy said. "I've been on the phone half the evening. I drove in from Sea Oat as fast as I could."

Doe turned quickly to the doctor.

"How is he?" she said, in a voice that was shrill and ragged at the edges.

He looked at me sternly and said, "May I speak with Mrs. Raines privately?"

"He's a friend," she said.

He didn't like that very much but it wasn't the proper time to argue the point. He said, "Doe, we're going to do the very best we can but I'm afraid that's not very much. Harry was shot in the forehead. They've done a scan and the bullet is lodged in the rear of the frontal lobe. It's inoperable."

She fell against him, her arms limp at her sides.

"I'm going to give you something to relax you," he said, but she started shaking her head violently.

"No, I'm not going to sleep through this. I've been protected enough in my life. I'm not a child, George."

"It won't put you to sleep, it will just take the edge off things a little."

"I want the edge. I want to feel it all. Don't you understand? This isn't your problem or Mr. Stoney's, it's mine. He's my husband and I will make whatever decisions are necessary here. I can't do that stoned out on a cot."

"Let her handle it her way," Donleavy said quietly.

Hanson was uncomfortable. He patted her shoulder. "As you wish," he said.

"May I see him?"

"Of course," Hanson said.

"I'll come along," Donleavy said, and followed them into the ICU.

The minute they were out of the room, Titan turned on me, his teeth showing.

"Keep out of this," he hissed, jabbing his finger in my face. "The one thing she don't need right now is you."

"That's up to her," I hissed back.

"I'm telling you, back off. Get out of her life. I blame all this on you, you and that bunch of stumblebums of Morehead's. This never should have happened—"

"Forget it!" I barked back. "You can't blame Morehead. Your mighty Committee screwed up. That's how Tagliani got in here."

"Damn you," he said in a threatening whisper. "We ain't smart college boys like you hotshot federals. So they got in! Morehead's job was to keep this element in line if they *did*."

"Screw you, Titan," I said vehemently. "You're just like the rest of these assholes who want to pass the buck to somebody else."

"I don't give a hoot owl's cross eyes what those wop bastards do to each other," Titan said, his voice rising to a shriek. "They want to kill each other off, that's goddamn good riddance, I say."

He was trembling with rage, the rage of a man whose power had been compromised.

"That ain't what I had to say to you, anyway," he went on. "I'll try appealing to your sense of honor, if you got any. Don't give the town reason to wag their tongues, doughboy. She surely don't need such as that at this time."

"Doe and I are old friends. Did it occur to you that I may be able to help?"

"Keep away from her!" he screamed.

"Mind your own fucking business," I said softly, and left the room.

"What was that all about?" Dutch asked as I joined them.

"Titan got a little out of line," I said.

"Titan doesn't get out of line," Dutch said.

"Wrong," I said. "He just did."

We hung around for fifteen or twenty minutes. It was obvious that Raines' time was running out, but the doctor was playing his prognosis close to the chest. Doe stayed in the unit with Raines while Titan and Donleavy were knee to knee, palavering in the waiting room, probably deciding who would replace Raines in the political structure. There were several uniformed police hanging around and there was nothing further we could do, so we moved on after I scribbled a brief note to Doe with some phone numbers on it and left it with a nurse.

It had cleared up outside. A warm summer wind had blown away the storm, leaving behind a beautiful starry night. Dutch, Stick, and I drove back to the park in silence, each of us in his own way trying to make sense out of what appeared to be a senseless holocaust plaguing Doomstown.

There was still a light fog hanging over the Quadrangle, like a wisp of cloud, but I could see across it to Warehouse Three, on the opposite side. Cobblestone walkways crisscrossed the park like an asterisk, intersecting at its center. One of them dissected the park and ran straight to the river's edge; another ran between the bank and Warehouse Three.

Plainclothesmen and uniformed cops were still examining the scene and had extended their yellow control ribbons around the entire park.

Raines had met his assailant about halfway between the back of the park, where Dutch's ear witnesses were searching for the lost necklace, and the river. I stood next to the chalked form on the walk and looked back and forth. Chip and his fiancée had been less than thirty yards away when Raines was shot.

"I wonder what direction Raines was walking in and where he was going," I mused aloud.

"His Mercedes is parked down behind the bank," Stick offered.

I walked the fifty yards or so down to the river's edge. What had once been a dock had been converted into a small fishing pier. The dark river swirled past its pillars, gurgling up small black whirlpools. The river walk ran from River Road, where it turned and coursed up an embankment to the highway above, along the riverbank, and behind three warehouses that had been converted into office buildings.

"Findley Enterprises is in Warehouse Three, next to the park, and Costello and Cohen have their offices in One. That's three buildings down on the end," Dutch offered.

I looked up and down the river, then back toward the museum and the spot where Raines was shot.

"Any ideas?" said Dutch.

I had a lot of ideas, all of them pure guesswork, none of them provable, and none I cared to share at that moment.

"Not really," I said. "How about you two?"

"Let's say Raines parked his car over at the bank and started across the park toward the Findley office," Stick said. "That young couple was twenty, thirty yards away, talking. The killer must have heard them. Seems to me whoever did the trick had to know the park pretty well."

"And knew which way Raines was coming, so he or she knew exactly where to wait," Dutch conjectured.

"And was pretty desperate," I concluded.

"How so?" said Dutch.

"To shoot him down with witnesses a few yards away," I said. "I call that taking a chance."

We walked back toward the bank, looking on all sides of the walkways, but found nothing else of interest. The locals had obviously worked the place over. I stood at the shooting site for a moment or two more.

"Could've been Nance," said the Stick. "Could've come down from Costello's office, waited until Raines parked his car, started across the park, done the deed, and run back to Costello's office."

"Maybe," I said. "A lot of maybes, as usual."

"Why don't we talk this out over a piece of pie and coffee," Dutch said. "This caught me in the middle of dinner."

"Suppose it wasn't Nance," I said. "Suppose it was somebody

who was so desperate they had to take a chance and blitz Raines on the spot. What would they do?"

"Run in the opposite direction from the witnesses," Dutch said. "Down toward the river."

"Yeah," I said. "And if they were real desperate, they might have ditched the weapon."

"In the river," Stick said.

"Exactly," I agreed.

"George Baker," both Stick and Dutch said in unison.

"Who's George Baker?" I asked

"The best black-water diver in these parts," said Dutch. "If there's a gun in the river, he'll find it."

"Think it's worth a chance?" I asked.

"Are you kidding?" said Stick. "George'd leave a movie queen's bed to go diving. It's how he gets his jollies."

"Then let's get him," I said.

"How about pie and coffee?" Dutch implored.

"Let's see if we can dig up Baker first," I said.

BLACK-WATER DIVE

Stick found Baker at home watching television. The diver, excited by the prospect of finding the murder weapon, promised to keep his mouth shut and be on the pier at first light. Coffee and pie brought Stick, Dutch, and me nothing but endless speculation. We packed it in early and I went to bed after checking the hospital and being told that Raines' condition was "guarded."

At five thirty a.m. I was back at the park with Stick, huddled over the river's edge in fog thicker than the previous night's, sipping black coffee from a plastic cup and listening to George Baker describe what he and his partner were about to do. Baker was a big man with a barrel chest, hulking shoulders, a neck like a spare tire, and black hair cut shorter than a buck private's. A telephone man by trade, he was a black-water diver by avocation and an auxiliary policeman, whatever that was, for the hell of it.

"It's dark down there," he said dramatically as he pulled on his wet suit. His patois, a blend of southern colloquial and old English, was as descriptive as it was archaic. He sounded like the hawker for an old medicine show.

"Yessir, dark and dangerous. Don't take much more'n a Mexico minute for a man to perish under these waters. A man cannot afford errors of the mind, for you don't make any miscalculations, least not more than once. Why, sir, I dive in waters so dark, even a torch will hardly cut their swarthy depths. The bottom is either sugar mud, which is shifty and quicksandy, or it's covered with old, rusty cables, the likes of an octopus, and old boat propellers, tin cans, and other such various obstacles from time past when this here was a pier for mighty ships of the sea. Why, say, at high noon, it's so dark at the depths of fifteen feet, I must, by needs, do everything by the touch of these here fingers."

He wobbled ten fingers at us, just in case we didn't know what a finger was, and stared at them himself with awe.

"Yessir," he said, "sometimes there ain't nothin' twixt me and the Almighty but a measly ol' fingerprint."

The bottom, Baker told us, sloped away from the bank for about thirty feet, then dropped off sharply into the channel. He would use what he called his "tender system," a ball of twine that he ran from pillar to pillar and used as a guide under water. His buddy diver, a scroungy-looking young man identified only as Whippet, who I later learned was a bootlegger by trade, kept track of his progress by means of a tie line around Baker's waist.

"If I get in trouble," said the master diver, "Whippet will endeavor to pull me up, careful but sure, in hopes that I will survive whatever calamity might befall me."

Baker also had a theory, derived from looking for more than just a few murder weapons in his time.

"A man most likely will throw the gun out in the water, such as flingin' a baseball," he said, "whereas a lady, who don't normally have much truck with guns, will tend to just drop the weapon straightaway, so as to get it out of hand as quick as is possible. I will operate from the edge of the channel in, thereby usin' the tide to my advantage."

"If I were guessing," I volunteered, "I'd say he or she dumped the gun fast, as soon as they reached the end of the walk. There were witnesses who heard the shot from fairly close by."

"Thank you, sir," Baker said formally. "I'll keep that in mind."

Fully dressed with mask and tanks, he could have modeled for a Hollywood monster, an enormous black bulk peering like an owl through his face mask. He clambered down the side of the fishing pier, vanished into the fog, and a moment later splashed into the water fifteen feet below us.

"If you got somethin' t'do, might's well get on with it," Whippet said, stuffing snuff under his lip. "This'll most likely take a while."

Stick and I groped our way through the fog, found a coffee shop, and took on breakfast.

"I got a crazy idea," I said.

He started to laugh. "Is that supposed to surprise me?" he asked. "Shoot."

"This is a real long shot, but how about checking the local gun shops. Start with the better ones. See if Donleavy, Seaborn, Raines, Sutter, or Logan, owns a .38 or something close to it."

"Raines?"

"He's got a wife," I said, without looking up from my eggs.

"Cover all the bases, don't you old buddy?" he asked coldly.

"No one is immune," I answered, just as coldly.

"I thought murder was off our beat."

"Anything that relates is our beat," I said. "Humor me on this, I've got an idea."

"Okay, you're humored. Want to tell me what it is?"

I gave him the short version of the idea before we were interrupted.

Charlie One Ear arrived bringing with him the autopsy reports on all the victims up to and including Tony Lukatis and Stitch Harper.

"The same gun killed Tagliani, Stinetto, O'Brian, Harper," he told us. "A .22. All of them shot to hell and gone except for Lukatis. He was shot only once, back of the head, with a .357. A .223 removed Stizano and his people."

"Coup de grace," I said.

"What?" Charlie One Ear asked.

"Just thinking out loud."

"So what else do you think?" he said.

"What I've always thought. We got an M-16, probably with a forty-millimeter grenade launcher mounted on it, that takes care of the Stizano massacre and Draganata. We got an American 180, sounds like a dentist drill, fires a hundred eighty rounds in six seconds, which takes care of the Tagliani kill, O'Brian, and the boys on the boat. The rope trick was used on Logeto and Della Norman. And we got a .357 that was used to put the insurance shots into Stinetto, Tagliani, and Lukatis. Not that big an arsenal for all the damage that's been done to date."

"How about Harry Raines?" Charlie One Ear asked.

"We won't know for sure until they get the slug out. Dutch says it was probably a .38 or close to it. That means it could be .357 or even a nine-millimeter. They're all about the same diameter."

"And Nance shoots a nine-millimeter Luger, right?" Stick asked.

"Nance didn't shoot Harry Raines."

He looked at me with surprise.

"How do you know that?"

"Instinct," I said. "Really, logic. First of all, he's not a contact killer. He likes to work from a distance. Second, he's a planner. He wouldn't ice his mark in a fog with two people twenty yards away. It's too risky. Nance is a pro. He's only made two mistakes that I know of."

"What were they?"

"He missed me twice," I said.

Dutch and our breakfast arrived at the table together. He had found us there to tell us that Harry Raines was dead.

"About forty-five minutes ago," the big man said, sinking into the booth beside me. "I been up all night. It's a sad, sad thing. Doe Raines is a wreck and Stony Titan is blaming everybody but the President. Donleavy finally stepped in to make the arrangements."

I listened but didn't hear any more. I was thinking about Doe and the devils that had shown themselves to her in the hospital, devils that could twist her mind into a private hell if they were not dealt with, and quickly. Strange how lovers and family always assume the guilt of death. Both DeeDee and Doe had lost loved ones in the same day and both were assuming guilt for the loss. I still wondered if Doe knew or cared that Tony Lukatis was dead. She had bigger things to deal with now.

"Does Chief know yet?" I asked finally.

"I dunno, that's probably Mr. Stoney's chore," said Dutch. The death of Harry Raines didn't seem to spoil his appetite. He ordered a breakfast that would have given me indigestion for a week.

"I can't believe it," Dutch said. "Sam Donleavy and I were talking about all this as it was happening."

"What time did he call you?" I asked.

"I called him," he said. "About five after eight."

"Where?"

"He lives in the condos out on Sea Oat, just before you cross over the bridge to the Isle of Sighs."

That gave Sam Donleavy an airtight alibi. I had talked to him at quarter to eight. Even the Stick at his best could not have driven the distance from Sea Oat to town in less than fifteen minutes. To drive both ways in twenty minutes was literally impossible.

"I've got something for you, Jake," Charlie One Ear said, breaking into my reverie. "Stick asked me to check out the Tagliani bank accounts. Three of those companies are foreign."

"Incorporated in Panama?" I said.

"Now, how'd you know that?" asked Dutch.

"Protected corporations," I said. "Which are they?"

"The Seaview Company, which owns the hotels; a company called Riviera, Incorporated, which does maid and janitorial service for the hotels and other clients; and another called the Rio Company, which is some kind of service outfit, although we couldn't find out much about it. The Thunder Point Marina and the Jalisco Shrimp Company are both owned by Abaca Corporation, which is a local company. The restaurant is a proprietorship."

"Bronicata the proprietor?"

"Yep."

"Makes sense," I said. "They need a few legitimate businesses as part of the washing machine."

Charlie One Ear, encouraged by my enthusiasm, left to see if he could dig up more facts.

Dutch's beeper started bugging us and he went to check it out. He returned, both amused and surprised.

"What now?" asked Stick.

"Everybody seems to be turning their cards up," he said. "Nose Graves made a wreck out of the Jalisco Shrimp Company not twenty minutes ago. Nobody's hurt but he spread the place all over the county. What's left is burning."

"Shit!" I said grimly. "It's starting."

"What's starting?" said Dutch.

"What I've been afraid of," I said. "Open warfare. If it's not stopped, Harry Raines won't be the only innocent victim. I've seen a gang war up close, in Cincy. It isn't pretty. It'll make the Tagliani massacres look like a harmless warm-up."

That put a crimp in the conversation for a moment. Then Dutch reached in his pocket and took out the tape recorder I had hung on Harry Raines' bed.

"I almost forgot," he said. "I retrieved this for you."

"Anything on it?" I asked.

"I haven't checked," he said.

"Do you know Graves did the Jalisco job for sure?" the Stick asked Dutch.

"Absolutely. That was the Mufalatta Kid on the horn," Dutch said. "Seems we did something right for a change. The Kid was shagging Graves and watched the whole thing happen."

He gathered up our checks. "I'll let the city pay for these," he said. "Let's go have a talk with the Kid."

"Where is he?" asked the Stick.

"Baby-sitting on Longnose Graves' doorstep," Dutch said, and his Kraut face broadened into the biggest smile I had seen since I got to Doomstown.

65

LONGNOSE GRAVES

The usual twenty-minute drive across Dunetown to Back O'Town took the Stick less than fifteen. He turned off the siren six or seven blocks from the scene and flew dead-stick the rest of the way in. Dutch smoked two cigarettes, back to back, without taking them out of his mouth once they were lit. He didn't say anything, just sat stiff-legged, puffing.

"Go a block past the club and pull in behind the drugstore across the street," Dutch told Stick as we neared the end of the journey. "Kid doesn't want we should turn him up to Graves' bunch."

"Gotcha," Stick said. He wheeled in behind the drugstore, stopped, braked, turned the car off, and was outside on his feet before I could pull mine out of the floorboards. All Dutch said was "Phew. He never drove like that with me before."

"He never drove any other way with me," I said. "You're damn lucky."

The drugstore was an antique, like the ones I remember from childhood, like Bucky's was, in downtown Dunetown, before it became Doomstown. It had a marble fountain top and wire-rung chairs and smelled of maraschino cherries and chocolate instead of vitamin pills and hair spray. A gray-haired black man behind the counter sized us up and nodded toward the Kid, who was sitting back from the front window, sipping something pink that looked medicinal. He was watching a two-story row house, which stood alone in the middle of the block. A vertical neon sign over the front door of the place said that it was the Saint Andrew's African Baptist Church.

"I didn't know he was the Reverend Graves," I said.

"Used to be the church," Mufalatta said. "When they moved to their new place, the sign ran the wrong way, so Nose bought it. He calls the place the Church."

"Doesn't that upset the Saint Andrew's African Baptist congregation?" I asked.

"Naw, he's head of the choir," the Kid said, and left it at that.

"Who's around?" the Stick asked.

"Two carloads of 'em just went inside," Mufalatta said. "Man, are they feelin' high. You never saw such grins in your life."

"How did they waste the shrimp company?" I asked.

"Just drove in, two cars of 'em, pulled up to the front door, got out, and checked to make sure the place was empty. Then they doused it with Molotov cocktails and tossed a couple sticks of dynamite in the front door as they was leaving. Man, the place went sky high."

We all stood there, staring across the street at the Church, wondering what to do next.

"If we're going to arrest him, don't we need a warrant?" I asked.

"Arrest them? Arrest who, man? Graves?" was the Kid's amazed response. "The four of us are gonna sashay in there and bust Nose Graves and maybe eight of the meanest motherfuckers south of Jersey City? Us four? Shit, man. Death with honor, *sí*; death by suicide, bull*shit*."

"Then why don't I just go in and have a talk with him," I suggested.

Mufalatta looked at me like I was certifiable. Dutch chuckled deep in his throat, like he had just heard a dirty joke. The Stick didn't do anything; he stood there and pro and conned the idea in his head. He broke the silence.

"Why?" he asked.

"He's being suckered," I said. "Maybe we can stop this craziness before anybody else dies."

"Do tell," said the Kid. "And you think he's gonna give a royal shit what you think, man?"

"What've we got to lose?" I said. "Stick and Dutch, keep an eye on our front and back doors. The Kid and I'll go in and gab with Graves."

"Absolutely crazy as shit," the Kid said.

"I'll second that," said Dutch.

"Hell, why not?" the Stick said. "Sometimes crazy shit like that works."

Dutch sighed. "Let's get some more backup over here," he said.

"Why?" I asked. "This isn't the gunfight at the O.K. Corral. We just want to talk."

"The man just blew up a business," Dutch reminded me. "If he knows he was seen doing it, he's not gonna be too receptive to any chitchat with the cops."

I shrugged. "Then we won't tell him yet," I said, and walked out the front door and across the street with Mufalatta legging it beside me.

"This is crazy, man," he said. "This guy has no fuse at all, okay? No fuse, man. You light him up, he blows all *over* the fuckin' place. They will hear it in West L.A. Shit, they will hear it West Fuckin' Ber*lin*, is what they'll do. You hear me talkin', man? Am I just makin' my gums bleed for fun?"

"I heard you, Kid," I said. "He's got a short fuse."

"No fuse, brother. None. N-o-n-e. None!"

We entered the club.

"Okay, okay," Mufalatta said as we walked into the dark stairwell. "Just let me get us to the man, okay? Let me do that because, see, I think in this case I have a gift of communication which you don't."

"How's that?" I said.

"Because you're a thick-headed, fuckin' honky, that's why, and this man don't even trust high yellows."

"Get us to the man," I agreed with a nod.

We walked up a short flight of steps to the main floor of the building. It was a cathedraled room with a pulpit at one end and pews shoved back in a semicircle to form a large dance floor. The room was tiered. On the second tier there were low-slung tables surrounded by large cushions. The color scheme was cardinal red and devil black. Four stereo speakers the size of billboards were booming almost visible sound waves. The music was so loud it hurt my Adam's apple. Not a ray of sunshine penetrated the once sacred interior.

Two black giants were sitting in wooden chairs at the top of the stairs. They looked both of us up and down, then one of them said rather pleasantly, "Sorry, gents, no action till four o'clock."

"It ain't that way," Mufalatta shouted. "We're here to talk with the man."

The two giants exchanged grins, then laughed loud enough to drown out the music. One of them yelled, "What you gonna do, turkey, ask him to boogie?"

"Yeah," I said, taking out my wallet and letting it fall open to my buzzer. "Here's our dance card."

"Shit," the Kid said. "There goes diplomatic relations down the fuckin' toilet."

The big guy doing the talking looked like I was waving a pretzel at him. He looked at Mufalatta, then me, trying to put us together, then pointed at me. "You stay right there, both a you," he said, and to his partner, "Keep an eye on them."

He turned and lumbered across the dance floor, up into the shadows. The other giant stood and glared at us alternately, his eyeballs clicking back and forth. Obviously he was a man who followed orders to the letter. When you're that big, you don't have to think.

There was a minute or two more of musical torture and then the music magically stopped.

"Up here," Ape One yelled down. "Do them first."

"On the wall," Ape Two said. "I'm gonna toss you."

He patted us down and took a .357 and a switchblade knife away from Mufalatta. All I had that looked threatening was a nail file, which he studied for several moments.

"It's a nail file," I said finally.

"No shit," he said. "I thought it was a toothpick."

Ape Two led us across the hardwood floor and up into the far corner of the room to the only booth in the place. Inside the booth was a round table and, behind it, a hand-carved chair big enough to suit the Queen. Graves was sitting in the chair with one leg draped over an arm. He was dressed like a Brazilian banker, in tan linen with a dark brown handkerchief draped from his jacket pocket and a brown-and-white-striped tie. Like Zapata, he wore sunglasses in the dark.

Several of his lieutenants slipped back into the shadows. They didn't go anywhere, they just became part of the ambience.

Graves leaned forward and pulled his glasses down slightly, peering over them.

"Well, what do you know, it's the dog lover."

I smiled. The Kid didn't do anything.

"You shouldn't do that," Graves said in a whispery rasp. "Come in a man's place flashing all that shit around."

Mufalatta smiled. "Well, what it was, King Kong and Mighty

Joe Young there didn't think looks was enough to get us an audience."

Graves smiled. He was a handsome man. Whoever had done the job on his nose had done him a favor.

"Who the fuck are you?" he said quietly.

"Feds," I told him.

He whistled softly through his teeth. "That's bad," he said. "Am I drafted?"

"Yeah, the marines can hardly wait," Mufalatta said.

"So, say your thing, man. What's it about?"

"Can we keep this between just a couple of us?" I asked.

Graves looked at Ape Two.

"They's totally clean," the black giant grunted.

Graves leaned back and waved his hands. "Okay," he said, "give us some air. You men drink?"

"Not right now," I said.

"You the talker, dog lover?" he asked, nodding toward me.

I said I was.

"So talk."

I didn't know how I was going to start or exactly what I was going to say. I had to wing it. Graves was no fool. If we were there because of the morning raid on Chevos' shrimp company, we would have come in force with warrants. We wanted to talk and he was all ears.

"Things come to me," I said. "Because of my business I hear things."

"And what's been comin' at you, man?" the lean, ebony mobster said, still smiling.

"It comes to me that a Cincinnati gangster named Tagliani and his outfit came down here to set up shop. They wanted the Front Street action, but they knew they had to get past you, one way or another. They may have had some local help moving in here— that's up for grabs right now—but one person Tagliani definitely did not have help from was Stoney Titan, and since you and Stoney have a deal, they couldn't ease you out. It comes to me that the Taglianis decided to try the water, find out just how tough you were, so they sent an Ohio hoodlum named Cherry McGee in to test you. He couldn't take you, so Tagliani managed to frame you, and after you did your clock, you came out and blew McGee up, along with a couple of his pistols.

"Meantime, they started taking over, squeezing in here and there. They started dealing heavy drugs, mostly cocaine, to service the big rollers from out of town, which, it comes to me, is not your style. They also had big money, and that's where they started hurting you. They were squeezing you out because they had the financing.

"So it comes to me that you decided to make one big move, a coke connection in South America that would net you maybe twenty, thirty mil on the street plus bite a big hole in their trade.

"Then, last Sunday, Tagliani hijacked your load, killed your people, and burned the boat, which left you without your goods and owing the connections that fronted you. So, it comes to me, you declared war and started wasting Taglianis. And then when Harry Raines got hot under the collar over all the shooting, you put him away."

I paused for a moment and then said, "That's the way it comes to me."

He took off the sunglasses and bored holes in me with cast-iron eyes.

"Dog lover, you're so full of shit you're contagious," Graves murmured, without humor. "Comes to you, my ass."

"I said that's the way it comes to me, I didn't say that's the way it was. But that's how it could be played, if enough people wanted it done that way."

He leaned back and toyed with the glasses. Now I had his interest.

"Okay," he whispered, "how do you think it was?"

"Well, here's the way it wasn't. I don't think you killed any of the Tagliani clan, except maybe McGee and some of his gang. And I don't think you put Harry Raines away. Not only that, but I can probably prove you didn't."

"That's damn nice of you, brother," he said. "What do you want me to do in return, marry your sister?"

"I want you to call off your guns, right now. Before the shooting really starts and a lot of people who don't have anything to do with this get wasted."

"You want we should stand in the middle of the boulevard and invite that fuckin' Nance to have target practice on us, that it?" his voice rasped.

"I'll take care of Nance," I said. "I got more reason than you. He's tried to kill me twice."

For some reason that impressed Graves. He said, "I'm not real clear on what it is you're offering me to do for what."

"If you hang up your guns, I'll see to it that the Taglianis do the same. Then all you have to do is sit back and let the Feds put the rest of the Tagliani clan away and it'll be all yours again."

"And the Feds're just gonna leave me alone, right?"

"That's the way it'll work out," I said.

"And what it is, you're just doin' this because you're a fine, upstanding dude that does good work, right? Shit, man, what you take me for? I wasn't out pickin' cotton when the brains were handed out."

"Look, I know about your deal with Mr. Stoney and I don't—"

"I ain't got no deal with Mr. Stoney," he said. "He don't deal, man, don't come grubbin' around with his hand out lookin' for part of the action, shit. That ain't his style. Me and Mr. Stoney have an understanding. If I fuck up, I get hammered. If I don't, everything's velvet."

"What I'm saying is, I'm after Tagliani. I don't care how you and Mr. Stoney run the town. It looked pretty good to me in the old days."

"You talked to Mr. Stoney about all this?"

"He'll figure it out by himself," I said. "Personally, I think you're getting suckered into this gunfight with Tagliani."

His smile vanished, but the voice didn't change.

"I don't get suckered, dog lover. That ain't my style."

"You want to listen?" I said bluntly.

He put his leg back on the floor and leaned over the table toward me. "Okay," he said, "we've come this far. Just don't piss me off."

"They need a fall guy for the whole enchilada."

"Who needs?"

"Maybe Chevos. Maybe Costello. Maybe even Bronicata, although I doubt it. Whoever knocked over twelve Taglianis so far this week. Somebody had to go down for it and they're setting you up to be the guy."

He leaned back in his chair, made a church steeple of his fingertips, and stared up at the dark ceiling. There was a lot to sort through, most of it guesswork on my part, and very little of it, if any, could be substantiated.

Without looking down, Graves whispered:

"Also I didn't kill McGee. Man, I was gonna whack that little cocksucker off but somebody else did the job for me."

That one caught me by surprise, although I did my best not to show it.

"I've had my people killed in this thing," he said. "Hard to forget."

355

"So why get more killed? It'll just get harder to forget. I understand people went down on both sides."

Pause.

"That's true," he agreed. Then, still looking at the ceiling, "I take the fifth on that cocaine shit. That's federal. Put that motherfucker back in the file."

"You're clean on that one too," I said. "If somebody else lifted the load, you're not guilty of violating anything. Whoever stole and brought it in, that's the guilty party."

He looked down at me and smiled. "You could be in the wrong game, dog lover," he said. "You oughta be a fixer."

"I used to be," I said.

"Well, shit, how about that."

"Can we talk about Leadbetter?" I asked. I wanted to know about the dead police chief. That was another coincidence I didn't believe in. Mufalatta was staring at me, open-mouthed, as I pushed it as far as it would go.

"What about him?"

"Was he giving you any trouble?"

Graves shook his head very slowly. "Him and Mr. Stoney," he said, entwining two fingers, "like that."

"Do you know why he was killed?"

"I heard it was an accident," he said.

"There's one other thing," I said. "Did Tony Lukatis ever do a job for you?"

"Shit, don't be a jiveass. I hardly knew the little motherfucker."

"You didn't like him, then?"

"I didn't think about him one way or the other."

"So he wasn't working for you on the Colombia run?"

"If there was a Colombia run, he wouldn't have been workin' for me, nohow. Okay?"

"Okay."

"So what the hell's the plan, baby? Do we wait for you to tell us the truce is on or what?"

"I need a couple of hours," I said.

"To do what?"

"Cool the situation down. Just stay low, that's all you got to do."

He stroked his jaw with a large, rawboned hand that sparkled with a diamond ring as big as the house I was born in. He started to chuckle in that whispery, gravel voice of his.

"I don't believe this, y'know. I mean, me trustin' a fuckin' honky Fed. What's your name, man?"

"Kilmer. Jake Kilmer."

"Like the poet?"

"You read poetry?" I said.

"Why not," he said. "I got class."

66
SHOOTOUT
IN BACK O' TOWN

"Okay, you got a deal," Graves said, offering me his hand. "We'll stay cool until you get Nance and the rest of them off the street. But they come lookin' for trouble, Kilmer, forget it. I ain't standing still for any motherfucker."

A phone rang somewhere in the darkness of the Church. It kept ringing persistently until it was finally answered. A voice in the darkness said, "It's for somebody named Kilmer. Is that either one of you?"

I stood up, followed by Graves' hard glance.

"I hope this ain't some kind of stand-up, 'cause if it is, man, you go down first."

"Probably my broker," I said, and followed a vague form back to the cash register. The phone was on the wall, an old-fashioned black coin-eater.

"Kilmer," I said.

It was Dutch. "Get your ass outta there now," he told me.

"We're doing fine here," I said.

"Kite Lange just called central from his car. He's following Nance and two carloads of Tagliani gunsels, and they're headed your way."

"Call in some blue and whites."

"I've done that but you got maybe a minute to get out of there before shooting's likely to start."

"Goddamn it," I said, "Nose has agreed to a cease-fire!"

"Then you better get your ass out here and tell that to your buddy Nance, 'cause he's about to come around the corner."

I slammed down the phone and stumbled through the darkness back to Graves' table.

357

"We got a problem," I said as calmly as I could. "Nance is on his way with two cars."

An S&W .38 appeared in Graves' fist. There was a lot of movement around us. The gun was a beauty, a Model 19 with a four-inch barrel, Pachmar grip, the cocking spur shaved off. Not fancy, all pro.

"What the fuck's goin' down here?" he hissed.

"That was our partner. One of our people spotted Nance and his bunch heading this way. Police cars are coming. Just stay inside, keep your heads down. Let us handle it."

"You ain't goin' nowhere till this gets unwound, dog lover."

An explosion ended the conversation. The front door erupted and yellow flames lashed up the stairwell, followed by bits and pieces of wood and glass that seemed to float lazily in the updraft.

The place shook like an earthquake had hit us.

The Kid dove sideways, out of Graves' line of fire, and pulled me with him. Graves couldn't have cared less about us, though. He dashed toward the door.

Handguns started popping down on the street. Then a shotgun bellowed and somebody screamed.

The Kid turned a service table on its side, smacked a leg off with his elbow, grabbed it like a club, and motioned me to follow him to a side door.

Another explosion. I looked back and saw a gaping hole in the side of the room. Light slashed through smoke and fire, showing me several men with guns, heading toward the front stairs, fire be damned. More gunfire. Another scream. Handguns were popping off all over the place. I could hear several sirens shrieking out on the street.

Heavy artillery boomed behind the door just as we got to it. The Kid kicked it open and came face to face with one of Turk Nance's goons. His Remington twelve-gauge had just blown a hole through one of Graves' men, who was tumbling down the stairs behind him. The Kid jumped back inside as the hoodlum swung the shotgun up. Mufalatta pulled the door shut, and dragged me to my knees beside him as the riot gun blew a six-inch plug out of the center of the door. The Kid counted to three and then slammed the door open again, right into the gunman's face. The shotgun barrel slid through the hole it had just made in the door. The Kid grabbed the barrel with one hand, pulled the door shut again, and wrenched the weapon from the gunman's hands. He reached through the hole, grabbed a handful of the hoodlum's shirt, pulled him against the shattered door, and slammed the butt end of the table leg into his chest. The gangster fell away from the door, gagging, and the Kid charged out, swinging the table leg like Lou Gehrig, and almost took off the goon's head. The gunman hit the stairs halfway down, bounced once, and piled up in the doorway.

We followed him down the stairs. The shotgun was an 870P police riot gun loaded with pellets, an awesome weapon. At the foot of the stairs we peered cautiously around the corner of the door. One of Nance's cars was parked twenty feet away. They saw the Kid's black face and every gun in the car opened up.

We jumped back as the doorjamb was blown to pieces.

"There's one of 'em outside the car on the other side," the Kid said. "I'm gonna squirrel the son of a bitch and get us a little breathin' room."

Squirreling is a useful trick. Fire a shotgun or any projectile weapon at less than a forty-five-degree angle into anything solid, and the bullet or pellets will ricochet exactly eight inches off that surface and stay at that height. That's just low enough to go under a car. The Kid got the shotgun ready, leaned around the corner, and cut loose twice.

Kow-boom! Kow-boom!

Forty-eight pellets sang off the sidewalk and showered under the car, tearing through the ankle and shin of the man on the other side. He went down screaming. The Kid took advantage of the hiatus to put another blast through the rear window. The car took off, with the wounded thug hanging on to the front door.

Outside, all hell had broken loose.

At least two of Nance's shooters and one of Graves' men were down in the street.

Pedestrians were cowering behind parked cars and in alleyways.

The Church was in the middle of a block with Gordon Street in front of it and Marsh Street behind. Empty lots on both sides. It was under siege. The front of the place was aflame, as was a police car sitting sideways in the middle of Gordon Street on blown-out tires.

Both ends of the street were clogged with blue and whites.

The mob car slammed on its brakes as it neared Gordon, and the human cargo hanging on to the door was vaulted end over end into the street. He lay there clutching his ankles until a volley of gunfire from the Church stilled him. The Nance car spun around and started back our way. As it did, Dutch Morehead pulled his Olds out of Marsh Street, into the lot, jumped out, and dashed for cover. The Kid shot off a rear tire and most of the rim as the sedan roared past. The Nance car lost control, tried to swerve out of the path of the Olds, slammed into the front end of the Dutchman's car, vaulted over it, and slid to a grinding halt on its side.

Nance's men started crawling out of doors and windows. Cops swarmed up from Marsh Street and were all over them.

The other car was nowhere to be seen. Then it suddenly burst backward out of an alley beside the drugstore and into Gordon Street, spun around on screaming brakes, and careened into the lot as the Stick's black Pontiac roared out of the alley in pursuit. Longnose Graves dashed from the door of the Church and emptied his pistol into the fleeing car.

As Nance's car passed our doorway, showering dirt and debris toward us, the Mufalatta Kid sent one burst into its rear window. He could handle a shotgun, all right, but it didn't slow down the escaping car. It cut left into Marsh, glanced off a police car, sideswiped a brick wall, and was gone, with Stick growling off after it.

Fire trucks and ambulances arrived. More confusion.

The Church was burning out of control. Graves' people tumbled out into the street, coughing and rubbing their eyes. A fast body count showed three of Nance's men dead to two of Graves' gunmen.

Graves was not in the roundup.

Dutch said, "He must've slipped us in the confusion."

I didn't believe that. I went back to the side door and ran upstairs. Smoke swirled through the Church. Flames were snapping at the far end of the room.

Graves was sitting on his wooden throne, tie askew, suit and face smoke-smeared, a bullet hole high in his left chest, his .38 aimed at the floor. He looked up with surprise as I stumbled through the smoke to the booth.

He raised the pistol and pointed it at my head. His rasping voice said, "Shit, dog lover, you don't know when you're well off."

"Why don't you get out of here while you can," I said.

"I ought to kill you on general principles," he said.

"What's stopping you?"

His finger squeezed and an electric shock sizzled through me. The hammer clicked harmlessly.

"Out of bullets, poet," he said, laughed, and threw the gun at my feet.

67

BODY COUNT

Dutch and I piled into the Kid's car and followed the ambulance to the hospital. It was like a front-line medcorps unit. Doctors, nurses, and attendants raced in and out of doors in bloodstained robes, while several of the wounded lay on stretchers in the hallway, waiting their turn in the emergency room.

"How bad is this one?" a hawk-faced nurse asked as they wheeled Graves in, a blood bottle stuck in his arm.

"Bullet in the chest and bleeding," the attendant said.

"Room three," she snapped officiously, and then to Graves, "Do you have hospitalization?"

Graves looked up at her and managed a smile.

"I'm on welfare, lady," he whispered. And they wheeled him away.

Kite Lange and Dutch filled us in on the particulars. Dutch had hardly finished his phone call to me when Nance and his sidekicks had whipped into the street. One car had gone in from Morgan Street, across the empty lot to the side door. Nance had driven straight to the front of the church, gunned down one of Graves' men, and thrown a stick of dynamite through the front door. Then all hell exploded. Lange, coming in close behind, rammed Nance's car and ruined his own in the process. Nance had headed up the alley beside the drugstore, only to run into Stick coming toward him, slammed into reverse, and backed out. We knew the rest of the story.

"My car's a wreck," Lange moaned.

"Your car was already a wreck," said the Kid. "We'll go to the city dump tomorrow and get you another one."

Dutch was as busy as a centipede with athlete's foot, assigning cops to the wounded and trying to get a final count on dead and injured. Miraculously, only one cop had been hurt in the melee. He had broken a toe jumping out of his burning patrol car. A quick count showed two of Graves' men dead, three shot or burned, and the boss himself fighting for his life. Five more had been arrested at the scene.

"We may be missing one or two more," volunteered the Kid. "I think there was thirteen of them, countin' Graves."

Nance had not fared well either. Three were dead, two more hanging on for dear life, two had minor wounds, and three were in custody.

"One of 'em looks like he got struck by lightning," Dutch said. "The whole top of his head's stove in."

"That was me," the Kid muttered.

"What'd you hit him with, a meat cleaver?" asked Dutch.

"Table leg."

"That's gonna look great on the report," Dutch said. "Anybody see how many there were in the getaway car with Nance?"

"Three or four," said the Kid.

"Not bad," I said. "This may have been Waterloo for both gangs. They've got to be running out of hoodlums about now."

"Let's hope Stick nailed Nance and the rest of his bunch," Dutch said.

"If anybody can, he can," I said.

I was right—and wrong.

A few minutes later an ambulance wheeled into emergency, followed by the Stick. The ambulance held three more of Turk Nance's gunmen, one of whom had literally lost his head in the shooting.

"That was me, too," Mufalatta murmured again.

"You had some day," Lange said.

No Nance.

"They headed for the interstate bridge," Stick explained. "I radioed ahead, had the bridge sealed off. They tried to go cross-country and hit a delivery truck. Nance was AWOL. I don't know what the hell happened to him, but I've put an all points out on him."

"We got the little s.o.b. this time," Dutch said. "We can nail him with murder, arson, creating a public nuisance, discharging firearms in the street . . ."

"Yeah," I said, "all we got to do is find him."

"How about Nose?" the Kid asked. "What do we charge him with? He was just protecting his ass."

"Concealed weapons?" Stick suggested.

"There wasn't anything concealed about them," Dutch said. "I don't know what we're gonna do about Nose. There's gotta be something we can stick him with."

"One thing for certain," Stick said, "it's sure as hell gonna attract a lot of people."

It did. Within thirty minutes Chief Walters, Titan, Donleavy, and several other dignitaries were in the emergency clinic, all asking questions. I had better things to do. I asked the Stick to run me back to the park to get my car and check on the progress of our black-water diver. As we started to leave, Titan grabbed my arm.

"What the hell happened over there?" he demanded.

"Ask Dutch," I said. "I'm busy."

"I'll bet my pension you shook up this ruckus," he said, his voice beginning to rise. He sounded like a dog whining.

"That's right. I attacked all twenty-five of them with my nail file," I said, and walked out.

A few doors down from emergency, a bronze casket was being loaded through the morgue entrance into a hearse. Doe Raines was standing alone, watching the procedure. I walked down to her. She was wearing a severe black suit and a black hat and was carrying a black purse. As usual, she was dressed impeccably for the occasion.

"I'm sorry," I said. "If it's any consolation, I really think Harry was one of the few people in this town who weren't involved in this whole mess. His only sin was naiveté."

She looked up at me. She was drifting aimlessly through a bad dream. Her makeup, heavier than usual, could not cover the grief lines around her eyes. Her voice, low and husky with sorrow, sounded like it was coming from someplace far, far away.

"It's been ghastly," she said in a tiny voice. "The newspapers in Atlanta and New York have been calling. TV stations. I don't know what to say."

"Let somebody else do the talking. Let Donleavy do it. Besides, when they get down here they're going to find a lot more to interest them than you."

"I've done a lot of thinking," she said. "Can we talk a little later on? I'll be at the funeral home until seven. Can we have a drink after that?"

"Sure."

"I'll be at the townhouse," she said. "It's on Palm right up the street from the hotel. The Breezes."

"I'll see you about seven thirty," I said.

"Yes, thank you," she murmured, shifting her attention back to the hearse.

I watched her drive away, remembering what DeeDee had said about Doe being a princess and everything always working out well for her.

The Stick drove back to the park like a human being, apparently having had enough action to hold him for an hour or two. The fog had lifted and a warm drizzle had started. We found Baker empty-handed.

"I have just about cleared the shelf," he said. "But I been thinking, this killer might just have thrown the gun up *under* the pier. For one thing, it would not have made as loud a sound such as throwing it out in the river would have."

"What's under there?" I asked.

"One helluva mess," Whippet said around his chewing tobacco.

"It's liken I told you, sir," Baker said. "Cables, old rope, ship propellers, just a lot of junk. The weapon could have slipped down amongst all that there, but it might be stuck close up to the surface of it also. I'll certainly give her a try."

"Thanks," I said.

I looked at my watch. It was barely one o'clock but it seemed like days since dawn. I sat down under a tree to think while the Stick went off for hot dogs and Cokes. Then I remembered the tape recorder. I took it out and rewound it. There was an hour's worth of tape, all of it full, none of it worth the bother. The Stick came back and we listened as we ate.

We could hear Raines' voice, muttering, sometimes yelling in agony. Once it sounded like he was giving football signals. Another time he said Doe's name very distinctly, but nothing before or after it. Nothing else was intelligible.

I looked at Seaborn's window several times, but if he was there, he wasn't showing himself. Someone had already placed a black wreath on the side door of Warehouse Three.

"What next?" the Stick asked.

"I'm going to sit here for a while while Baker plumbs the murky depths," I said.

"It's swarthy depths," said the Stick. "He's plumbing the swarthy depths."

"Right, swarthy," I said.

We watched Baker's air bubbles playing on the surface of the river while I mentally catalogued the events of the previous five days. Ideas were forming slowly. There's a thin line between what is logically true and what is fact, what can be proven and what can't. Most of my ideas were logically true. Proving them was going to be touchy. I decided to go for broke, throw the long bomb, and break up the ballgame. It was a risky plan but Stick loved it. I knew he would. It appealed to every perverse bone in his body.

Facing Nose Graves had been nervy. Now it was time to try something rash.

68

MONEY TALK

It was nearly five when I went to the bank. It was closed but I had been watching the place for two hours and I knew Seaborn was still there. Now I could see him, through the double glass doors, sitting back in his office behind that massive desk, talking frantically into the phone.

I tapped on the front door. A bank guard, swaybacked by time, shuffled slowly up, tried to talk to me through the door, and gave up. I could have driven to Key West in the time it took him to open the door. He fiddled with his keys, took two or three stabs at the latch before he got the key in, and finally got the door open a sliver.

"We're closed," he said, in a patronizing voice that sounded like it was squeezed from a balloon. "Open at nine in the morning."

"I've got an appointment with Mr. Seaborn," I said. I was getting almost casual about lying.

He looked me up and down, sizing me up. "I'll check with the president," he said. "What was the name?"

"Kilmer. It still is."

"Huh?"

"Never mind," I said.

He closed and locked the door and shuffled across a wide, cold, marble lobby to the office in the back. I could see his stooped frame, silhouetted in Seaborn's doorway. Finally he turned and slue-footed back to the door. He didn't have a fast bone in his body.

He opened it another sliver.

"The president says he's busy and—"

I had my wallet out and I flashed my buzzer as I shoved past the old gentleman. "The hell with protocol," I said. "This is business."

Seaborn looked up wide-eyed when I entered the office. I closed the door behind me and leaned against it. He looked out the window, then back at me, his face doing every number in the book as he tried to change his expression from fear to anger.

"What do you mean by this?" he demanded. "This is the second time in two days you've intruded on me without—"

"I didn't intrude on you yesterday," I said, without waiting for him to finish. "I came to tell you your secretary had a death in the family."

"What are you doing here now?"

"I thought we could have a little talk, Mr. Seaborn, just you and me."

"About what?"

"About Franco Tagliani, who called himself Frank Turner. About Lou Cohen's banking habits. About Harry Raines, who got himself killed right over there." I nodded toward the window. He followed my gaze, but looked up instead of out, toward the top floor of Warehouse Three. Heavy storm clouds were brewing again and it was dark enough for lights but there weren't any. Nobody was home. The boss was dead.

Seaborn's nervous fingers rippled up and down the desk as if it were a concert piano.

"I hardly knew Mr. Turner," he said. "And I don't know anything about poor Harry's death." He paused for a minute and then said, "Perhaps I should summon my lawyer."

"You could do that. Or you and I could have a private little chat. Just the two of us. That's if you want to cooperate. Otherwise, you don't have to call your lawyer, I'll leave. Somebody else will come back; that's when you'll need your lawyer. That's when they read you your rights and all that stuff you see in the movies."

He turned ash gray.

"What is it, then?" he said, in a faltering voice that was rapidly losing what little character it had. He looked back over at the warehouse.

"There's nobody over there," I said. "The place is closed. Another death in the family. So what's it going to be? Talk? Or lawyers?"

"Ahem. We can . . . certainly . . . start . . . uh . . ."

"Look here, Mr. Seaborn, there are some things I know, and some things I think I know, and some things I'm strictly guessing at. I think maybe you can eliminate some of my guesswork."

He didn't say anything. He sat there like a man with his head in the guillotine, waiting for the blade to drop.

"I repeat," Seaborn said, putting a little strength back in his voice. "I knew the man as Turner. He was just another business-man. We were actively soliciting new business and capital into the community, that's no secret. And he made us a very attractive offer."

"No strings attached, right?"

He paused for a minute and said, "Right."

"Who proposed the banking arrangements?" I asked.

"What do you mean?"

"This is what I know, Mr. Seaborn. I know that Tagliani did his banking with you. I know that Lou Cohen was the bagman for the operation and made all the cash deposits directly to you. I also know that a lot of that cash came from pimping, gambling, and narcotics, and that classifies it as *ill-gotten gains*, which is dirty money, and that means we can confiscate it, and any other money made through the use of it, by anybody connected to them."

"I don't know where his money came from," Seaborn said.

"Cohen made enormous cash deposits to you almost every day. You didn't find that odd?"

"It's not my business to question my customers," he said.

"It's your business to report all deposits over ten thousand dollars to the IRS, isn't it?"

That stumped him. He looked out the window again. I followed his gaze. I could see Stick down on the pier, talking to Whippet.

"I assure you," he said, after a long pause, "that there was nothing illegal in his banking transactions. It would be a violation of confidence to discuss it any further."

"At least three of the accounts are Panamanian mirror ac-counts," I said.

"Still none of my business and perfectly legal," he said, too quickly.

He was feeling stronger and putting up a pretty good fight. I had only two cards left to play.

"What about the Rio Company?" I said.

"What about it?" he said. "It's one of their corporations. They have dozens. I really don't know for what purpose. I was not Cohen's confidante, I was simply his banker."

He seemed sincere enough. So I played my last ace.

"How about the pyramid accounts?" I asked.

This time he jumped as if a flea had bitten his ass.

"I told you, I don't know anything about their business," he said, almost in a whisper.

I reached into my pocket and took out the tape recorder, punched the play button, and sat it on the edge of the desk. The heart monitor was beeping a monotonous background to Harry Raines' strained breathing. He was muttering, then a pause, then he cried out, "Doe!"

Seaborn's eyes bulged. His Adam's apple was doing a little dance.

I turned the player off.

"He said a lot before he died," I lied.

Seaborn's tough shell began to peel away. He stared at the recorder as if it were a black widow spider crawling across the desk toward him.

"We were talking about what I know," I said. "I know you called Sam Donleavy at Babs Thomas' party a little after seven. I know you were in the bank because your lights were seen by two witnesses. I know that when Harry Raines was shot, he was either walking from his office in the warehouse toward here, or from here toward his office. It's illogical to think he was meeting somebody in the park, it was too foggy. Whoever shot him was either waiting for him or caught up with him."

His fingers started playing on the desk again.

I said, "He came here and braced you about Tagliani. You broke down, and before it was over, you'd told him the whole story. He threatened to expose you, and when he left, you went out the back door of the bank, followed him, and shot him."

His face turned purple. "You're insane!" he screamed. "I don't even own a gun. And I didn't have time to run after him. I was still sitting right here when—"

He stopped babbling and fell back in his chair.

"When you heard the shot," I said.

He sat dead still for a full minute; then his face went to pieces and he nodded.

"I swear to God I don't know who shot Harry," he said, almost whimpering. "I've done nothing illegal. There was nothing illegal in the way Cohen's money was handled."

"It's a subterfuge," I said.

"You're guessing," he said. "Besides, that's not what Harry was so angry about."

"He was angry because you'd gotten into bed with the wrong people, right?" I said.

"That's as good a way of putting it as any," he said.

"What did you tell Sam Donleavy on the phone?"

"I told him . . . I told him Harry knew everything. I couldn't help it. Harry came here and he was insane with anger. Abusive. He could always intimidate me with that cold stare of his, anyway. I don't know why he suddenly got so upset. He went crazy. I told him everything. I tried to make him understand how it happened, that we didn't know who Turner really was until it was too late. He was screaming about trust and loyalty."

"What did Donleavy say?" I asked.

"He talked to Harry."

"Raines was here when you called the Thomas woman's apartment?" I said with surprise.

"Yes."

"And . . . ?"

"Sam had to go out to his place and wait for a phone call. He said he'd call us when he got there. About forty minutes later he called back."

"Did you talk to him?"

Seaborn nodded. "Yes. He told me he had to talk to Dutch Morehead at eight o'clock and that he would ask Harry to come out to his place and they'd have it out. He said he felt Harry would be reasonable, that we'd done nothing really wrong, nothing illegal. Then he talked to Harry."

"Did Raines say anything?"

"He just listened for a minute and then said, 'All right, I'll see you there.' Then he hung up and left. He didn't say anything else to me, just turned around and stalked out of here. That's the way Harry Raines was. He couldn't forgive anything. Mister Perfect. All he ever cared about was his career, his goddamn career. He wouldn't have been anything if he hadn't married Findley's money."

"And you were sitting here all by yourself when he was shot," I said.

He nodded.

"That's your alibi, is it? Mister, if I were the jury, you'd have one foot strapped in the chair already. You have a motive, you had the opportunity, and you haven't got an alibi."

His shoulders sagged. He looked out the window again and then dry-washed his hands, like a funeral director pitching for the solid copper casket. Sweat twinkled on his upper lip and across his forehead.

"I didn't kill Harry Raines," he repeated. "Neither did Sam. He was miles away when it happened. We don't know who killed him or why. I assumed it had something to do with these other killings."

"I'm sure it does, in some way or another," I said.

The phone rang, startling both of us. He stared at it for several rings, then picked it up as if he were afraid it would burn him.

"Hello? Yes . . ." He looked over at me wild-eyed and mouthed the word "Sam."

I held out my hand and he gave me the phone.

"Sam, this is Jake Kilmer."

Silence. Ten or twenty seconds of silence. When he finally answered he was quite pleasant.

"Sorry about our lunch date, old man," he said.

"It's been a pretty grim day all the way around," I said. I looked up at the warehouse. The lights in the corner office were on. "Where are you now?"

"As a matter of fact, I'm in my office. You can see it from Charlie's window. The river corner."

"Do you have a minute or two now?" I asked.

Another silence.

"I was planning to go over to the funeral home," he said. "But I can take a few minutes."

"I'll be right over," I said. I gave the phone back to Seaborn.

"He hung up," Seaborn said, with surprise.

"I'm sure he found out what he wanted to know."

"What do you mean?"

"He wanted to know who you were talking to."

Seaborn looked over at the warehouse. His face caved in.

"What do we do now?" he said, almost to himself.

"Go home, Mr. Seaborn," I said. "You can't do anything here, so go on home."

He stared at the big, bare desktop for a second and then said, "Yes, I suppose so."

We left the bank together. Seaborn went to his car; I returned to the pier.

Baker was sitting on the edge of the concrete dock sipping coffee from a Thermos.

"No luck, eh?" I said.

He shook his head. "I'll make one more attempt before dark," Baker said.

"I appreciate your effort, Mr. Baker," I said, then to Stick, "Did you find out what I wanted to know?"

"Nothing to it. A silver-plated S&W .38, two-inch barrel, black handles."

"I'm going upstairs," I said. "You got the number?"

"Yep."

"Give me fifteen minutes."

"You got it."

As I turned to leave, he said, "Jake?"

"Yeah?"

"Love your style," he said with a grin.

69

THANK YOU, MA BELL

Number Three Warehouse was a three-story brick building dating back to the late 1700s with nothing between it and the river but the narrow cobblestone walkway behind it leading from the park. A small sign over the wreath told me the company was closed because of Harry Raines' death. The door was unlocked.

I remembered coming there with Teddy and marveling at how clean and polished everything was. Nothing had changed. The brass hand railings and doorknobs were dazzling and the wood looked oiled and elegant. There was about the place, as there is with most old buildings, that kind of musky odor that comes with age and care.

Donleavy's office occupied most of one corner of the third floor, overlooking both park and river. He was wearing his dark blue mourning suit but had taken off the jacket and was in his shirtsleeves. The air conditioning was off and he had the office windows open; although the rain had stopped and the sun had peeked out before dropping to the horizon, it was still warm and muggy in the office. His smile was sad but sincere and his handshake was so vigorous it was almost painful.

"That was quick" was his greeting. "Sorry it's so hot in here. The air conditioning's been off all day."

I told him I could live with it and peeled my jacket off too.

"I'll just put on the answering machine so we won't be disturbed," he said.

"Would you mind leaving the line open?" I said. "I don't have my beeper with me. I had to leave this number."

"No problem," he said amiably.

From his window I could see the park below. A small group of people clustered around the spot where Harry Raines was shot and a couple of pretty girls sat on one of the park benches, giggling and knocking shoulders. The river sparkled brightly in the dying sun.

On the other side of the park was the darkened Seacoast National Bank. It reminded me of DeeDee Lukatis, her own grief all but forgotten in the wake of Harry Raines' death, and the bitter irony that linked Doe and DeeDee with death. Altogether, a sad view on this particular day.

"The last twenty-four hours have been insane," Donleavy said with a sigh.

"Yeah," I said, watching George Baker appear over the side of the pier, pull off his face mask, and start talking to Stick. "It's been one thing after another."

He followed my gaze down to the waterfront.

"I hear they've been diving down there all day," he said.

"We're looking for the gun that killed Harry Raines."

"What makes you think it's in the river?" he asked.

"Logic," I said.

"Logic?"

"Sometimes it's all we have to go on. A young couple was nearby and heard the shot. She screamed. I figure the killer ran in the opposite direction, toward the river. Not knowing who else might be nearby in the fog, he tossed the gun in the river."

"Any luck so far?" he queried, showing only mild interest.

"Not yet," I said.

"You say 'he.' Are you sure the killer is a man?"

"Figure of speech," I said. "It could be a woman."

"Humph," he said, and dismissed the subject of murder temporarily. "I was thinking," he said. "Perhaps these mobsters had phony credit profiles. Maybe that's how they got by us. It's not uncommon, you know."

He reached into a small refrigerator, took out a couple of Cokes, popped the tops off them, and handed me one.

"It's possible," I said, although it was obvious I didn't believe it.

"Well, I'm jumping ahead of you," he said. "You should be doing the talking."

"Did you ever find that book with those dates?" I asked.

His eyes rolled with embarrassment.

"My God," he said, "with everything that's been happening, I completely forgot it. I'll make a note to myself to dig it up."

"That's all right," I said. "I may not need the information after all."

Baker slid down over the side of the pier and dropped out of view. Good man, he was making one last effort.

"Do you think Harry's death is connected to these other killings?" Donleavy asked.

"It seems likely, doesn't it?"

"I wouldn't know. I don't know much about police work."

"I thought maybe being a lawyer . . ." I said, and let the sentence hang.

"I went to law school but I never practiced law," he said. "Harry asked me to come on board straight out of college. I've never really worked anywhere else."

"Well," I said, "let's just say I'm not real big on coincidence. It happens, but it isn't logical, it's the long shot. Logic is simply using all the facts you have in order to draw a conclusion."

"Seems to me there's a danger in that," he said. "You tend to look only for the evidence to prove the conclusion."

"I suppose," I said, noncommittally. "Anyway, logically speaking, Harry Raines' death would seem to be connected to the Tagliani massacres."

"That's a rather gruesome way of putting it." He shuddered.

"Gruesome work," I said. "Murder always is."

"Why would they want to kill Harry?"

"It's the way things happen. One thing leads to another. One murder leads to another."

"So you think these mobsters did it all," he said, making it a statement rather than a question.

I looked back at him. The park was growing dark.

"No," I said.

"But you said—"

"I said I thought they were connected. I don't think the same person killed the Taglianis and Harry Raines."

"Oh. Logic again?" he said. His mouth was iron-bent in a smile.

He opened a walnut cigar box on his desk and offered me one of those thin cheroots, the kind riverboat gamblers in costume dramas always seem to prefer, accepted my refusal with a shrug, and peeled the wrapper from his own.

"So what does logic tell you about all this?" he asked as he lit the cigar.

I sat down on the windowsill.

"First, I'd say Raines was obviously coming over here when he got shot," I said.

"That certainly seems logical," Donleavy said. "He was probably parked in the company lot."

"He was parked behind the bank."

"Well, he still maintains his office here. Maybe he was coming over to get something."

I went on. "Second, all the Tagliani killings were well planned. Daring, perhaps, but infinitely well planned and executed. That isn't logic, that's fact. Logic tells me Raines' death wasn't. It has all the earmarks of a sudden move, even a desperate one."

"How so?"

"Because the killer couldn't plan on it being foggy, so he must have decided to *use* the fog, and that means the killer had to know exactly where Raines was going to be and the exact moment he was going to be there. As our witness said, 'You couldn't see your hand in front of your face.' "

"Perhaps he followed Harry," Donleavy suggested.

"Yeah, except our ear witnesses only heard one person, which leads me to believe the killer was waiting for Raines."

"Interesting," Donleavy said, contemplating the tip of his cigar for a moment. He then added, "Look, Jake, I may as well tell you, Harry was on his way out to my place. He was very angry. He and Charlie Seaborn had words. I called Charlie just after I talked to you. Harry was there. I told him I thought at worst we were guilty of poor judgment and he agreed to come and talk it out, once and for all."

"Did Raines have a bad temper?" I asked.

"Only when he felt threatened. He couldn't stand being intimidated, by anything or anybody."

"How about Seaborn? How upset was he?"

He chuckled. "Charlie's easily upset, a worrywart. But he certainly wasn't distraught enough to kill anybody."

"Perhaps there was a problem beyond just bad judgment," I suggested.

"What do you mean?"

"Ever hear of the Rio Company?" I asked.

His expression didn't change.

"The what?" he said.

"Rio Company," I repeated.

He shook his head. "No, should I have?"

I explained to him about the Panamanian Mirror Rule and Virgin Island accounts and that whole rigamarole. Donleavy was a lawyer, I was sure he knew what it was all about. I guess I wanted to make sure he knew that I knew.

"The Rio Company is what we call a Hollywood box," I said. "It's like a street on a sound stage, all front with nothing behind it. It's usually used as a payoff."

"A payoff? For what?"

"Favors, hush money, politicians, illegal lobbies, bad cops. They have a lot of palms to cross in their business."

"Doesn't cash work anymore?" he said, laughing.

"This isn't the old days," I said. "We're not talking about a few Ben Franklins here and there, we're talking about hundreds of thousands of dollars a week. The trick is how to hide it. The Hollywood box is one good way. They pay off their graft with dirty money and use the banks to clean it along the way."

"And this Rio Company was used for that purpose, eh?" he said.

I nodded.

"Are you implying that Charlie Seaborn was involved in all this?" he said, his face clouding with concern.

"I'm not implying anything. But his bank is being used as the instrument. He helped set up a rather elaborate subterfuge to help make it work. And a lot of the money that went through those accounts is what is called ill-gotten gains. It can be confiscated under the RICO act. I'm not sure how deeply involved Seaborn is. He may be guilty only of stupidity. But he could be on the sleeve."

"The sleeve?"

"The take, part of the payoff. He could be getting a piece of the Rio Company—that's if he knew what he was doing and Tagliani felt it necessary to put him on the sleeve. I don't know the answer to that yet."

"What do you think?"

"I don't think he was."

"Why?"

"Too much to lose. I think Seaborn's indiscretion was that it looked good for the bank and good for the town and he didn't think about the consequences. Seaborn's a small-town banker. It probably never occurred to him that what he was involved in was illegal until it was too late to get out. That's the way it usually happens."

"Who else was getting paid off?" Donleavy asked, leaning across his desk. "What cops? What politicians?"

"I'm working on that."

"Any ideas?"

"A few."

"Care to share them?" he asked. "I assure you, I am as interested in resolving this mess as you are."

"I'm sure you are," I said.

He was leaning on the desk now, staring intently at me.

"Any more logic?" he asked, still smiling.

"I've been thinking a lot about Raines' death," I said. "Trying to narrow down the possibilities."

"Have you come up with anything?"

"Yeah," I said. "Logic tells me that there's only one person who could have killed Harry Raines."

"And who's that?" he asked eagerly.

"This is going to sound crazy," I said.

"Try me."

"It seems to me the only person who could have killed Harry Raines was you."

"Me!" he gasped, and started to laugh. "Well, except for the fact that I was at my place on Sea Oat Island twenty miles from here and couldn't have done it, how did you come up with such a notion?"

"Yeah, I know," I said. "You have two alibis, me and Dutch. And yet, I have this thing about the logic of the situation. According to Seaborn, you were the last one who spoke with Harry Raines before he was killed. He left Seaborn's office without even saying good-bye and he was gunned down two minutes later. That makes you the only one who *could* have known exactly where he was going, and when."

"Now how would I have known that?" he demanded.

"When you talked to Raines, you must have told him to come here, not to your condo. You knew he'd walk straight across the park. All you had to do was go down and wait for him."

His eyes were beginning to bob like fishing corks on the sea. His white shirt front was stained dark gray with sweat. He jumped up.

"Christ, I think you're serious," he said angrily.

"Deadly so," I said.

"You're out of your mind, Kilmer," he snarled. "My God, talk about trying to prove a preconceived notion! Barring the fact that I *couldn't* have done it, what reason would I have had for killing my best friend? A disagreement over an error in judgment? Don't be ridiculous."

I could have given him a lot of stereotyped reasons—greed, power, fear of Raines—but they would have been simple answers. They didn't cover the abstractions.

He sat back down, put his feet on his desk, and glared at me over the end of his cigar.

"Well?" he challenged.

"Let's forget the obvious and deal with the abstractions," I said.

"What the hell do you mean, abstractions?" he said.

"Look, I understand you, Donleavy," I said. "There was a time when I could've been in the same boat, doing things the way I was told to do them, or expected to do them, running the show in the same old ways, with an occasional pat on the head. I also know that in the end I would have had to make a name for myself, to prove I was worth the trust, that I wasn't just somebody's lover or best friend.

"The thing is, you were smarter than I was. You had it figured out from the beginning. You knew the power was given and you knew it could be taken away. I learned that lesson the hard way. Hell, I never did know the rules.

"You were given the power, the day-to-day business of running Findley Enterprises. You got it from Raines, who got it from Chief, and you ran it the way it was always run, the way the Findleys had run things since Oglethorpe was governor. But sooner or later, Donleavy, you had to prove your value, not only to everyone else, but to yourself. You had to prove you weren't a sycophant, just another jock with a rich friend. And not just *any* rich friend. Harry Raines lived by the rules. He managed the Findley businesses brilliantly, got himself elected state senator, moved a mountain by swaying public opinion in favor of the pari-mutuel laws, and looked like a shoo-in to be the next governor. A tough act to follow. You had to show Dunetown that Sam Donleavy could move a mountain or two himself."

"Big deal," Donleavy snapped. "Since when is ambition a crime?"

"There's nothing wrong with ambition," I said. "It's all in how you handle it."

"And just what do you know about how I handle things?"

"I know that Raines was a clone of the old guard. I think when the opportunity presented itself, you saw yourself as a harbinger of the new. Dunetown was growing, and suddenly you had a chance to revitalize the town—before the track was even finished. After all, tourist trade was booming; the city was growing faster than flies in a dung heap. What you needed was to pump fresh money into the system that had been passing the same old tired bucks back and forth for centuries. Then a windfall blew your way. A chance to develop the beach with new hotels, condos on the waterfront, subdivisions in the swamplands. Dunetown to Boomtown, courtesy of Sam Donleavy.

"Except the dream turned into a nightmare. Dunetown became Doomstown, because the opportunity was spelled T-a-g-l-i-a-n-i—"

"You're plowing old ground," he snapped, cutting off the sentence.

I ignored him and kept plowing.

"And when you found out you were in bed with La Cosa Nostra, you had to make one helluva decision. Tell Raines? Risk his wrath? Or ride it out? What did you have to lose? Tagliani was reclusive, his people were running legitimate businesses, everything was coming up sevens for you, so why rock the boat, right, Sam?"

He hadn't moved. He was twisting the cheroot between his lips, staring straight into my eyes.

"So far, nothing you've said is incriminating, immoral, or illegal," he said.

"Right. But you forgot one thing—the Golden Rule of Findley. They didn't give a doodly-shit whether it was immoral, illegal, incriminating, irregular, or anything else. The unwritten rule of Findley was that Harry was going to be the next governor and your job was to cover his ass, not grease your own. You fucked up, Sam. When you made your deal with Tagliani, you jeopardized Harry Raines' political career and padded your own, and that was an error Raines would never forgive. It was imperative that Tagliani's real identity be protected, not for him, but for *you.* You needed to keep that power until you established your own power base. Then the war with the Taglianis broke out and you ran out of time. Like I said, the power is given and the power is taken away."

"Nobody has taken anything away from me!" he said, rising up as though he had grown an inch.

It was time to go for the jugular.

"That's a lie," I said. "You committed the big sin. You betrayed Raines' trust. He knew Seaborn was too naive to get as deeply involved as he was on his own, and he really didn't have any hold over Seaborn, anyway. But you? You he had by the short hairs. Harry was the only person in the world who could destroy you, and he was going to do it. It wasn't the killer who said 'You're finished' to Harry Raines down there in the fog; it was Harry Raines, saying it to you. So you shot him."

His expression didn't change. He blew a thin stream of blue smoke out into the room and watched it swirl away in the breeze from the windows, and then he laughed in my face.

"Nobody'll believe that hot air," he sneered. "You couldn't get that story into small claims court if you had Clarence Darrow, John Marshall, and Oliver Wendell Holmes on your side."

I ignored him. I said, "The irony of all this is that Raines might still be alive if it weren't for a horse with a game leg and his crooked owner. It was the death of the horse, the shock of learning that a race had been fixed and Tagliani knew it, that woke Raines up."

The phone gave me a breather. Its buzzer startled Donleavy. He snatched it up, said, "Hello," paused, and then handed the receiver to me.

"Kilmer," I said.

It was the Stick. "You were right," he said. "I dialed the other number."

"Any other news?"

"Not yet. Baker's doing his best. You want me to come up now?"

"That sounds good, thanks," I said. I gave the phone back to Donleavy.

"Now that your course in Psych 101 is over," Donleavy said, slamming down the phone, "maybe you'd like to tell me how I'm supposed to have gotten here from Sea Oat. Did Peter Pan fly me over?"

"You never went home," I said. "You came straight here from the Thomas cocktail party."

I took out the card he had given me the night before, the one with his home phone number on it, and picked up the phone. One of the dozen or so yellow lights on its base lit up as I dialed the number. When it started to ring, the light beside it gleamed.

He stared down at it dumbly.

"Pick it up," I said.

He hesitated for a moment and then lifted the phone.

"It's called call-forwarding," I said, the two of us staring at each other across the desk. "Courtesy of Ma Bell. If you want to forward your calls to another number, you punch in a code on your home phone, followed by the new phone number. The calls are forwarded automatically. Obviously you use it all the time; your home phone's on it right now. That was your home number I just dialed."

He wasn't talking. The muscles under his ear were jerking with every heartbeat. He tapped the ash off the cigar without taking his eyes off me. I went on:

"When you left the party last night, you came here instead of going home. You knew Raines was in Seaborn's office; you had talked to him when Seaborn called you at Babs' party. You also knew Raines would intimidate Seaborn enough to get the whole story. You probably had your gun there in the desk, or in the car. After I called you, you called Seaborn's office again, told Harry you'd meet him over here. Then you went downstairs and took the walkway through the park toward the bank. When he came up on you and said, 'You're finished,' you knew your career was flushed, so you shot him. The girl screamed, you ran back toward the river, dumped the gun, and came back here in time to get Dutch's call."

He sighed and shook his head. "Well," he said, "I must admit you've got quite the imagination. But I can see why you don't practice law. You couldn't get anywhere with that outrageous bunch of circumstantial bullshit."

The office door opened and the Stick meandered in, his hat perched on the back of his head as usual.

"Who the hell are you?" Donleavy demanded.

"He's with me," I said, and to the Stick, "Did you get it?"

He smiled and took a package out of his jacket pocket. It was a Baggie containing a very wet silver-plated S&W .38, with black rubber pistol grips. I looked at it. There was a number scratched on a piece of tape on the side of the bag.

"The number of your .38—is it 7906549?" I asked Donleavy.

"What .38?" he demanded.

"The one you bought on February third of last year at Odum's Sport Shop on Third Street," Stick said. "Mr. Odum remembers it very well. The only thing he had to look up was the exact day and the serial number."

"This is hard evidence," I said. "There's nothing circumstantial about a murder weapon."

"That gun was stolen from me months ago," he squealed.

"Tell it to the judge," I said.

"Let me see that," he demanded.

"When we get downtown," I said. "You want to book the man, Stick?"

"Delighted," he said, grinning. "What's the charge?"

"Murder in the first," I said. "Let's go all the way."

Stick took off his hat and peered into it. He had a list of rights printed on a card taped to the inside of the crown and started reading them to Donleavy.

"You have a right to remain silent—"

Donleavy swatted the hat out of his hands. "The hell with that," he snarled, reaching for the phone.

I laid a forefinger on the receiver. "You can make your call from the tank like everybody else does," I said.

The Stick took out a pair of cuffs and twisted Donleavy rudely around. "Normally we wouldn't need these," he said quietly in Donleavy's ear as he snapped on the cuffs. "That was a mistake, doing that thing with my hat. Your manners are for shit."

"Hell," I said, "we all make mistakes. Look at poor old Harry, he wrote his own epitaph: 'Here lies Harry Raines. He trusted the wrong man.' "

Donleavy was smart enough to keep his mouth shut. We escorted him downstairs and turned him over to two patrolmen in a blue and white and told them we'd meet them at the station.

"What do we do now?" Stick asked.

"Pray," I said.

We didn't have to. George Baker came running across the park as we started back toward our cars. He was still in his wet suit, although he had changed his flippers for boots.

"Gotcha a present," he said, and handed me an S&W .38, black handles, two-inch barrel. It was wrapped in a cloth to protect whatever fingerprints might be on it. I checked the registration. It was Donleavy's gun.

"I assure you, that's the weapon," Baker said proudly. "It has not been underwater long enough to gather rust."

"Thank you, Mr. Baker," I said with a smile. "You just saved my ass."

"Well now, sir, that's a compliment which I will certainly not liken to forget."

I gave Stick the Baggie he had given me in Donleavy's office, the one with the other S&W silver-plated .38 in it.

"Where did you get this one?" I asked Stick.

"A friend of mine on Front Street," he said.

"Beautiful," I said.

"That was one helluva play up there," he said. "Remind me never to play poker with you."

"I don't play poker," I said.

"Love your style, man," said the Stick.

MURDER ONE

I was feeling great when we got to the county courthouse. The stately brick antique stood alone in the center of a city square surrounded by ancient oaks big enough to pass for California redwoods, and palm trees, which seemed somehow cheap and out of place beside them. The old place seemed to groan under its burden of history. One story had it that Button Gwinnett had drafted his amendments to the Declaration of Independence in one of its second-story offices. Another that, on Christmas Eve, 1864, in a secret meeting in one of the courtrooms, Sean Findley, Chief's grandfather, had turned Dunetown over to General Sherman without a shot, after Sherman agreed to spare the city from the torch. It was a story Teddy loved to tell, although the way he told it, old Sean's role in the surrender came off more selfish than patriotic. Others apparently thought so too. The old man was assassinated on the front steps of this same courthouse as he was being inaugurated as Dunetown's first postwar mayor.

So much for history.

The DA's suite was on the first floor, protected by a frost-paneled door and little else. The door to Galavanti's office stood open. The tough little district attorney was poring over a sheaf of legal documents as thick as an encyclopedia, her Ben Franklin glasses perched on the end of her nose. I leaned on the edge of the door and rattled my fingers on the jamb.

"Hi, kiddo," I said. "Send anybody to the chair today?"

She glowered at me over the top of her glasses.

"I'm not your kiddo, Mr. Kilmer," she said. "We're not that familiar. How about the Harry Raines tape?"

"A bust," I said. "Nothing but a lot of rataratarata."

She narrowed her eyes as if she didn't believe me and said, "I should have guessed that would happen."

"Now that's no way to talk to someone who just laid the biggest case in the county's history right in your lap," I said.

She leaned back, still staring warily at me.

"And just what case is that?"

I paused a little for effect, then said, "The State versus Sam Donleavy."

She leaned forward so quickly that her chair almost rolled out from under her.

"You busted Sam Donleavy?" she said, her tone sounding like I had just accused Billy Graham of indecent exposure.

"He's being booked right now," I said, as casually as I could make it.

"On what charge?"

"First-degree murder."

She jumped up, all five feet of her, and stood with her mouth dangling open.

I held up a forefinger and repeated the news: "Murder one."

She gulped. I had never heard anybody gulp before, but she definitely gulped.

"Who the hell did he kill?"

"How about Harry Raines for starters?"

"Oh my God!" she said, and the "God" stretched out for several seconds.

I walked into her office and dropped the Baggie-cased .38 on her desk.

"I'd feel better giving this to you than the Keystone Kops down in homicide. It's the gun Donleavy used to do the trick. We dug it out of the river about half an hour ago."

"Harry Raines," she said with awe, staring at the .38.

"Donleavy has an alibi but it won't hold water," I continued. She hadn't caught up with me yet.

"Harry Raines?" she repeated, still staring at the gun, as though she expected it to say something back.

"You may have a little trouble proving premeditation," I went on. "I don't think the idea occurred to him until about thirty minutes before he did it . . ."

This time she heard me and cut me off in midsentence. "That's plenty of time," she said quickly. "Hell, if he gave it five minutes' thought, that's premeditation enough for me."

"If you can make it work in court, that's okay by me."

"Why did he do it?"

I gave her the basic details as quickly as I could, including background on the pyramid accounts, the Hollywood boxes, and Seaborn's questionably benign role in the matter.

"So the motive was fear of exposure by Raines," she said. "Seems to me he was on borrowed time, anyway. Tagliani would have surfaced sooner or later."

"By that time Donleavy hoped to have established such a strong power base of his own that he could override his 'error in judgment.' That's what he likes to call it."

"What do you call it?" she asked.

"Graft," I said. "Besides, as I told Donleavy, murder leads to murder."

"You mean he killed somebody else?" she asked, her eyebrows flirting with the ceiling.

"Accessory," I said.

"Before or after the fact?"

"Both."

"Who was it?"

"Ike Leadbetter."

"Ike Leadbetter! Ike *Leadbetter*!"

"Yeah, you remember him, don't you? He used to be chief of police."

"Leadbetter's death was an accident," she said.

"Only because you couldn't prove otherwise," I told her.

She closed one eye and gave me her sternest look. "Don't get uppity with me," she said.

"Dutch Morehead thinks it was murder and I'm inclined to agree. At first I figured Dutch was angry and wanted to make a case out of the Leadbetter drowning. It wasn't Tagliani's style to kill a police chief, particularly when Tagliani was on the dodge. And there weren't any other likely suspects. Then I thought better of it."

"Oh? How come?"

"I don't believe in accidents any more than Dutch does. Not in this town. Not when the police chief is the victim."

"Why was Leadbetter killed?" she asked.

"Look, Ms. Galavanti, if one person in this town was likely to make Tagliani, it was Leadbetter. He had done some time on the force in Atlantic City before coming here, so he was more than just a little familiar with LCN and how it operates."

"You think Leadbetter recognized Tagliani?" she said.

"Right, and Leadbetter went to Donleavy with it, the natural thing to do. After all, Donleavy was Harry Raines' personal choice to head the Committee. Donleavy was facing exposure himself, so he panicked and took it to Tagliani, who had Leadbetter burned. That's when Rio was set up and Tagliani put Donleavy on the sleeve."

"And had him on the hook forever," Galavanti said.

"You get an A in the course. Want to try Cherry McGee next?"

"Cherry McGee? How about the Kennedys and Anwar Sadat?" she said. "Let's not leave anybody out."

"You want to finish the story for me?" I said.

"Go ahead, you're doing great," she said. "Except that Longnose Graves killed Cherry McGee and his hoodlums." She paused for a moment, then added, "Didn't he?"

"Nope."

"Humph," she said. "I'll admit we tried everything but prayer to hang it on Graves."

"And couldn't," I said, "because he didn't do it. At least Graves says he didn't and I'm inclined to believe him."

"Why?"

"I kind of like him."

"Well, that's one hell of a good, legitimate reason," she said caustically.

"Why would he deny it?" I said. "Everybody thinks he did it anyway, and he wanted to. Somebody beat him to it."

"Any ideas?" she asked, then, waving her hand vigorously in front of her face, said, "How silly of me, I'm sure you do."

"Same cast," I said.

"Are you saying Tagliani killed his own man?"

"Cherry McGee and Graves were in a Mexican standoff and Donleavy was on the spot again. He had to stop all the shooting before Raines got nervous. When Tagliani couldn't nail Graves, he eliminated McGee. McGee was a hired hand, he wasn't family. Tagliani couldn't have cared less."

She whistled softly through her teeth. "Can we prove any of this?" she asked.

"Donleavy and Seaborn may break down and unload it all," I said. "But if you're as good as they say you are, it doesn't make any difference. Donleavy can only hang once, and most of the Taglianis who were involved are probably dead."

She looked at me like she was waiting for a second shoe to drop. Finally she said, "Well?"

"Well what?"

"Well, what do you want out of all this?"

I said, "Cohen, alive and spilling his guts. Then I'll have my RICO case. It would help me a lot if you got a court order to freeze the pyramid account until we can get into it. I'd like to know nobody's going to push the erase button on the computer before we get there."

"I'll take care of that in short order," she said, running in high gear, her eyes as bright as a Mexican sunrise. "Nobody's going to believe this," she said, standing up and flipping her glasses on the desk.

"There is one more little favor . . ." I began.

She eyed me slyly. "I knew it," she said.

"Did either Winslow or Lukatis have any priors?" I asked.

"I wish you'd let me in on this thing you have about Lukatis."

"It's personal," I said.

She pondered my question a little longer.

"Yes, there was a case on the books against Winslow," she said finally.

"For what?"

"Controlled substance."

"What happened to it?"

"Dead-docketed."

"For . . . ?"

"Lack of evidence."

"Ah, good old lack of evidence," I said.

"Look," she said, "if I don't have the goods, I can't go to the grand jury. My buck and wing is terrible."

"I'm not blaming you," I said quickly. "Was it dropped before or after the trip with Lukatis?"

"I really don't remember."

"Guess."

"You son of a bitch."

"Well?"

"Probably after."

"Beautiful. And Titan asked you to drop the case, right?"

She had to think about that one for a while.

"Not exactly," she said. "He just didn't come up with the goods for an indictment."

"Fair enough," I said. "Okay, we're even, kiddo. By the way, I suggest you push for a no bond on Donleavy. If I'm right, he probably has half a million dollars waiting for him in Panama. If he gets on the street, he'll turn rabbit."

"Over my dead body," she snapped.

"Don't say that," I groaned. "We've got enough of them already. Who knows, kiddo, you just might ride the Raines case into the governor's mansion."

I winked at her as she scurried by and headed for the booking desk.

71

NANCE SHOWS HIS STRIPE

The Breezes reeked of money. The conservative, two-story town-houses were Williamsburg gray with scarlet trim, and the walkways wound through ferns and flowering bushes that looked almost too good to be real. Some intelligent contractor had left a lot of old oaks and pines on the development and there wasn't a car in sight; the garages were obviously built facing away from the street. The lawn looked like it had been hand-trimmed with cuticle scissors.

There was a combined exit and entrance in the high iron-spike fence that enclosed the compound. It was divided by an island with a guardhouse and around-the-clock guards. The one on duty, a tall black weightlifter type, was starched into his tan uniform, and his black boots glistened like a showroom Ferrari.

He looked at me through no-shit eyes and shifted his chewing gum from one cheek to the other. He didn't say anything.

"My name's Kilmer, to see Mrs. Raines," I said.

He checked over his clipboard, leafing through several sheets of paper, and shook his head.

"Not on the list," he said.

"Would you give her a call? She probably forgot. It's been a rough day for her."

"I got a 'no disturb' on that unit," he said.

"She's expecting me," I said, trying not to lose my temper.

"There's no Kilmer on the list and I got a 'no disturb' on that unit," he said, politely but firmly. "Why don't you go someplace and call her, tell her to call the gate and clear you."

I showed him my card and his eyes stuck on the first line—

"Agent—U.S. Government"—and stayed there until he looked back up.

"My brother's a city cop," he said, looking out the window at nothing in particular. "He's taking the Bureau exams in the fall."

"Fantastic. You know what's going on up there at Mrs. Raines' place, don't you?"

"You mean about Mr. Raines?"

"Yeah."

"Terrible thing." He looked back at the buzzer and asked, "This official?"

"What else?" I said in my official voice.

"They got tough rules here, buddy. Nobody, not *nobody*, goes in without a call from the gate first. It's in the lease."

"Like I said, she's expecting me; probably forgot to give you the name with everything else that's going on. Why don't I ride through?"

"Hell, I'll just call her," he said. "Guest parking is to the right, behind those palmettos."

I pulled in and parked in the guest lot, which was so clean and neat it looked sterilized. When I got back, the guard had his grin on.

"A-okay," he said, making a circle with thumb and forefinger. "You were right, she forgot. First walk on the left, second unit down, 3-C."

I thanked him and headed for 3-C. The place was as quiet as the bottom of a lake. No night birds, no wind, no nothing. Pebbles crunched under my feet when I reached the cul-de-sac. It was a class operation, all right. Each condo had its own pool. There wasn't a speck of trash anywhere. Soft bug-repellent lights shed a flat, shadowless glow over the grounds.

Three-C stood back from the gravel road at the end of two rows of azaleas. It seemed as though all the lights in the house were on; the place looked like a cathedral on Christmas Eve. I pressed the doorbell and chimes played a melody under my thumb. Chains rattled, dead bolts clattered, the door swung open, and she was standing there.

The events of the last twenty-four hours had taken their toll. Her eyes were puffed, her face drawn and sallow. Grief had erased her tan and replaced it with a gray mirror of death. She closed the door behind me and retreated to a neutral corner of the room, as though she were afraid I had some contagious disorder.

"I'm glad you're here," she said, in a voice that had lost its youth.

"Glad to help," I said.

"Nobody can help," she said.

"You want to talk it out?" I suggested. "It helps, I'm told."

"But not for you, is that it?"

I thought about what she'd said. It was true, there were few people in the world I could talk to. A hazard of the profession.

"I guess not," I said. "Nobody trusts a cop."

"It's hard to realize that's what you do."

I looked around the place. It was a man's room, no frills, no bright colors. The color scheme was tan and black and the antique furniture was heavy and oppressive. The walls were jammed with photographs, plaques, awards, all the paraphernalia of success, squeezed into narrow, shiny brass frames. The room said a lot about Harry Raines; there was a sense of monotonous order about it, an almost urgent herald of accomplishment. A single flower would have helped immensely.

Oddly, Doe was in only one of the pictures, a group shot obviously taken the day the track opened. The rest were all business, mostly the business of politics or racing: Raines in the winner's circle with a jockey and racehorse; Raines looking ill-at-ease beside a Little League ball club; Raines with the Capitol dome in Washington soaring up behind him; Raines posing with senators, congressmen, governors, generals, mayors, kids, and at least one president.

"Didn't he ever smile?" I asked, looking at his stern, almost relentless stare.

"Harry wasn't much for smiling. He thought it a sign of weakness," Doe said.

"What a shame," I said. "He looks so unhappy in these photographs."

"Dissatisfied," she said. Resentment crept into her tone. "He was never satisfied. Even winning didn't satisfy him. All he thought about was the next challenge, the next victory, another plaque for his wall. This was his place, not mine. I'm only here because it's convenient. As soon as this is all over, I'm getting rid of it. I'm sick to death of memorials, and that's all this house is now."

"How about you, did you satisfy him?"

"In what way?" she asked, her brow gathering up in a frown.

"I mean, were you happy together?"

She shrugged.

"We had all the happiness money can buy," she said ruefully, "and none of the fun that goes with it."

"I'm sorry," I said, feeling impotent to deal with her grief. "I'm sorry things have turned so bad for you."

She sat down primly, her hands clasped in her lap, and stared at the floor.

"Oh, Jake, what happened to it all?" she said, without looking up. "Why did it shrivel up and die like that? Why were we betrayed so? You, Teddy, Chief, all the things that had meaning for me were ripped out of my life."

"We all took a beating," I said. "Poor old Teddy got the worst of it."

"Teddy," she said. "Dear, sweet Teddy. He didn't give a damn for the Findley tradition. In one of his letters from Vietnam he said that when you two got back, he was going to buy a piece of land out on Oceanby and the two of you were going to become beach bums. He said he was tired of being a Findley. It was all just a big joke to him."

"We talked about that a lot," I said. "Sometimes I think he was halfway serious."

"He was serious," she said, sitting up for a moment. "Can't you just see it? The three of us out there telling the world to drop dead?" She looked up at me and tried to bend the corners of her mouth into a smile. "You see, I always knew you'd come back here, Jake. Sooner or later Teddy would get you back for me. Only what I thought was, it was a glorious fantasy, not a nightmare. Then Teddy died and the nightmare started and it never ended and it keeps getting worse."

She picked at a speck of dust for a moment and then said, "The gods are perverse. They give lollipops to children and take them away after the first lick."

I wanted to disagree with her, but I couldn't. What she said was true. It's called growing up. In her own way, Doe had resisted that. Now it was all catching up to her at once and I felt suddenly burdened by her sadness. Not because of Raines' death—there was nothing to be done about that—but because of what they didn't have when he was alive; because the bright promises of youth had become elusive; because the promises of the heart had been broken. I remembered Mufalatta's story about the two violins. She was playing a sad tune and my violin was answering.

"Harry knew from the start that he was second choice," she went on. "I never deceived him about that. But I tried. In the beginning we both tried real hard. Then Chief got more and more demanding and Titan started talking politics and Harry started changing, day by day by day, and pretty soon I was just part of the territory to him. Just another plaque on the wall. I wanted the commitment, Jake. Oh God, how I wanted that. And now I want him back. I want to tell him I'm sorry, that it was all a . . . a . . ."

She shook her head, trying to find a way to end the sentence, so I ended it for her.

"An error in judgment?" I suggested.

She looked up at me and said, "An error in judgment? What a cheap way to sum up a life."

I was trying to think of a way to tell her about Sam Donleavy, but I didn't have a chance to get around to it.

"I can't stay here, Jake," she said, staring at the pictures on the wall. "Every place I look I see him." She looked at me. "Drive me out to Windsong, will you, please? Get me out of here."

"Let's go," I said. I could tell her on the way out.

She did whatever women do before they leave the house—it seemed like an eternity of puttering around—then we left and walked back to my car. We didn't say anything but she clung to my arm so hard it hurt.

The security guard flagged me down as we drove toward the island.

"You got somebody waiting for you?" he asked.

"Why do you ask?"

"There's this black sedan down to the right. Pulled up just after you went in. He's been down there ever since."

I squinted through the dark and could see the car, half a block away, sitting on our side of the street. It could have been one of Dutch's hooligans, but I didn't recognize the car.

"Can you tell how many there are?"

"Just the one," he said.

"Maybe he's sleeping one off," I said.

"Yeah, well, just thought I'd mention it," the guard said.

"Thanks."

"My pleasure."

I pulled out of the security drive and turned left, away from the parked car. It pulled away from the curb without showing any lights and fell in behind us. I drifted, letting it pull closer. As usual, my gun was in the trunk.

"Hook up," I told Doe.

"What?" she asked.

"Your safety belt. Hook it up, and hang on."

She groped for the belt and snapped it across her lap.

"What's the matter?" she asked, urgency creeping into her voice.

"We've got company," I said, hooking up my own belt. "Just hang on. It'll be like the old days in the dune buggy."

I waited until the car was ten feet behind me, then slammed down the gas pedal and twisted the steering wheel. The car leaped forward, its tires tortured by the asphalt, and then spun around. I hit the brakes, straightened it out, and left rubber all over Palm Drive as I headed in the other direction.

The other driver was faster than I figured. He swerved and hit my left rear fender. I lost control for a moment, spun wheels, hit gas and brakes trying to get it back, leaped over the banquette, missed an alcove of garbage cans and Dempster Dumpsters, and wasted about thirty feet of the fence surrounding the compound. My car came to a grinding halt, its ruined radiator hissing crazily.

I fumbled with the keys, got them out of the ignition, jumped out, and ran back toward the trunk. The other car did a wheely and headed back toward me, stopping ten feet away. I was still struggling with the trunk latch when I heard Turk Nance say from behind me:

"You need driving lessons."

While we were looking for him, Nance had followed me.

Doe was out of the car and beside me.

"Get back in the car," I said as quietly as I could.

"What's going on?" she squealed.

Too late. Nance was standing in front of me, his Luger, at arm's length, pointed at my face, his reptile eyes dancing gleefully, his tongue searching his lips.

I reacted. Without thinking. Without figuring the odds. Without thinking about Doe.

It was like an orgasm, a great flood of relief. All my frustrations and anger boiled up out of me into a blind, uncontrollable rage. Nance was more than just a psychotic who had killed people I knew and who'd tried to kill me. He was every broken promise, every shattered dream, every pissed-away value in the last twenty years of my life.

I didn't think. I grabbed the gun by the barrel and twisted hard, heard the shot and felt the heat surge through the barrel, burn my hand, and howl off down the street. I hit him, knocked him into the alcove of garbage cans, hit him again, kneed him, thrashed him back and forth, from one wall to the other, and then hit him again and kneed him again. He started to fall and I held him up and kept hitting him. I could hear Doe screaming my name hysterically but I couldn't stop. Every punch felt good, every kick. He started screaming, trying to get away from me. His shirt tore and he fell to his knees and scrambled toward the street like a crab. I slammed my foot down on his ankle to stop him, twisted it, and hit him in the back of the head several times with my fist until my hand was burning with pain. I dragged him up and kicked him in the small of his back and he vaulted in a clean diver's arc into the garbage cans.

It wasn't enough. I snatched up a garbage pail lid and slammed it down on his head, three, four, five times, until it was a mangled wreck, then threw it away, dragged him to his feet, and jammed my knee into his groin again. I grabbed a fistful of his shirt, held him, and hit him half a dozen more times, short, hard shots, straight to the face. I hit him until he was a bloody, limp rag.

Doe was leaning against the wall, her hands stifling her screams, her eyes crazy with fear and shock.

"Stop it, Jake, for God's sake, please stop it!" she cried.

I dragged him up and threw him across the hood of the car, picked up his Luger, and jammed it into his throat.

The entire exhibition had taken about thirty seconds.

"You fucking Mongoloid!" I screamed in his ear. "That's three strikes. You're out."

"No, no, no!" Doe screamed.

The security guard was in the street, blowing his whistle, not sure whether to pull his gun or not.

"Call this number," I yelled to him, and barked out the number of the Warehouse. I repeated it.

"You got that?" I demanded.

"Yes, sir!"

"You call it now, tell whoever answers that Jake Kilmer wants company and not to waste time getting here."

"Yes, sir." He dashed back inside the security house.

Nance wasn't alone. Nance was never alone. Nance was a company man; he liked people around.

"Run back inside the compound," I told Doe.

"But—"

"Do it now. This creep isn't alone. Just get inside and stay there until—"

Headlights ended that sentence. The car moved toward us from a block away. I gripped the Luger in two hands and blew out a headlight. The car picked up speed and stopped an inch in front of mine. I aimed at the other light and a voice behind me said: "Drop it, or the girl goes down."

Nance tried to gargle something through swollen, bloody lips. I dragged him off the hood and threw him on the ground, dropped the clip out of his gun, and threw it at him with everything I had. It hit him in the side and clattered harmlessly across the sidewalk.

A moment later something just as hard hit me in the back of the head. The street turned on end. Doe spun around me like a doll on a merry-go-round. The lights went out.

72

FLASHBACK: NAM DIARY, END OF TOUR

The 556th day: *We been on the ass of this crazy schoolteacher named Nim who's been raising hell up and down the river and has maybe a hundred slopes tagging after him now. HQ says he's getting to be some kind of God to these people and to terminate the cocksucker posthaste. I mean, there's five of us on this CRIP team, right, and we're gonna bust this crazy bastard and a hundred or so nuts that are hanging out with him?*

So I tell HQ I need about fifty, sixty first-class hunters, Kit Carsons'll do fine, but I ain't running up against this fuckin' army of Nim's with a five-man team, I don't care how good we are, and I'll tell you this, we're the best they got down here, goddamn it. Between the five of us, I'd say we got probably three hundred fuckin' scalps. Not bad for six months on the line, five guys. Corrigan, French Dip, Squeak, Joe Fineman, and me. Five guys, one head. We're charmed. We got this daily bet, we start off with a bill apiece and each add a twenty every day we're dry. First one gets his kill, takes the pot. It ain't ever gone over eight hundred, that's four days.

So anyway, we go down to meet the riverboat today and pick up this bunch of sharpshooters HQ sent down, and the boat crew says the war's gonna be over any day now and I say, "Sure, I've heard that before," but the team, they all buy it and they get a couple jugs of Black Jack from the black market guy on board and while I don't put up with drinking out here I figure, what the hell, we got all these wild-eyed slopes from HQ, why not, they deserve it. So the rest of the team, they get juiced up to the eyeballs and I have to sit guard all night to make sure this asshole Nim don't come crawling up on us, blitz us all. The slopes are okay in the daylight, face to face, that kind of fighting. I don't trust them at night when I can't see them, so I sit up.

All night I keep thinking about the cease-fire and about what that lieutenant, what was his name, Harris? said, that night in Dau Tieng, about going back to the World and bowling every night and all. Shit.

Turns out it was a false alarm, about the cease-fire, I mean.

Another day of grace.

The 558th day: *It was beautiful. Last night we catch up to Nim just before sunset and we blitz the shit out of his whole fuckin' bunch. We have them boxed in and we have a fuckin' field day. The Carsons are crazy motherfuckers. They cut heads, drink blood, I mean really rubber-room crazy. We get in close enough, the team is having some real sport. We all managed to acquire these Remington pumps from the juice man upriver, and so the deal is, this time we have to use shotguns to win the pot. So anyway we load up with rifle slugs; it's about an inch around and weighs about three ounces and it's rifled so you get a little spin on it and when it hits anything solid it fuckin' blows up. You hit one of those motherfuckers dead center, the body being mostly water, it's like shooting a fuckin' watermelon. We call them splashers.*

Anyway, it was like shooting skeet. So I take the pot. We just put it up this morning, six hundred bucks. Nine scalps. A good day's work. The only problem is, this Nim and about twenty of his gooks got away from us.

So this morning we track them into this little valley with a hump in the middle, looks like a tit in a cake pan. Lots of trees, I call in some air and we do a little Macing. It's hotter than a whore's mattress and we spread out around the perimeter and we give the fuckers a little while and that gas starts mixing with their sweat, next thing you know one of these Kit Carsons, he stands up, starts sniffing the air like a hyena, points down in the bush, here comes about fifteen of them, beating the shit out of themselves because of the Mace, crying. The Kit Carson, he up and blows the first one away, just like that if you please, and then he tells the rest of them to get their hands behind their heads like good little gooks. Man, they took a beating, all covered with Mace burns, their eyes all bugged out. Whipped dogs, man, they got as much fight left in them as a guppy. So we figure we're lookin' at, what, five, six of them that are left maybe. Fuckin' Nim ain't in the group.

I got this American 180, a neat little submachine I won in a poker game with some civilian types up in Saigon, shoots .22's but, like, thirty rounds a second. You could drill a hole in a brick wall with this mother-fucker. That's what it sounds like, a dentist's drill:

Brrrttt, brrttttt.

Like that. Jesus, what a nice piece of work. Two of these, the Alamo would have never fallen. So what it is, you learn to do things quick over here, know what I mean? You move fast, shake 'em up, they'll tell you anything you want to know. The thing is, you don't spend a lot of time thinking, you just do it, see. I call one of these little bastards over, he gets about four feet away, I give him a burst.

Brrttttt.

He hits the dirt, jerks once, it's all over. I call out the second one, ask him where this fucker Nim is, he starts thinking about it . . .

Brrttttt.

Another one down. The third one I point at tells us all of it. The slopes don't call me Monsieur Morte for nothing. What it is, there's this pool at the foot of the hill and Nim's holed up there in a cave. I call the air back and this time he comes in and lands and the pilot, who is this fuckin' rosy-cheeked bastard about twelve years old, he jumps out, says, "Where's the lieutenant?" and I tell him there ain't any lieutenant, I'm a sergeant and I'm in charge and what's his problem, and he says the cease-fire is tonight and it's official, all that shit, and he wants to call the whole thing off. "What the hell," he says, "it's only a few more hours," and I say, "Listen, you fuckin' wimp, we been following this little bastard for days and we're goin' in there and get the motherfucker, so let's get on with it." He gets the color of a goddamn beet and he says, "I'm putting you on report. What's your name, mister?" and I say, "Just tell them Monsieur Morte insulted you, that a Pall Mall'll get you a kick in the ass and that's all it'll get you," and he says, "Don't give me any of that Wild West shit, what's your name?" and I say, "Parver, P-a-r-v-e-r," and I spell it for him and then I say, "And either you're gonna fly that fuckin' bird or one of us will. We're goin' over that hump and my people ain't wadin' through a lot of fuckin' Mace to get there."

Anyway, before it was over, we were in the chopper and we go over the hump and the pool's down there, like the gook says, and there's little gray wisps of Mace, still hanging in there, like stringy strands of cotton. So we drop a string down and three of us drop into the pit there, we beat it over to the cave and we look in and this fuckin' Nim is sitting maybe twenty feet from the cave entrance. What a mess! His legs are crossed at the ankles, he's naked as a fuckin' flounder. His body is covered with these scorched sores, his eyes are swollen shut, and he's foaming at the fuckin' mouth from all the Mace, like a goddamn mad dog. Fuckin' forty-five-year-old schoolteacher thinks he's Fidel Castro or something, and the fucker's still breathing but blind as a bridegroom. All of a sudden he starts reaching around for his weapon, which is an M-16 and you know where he got that, *the little bastard, so I step in behind him and*

Brrttttt.

Lights out, spook. Then, and I don't know why I did it, maybe it was because, you know, it's the last day of the fuckin' war, you want to try to get in as much as you can, I take Fineman's machete and lop that slope's head off, swock, *just like that, pretty as you please. Fineman almost pukes, can you believe that? All he's seen, for Christ sake. I throw the trophy in this ammo bag, take it back for the rest of them to see. What the hell, they have a right. Call it spoils of war.*

The last day: *This time the scuttlebutt's true. We get back to the river and it's all over. Everybody's cheering, singing songs, drinking, and the black market man is giving away booze. I never thought I'd live to see the day. They're settin' off rockets and flares, shooting up shit, like the Fourth of Fuckin' July, and all I'm doin', I'm sittin' there thinkin' about what that lieutenant said, about bowling. Only he didn't talk about what happens when it's over, maybe none of us thought it ever would be. Thing is, we're goin' back to the World, man, whether we like it or not. It's all over. No more grace.*

ZAPATA SAVES THE DAY

The call came in at 8:04.

The Warehouse was already babbling with activity. Dutch was quizzing Lange, Cowboy Lewis, and Pancho Callahan. Charlie One Ear took the call.

Callahan was doing most of the talking.

"We all showed up at city pier together, no more than thirty minutes ago," he told Dutch. "Kite there was following Bronicata, and Cowboy

was on Chevos. I had Costello. Zapata was there, too, doing something, I don't know what. All of a sudden all four of us are watching each other and the three of them are tooting out into the bay on Costello's boat."

"Cute. So right now we're standing on empty, that it?" Dutch said.

"Well, Zapata powdered. I don't know where he went. One minute he was there, the next minute he wasn't."

"We woulda followed Costello and them but we couldn't find a rowboat to rent," Kite Lange said.

"Hilarious," said Dutch. "You auditioning for the Comedy Hour?"

Charlie One Ear burst through the door.

"What's bugging you?" Dutch asked.

"A security guard over at the Breezes just called. That's where Harry Raines and his wife lived. He says Jake Kilmer and the Raines woman were attacked leaving the place and were shoved in a car at gunpoint."

"When?" Dutch roared.

"About two minutes ago."

"Jake Kilmer was with Doe Raines?" Dutch said.

"That's what the man said. It's a late Eldorado, cinnamon-colored, too far off to get a license. They headed east on Palm."

"Did you get an APB out on that?" Dutch demanded.

"You want to stop every Cadillac in town?" Charlie One Ear asked with surprise.

"How the hell many cinnamon Eldorados do you think we got in town?" Dutch yelled, snatching up the phone and calling central radio.

The Stick was next to appear in the doorway.

"What the hell's going on?" he asked.

"It appears that Nance and his bunch have lifted Jake Kilmer and Harry Raines' widow," Pancho Callahan said.

"Nance kidnapped them?"

"It don't sound like no scavenger hunt," said Lange.

Charlie One Ear said, "It sounds straight. Jake's car is still out there. Apparently it's permanently imbedded in the security fence. The security man checked the license for me. I've got a blue and white on the way to make sure somebody isn't giving us the finger."

"Speaking of fingers, right now we ain't got a finger on anybody in the mob, that right?" Stick exclaimed.

"Chino and Salvatore are still on the range somewhere. Shall we try to raise them?" Charlie One Ear replied.

Dutch slammed down the phone. "Okay," he said. "There's gonna be a lot of pissed-off Cadillac owners in town, but maybe we'll luck out and nab them before they get too far."

Five minutes later Zapata answered his page. Stick snatched up the phone.

"Chino, it's Stick. Where the hell are you?"

"Outside one of these strip joints on Front," he answered.

"What are you doing there?"

"Watching Silo Murphy, the one they call Weasel."

"You got Murphy in sight right now?" the Stick said.

"Yeah. He didn't go on the boat ride, so I stuck with him. Salvatore's still trying to get a line on that fuckhead Nance."

"I'm on my way," said Stick. "If he leaves, follow him and keep me cued through central. What's your number?"

"Seventy-three. What's goin' on?"

"Ten minutes. Tell you when I get there," said Stick. He slammed down the phone and headed for the door.

In Dutch's office the rest of the SOB's were also wrestling with the problem.

"How about the traffic chopper," suggested Cowboy Lewis. "Maybe we can run down Costello's cruiser."

"Good idea, get on it," said Dutch. "So where do we stand right now?"

"Salvatore and Zapata are still on the street," said Charlie One Ear. "Mufalatta's on the range rounding up the rest of the Graves gang. The rest of us are here."

"Where'd the Stick go?" demanded Dutch.

"He's checking on Chino," said Charlie One Ear.

"Not anymore," said Callahan. "He just went out the door like his underwear was on fire."

"Sheiss, what next!" cried the Dutchman.

I came around with elephants thundering in one ear and out the other and the bitter-salty taste of blood in my mouth. I was stretched out on a fairly comfortable Naugahyde sofa. Doe was sitting beside me, bathing my aching head with a wet cloth.

"Oh, thank God!" she said as I opened my eyes.

"You okay?" I asked.

"I'm fine. It's you they knocked out."

"Where are we?"

"I'm not sure. They blindfolded me," she said. "We're near the water, though, I can smell it."

My nose had been knocked out of commission along with half of my other senses. I couldn't have smelled my hair if it was on fire.

"How long did it take to get here?"

"Twenty minutes, thirty maybe. I've never been very good about time and I don't have a watch on."

"My God, how long have I been out?"

"Another ten."

"They must've hit me with a poleaxe."

"Actually it was a little black stick one of them had strapped to his wrist."

"Just a plain old-fashioned sap," I said. "Just like me."

I sat up slowly, so my head wouldn't fall off, got my feet on the floor, and sat very still to keep from vomiting. Eventually the nausea went away. The room was small and tidy and looked like a doctor's office, without the medical journals and four-year-old *National Geographic*s strewn everywhere. The only light in the room came from a table lamp made from a wooden anchor with "Saint Augustine, Florida, 1981" hand-painted on it. The room had two windows, both heavily draped, and there was a TV monitor camera mounted high in one corner.

I decided to see if I could stand up. That brought some activity from the other room. The door opened. I could tell from the silhouette that it was Nance. I didn't realize how badly I had beaten him until he turned sideways and the light from the other room fell across his face. Both eyes were swollen to slits, he had bruises and gashes down both sides of his face, he was limping, and there was a cut that had swollen to the size of an egg on the corner of his mouth, surrounded by a blue-gray bruise that spread almost to his ear. He was a wreck. I felt better when I saw him.

"Hi, Nance," I said. "Been a real shitty day for you, hasn't it?"

He made animal noises in his throat and started toward me but a hairy paw against his chest stopped him. Arthur Pravano, the one they called Sweetheart, stepped past him.

"Don't make any more trouble," he said to Nance. Sweetheart leaned on the doorjamb and stared at me.

"Well, well," I said, "the pool's getting full."

"You talk awfully big for a man with his balls in the ringer," said Nance.

"Go on outside," Pravano said, and Nance bristled for a second, then turned and vanished from the doorway.

"You ought to do something about him," I said, "like give him a brain transplant for Christmas."

"Big-mouth Fed," he said, shaking his head. "You got about as much time left as an ice cube in a frying pan."

"No less than you," I replied, although I was sorry the moment I said it. They were all in it up to their eyeballs. Murder, kidnapping, arson—all could be proven, regardless of whether or not we broke down Cohen, Donleavy, and Seaborn and opened up the pyramid. They were all smart enough to know you can only hang once. One or two more murders couldn't have bothered them less, so I cut the smart talk and hoped that Doe wouldn't figure it out too.

"So why are we here?" I asked.

"It's a scientific experiment," Pravano said. "We want to see how long it takes for a Fed to wet his pants."

"There's a lady in the room," I said.

"She's got rotten taste," he snarled.

"Your dance partner's no trophy winner," I snapped back.

He let it pass. "Don't try nothing spectacular, okay, to impress the lady, like the thing with Turk back there in town. Keep away from the windows. Don't make no racket, bust up the furniture, start no fires, that kind of shit. We got people outside and people watching that." He jerked a thumb toward the monitor. "You fuck with that, I'll let Turk come in and blow off your goddamn balls, if you got any."

He left.

"Who was that!" Doe cried.

"One of the Seven Dwarfs," I said, and tried a chuckle. It sounded more like a dirge.

Zapata was sitting sidesaddle on his hog, smoking a Fatima and watching the traffic go by, when Stick got there.

"He's in that strip joint over there, drinking Scotch and checking crotch," the Mexican said. "What the hell's going on?"

"Costello and his bunch ditched the boys. They're out pleasure cruising on Costello's boat."

"I know. I been watching this Weasel 'cause I heard him and Nance were, y'know, kinda tight, if that psycho has any friends. Anyways, he don't go on the boat. So I figure maybe he's gonna meet Nance and I shag him. He comes over here. Is that what it's all about?"

"Dutch wants to have a talk with Weasel," Stick said. "Let's go over and see can we ease him out of there without starting a riot."

The girl on stage was all legs. Legs and purple hair with a white streak, front to back, dyed on one side; a punk stripper who looked about as sexy as a stuffed flounder. Weasel Murphy was sitting at the bar, as close to the action as he could get without getting his nose caught in her G-string. A pair of worn-out speakers were thumping out a scratched version of "Night Life" as the punker peeled off her bra and let her ample bosom flop out. The Prussian army could have marched in and Murphy would have missed it. He had eyes only for the Purple People Eater.

"Wanna just put the arm on him?" said Chino.

"Dutch says try to avoid a ruckus," Stick said.

"What do we do?"

They sat down at a table the size of a birdbath near the door to think it over. Purple People Eater was snapping her bra like a slingshot in Murphy's face. He stuffed a five-dollar bill in the tip glass and she kneeled down in front of him, pulled her G-string down to the bar, and let it snap back. He tucked a twenty in the string, dead center. She ended her performance by seducing an imaginary pony, complete with squeals of delight and instructions to the invisible animal. Murphy was wired so tight he was humming.

One of the B-girls slid a chair over to the table and sat down backward. The runs in her hose looked like black varicose veins. This one had orange hair, no streak. It looked like it had been cut with pruning shears. She ran a finger along the brim of Stick's hat.

"Love it," she said. "I didn't think anybody wore those anymore."

"It was my grandfather's," Stick said. "How'd you like to make an easy twenty?"

"We're not allowed to do that," she said coyly. "Just have a drink with the customers."

"You don't even have to do that," said Stick. "See that dude at the bar, the one who's sweating so hard?"

"You mean the one that looks like a possum?"

"Close enough. See, what's happening, we got this bowling club and we just voted him in but he don't know it yet."

"You're into bowling?" she said. She made it sound like child molestation.

"Yeah. Anyway, see, we're gonna put the snatch on him, take him out to my boat. The rest of the guys are out there waiting and we're gonna surprise him, tell him he's in, y'know."

"Sounds like a real great party," she said, and yawned.

"What we'd like, see, all you have to do is get him out the side door there, onto Jackson Street. We'll take it from there."

"This ain't some kidnapping or something?" she said suspiciously. "I mean, I ain't goin' to the freezer for some snatch job."

"Look at him," Zapata said. "His own mother wouldn't kidnap him."

"So how do I get him outside?" she asked.

"For twenty bucks, you can write the script. When he goes through the door, you get the double saw."

She thought about it for a minute.

"He's a big spender," she said. "The boss might get pissed with me."

Stick took out a twenty and wrapped it around his little finger.

"When's the last time the boss laid twenty on you for walking to the door?"

She eyed the twenty, eyed Murphy, who was catching his breath between acts, and looked back at the twenty.

"I'll see what I can do," she said.

"The Jackson Street entrance. The twenty'll be right here on my pinky."

She giggled. "Pinky! Jesus, I haven't heard that since I was in the fourth grade."

Stick and Zapata went outside and Stick pulled his car around the corner and parked near the door.

"This seems like a lot of time and money when we could just bust his ass and haul him in."

"Dutch doesn't want a fuss."

"Yeah, you told me. How do we do this? We just cold-cock the son of a bitch or what?"

Stick took out a pair of thumb cuffs.

"When he gets outside, bump into him and knock him into me. I'll grab him from behind, get his arms behind him, and thumb-cuff him, throw him in the car."

"My hog's around the corner."

"I'll see you out at the Warehouse."

"Okay, but it seems like a lot of hassle."

They waited about five minutes; then the door opened and the orange-haired punker and Murphy came out. He was wrapped around her like kudzu around a telephone pole. Zapata bumped into them and the girl stepped back and Stick grabbed both his elbows and jerked them back, slid his hands down Murphy's arms to his wrist, and twisted both of Murphy's hands inward. Murphy hollered and jerked forward, and as he did, Stick snapped the tiny cuffs on his thumbs, twisted him around, and shoved him into the back seat of the car. The girl saw the wire-caged windows.

"Goddamn it, you're the heat, you goddamn lying—"

Stick dangled the twenty in front of her. She snatched it out of his hand and stuffed it down her bosom.

"Better than busting up the place, ain't it?" Zapata said as Stick tipped his hat, jumped into his car, and sped off.

"He's like that," Zapata said, walking toward his hog. "Impetuous."

"What d'ya mean, you snatched Weasel Murphy?" Dutch bellowed after Zapata had finished his story.

"He said you wanted we should hustle Weasel outta that joint and bring him out here on the QT. So that's what we did. He shoulda been here by now, he got two minutes' head start on me."

"Maybe it's the international Simon Says sweepstakes," Kite Lange said.

"Will you stop with the wisecracks, Lange," Dutch grumbled. "Things're bad enough without you imitating Milton Berle. What I wanna know is, where the hell's Stick and Murphy?"

"Perhaps I should put out an all points on Parver's vehicle," Charlie One Ear suggested.

"Why don't we just bust everybody in town," Callahan said. "We can put them in the football stadium and let them go one at a time."

Dutch buried his face in his hands. "What is it, is the heat getting everybody?" he moaned. "I shoulda known when I was lucky, I should of stayed in the army."

74

CHRISTMAS CREEK

The thirty-horsepower motor growled vibrantly behind him as Stick guided the sailboat out of the mouth of South River and into the bay. Buccaneer Point was two miles away. Five miles beyond it was Jericho Island, where a sliver of creek, two or three hundred yards wide and a quarter of a mile long, sliced the small offshore island into Big Jericho and Little Jericho. Stick set his course for Jericho.

Clouds played with the face of a full moon and night birds chattered at them as the sleek sailboat cruised away from land, its sails furled, powered by the engine. Stick flicked on the night light over his compass. It was 8:45. He would be there in another fifteen minutes. He checked his tide chart. High tide was at 9:57. The bar would be perfect.

Weasel Murphy was crunched down against the cabin wall, his thumbs still shackled behind him.

"I already told you," the rodent-faced gunman said arrogantly, "I don't know nothin' about nothin'."

"Right," said Stick.

"I get seasick; that's why I didn't go along on the boat. You can't understand plain English?"

"You start getting sick," said the Stick, "you better stick your head over the side. Puke in my boat and I'll use you for a mop and throw you overboard."

"Fuck you," Murphy growled, but his arrogance was less than convincing.

"Cute," Stick said. "I admire your stuff."

"How many times I gotta tell you," Murphy said, "I don't know nothin' about snatching no Fed, or the Raines dame. That's all news t'me."

"Where's Costello heading on that schooner of his?"

"I told you, I don't fuckin' know! They was just goin' out to have dinner and get away for a few hours. We was all tired of looking up some cop's nose every time we turned around."

He shifted slightly.

"Where the hell are we going?" he demanded.

"Up the lazy river," Stick said.

"You're a full-out loony, you know that. You need about fifty more cards to fill out your deck."

"Big talk from a man who can't even scratch his nose," Stick said.

"Look, these things are killing my thumbs," Murphy said. "Can you at least loosen them a little? My whole damn arm's goin' to sleep."

"I want to know where Kilmer is and where Costello's going. You just tell me that, we turn around and head for home."

"Shit, man, how many ways can I—"

"You already have," the Stick said. "You're beginning to annoy me. If you won't tell me what I want to know, keep your mouth shut or I'll put my foot in it."

They went on. The only sound now was the bow of the boat slicing through the water, and the occasional slap of a wave as it rolled up into a whitehead and peaked. Stick was using running lights, although occasionally he snapped on a powerful searchlight for a look around. Otherwise he watched his compass and smoked and said nothing.

At 9:05 he passed the north point of Big Jericho, swung the trim boat in toward land, and followed the beach around to the south. A minute or two later the moon peered out from behind the clouds and in its gray half-light he could see the mouth of Christmas Creek. He turned into it, cut back the motor, and switched the spotlight on again. He swept it back and forth. Murphy straightened up and peered over the gunwale. A large heron thrashed its wings nearby and flapped noisily away. Startled by the sudden and unexpected sound, Murphy slumped down again.

Then he heard the sounds for the first time.

A sudden whirlpool of movement in the water near the boat.

"What'sat?" he asked, sitting up again. "Hey, there it goes again. You hear that?"

The Stick said nothing.

The sounds continued. There seemed to be a lot of turbulence in the water around the boat. Then there was a splash and something thunked the side of the sailboat.

"Don't you hear it?" Murphy croaked, staring wide-eyed at the circle of light from the spotlight. The Stick still didn't answer.

Stick had stopped in an all-night supermarket on the way to the boat-house and bought a large beef shoulder. It had been soaking in a bucket of warm water near his feet. Now he took it out, laid it on the rear bulkhead, and slashed several deep gashes in it with a rusty machete. Blood crept out of the crevices, seeping slowly into the seams between the boards.

There was a loud splash near the stern, then another, even louder, just beyond the bow. Fear began as a worm in Murphy's stomach, a twisty little jolt. He began to look feverishly at each new tremor in the water, but he could see nothing but swirls on the surface of the creek.

Then he thought he saw a gray triangle cut the surface ten feet away.

"What was that?" he asked.

The worm became a snake. It crawled up through his chest and stuck in his throat. His mouth dried up.

"This is a little nature trip, Weasel," Stick said, taking a grappling hook from the bulkhead storage box and burying its hooks in the beef shoulder. He wrapped a thick nylon fishing line around it several times and tied it in a half hitch. "Ever hear of Christmas Creek?"

"I told you, I get seasick. I don't have nothin' to do with the fuckin' ocean." His voice was losing its bravado.

Stick saw the bar dead ahead, a slender strip of sand, barely a foot above water.

"Well, you're right in the middle of it. This is it, this is Christmas Creek," Stick said. "One of the local ecological wonders."

There was another, more vigorous splash off the starboard bow and this time Murphy saw it clearly, a shiny gray dorsal fin. It sliced the surface for an instant and then disappeared in a swirl.

"Good Christ, those're sharks," Murphy gasped.

"I was about to tell you," said Stick. "This is a breeding ground for gray sharks and makos, and this is the month for it. That's why they're so fidgety. I'd guess there are probably, oh hell, two, three hundred sharks within spitting distance of the boat right now."

The first shark Murphy actually saw breached water three feet away, rolled over on its side, and dove again.

It was half the length of the sailboat!

"Sweet Jesus," Murphy muttered to himself. He was still trying to maintain his tough facade, but his eyes mirrored his growing fear. He dropped back onto the floor of the cockpit and cowered there.

"This bloody piece of beef here will drive them crazy," Stick continued. "I thought I'd just give 'em a snack, let you see one of the wonders of the world."

Murphy hunched down lower.

"C'mon, fella, watch the show," said Stick. He reached down and pulled Murphy up and slammed him against the bulkhead. He threw the piece of meat overboard, holding it by the nylon cord. It had hardly hit before the creek was churned into bubbles. The water looked like it was boiling. The frenzied killers streaked to the bloody morsel. Their tails whipped out of the water. Fins seemed to be slashing all over the creek. The creatures surfaced in their frenzy, their black marble eyes bulging with excitement, their ragged mouths blood-smeared from ripping at the beef shoulder. A great, ugly mako breached the surface, twisted violently in the water, then suddenly lurched into the air as a large gray disemboweled it, the attacker thrashing its head back and forth as it tore a great chunk from the other shark's belly. More blood churned to the surface. A half dozen more sharks converged on the mako, ripping it to shreds. Then one of them turned and charged the sailboat.

Murphy screamed, a full-fledged, bloodcurdling scream.

The big gray turned at the last moment and scraped down the side of the sailboat.

All Murphy saw were insane eyes and gleaming teeth.

Within seconds the hook was empty. Stick pulled it back in.

"Lookit that, they even gnawed at the hooks," Stick said with a chuckle.

"What're we doin' here?" Murphy whispered, as though he were afraid he would disturb the predators.

"I'll tell you, when these bastards are horny, they're downright unreasonable," Stick rambled on.

He swung the sailboat in a tight arc, pulling as close to the sandbar as he could. He knew the creek well; knew, too, that the bar dropped off sharply on its north side, sharply enough to get in tight. Stick grabbed the back of Murphy's shirt and hauled him to his feet.

"What the hell are you doing? Lemme alone, lemmee . . ." the mobster howled.

The boat nudged the bar.

Stick threw him over the side.

Murphy shrieked. He landed on his side in the soft sand, rolled over, still screaming, scrambled to his feet, and sloshed through ankle-deep sand to the middle of the bar. He stood there, his hands behind his back, his eyes bulging with fear, watching the fins circle his diminishing island.

"For God's sakes, what'd I do? I didn't do nothin'! Get me offa here. Jesus, Mary, and Joseph, please, get me offa here!"

407

Stick leaned toward him. "Now listen good, Weasel. The tide's coming in. This bar lies very low in the water. Another five, six minutes, the water will cover it. At full tide, in about forty-five minutes, it'll be up to your waist. Do you get the drift?"

Murphy looked around, wide-eyed. There were sharks all over the place, circling the tiny island as if they could smell him.

"Here, I'll give you a break," Stick said. "You won't have to look at them."

Stick turned the spotlight off.

"No-o-o," Murphy moaned.

The moon dipped behind the clouds. Murphy was rooted to his spot. He was beyond fear now, afraid to move in any direction. He squinted into the darkness but it was too dark to see anything.

But he could hear them.

"Get me offa here, please," Murphy pleaded. There was no bravado left.

Stick replied, "The tide's coming in, Weasel. In two or three minutes you'll feel it around your ankles."

Murphy's feet squirmed beneath him. He had trouble catching his breath. He was overwhelmed with fear. Then he felt the first cold, wet fingers seeping through the soles of his shoes, down through the shoelace holes, around the tongues of his expensive brogans, clutching at his feet.

Murphy suddenly started to babble. He couldn't talk fast enough. His words tumbled over each other and he started to stutter:

"They'regointoThunderPoint! To Chevos' p-p-p-place! They went out-ontheboat to celebrate . . ."

"Celebrate what?"

"Costello's the new capo di capi.*"*

"When are they coming in?"

"They're due to get to the marina about t-t-ten . . ."

"How do you know that?"

"That's when I'm supposed to be back. I g-g-got a coupla hours off 'cause I get seasick."

"Who's going to be there?"

"It's everybody. It's the wholegoddamnw-w-works, except maybe for Nance. I . . . I sweartoG-G-God I don't know where he is. Please, oh, God, please get me offa here. That's all I know. All I know, I swear on my mother's eyes, I don't know another f-f-fuckin' thing. Jesus, man, I'll p-p-pay you. What d'ya want? You want my car? I got a brand-new Chrysler convertible it's yours. Damn it, please . . ."

"That's better, Weasel. Okay, start walking this way."

"I can't, not in the dark, don't do . . ."

"Just walk toward my voice."

"I can't m-m-move!"

"I'll keep talking and you keep walking and if you don't lose your cool, you'll make it over here. But you better stop fuckin' around, Weasel, because the tide doesn't stop. It's gonna get deeper and . . ."

"I'm walkin', I'm walkin'. Can I have the light, can I please have the fuckin' light?"

Murphy was dragging one foot after the other through the sandy water. Each step seemed to take him deeper.

"I'm going wrong!" he yelled at the darkness. "The water's up to my shins!"

"I warned you about the tide, Weasel. Just keep coming. You're doing fine, but don't stop. If you stop, they'll be on top of you in another five minutes."

Murphy took another step and the water swirled around his knees. He began to get sick to his stomach. He started running, lost his balance, and fell face down in the cold salt water. He scrambled frantically, trying to get his knees under him, but with his hands shackled behind him he had trouble. He swallowed a mouthful of water, then got his head up, coughing and gulping for air.

"Where are ya?" Murphy screamed when he finally regained his footing.

He heard the sailboat's motor, then realized it was moving away *from him!*

"Hey!" Murphy screamed. "H-e-e-e-y!"

The sound of the motor grew dimmer and dimmer. The thrashing of the sharks was drawing closer. The water was almost up to his waist.

The last human voice Murphy heard was the Stick's, far off in the blackness of night. The man's singing! *Murphy cried out to himself.*

"Up a lazy river, by the old mill run . . ."

GOOD-BYE HIT

An hour crept by. It seemed like four or five. At first the TV monitor discouraged conversation. I figured the room had to be bugged. After I got my wits together I decided to give it a test. I looked straight into the camera and said, "Would it be too much to ask for a glass of water?" Nothing had happened, so I kicked on the door. Sweetheart Pravano answered my summons. He was still wearing the battle scars from the fight at the Warehouse: a mouse on his right eye and a four-inch gash in his jaw. He glared at me when I made the request and shut the door in my face, but a minute or two later a young kid who was wearing both suspenders and a belt, as well as an empty shoulder holster under his arm, brought us each a glass of ice water. Then they left us alone.

"What do you think they're going to do with us?" Doe asked.

"I don't know," I said, quite honestly.

During the remainder of that hour Doe and I talked quietly but steadily. I explained who Tagliani was, although she seemed to have a vague notion already. I also told her Tony Lukatis had been slain hijacking the cocaine shipment, which she didn't know, although the information didn't seem to upset her too much.

"So you knew about Tony?" she said. "That was over such a long time ago. Poor Tony. He wanted so desperately to make something of himself, to be more than . . ." She tried to explain Lukatis' obsession, but it wouldn't come out.

"I can understand that," I said. "He just picked the wrong way to do it."

"Was he involved with these people?"

I shook my head. "I don't think so," I said, but didn't take it any farther. I still didn't know who he *was* involved with.

"I guess I was the cause of all that, too," she said, and started to cry. "I caused it all."

"No, that's not true," I said. "You were a pawn in the game, like a lot of us."

"It was all over between us before he ever got in trouble," Doe went on, purging the memory of Lukatis. "He wouldn't accept that. He kept calling, sending me cards, leaving little gifts. Then I saw him one day and he told me things were going to be different. He called it his big score. I had no idea he was going to . . ." She let the sentence drift off. She was having a lot of trouble finishing sentences.

That's when I told her about Sam Donleavy. Her shoulders sagged as the story unfolded. Tears welled in her eyes. The shock of disbelief pulled at her face, like the heavy hand of time. I took

her in my arms and held her as tightly as I could and let her sob
it out.

Then I heard the throb of heavy engines outside. There was a
lot of yelling and laughter, people entering the other room. A
few minutes later there was what sounded like an angry exchange,
although I couldn't tell for sure who was talking to whom, or what
the rhubarb was all about. Then the door opened.

*The lights of Thunder Point Marina twinkled like stars on the bay a half
mile away. Stick hunched down in the cockpit of the sailboat, his hat pulled
down over his eyes so the wind wouldn't blow it off. There was a strong
wind coming in from the southeast and the sails were full, billowed out
like shrouds above him in the darkness. He had the sheets pulled in as
tight as he could and the boat was keeled low in the water. The waves
bounded past his elbow like a river on a rampage.*

*For ten minutes he had been watching Costello's yacht as it sailed into
the inlet from open water and headed for the marina. Now it was pulling
into the dock.*

*He set the tiller, tied it down, reached under the seat, and pulled out
a waterproof bag. First he took out the .357 and checked the chamber. It
was loaded with controlled-expansion treasury rounds. Then the 180, his
little jewel. He checked the silencer and snapped a 180-round drum into
the chamber, mentally ticking off his firepower as he did. He turned on
the laser scope and watched the little red dot dance across the swollen sails.
Next came the M-16, the old standby, fully loaded with a thirty-shot clip.
He took a forty-millimeter grenade from the bag and inserted it in the
grenade launcher under the barrel. Finally he got the ammo bag, which
held two drums for the 180, six clips for the 16, six grenades, and five
quick-loads for the Magnum.*

Not bad. Seven grenades and 786 rounds of ammo.

*He mentally counted the enemy: Costello, Bronicata, Chevos, and two
other gunmen on the boat. Nance, Sweetheart Pravano, and at least four
others he could think of inside the marina, and two guards with sawed-
off shotguns on the dock.*

*Thirteen. About sixty rounds per man plus the grenades. Piece of cake.
He'd been up against a lot worse.*

*He adjusted the night sight on the M-16 and checked out the deck of
the yacht. There they were: Costello, Chevos, Bronicata, Drack Moreno,
all the heavyweights but Nance and Pravano, who had to be inside somewhere, and Cohen, who was probably home in bed.*

Beautiful, he thought. The timing couldn't be better. Just one big happy family.

That was fine about Cohen. Cohen belonged to Jake. The rest of them were his. He started smearing black shoe polish on his face.

This time it was Dutch who snatched up the phone when it rang. He was waiting for the call. It was Cowboy Lewis, patched in from the police helicopter.

"We spotted 'em, Dutch. Costello's barge is pullin' into the private dock on the back of Thunder Point Marina right now."

"You sure it's him?"

"It is unless he cloned that boat of his. Ain't another one around here like it."

"How far away are you?"

"Half a mile, maybe."

"Can you get down low enough to check the parking lot for that cinnamon Eldorado without getting your kiester blown off?"

"We'll have to use lights."

"Okay, but be careful. We're heading out there anyway, just in case. I'm tired of sitting on my duster back here."

"See ya," said Lewis.

Stick trimmed his sails and slid quietly past the end of the dock. The two guards were leaning against the side of the yacht, talking.

Stick studied the layout. The marina was to his left, separated from the private dock by a concrete wharf and twenty feet of water. A walkway led from the dock up to the house.

A hundred meters maybe, no more, from dock to house.

Plenty of trees for cover plus a terraced lawn that led down to the water.

Two big lights on a pole at the end of the dock. Fuck it, no problem.

The house itself was one-story. That was good. No high ground for them. He swept the house with his night scope, planning his attack. From left to right, he made the kitchen, with a sliding panel out to a terrace; the main room, big, with a cathedral ceiling; a bedroom with a large picture window overlooking the water, and a circular waterbed in the center of it; and a smaller room at the end of the house. At first he thought that room was dark; then he saw a sliver of light streaming through the drapes. That's where they had to be. And they were here. He knew that because Nance was here.

He counted heads.

Three in the kitchen, including Bronicata.
Five in the living room, including Moreno and Pravano.
Chevos, Nance, and Costello in the bedroom.
Eleven, just as he had figured. He still had the touch.
Behind him, out over the bay somewhere, he heard a chopper whop-
whop-whopping. *He ignored it. He swung around, headed straight for
the pier, and pulled in his sails. He tied down the tiller, slung the ammo
bag over his shoulder, grabbed the 180 and M-16, and clambered over
the cabin to the front of his boat, stretched out on the deck, and got the
submachine gun ready. The sailboat sliced through the water and sailed
into the orb of light from the two big dock lights.*

The door opened and Costello was standing there.

He looked like Yankee Doodle Dandy: white slacks, a blue blazer,
a red silk scarf flouncing around his neck.

"Well, well," I said, "it's Captain America."

By that time I was ready to take on the Russian army.

"You just never give up, do you, Kilmer?" he said, in that flat,
no-nonsense lawyer's voice of his.

"Offhand, I'd say your little bubble has blown sky high," I said.

"You talk big for a man who could be sixty seconds from his
own funeral," he said. "Notice I said could be. I'm all that's standing between Nance and a bullet in your head."

I ignored the threat. "You're going across, Costello. First murder, now kidnapping. I've been wrong about you. I thought you
were smarter than the rest of these wahoos. You just wear cuter
clothes."

Doe was hanging on to my hand like a drowning woman.

"Why don't you let her go?" I said. "This is between us boys."

"I didn't have anything to do with this," he said. "I've been out
on the water for the past four hours. My cuffs are clean."

"I can hardly wait to see the look on the jury's face when you
run that one by them."

He pulled a chair over and sat down in front of us.

"The monitor's turned off," he said. "So we can talk straight.
First of all, Nance and you have had this hard-on for each other
for a couple of years. I'm not responsible for his actions. And
from the looks of him, you could be looking at a case of police
brutality, anyway."

"And what's the lady here guilty of, holding my coat while I
did it?"

"I'll admit that bringing you two out here was bad judgment on somebody's part, but we can work all this out."

"Good, I'm glad you see it that way," I said. "If you'll just arrange for a ride back to town, we'll be leaving."

"Not quite."

"You're skating on no ice, Costello. You may not be guilty of kidnapping, but holding us against our will sure as hell makes you an accessory."

"I'm just trying to arrange a negotiation here," he said, holding his hands out at his sides and smiling. "So everybody comes out happy."

"There's no way that can happen."

"You're all bluff, Kilmer. Right now you couldn't lick a postage stamp in a court of law, and you know it."

"I've got Donleavy cold for murder one," I said. "And I've got Seaborn and his bank against the wall. Before it's over, they'll both be singing like Pavarotti."

"I never had anything to do with either one of them," Costello said. "I may have said hello once or twice."

"Oh, I get it. It's Save Costello's Ass Week, that's what we're talking about here? Okay, here are my terms. You give us Nance for murder and kidnapping, Cohen and his books for violation of the RICO acts, Chevos for smuggling and accessory to murder, and you become a friendly witness for the Fed. I'll see if maybe we can't get you off with five to ten."

"Dream on," he said with a laugh. It was his last.

The chopper was bearing in, coming closer.

Whah, whah, whah, whah . . .

Christ, he thought, just like the old days.

The guards didn't even hear the boat until it bumped the dock. He was ready.

"What the hell's that?" one of them said. They both turned toward the boat.

The laser's red pinpoint settled over the heart of the first one. He still had his shotgun over his shoulder.

Brrddtttt.

He went down like an elephant stepped on him. The other one started to scramble. He didn't have time to yell; he made a dash for the trees. Stick squirreled a burst into the sidewalk, twenty meters in front of him.

A dozen rounds whined off the walk and tore through his legs. He went down on his face. The second burst finished him.

Stick jumped ashore and ran toward the house. He blitzed the two big lights as he ran. The chopper was getting louder but Stick was committed. He didn't need any air for this one. This one was a piece of cake. Piece of fuckin' cake.

He dropped behind a tree, twenty yards from the door to the main room, swung the M-16 up, and checked the kitchen and the living room one more time. Bronicata was leaning over a large pot, sipping something from a spoon. The other two were standing next to him.

The five were still in the living room, gabbing. No women, thank God.

He swung the M-16 around and launched a grenade into the center of the big room.

It happened fast.

Chevos opened the door and said, "There's a helicopter coming in from the bay, flying pretty low."

"Probably some businessman coming home late for dinner," Costello said.

I could see through the door into a bedroom. Nance was sitting on a large, round waterbed, holding an icepack against his jaw. Beyond that there was a large, high-ceilinged room with half a dozen or so goons, and beyond that the kitchen. Bronicata was cooking something. Just a nice domestic get-together. The boys' night out.

Suddenly the living room erupted in a garish orange flash. The explosion followed an instant later and blew the room to pieces.

After that, everything happened so fast, I remember it almost like a series of still pictures.

Sweetheart Pravano was lifted four feet off the ground and thrown against the wall. His face was gone.

Another hoodlum went out the back window head first as if he had been bounced off a trampoline.

Another fell to his knees in the middle of the room, clutching a bloody mess that had been his chest a moment before, and fell forward screaming, "Mother!"

Bits and pieces of furniture were thrown around the room like dust.

In the kitchen Bronicata was almost knocked into his soup pan.

The explosion blew Chevos' face forward into the room.

I grabbed Doe, twisted her around, and went to the floor on top of her.

Costello was knocked off his chair.

An M-16 started chattering.

Bronicata did a toe dance in the kitchen while his pots and pans exploded around him, then fell across the hot stove as if embracing it.

His two pals were slammed against the wall and riddled.

In the other room Nance whirled and dropped to his knees behind the bed.

Chevos was on his knees, a .32 in his fist, his glasses hanging from one ear, hissing like a snake.

Costello rolled over and shook his head.

The smell of gunpowder flooded the room.

Nance turned toward me, his smashed face curdled with hate, his Luger in his hand.

I dragged Doe to her feet and pushed her toward the far corner of the room, away from the doorway.

The Luger roared and I felt the round twirl through my arm and hit the wall beyond. I knocked Chevos' glasses off, grabbed his arm, and twisted him around, turning his gun hand down and away from his body.

The M-16 thunked again and the waterbed erupted. Geysers of water plumed up from it. Nance dove face down on the floor, huddling by the bed.

Costello pulled a .38 and leaped for the corner, grabbing at Doe.

I got the .32 away from Chevos, shoved him out of the way, jumped across the room, got a handful of Costello's jacket, and threw him against the other wall. It didn't stop him. His lips curled back and he swung the .38 up. I shot him twice in the chest. He fell back against the wall and dropped to his knees. The gun bounced out of his hand. His knuckles rested on the floor. He stared at my belt buckle; then his mouth went slack and dropped open.

The window beside me burst open. The drapes crashed down, and then I heard the dentist's drill, an inch from my ear, hum its tune.

Brrdddtttt.

So much for Chevos.

I stuffed a handkerchief inside my jacket. The bullet wound burned. I could smell the almond odor of arsenic. The Stick jumped

through the window with the grace of a dancer, the 180 submachine gun in one hand, the M-16 in the other. He held a finger
to his lips and pointed toward Nance's room.

We heard footsteps run across broken glass and debris and
smash a window. Stick jammed the 180 under his arm, pulled a
.357 out of his belt, tossed it to me, and dove through the doorway
into the bedroom, the chattering 180 back in hand as he went.

"He's heading for the water," Stick yelled, and went over the
windowsill and into a garden behind the place. "Stay with the girl.
He's mine."

A shot whined between us and smacked the windowsill. Stick
hunched down and took off in a crouch, jumping this way and
that, threading his way through the trees. He didn't make a sound.

I went back into the other room. Doe was facing the wall with
her hands over her face. I led her outside, to the side of the house
away from the shooting.

"Stay right here, don't move," I said. "You'll be safe here. I've
got to check the rest of the house."

She nodded but her eyes didn't like the idea.

I went back inside.

A quick check turned up ten bodies in the house. Nobody had
survived. The bomb, or whatever it was, and the burst from the
M-16 right after it, had killed five gunmen in the living room and
three in the kitchen.

There was a shot outside.

A muffled burst of M-16 fire.

I checked the .357 and half ran, half stumbled out the back
door. Another burst, down near the water.

I started after them.

Nance was out on the dock. He started to get aboard the yacht.
I heard the *pumf* of the grenade launcher, and the back end of
the yacht erupted. Nance was blown back onto the dock. He got
to his feet, kept running away from Stick. The big luxury boat
started to burn. In the light of the flames, I saw Nance scramble
aboard a sailboat at the end of the dock, her sails furled loosely
around the boom.

The Stick was hunched near the bowline. He moved away from
me, toward the shadows on the far side of the sailboat. Then
suddenly he leaped over its side.

His submachine gun was chattering.

Nance got off three shots before he started his dance. He went
up on his toes, spun around, slapping his body as if bugs were

biting him. His hands flew over his head, and he fell backward onto the deck like a side of beef. One foot kicked halfheartedly and he went limp.

I picked up the M-16 and ran out onto the dock. The Stick was walking awkwardly toward the stern, where Nance was lying.

"Stick!" I yelled.

He turned and crouched in a single move; then his shoulders drew up suddenly, his knees buckled, and he fell over onto the deck.

I jumped aboard the sailboat and ran back toward the stern, where he was lying. I was ten feet from him when he raised up and lifted the 180. For a second I thought he was going to shoot me. I just froze there. He swung it up, to my left, and squeezed off two or three bursts. The bullets chewed a ragged line up the mast. Bits and pieces of wood flew out of it, followed by streams of white crystals. They poured out of the bullet holes in the shattered mast, sparkling like snowflakes, were caught in the wind and whisked away, out over the bay and into the darkness. Stick sighed and his head fell back on the deck.

I leaned over him. His eyes were turning gray.

He flashed that crazy smile.

"Wasn't it . . . one helluva . . . blast," he said, in a funny, tired, faraway voice, "while it lasted? Huh, Jake?"

"It was one helluva blast."

His lips moved but he didn't say anything.

"You did it all, didn't you? Took on the whole Tagliani clan?" I said.

He didn't answer. All he said was "Burn . . . boat, 'kay?"

The Stick winked, then sighed, and it was all over.

Up near Chevos' compound, I could hear sirens and see red and blue reflections through the trees. People shouting. Doors slamming.

I turned Nance over. Half a dozen slugs had removed most of his chest. He wouldn't be soaking any more slugs in arsenic. The look frozen on his face was pure terror, the mask of a man who had died in fear. That's one I owed that I'd never repay.

I checked over the mast. It was on hinges, the kind that can be lowered for repairs and going under low bridges. I examined it closely, then picked up the machine pistol and racked the mast with gunfire. I started at the base and let the .22-caliber slugs tear it to pieces. As the slugs ripped up the birch pole, the shining white crystals sifted out, sparkling as the wind caught them and tossed them, twinkling, out over the water. I kept shooting until the gun was empty. The powder poured out. I sat down next to Stick and watched twenty-four million dollars' worth of cocaine dance on the wind and dissolve in the sea. It took a while.

I rolled Nance's body off the deck and watched it splash into the bay. Then I carried Stick ashore and fired a grenade into the engine of his sailboat. The back end of the sleek craft exploded, then burst into flames. I threw the M-16 and the 180 as far out into the bay as I could fling them and headed back up the hill to see what was happening.

76

VOTE OF CONFIDENCE

I labored back up the hill toward the big cottage, lit now by the roving searchlights of a chopper that hovered a few feet a-bove the roof. There were a lot of red and blue lights flashing, by now standard procedure every time the SOB's showed up anyplace.

A small fire was burning in one of the rooms and I could hear the throaty blast from a fire extinguisher. There was a lot of smoke and broken glass around the place. As I passed the kitchen window I got a brief look at the inside of the house. I could see down the length of the five-room cottage. I didn't stop to count bodies, I knew the score already.

The chopper swung away from the house and dropped down into a corner of the parking lot, throwing shards of glass and dirt in little waves below it. Cowboy Lewis jumped out and dashed from under the whirring blades.

I found Doe in the back, standing with Dutch. Her eyes were as round as quarters and she was trembling. I'm sure she was as confused as she was stunned by the sudden explosion of activity and by the destruction. I walked straight over to her and an instant later she was huddled against me, burrowing into my chest with her nose, like a puppy.

"What in hell happened?" Dutch asked as the rest of the group began to gather around us. He sounded like he was in shock. I realized it was the first time I had seen all of the hooligans together at one time. All but one.

"Nance lifted Mrs. Raines and me off the street in front of her townhouse," I answered. "Stick hit the place and got us out. Just that simple."

I looked back down the hill.

"We need to get somebody down there," I said. You could hardly hear my voice. "Stick's lying at the bottom of the hill."

"Is he dead?" Salvatore asked.

"Yeah." I nodded.

"Aw, shit," Cowboy Lewis said. "Aw, *shit!*"

He started down the hill and Dutch tried to stop him. "We got an ambulance on the way, Cowboy," he said gently.

"I'm gonna get him. Fuck the ambulance."

"I'll go along," Charlie One Ear said, and followed him through the smoke.

Callahan strolled out of the wreckage looking startled, with Kite Lange behind him carrying the extinguisher. "All dead in there," he said incredulously. "Every last one of 'em. I count ten. Biggest total yet."

"Why in hell would they kidnap you?" Salvatore said.

"Costello wanted to make a deal. He was willing to turn up Nance and Chevos and dump Sam Donleavy and Charles Seaborn if I'd get him off the hook."

"Otherwise?"

"He was going to kill us."

Dutch squinted his eyes and looked down his nose at me.

"How's that again?"

I had started another lie. I was getting pretty good at it by now.

"Let me give you the scenario, okay? Nance and Chevos were going to throw in with Bronicata and Cohen, get rid of the rest of the family, and take over the town. Nance was the official shooter. I don't know the reasons—what difference does it make anyhow? There's none of them left to disagree. Any problems with that?"

Dutch humphed and shuffled his feet around a bit.

"How about Nance?" Mufalatta asked.

"He's floating around in the bay," I said. "Stick's last official act."

"We got the weapons? Any of that?" Dutch asked.

"They fell in the bay," I said.

They all looked at each other, then back at Dutch, and then at me.

"How about the toot?" Zapata asked.

"In the mast of the sailboat that's burning down there," I said. "By now it's either in the bay or turned to charcoal."

I looked at each of the hooligans in turn, waiting for comments. Only Dutch spoke up.

"It ain't gonna work," he said. "There's holes in it."

"Fuck the holes," Salvatore said.

"It'll work," I said.

"How about Titan? Chief?"

"I'll take care of that."

"It's some story," Dutch said, shaking his head.

"You got a better one?" I asked.

Cowboy came back up the hill with Stick over his shoulder. He laid him on the grass away from the building and started to take off his Windbreaker.

"Don't do that," I said. "Don't cover him up."

He hesitated for a moment before nodding. "Whatever you say," he replied.

"Anybody else got any problems with the story?" I asked.

"What story?" Cowboy asked. "I missed it."

I repeated it for Cowboy and Charlie One Ear. Charlie One Ear raised his eyebrows and greeted the outcome with a wry smile. But his answer was instantaneous.

"I don't see a problem," he said. One by one they all chimed in. No problem, they agreed.

"I've got to get the lady home," I said. "Anybody got a car I can use?"

Half a dozen sets of car keys were offered. I took Dutch Morehead's sedan. It was the only one I was sure was clean.

As we were walking away, the Mufalatta Kid said, "Hey, Kilmer?"

I turned around. "Yeah?"

"We're gonna need to replace Stick. You ought to think about that."

"Thanks. I'll do that," I said. And smiled for the first time in several hours.

77

RETURN TO WINDSONG

When we got to the end of the lane leading to Windsong, Stonewall Titan's black limousine was parked in the drive. Luke Burger, the sheriff's man, was leaning against the hood of the car. He didn't take his eyes off me from the moment I stepped out of the car I had borrowed from Dutch.

I started toward the house and he said, "Just a minute there. Gonna have to pat you down."

"Don't even think about it," I said, without looking at him or slowing down. I'd had enough of hard talk and tough people for one night. I put an arm around Doe, led her across the long green lawn to the house, around the porch, and up the front steps to the door. Warren, the family retainer, opened it before I got a hand on the doorknob, as if a psychic doorbell had rung inside his head. He was older and grayer and arthritis had slowed him down, but he was as starched and precise as ever.

"Good evening, sir," he said with a smile, as if it were twenty years ago and I was dropping by for dinner. Then he looked closer at both of us and added, "Gracious, are you all right?"

"We're okay," I said as we went into the broad entrance hall. I had feared coming back to this house with its ghosts, long gone. But now I had too many other things on my mind, and so there was only curiosity. I figured the years would have distorted my memory of the place, but there were few surprises. I doubt that a single picture, vase, or stick of furniture had been moved in two decades. It was like a museum, preserving the past for future generations of Findleys, generations that would no longer carry the name, which had died with Teddy. Warren led us through the sprawling entrance hall with its twin curved staircases at the far end, and into a sitting room large enough to accommodate a Legionnaires' convention.

Chief and Titan were waiting there. It was a room cloyed by nostalgia, all wicker and antiques, its tabletops choked with framed pictures of every size and shape—laughing pictures of Doe and Teddy as children, teenagers, college kids, and finally adults, if in fact they had ever grown up.

The old man looked up from his wheelchair with almost orgasmic relief when Doe came into the room. He held out his arms and she rushed into them, as if she had just returned from a long trip. Titan stood in front of the dormant fireplace, smoking a short, stubby cigar which he held between two fingers like a cigarette. You could almost feel the relief in the room, like a warm breeze seeping through the shuttered windows.

Chief was the first to speak. He looked at me over Doe's shoulder.

"Thank you," he whispered. "You're a brave man."

"Not really," I said. "It was my stupidity that got us into trouble in the first place."

Doe said, "We're back, Daddy. That's all that matters."

"We'll make it up to you, son," Chief said, hanging on to her as if he were afraid the tide was going to rush in and carry her away.

"You don't owe me anything," I said. "It was Stick who bailed us out."

"Stick?" Chief said.

Both he and Titan tried to cover their surprise, but they were not very good actors.

"A cop. You probably know him better as Mickey Parver," I said, when it had sunk in.

"What happened out there, doughboy?" Titan asked. "There hasn't been much in the way of radio communication for the last two hours."

"We were too busy to bother," I said curtly.

I gave them a sketchy report on what had happened from the time we left the Breezes until the shooting was over.

"Costello, Bronicata, Chevos, and Turk Nance are all dead, along with nine of their gunslingers," I said.

"My God," Chief whispered, clutching Doe even tighter.

"The four of them were behind the Tagliani killings," I went on. "My guess is that Nance did most of the work, although we'll never know for sure."

Titan looked up as if a bee had stung him, then said, "Well, I'll be damned."

"It will all work out because Parver didn't make it," I said. "He went down saving me and Doe."

Titan stared at me. A long minute crept by before he said, "What do you mean, it will work out?"

"I mean for the record, it will work out."

"I thought you just said Costello was behind it all, doughboy," Titan said cautiously.

"I think I can sell the idea. Who's around to argue, right?"

Doe looked at me with curiosity.

"I don't understand," she said.

"We don't need to talk about this right now," Chief said.

"Talk about what? You couldn't get me out of the room now if you tried!" she protested.

"Let it pass," Titan said, looking at his feet.

"No!" Doe said. She stood up. "What is this all about?"

Chief said, "It's nothing, baby. Just business."

"What kind of business?" she persisted.

I said, "The business of murder." I wanted her to know. I wanted all the dark corners swept clean, once and for all.

"Tell her," said Chief. He was too old and tired to argue.

"The thing is, we know better, don't we, Mr. Stoney?" I said.

Titan turned his back to me and stared into the empty fireplace.

"Parver was an agent of the Freeze, the same outfit I'm in, but he was assigned to Dutch Morehead and his squad," I said. "Stick claimed he didn't know anything about the Cincinnati Triad until my boss, Cisco Mazzola, tumbled on to it a month or so ago. It went by me at the time. I've never been much on filing reports. That was one of my mistakes."

"You mean you're capable of making a mistake?" Titan asked caustically.

"Oh, I made a lot of them," I said. "We all did."

"For instance?" Titan asked.

"For instance, I had a five-man team in Cincinnati for three years working on the Tagliani case. There were pictures, newspaper clippings, snitch reports, and a link analysis on the Triad in our confidential files. Stick had spent six months studying our computer reports before he came here. He knew all about Tagliani and his bunch. Stick made the Triad right after he got here. Had to be. The question is, who did he take the information to?"

Nobody said anything. Doe still looked confused.

"No takers?" I said. "Okay, I'll try. I think he came to you, Mr. Stoney. You're the logical one, not Dutch. You're the one with the iron hand. You represented the law on the Committee."

He didn't say anything, he kept staring at the fireplace.

"So you asked Parver to kill Tagliani," I finished.

Titan turned around and glared hard at me from across the room.

"Now why would he do a damn fool thing like that?" Doe said, getting defensive.

"Two reasons, I can think of. To protect Harry Raines' career, and to break the Triad's back."

"Hah," said Titan, "I'm not a miracle worker."

"You're just finding that out," I said, and before he could respond, I went on, "I think you honestly believed by getting rid of Tagliani, you could run the Triad off, the old 'get out of town before sunset' routine, but it was a risky move. Then you found out I was coming down here and the whole story would come out, so you cut Stick loose in desperation. You knew the press here would buy anything they were told. You could write the killing off as some kook slaying, or better still, you could let Graves be the fall guy. As long as it couldn't be proven, he didn't give a damn. He never even denied killing Cherry McGee, even though it was Tagliani who had the job done. And Stick cased that set-up by hijacking Graves' cocaine shipment. That provided the final motive, if one was needed at all."

Doe stared at me, her expression changing from bewilderment to disbelief.

"That's just plain crazy," she said. "Isn't that so, Mr. Stoney?"

Titan sneered at the idea.

"I'll admit, it was a rather naive notion on your part," I said. "It's understandable, though. You thought you were still playing by your rules; if you need to get rid of someone, do it the quickest way possible, like framing Tony Lukatis because he was a potential threat to Raines. Or suggesting Stick use him on the hijacking run and then get rid of him. Graves' people and Tony were both shot with the same gun—Stick's. Aw, hell, I guess when you've run a town for forty years, playing God comes easy."

Doe, still confused, looked at me and said, "Whose side are you on, Jake?"

"Nobody's. I'm just a simple cop trying to do his job. It's really none of my affair anyway, except I contributed to it."

"How?" she asked.

"By convincing myself that Nance was the killer because I wanted him to be. For awhile I even tried to build a case against Harry, because I wanted you."

"You did that?" she said, moving away from me.

"Yeah," I said, "we all did a little God playing. Stick certainly did his share. And you, Mr. Stoney."

"That's good thinkin', doughboy," said Titan. "There's only one thing wrong with it."

"And what's that?" I asked.

"It wasn't my idea at all," he said, pausing for effect, and then his lip curled up in a smile. "It was Parver's idea from the start."

"Why?" I demanded. "What did he want out of it?"

"Not one damn thing," Titan said. "Besides, if what you say's true, how come he didn't stop at just Tagliani?"

I didn't have an answer for that, and still don't. I shrugged my shoulders. "I don't know. It's moot, anyway. None of this can ever be proven."

Chief finally spoke up. "Then why bring it up?" he said sternly.

"Yes," Doe said, moving closer to her father, "why bring it up?"

I sensed that suddenly I was no longer the hero.

"Because it's his game now," said Titan. "He has all the cards, right, doughboy?"

"Is that it? Doe asked angrily. "You were in this for yourself all the time?"

"Yeah, doughboy," said Titan. "What do you want out of it?"

I thought about it for a moment, looking at Doe, standing beside her beloved Chief, as she always would. At Titan, with his bulldog jaw jutting out at me, invincible to the end. Their allegiance to each other was clear. I was the outsider, as I had always been. I don't think it occurred to any of them that in the end they not only had lost their precious town but cost Harry Raines his life. They would never stand accountable for their actions—I guess that's one of the perks that comes with power.

"The same thing Stick wanted," I said. "Nothing."

I turned and walked out.

78

EULOGY

Driving away from Windsong, I felt a sense of relief, not so much at leaving the place but because I had feared coming back to that house with all its ghosts, and now the fear was gone. If there were ghosts at Windsong, they were keeping alive a memory of laughter and youth and a time that was as sweet as the remembered taste of hot dogs and burnt marshmallows, and the smell of campfires on the beach. If I had learned nothing else in coming back to this house, I had learned to treasure those moments of my life, not trample them in despair. And if that fleeting time, twenty years ago, was to be the only green summer of my life, at least it was mine. Nobody could ever take that away from me.

Cisco blew in the next morning, raising merry hell.

It was easy to lay the Tagliani massacre off on Nance, Costello, and Chevos; there was nobody of consequence left to argue about it. Costello had kept Cohen at arm's length, so Cohen was in the dark. Since they were part of the conspiracy, Titan and Chief also had to go along. Besides, people hear what they want to hear. A hero cop is always good copy.

To Dutch and the rest of the SOB's, it was a state secret, never to be shared outside the team. As for Cisco, he kept mum, too, although he was still bugging me for my report two months later. I never filed it. So what else is new? But he wanted to know. He wanted answers to all the questions. And though I didn't answer a lot of them, and couldn't answer some, one thing kept bugging him until he finally put the question straight to me.

"You didn't get emotionally involved in this thing, did you, Jake?" he asked, over one of his breakfasts of garbage and vitamin pills.

"What do you mean?" I replied.

"I mean, you didn't have something going with the Raines dame, did you?"

I thought about that for a long time before I said no.

I don't really think that was a lie. It should have been obvious to me all along that a dalliance with a football player could never last, any more than one with a lifeguard. For me, the patterns of Dunetown now fit together like the pieces of a jigsaw puzzle. Chief had erased me from Doe's life, just as Titan had erased Tony Lukatis; Harry Raines had filled the spot left by Teddy Findley, just as Sam Donleavy had taken the place once reserved for me. In the end, when the puzzle was complete, the picture was all sound and fury, and the irony was that Tagliani, who was never really a part of it, was the catalyst that brought it all tumbling down. Uncle Franco had come to Dunetown seeking the same kinds of things we all want. He thought he could buy respectability. All he bought was the long, dark, forever tunnel. The one with no light at the end.

Looking back on it now, I think maybe the Stick, in his own way, was looking for the same things too. I'll never know the answer to that, but I'd like to think that he wanted to put some sense of order back in his life, to find something of value to replace the values he had lost in that faraway place all of us would like to forget and never will. Or maybe he had simply lost that dream forever. Maybe he was just doing what he did best, the best way he knew how. Whatever he wanted, I hope he found it. I hope death is kinder to him than life and, like all our fallen comrades, he is in some special place reserved for those who stalked the rim of hell and never came back.

One thing for damn sure, Stick had one fine sendoff. He was buried in that beat-up hat of his. The hooligans were the pallbearers and there was an honor guard and Dutch read a eulogy that had everybody weeping. And there was a bugler playing taps, and another, off somewhere in the cemetery, echoing its sad eloquence. Everybody was there but Doe. Beautiful Doe, elusive to the end. But DeeDee Lukatis was there, and Lark, and Cisco. And Chief Findley and Stonewall Titan showed up. Salvatore even wore a tie.

WILLIAM DIEHL is a former reporter for the *Atlanta Constitution* and one-time managing editor of *Atlanta Magazine*. He is the author of *Sharkey's Machine* and *Chameleon* and is currently at work on his fourth novel. He lives off the coast of Georgia with his wife, Virginia Gunn.